CW01603534

DANGEROUS Embrace

DANA MASON

Copyright © 2012 Dana Mason
All rights reserved. Except as permitted under the U.S. Copyright Act of 1976, no part of this publication may be reproduced, distributed, or transmitted in any form or by any means, or stored in a database or retrieval system, without prior permission of the publisher.

Sapphire Star Publishing
www.sapphirestarpublishing.com
First Sapphire Star Publishing trade paperback edition, October 2012

The characters and events in this book are fictitious. Names, characters, places, and plots are a product of the author's imagination. Any similarity to real persons, living or dead, is coincidental and not intended by the author.

ISBN: 978-1-938404-23-8

Cover Image by Shoots

www.sapphirestarpublishing.com/danamason

Dedication

Jim, you are my home.

Acknowledgements

I want to thank my family, Jim, Lizzie, Kaitlin and Trevor—you have been so patient and understanding. Thank you for sharing this with me. I love you and the support you've given me. Please remember, dreams do come true—promise to never give up on what you really want.

Thank you to my extended family and friends who have sent countless tweets and shared countless posts on Facebook. I'll never forget the support you've given me.

Jennifer, you are not only a friend but a sister. Thank you for keeping it real and keeping me grounded. Honesty is the mark of a true friend.

Michelle, you have had a stand-out role in all of the most important days of my life, including this one. I love you. Thank you for always being there for me.

Natasha Alexander, thank you for sticking around when I needed a friend who understands what this truly means to a writer.

Jenny, Kelley, Lani, Jason and Darlene, you've been fabulous cheerleaders. Thank you for all the enthusiasm and support.

Valerie Neumark, thank you for sharing your talent and time. Thank you for caring and for the support you have shown. Thank you for pushing me to want more.

To all of my parents, thank you for teaching me the values that get me through every day. You have each had a role in showing me the importance of loyalty, resilience, resourcefulness, and most important, the ability to laugh at myself.

To Amy and Katie at Sapphire Star Publishing, thank you for caring about this story as much as I do. Your dedication and attention has meant so much to me. Thank you for painstakingly walking me through the editing and publication process. I couldn't imagine doing this without you.

I must also thank the Vaca Arts Council for welcoming me into their family and for all the support they've shown.

Chapter One

The sky was on fire. At least, Sarah Jennings thought the orange glow resembled fire when she stepped out of the double, glass doors of Oakbrook Elementary School. Even with fire in the sky, the deserted school grounds were too dark for her taste.

She hated being the last teacher to leave. How stupid of her not to check the time, but she couldn't refuse when parents showed up unannounced at her classroom door. Not even when it got her behind. It'd been a shock to see Noah's mom and dad together. Especially knowing they were going through a terrible divorce. Noah looked more shell-shocked and withdrawn every day since school had started. Of course she put everything on hold to give them her undivided attention. She'd hoped this was a sign they were going to make him a priority and stop the petty fighting.

Sarah's eyes scanned the grounds again before turning toward the parking lot. She kept her pace normal. She wouldn't let old fear push her to run to her car like a coward. She wasn't in the city anymore. This neighborhood was safe and quiet, and she needed to just breathe through it and move ahead.

In college, the dark, foggy San Francisco nights left her in a constant state of fear. Always afraid she'd been found, running through parking garages, looking for stalkers hidden in shadowed corners. She wouldn't live like that now. It'd been too long, and she given up too much already.

Sarah gripped the purse on her shoulder and turned toward the ramp leading to the parking lot.

The school sat on a hillside, and the walkway connected the school grounds with the teachers' lot. A waist-high, metal handrail bordered the elevated ramp with a ten-foot drop down to a gravel hillside.

Sarah started across, but stopped when a tingling sensation attacked her scalp. She waited and listened, her pulse a little quicker than a few minutes ago. That's when she heard running footsteps.

She looked up and met his eyes, a sick smile spread across his face. Fear dripped down her spine like a drop of cold water, and she knew she was in trouble. He moved fast considering his bulk, and as he got closer, his piercing glare became more menacing.

Sarah froze.

Breath caught in her throat and her body wouldn't react to the fear. She'd always been a deer in the headlights type of person, and now she'd been caught off guard.

His shoulder slammed her chest, sending her against the metal handrail. He gripped her knees and lifted, sending her toppling backwards. She reached out for the rail too late. Her world turned upside and she couldn't grasp anything to prevent the fall.

Sarah wasn't sure what brought her out of the unconscious state. It could have been his weight pressing down on her, or his clammy hands touching her, or the sound of her skirt being ripped open.

No...she didn't feel any of that. Panic left her paralyzed and numb. She didn't feel his hot mouth when he licked and bit her breasts. She watched the scene play out like a film instead. Her mind too distant, too frightened to allow her to feel anything.

Sarah couldn't say which hurt worse, watching or feeling.

One of her arms lay twisted unnaturally at her side, the other restrained above her head, but she didn't fight.

She didn't move.

Tears ran down her face and quiet whimpers escaped her lips. This was wrong—she was wrong for not fighting. She could not let another man break her.

"No!" Not again—she was stronger, more powerful now and would not lose herself again.

His nails scratched and clawed at her, ripping her panties off, the material cutting her skin when he yanked them away.

"No!" she screamed again as her senses came back to life. Now she felt every injury, from her twisted arm, to the burning cuts up her back. His whiskey and cigarette breath wafted into her nose, and she had to swallow back the bile that collected in her throat.

"Get off me!" She grunted and kicked out, arching to throw him off. Adrenalin pushed her body into overdrive, thrusting her heart to a manic pace. She lifted up again, kicking with her bare feet at anything within reach.

He shifted, sliding one leg between her knees and the other over her right leg, relieving some of the pressure on her body. She inhaled a gasping breath, but when he punched his fingers between her thighs, her panic spiked.

Oh God, no! She could feel him—his fingers, his hand—forcing her thighs apart. She kicked off hard, arching again to push him off.

When he teetered sideways, she rammed her knee into his groin. He cursed and withdrew his hands to grab himself.

With her right hand free, she hit and flailed at his face, scratching, pushing, and smacking him everywhere.

She jerked and tried to scoot away, fighting to get free. She managed to get one leg out from under him. She lifted it and came down on his hip with her heel over and over as hard as she could.

The attacker tried to scramble back over her, but she kept kicking and pushing with her free foot, landing several blows to his lower back and hip. She continued to fight, screaming with each blow.

"No—get off me!"

Her vision tainted red, her jaw clenched like a vice, and her pulse pounded like a base drum in her ears. Sarah kicked out again with all her power, while using her uninjured hand to push until he was off her.

With her legs free, Sarah lifted up and kicked out, putting her weight behind the kick. He cried out this time as he reached for his lower back. She jolted upright and jumped up, the gravel pinching her bare feet.

As she gained her balance, he grabbed her injured arm and tried to pull her back down. Pain almost forced her surrender, but Sarah fisted her right hand and plunged it into his face. She felt the crack. When she pulled her fist away, blood gushed from his nose.

She took off running into the darkness without looking back. Her feet pounded harder and harder, letting the distance grow between her and her attacker.

The air was knocked from her lungs when she plowed into him. He felt more like a brick wall than a person, until she knocked them both off their feet. His arms came around her as they skidded to the pavement together. They hit the ground, but she only felt his secure grip.

She fought hard again. Punching at his chest and pushing with her uninjured hand, but his words made her stop.

"Hey, hey, you okay?"

Despite the concern in his voice, her panic spiked again.

He loosened his grip when Sarah pushed away.

"It's okay," he said, and in the glow of the streetlight, she found a pair of intense, blue eyes staring back at her.

A scream bubbled in the back of her throat, and her entire body vibrated with fear. He said something again, but she couldn't hear him over her own cries.

"Where is he?" She finally heard when their eyes locked on each other's again.

Her breath came out in gasps. She shook her head and began to sob.

The man holding her, shifted and placed her on the concrete next to him. Sarah felt hands on her shoulders and jumped, ready to fight again.

"It's okay," a woman's voice said, soft and hesitant.

"Mom, help her." The man got to his feet. "I'll be right back. Here's my phone, call 911." He pulled off his jacket and laid it over Sarah's shoulders.

The woman reached out for him. "No, Mark, don't—"

"I'll be right back," he said, and rushed into the dark in the direction Sarah had come.

Sarah hugged herself and dropped her head, trying to breathe. When the jacket fell off her shoulder, she looked down at her ripped clothes just as her vision narrowed into a dark tunnel.

Chapter Two

Sarah pried open her heavy eyelids and turned, trying to focus on the clock.

"Ow, dammit!" She clenched her teeth and looked down at the sling tied to her arm. The smothering realization pressed on her chest. When the nausea hit, she flung the covers off and rushed to the bathroom, fighting to get to the toilet before her stomach heaved.

When the painful dry heaving stopped, she lay back on the cold tile floor, exhausted, and waited for the room to stop spinning. Her ragged breaths roared in her ears and seemed to echo in the quiet room. When her breathing slowed, the silence ebbed around her in waves, but when footsteps approached the bathroom door, she tensed again.

A bead of sweat dripped down her scalp, and at the same time someone tapped at the door. Her pulse spiked, and she fought like hell to remember who brought her home from the hospital.

She closed her eyes.

"Who's there?" The waver in her voice pissed her off. *Gawd – please don't let me be pathetic in front of whoever this is.*

A hesitant and completely unfamiliar man's voice said, "Are you all right? Do you need something?"

Sarah sucked in a hard breath. "Um..." She exhaled slowly. "Who are you?"

"Mark Summors."

She stiffened and tried to sit up.

"Do I know you?" she asked, her voice pitching.

"I can explain if you open the door."

She steadied herself against the bathtub. The sling had slipped up her arm, exposing the trail of bruises. She swallowed another wave of nausea and tried to put the pieces together. *Mark Summors?*

She glanced around for something to use as a weapon just in case. Then she wanted to laugh—and cry. Who the hell was she kidding? She rolled her eyes. *Good plan, Sarah, take on a strange guy with a toilet brush.*

"Can I come in?" His voice was muffled as if he was resting his face against the door.

"Go ahead." She clamped her mouth closed to suppress a shiver and mumbled, "It's unlocked."

The door eased open and a cup of water shot out at her.

"Oh, thank you," she cried out, relieved to wash the disgusting film out of her mouth. She snatched the cup out of his hand and gulped it, letting her eyes lift above the rim to see his face.

"Ah." Sarah choked and inhaled the water. She set the cup down, almost upending it as she dropped it.

"Oh my God!" She would never forget those intense, blue eyes, just like she would never forget the smell of her attacker's breath. They were all thrown together in the same horrifying memory.

He waved in surrender, his eyebrows drawn together. "I'm sorry...I'll explain, but you have to calm down."

She shook her head, still coughing. "Don't tell me to calm down. Why are you here, in my house..."

"You didn't have an emergency contact, and I couldn't leave you alone."

She cleared her throat. "Since when—what time is it?"

"My mom and I brought you home from the hospital at about three this morning."

"Three o'clock—what time is it now?"

He glanced at his watch. "Almost midnight."

She rubbed at her throat. "So, it's Saturday...Sunday?"

"It'll be Sunday in ten minutes. You slept through Saturday. Do you want help getting off the floor?" He held his hand out for her.

She looked at his face, and then his hand. "Ah, thanks, but I can manage on my own."

He backed up a step as Sarah tried to push herself up.

When she winced, he stepped forward and reached out for her. She jerked away and fell back against the tub. Heat rushed her cheeks, and she couldn't take her eyes off the floor to look at him again. She hugged herself, trying to stop the fluttering spasms taking over her body.

Mark stepped back, mumbling an apology. "I'll just...give you some privacy."

She watched his feet inch back out of the room. "Thanks."

With her good hand, she braced herself against the edge of the bathtub and lifted up off the floor.

She closed the door and looked in the mirror. *What a mess.* Besides the bruises on her arms, her left shoulder was black from the top of her elbow to the base of her neck, and it hurt like hell. The sight was cringeworthy for sure. If it didn't hurt so much, she would've thought someone painted it on. The tenderness made it impossible to touch, and beyond the bruising, fine, red scratches covered one side of her face and neck.

Bruises also colored her cheekbones, the black and purple standing out against her pale skin. She reached up and picked a twig out of one of her curls. With a quickened pulse, she ran a finger along the angry scratch that traveled her jaw and remembered waking up in the bushes.

Sleeping for an entire day didn't make this less real. It had not been a bad dream. The bubble of safety she'd envision around her had burst. *How did this keep happening?* For some reason she'd thought a stranger attack would be less painful, but she never imagined she'd have the opportunity to compare.

She shook off the anxiety and took a deep breath, then gingerly took off the sling and slipped on her robe. Before tying the front, she stopped and plucked at the hem of her tank top. *Uh—how?*

Think, Sarah, how did you get inside the house? How did you change your clothes? She remembered Mark helping her out of the car, but nothing else.

Sarah crept to the side of her bed, looking for her slippers. Sitting on the tiled bathroom floor had made her body rigid with cold, and now every injury throbbed as she inched through her bedroom.

The aroma of fresh brewed coffee drifted in.

"Oh thank God," she whispered, following the scent. She hobbled out of her bedroom through the living room, toward the kitchen where Mark sat waiting and the coffee pot percolated softly.

She looked at the unfinished coffee. "Thank you."

"I wasn't sure you would want coffee, but I thought just in case..." He shrugged his shoulders, making his uneasiness known.

"Coffee should help clear the fog." She hesitated and struggled to pull herself up on one of the barstools with her good arm. When she was seated comfortably, she looked at him and then down at herself.

She tugged her robe closed. "I don't remember much."

He gave her a sheepish grin. "Yeah, my mom helped you get dressed when we got here."

"Right...your mom is Beth Summors." She nodded now as the memory cleared some. "She runs the after-school center next to the school."

He pressed his lips together and nodded. "I was picking her up from work. How's the shoulder feel?"

"It'll be fine. I'm not sure what the sling was for..."

"You don't remember having your shoulder pushed back into the socket?"

She shook her head.

"It was dislocated." His expression darkened as he said it. "Does it hurt? You have a prescription of pain killers if you need something." Mark gestured toward the pill bottle next to the coffee pot.

"Ah, no."

It was obvious her refusal worried him.

"I want to be clearheaded for a while before I go numb again. It's a pretty weird feeling, you know, waking up with a strange man in my house—and not knowing what day it is." She narrowed her eyes and said, "Why are you here?"

"We didn't want to leave you alone and you wouldn't let us call anyone."

"Thanks for staying." She looked around now, too embarrassed to admit just how grateful she was to have someone there with her. "Beth isn't here?"

"I finally talked her into going home. She's a caretaker by nature and wouldn't agree to leave you until I promised to stay."

"I'm sorry to have caused you so much trouble. I appreciate it, but I could've managed." She tried to sound stronger than she felt. Normally being alone with a stranger in her house would make her uncomfortable, but she was too relieved to be uncomfortable.

"I'm glad we were there to help, and I'm glad you're...okay." The softness of his voice made her feel a little guilty for questioning him.

She got to her feet and walked stiffly over to the coffee pot to pour a cup. "Would you like some?"

"Sit down. I'll get it."

"I can handle..."

"I've got it." He wrestled the pot from her hands and filled two mugs.

Sarah stared at him, not sure how to respond to his manhandling her coffee carafe.

"I'm not completely helpless," she said, struggling to get back onto the barstool.

"No—yeah." He gestured to the stool. "You've got everything under control."

He actually had the nerve to smile at her when he said it. As if she cared about the cute little dimple on his left cheek.

"Well, Mark, thanks again for your help. Sorry you can't stay longer, but I need to get back to bed."

Mark ran a hand through his short, chocolate brown hair. "Sorry. I really am only trying to help." His eyebrows drew together. "Do you even remember what happened to you last night?"

She lowered her eyes and fought the slow suffocating pressure that overcame her. The things that might have happened...

"Are you okay?"

"Yes...fine."

"Do you remember anything?" His voice softened again, and she glanced up at him.

"Some. *Enough.* It's kind of fuzzy though."

"I'm not surprised, between the trauma and the drugs they sedated you with."

"They sedated me?"

"Yeah...you were pretty out of it. Do you remember being at the hospital, talking to the police?"

She shook her head. "Not really."

He sat quietly for a long moment, and then said, "Do you have someone who can stay with you?"

"I don't need help." She thought about calling her mother and cringed. She didn't have the strength to deal with that invasion. "I'll be fine on my own."

"You don't have any family?"

"Not nearby. My parents live out of state."

"I'll sleep on the sofa tonight. You can call someone in the morning to come help you."

She jerked her head up to look at him. "No—no, I've imposed too much already." Her eyes traveled his face, taking in the dark circles and disheveled hair. "You look completely exhausted and I'm—I *will* be fine."

Mark rubbed at the scruff on his chin. "Yeah, I must look pretty frightening myself. I stayed awake, thought you would need someone when you woke up."

Sarah started to refuse again, but before she could, she saw the concern etched in the lines of his face. A complete stranger—the emotion and the fear for her was all there in his deep blue eyes. As she looked at him, she couldn't deny the sincerity she read on his face and felt as if she needed to comfort him. What had he gone through over the last two days? She would have said something to show her gratitude, but she was too busy fighting tears. Usually she guarded herself better around people.

"I'm sorry," he said in reaction to her tears.

"No, I am." She cleared her throat and waved off his apology. "I'm sorry you've been dragged into this mess. I'm sure your wife is furious with you."

"No, she doesn't know anything about it."

"What? Your wife doesn't know where you are?" she shot back at him, her face getting hot.

He raised his hand in defense. "My ex-wife, sorry, didn't mean to confuse you. I'm divorced."

"Oh," she said, lifting a hand to her chest. "I was about to feel even more guilty. I'm not comfortable with you uprooting your life to babysit me. You don't even know me."

"There's no need to feel guilty at all," he said with a little more force in his voice. "I'm not comfortable leaving until I know you're going to be okay and...*safe*." Mark hesitated a little too long on the word safe.

Sarah's pulse kicked up in reaction to the look on his face.

He waited a heartbeat before he said, "I don't think you fully understand the situation."

Chapter Three

"What do you mean by situation?" Sarah asked, wide-eyed.

"The guy who attacked you took your wallet and keys."

The force of what he said sunk in slowly.

"He took my wallet *and* my keys?" Her stomach rolled and coffee burned the back of her throat. With her hand over her mouth, she tried to swallow back the sick.

"I'm not going to let anyone hurt you," Mark said when Sarah slid off the barstool and headed back to the bathroom.

Her second round of fear-induced vomiting and the cold tile floor gave her a sense of déjà vu. She was seriously failing at the "not being pathetic in front of people" thing.

With a moan, she lay back on the hard floor, shivering and trying to catch her breath. She'd been nearly raped by some maniac, and now that maniac had her keys and address.

Mark approached the bathroom door and tapped. "Do you need my help?"

"No."

"I brought you more water."

"Okay, come in." She sat up slowly, feeling every bruise on her body, and reached for the cup. "Thanks," she whispered, trying not to grimace.

"I guess this is a reaction to the sedatives."

"Ha, maybe," she lied.

"Can I help you up?"

"If you don't mind." She squeezed her eyes closed and waved him off. "No, I'm fine."

"Don't be scared of me. I'm not going to hurt you."

Her eyes popped open and met his, "I'm not scared!"

"I know...I'm just trying to help."

She shook her head, feeling foolish for snapping at him. "I'm sorry," she muttered. "Will you please help me get up?"

Mark leaned closer, reaching without touching her, as if waiting for her to pull away. He looked like he was approaching a feral cat. She inhaled and held her breath reaching for his shoulder with her trembling right hand. Then she lifted her left hand and laid it on his arm above his elbow. He held her behind her shoulders and under her arms, but kept a comfortable distance between them.

Despite his gentleness, his touch made her apprehensive. She braced for more pain, but he held still.

"Try to relax, Sarah. Tension will only make the pain worse."

Hearing her name helped her focus. She exhaled slowly and relaxed a little. When Mark pulled her up, she fought the urge to lean into his warm chest.

Steady on her feet, she whispered a quiet thank you, and he backed out of the room.

She adjusted her robe and looked at her reflection. *Okay, Sarah, hold it together a little longer.* With a nod to the mirror, she left the bathroom striving for confidence, but suspected Mark saw right through her facade. She gave him a weary smile when she entered the kitchen. "I'm okay."

"How's the arm?"

"It hurts." Heat flooded her face at the admission.

"Are you ready to take something for the pain now?"

"No, I need to know everything before I fall into another medicated stupor."

"Do you think your stomach is settled enough? I'm not sure how much more your body can take."

"I am fine. I'm stronger than I look, and a little puking never killed anyone." She took a deep breath and tried to relax. "Sorry, but once I hear everything, I can relax." She carefully lifted herself back up onto the barstool.

"Are you *fine* enough to eat something?"

He smiled, and Sarah realized she should give him more credit. She wasn't an easy patient to treat, but he was relentless. She started to refuse, but he was already pulling things from her pantry.

"Soup and crackers okay with you?"

"Yeah...fine."

She didn't like that Mark moved around her kitchen as if he lived there. Clearly his mother wasn't the only caretaker in the family. Most men wouldn't bother making her soup. It was a sweet gesture, staying there with her was a sweet thing to do. And let's face it, if he wasn't here, she'd still be shivering on the bathroom floor, likely sobbing in self-pity.

"You should tell me the rest." She fought to keep her voice level. "I guess it's safe to assume he wasn't caught, and it's only a matter of time before he figures out he has complete access to me and my home."

"No, he wasn't caught." He turned toward her. "But he doesn't have access to you or your home."

Surprised, Sarah looked up at him. His gaze was so intense she had to turn away. His level of intensity told her one thing for sure—she had to leave. Pack her bags and leave her home. Again. *Oh, God*—the thought of running away broke her heart. Especially now that she'd finally found a place she really loved.

"He can't get to you," Mark said, pulling her from her thoughts.

"I'm sorry?"

"He won't get through me." His jaw tensed and determination flitted across his face. "I've already taken precautions to protect you."

She stared at him now, holding her breath, not sure she understood what he was telling her.

He turned back toward the stove, and she focused her eyes on his broad shoulders, trying like hell to make sense out of what he said. She slid off the stool and walked to the stove. He towered over her five feet seven inches by at least another five inches.

When she leaned against the counter next to him, he glanced at her and then back at the pot.

"Exactly what precautions are you talking about?"

"Soup's ready," he said, and reached over her head to grab a bowl off the shelf.

The closeness forced her to back away, but not before she took in his musky, sandalwood scent.

She walked back to the stool as he placed a bowl of soup down in front of her. "You're avoiding my question."

"I'll talk, you eat."

Sarah took a couple of spoonfuls of soup, and some of her tension melted away. She ate in silence for a few minutes before she glared up at him with one eyebrow arched in question.

He held his hands out palms up and said, "I didn't want you to have to worry—let's just say I took care of some security issues for you."

She dropped her spoon, and it sank into the soup when she placed her palms down on the bar, fighting for the courage she needed to put this man in his place. She would not let him act like she was some stupid woman who couldn't take care of herself. She'd always taken care of herself.

"Are you ready for your pain meds yet? Now that you've eaten they shouldn't upset your stomach."

"No. You need to finish telling me everything so I can protect *myself*."

"Don't worry. I've taken care of your security."

"What are you talking about?"

"I changed your locks."

"Oh." She wasn't sure how she felt about that. *No, not true,* she knew exactly how she felt about that—she didn't like it at all. "Thank you for taking liberties without my permission."

"I also installed a security system on your house."

"Wait...what? Did I hear that right?" She took in his posture and narrowed her eyes. What an arrogant S.O.B. What made him think she needed him to come in and save her—rescue her like some pathetic little twit?

She slid off her barstool and paced the length of her kitchen, fighting to keep from screaming in frustration. "So who died and made you God?"

"Whoa, what's the problem?"

She threw her uninjured arm in the air. "You had no right to come into my home and do this. I don't even know you."

"I guess I should have just left you unprotected."

She leaned closer to him. "I don't need a knight in shining armor to come in here and take over."

His brows shot up. "Take over—what the hell are you talking about? I'm trying to help. Most people would be grateful." He leaned in too, getting even closer. "Sorry for considering your safety and not leaving you to deal with it alone."

It took everything she had not to retreat from his glare, but she refused to back off. This was her house—her life. "I didn't sign anything. I didn't agree to any of this."

Mark must have seen a spark of fear in her eyes. His expression softened and he backed off. "You're right." He turned his back on her and walked toward the living room. "I'll take it out. Sorry for inconveniencing you with my help."

When the front door opened, she wished for a hole to crawl into—a place where she could be alone and think. If he had intended to make her feel bad, mission accomplished. She had every right to be angry, but did she have a reason to be nasty to him after taking care of her and staying with her? What kind of man does this?

She rested her hand on her forehead and took several shaky breaths. She didn't need him—did she? God, why did he have to be so helpful and caring? Sarah pushed back the emotion and stepped into the living room when Mark returned with his toolbox.

He set the box down and squatted next to it. The smile she'd seen on him earlier with that cute little-boy dimple was a complete contrast to his football player physique He looked so strong. She envied that and knew she couldn't wonder at him thinking her weak when being compared to him. His shoulders broadened as his irritation increased, making him look even bigger, surlier. But his exhaustion was prevalent too, with dark, sunken, tired eyes. It was hard to be angry with a man who stayed up for two days because he thought she might need him when she woke up. How does one respond to something like that? It was like ambush thoughtfulness. She wasn't prepared to deal with someone like that, or someone so...considerate.

She blew the bangs out of her eyes and approached him. "I'm sorry...if I seem ungrateful."

"Forget it. I'm outta your hair in three seconds."

"I appreciate that you want to help me. Just..." She held out her hand. "Please stop...for a second."

He glanced up at her.

Her heart pounded in her chest at the thought of accepting his help, but she had to think reasonably here. "I may be irrational sometimes, but I'm not stupid. I know the security system is a good idea. I just wish you would have asked me first."

They were quiet for a moment, which gave her time to push her uneasiness away. She walked over and sat on the sofa, wanting to be eye-to-eye with him. "I apologize for my reaction, but this"—she gestured to the toolbox—"caught me off guard."

"You know," he said, "I didn't intend for this to cost you money. I own a security agency. I did all the installation myself."

"I appreciate that, but I'm capable of paying for it myself."

"Fine, whatever. If it makes you feel less handled, I'll send you a bill."

She nodded and hoped her meager smile was enough of a truce sign for him. "Okay, tha—thank you."

He closed and locked the toolbox, and then set it next to the front door. Sarah took a couple more deep breaths and focused on what to do next. She couldn't believe how foggy and weighed down she felt after all that sleep she'd gotten.

When Mark turned toward her, she got a good look at his now slumped shoulders and felt really bad. Her behavior, her bitching, was embarrassing. How manic and unreasonable she must have seemed to him.

"Why don't you go home and get some rest." She stood and closed her robe, pulling the strap tighter, not sure what to do with her hands.

Mark nodded, but stared at her cautiously as he tugged his wallet out and removed a business card. "These are my home, cell, and office numbers. Call me if you need anything."

She thought he looked worried, but considering how rude she'd been, he probably just wanted to get away from her. "That's nice...thank you."

He picked up his jacket to pull it on.

"Are you all right to drive? You look exhausted," she said, watching his slow movements, now worried about him.

"I'm okay, it's not that far. Just please call me if you need something. I can be here in a few minutes."

"I will," she said.

He stepped outside, and Sarah's eyes landed on her truck in the driveway. "How did my truck get here from the school?"

"My mom and dad picked it up and brought it over."

Her eyebrows shot up. "How—if my keys were stolen?"

"The hide-a-key in the rear wheel well," he said, pointing to the back of the small Toyota pickup. "You didn't know that?"

She nodded. "Right...forgot, sorry. I guess that's another thing I owe you for."

"I'm not trying to rack up the favors here." His voice hardened. "You act like I have some ulterior motive."

"No—no, I don't," she snapped. "Why are you so defensive?"

"I'm not used to being accused of things when I help people."

"If you were paying attention, you would know I was only trying to thank you." She turned and stormed into the house before closing and locking the door.

Once Mark was inside his truck, he rested his head back and closed his eyes.

"What the hell was that about?" he muttered, lifting his head to stare at her closed front door. "Try to do something nice and look where it gets you."

As irritating as she was, he couldn't help but worry about her. She was alone—no help, no protection, and no family to check on her. He glanced around her dark front yard. She didn't even have proper lighting in the long, circular drive. Tall hedges blocked the neighbor's view completely, hiding the house and most of the driveway. The place was beautiful but private to the point of being dangerous. If the son of a bitch got passed his security system, nobody would hear or see a thing. He hadn't even taught her how to use the system.

Mark watched the house until her lights clicked off inside. He gave it another couple of minutes and then drove directly to Summors Security. He stepped into his office and plopped into his desk chair. He should've gone straight home and crashed, but his nerves were too on edge.

He picked up the receiver and dialed his dispatcher's extension. "Seth?"

"What are you doing here this late?" Seth asked.

"I'm on my way home. I need you to do me a favor."

"What do you need?"

"That system I installed today, at the Jennings' house, 248 Hartford."

"Yeah, I got the work order right here."

"The homeowner, Sarah Jennings, hasn't been given proper instructions on how to use the system yet."

"You want me to make an appointment?"

"No, but if the alarm sounds, don't wait to call 911. I didn't give her the password yet or codes, but she may try to figure it out. Either way, don't hesitate to call the police—and me if you get anything."

"Expecting trouble?"

Mark looked up when a figure blocked the window in his office door. Leaning back in his chair, he waved at Shane to come in. "Just being cautious."

"I'll do it."

"Thanks, Seth. I'm outta here in ten."

"Get some rest," Seth said before disconnecting.

"So...how's the girl?" Shane asked.

Mark shook his head. "Irritating as hell. I can't fucking believe I left without showing her how to use the system."

Shane smirked. "I guess you're not off the hook yet."

"No...I'm gonna keep an eye on her. I have a bad feeling about this whole situation."

"Of course you do."

"Shut up." Mark chuckled, and then frowned, his eyes focusing on the desktop. "She's such a fighter. She never gave up. Not while fighting that asshole attacker and not while being treated in the hospital. With her arm in a sling and after being beaten black and blue, she wouldn't call anyone to help. She clung to me while they were treating her...and I knew she was scared, but she was so strong." He finally looked up and shook his head at Shane. "If you would've seen her, you'd want to help her too."

"She's lucky to be alive. That jerk could've killed her," Shane said.

Mark chuckled again, and a sense of pride seeped into his heart. "About now, I bet that son of a bitch is feeling lucky he got away from her. She's a hell of a lot tougher than she looks, and he left behind a lot more blood than she did."

"Hopefully he doesn't come back to finish the job."

Mark cringed at the thought. "That's why I want to keep an eye on her."

"I got time, you want my help?"

"No...you're on a break."

"I'm bored as hell. Watching security monitors all night is under my pay grade, if you know what I mean."

Mark knew that was true. Shane didn't like sitting around, but after being injured on his last job, he needed to take it easy for a while. Shane was one of his best agents and his best friend. Mark wouldn't jeopardize Shane's recovery because he was bored. "I'll let you know if something minor comes up."

"Twenty years we've been friends and now you're pulling rank on me?"

"Forget it. You can't guilt me into putting you back in the field. I need you healthy."

"Right. Thanks." Shane bolted from the chair and stormed out of the office.

Mark dropped his head in his hands and cursed under his breath. He was two for two. Who else could he piss off before daylight? He lifted his head and went back to the computer, trying to answer a few emails before he crashed.

Driving home, his only thoughts were of sleep. He closed the front door, looked around his empty house, and glowered. The stagnant air made the place seem empty of life. He hated that. When he and Ali bought the place, he never envisioned it empty. He dropped his keys on the bar and hobbled up the stairs toward his bed.

Chapter Four

The shrill ring of his phone pulled Mark from a deep sleep. He glanced at the clock and grabbed the receiver off the nightstand.

"What?"

"Hello to you too," Ali said, her annoyance obvious.

"I'm sleeping, what kind of greeting did you expect?"

"First of all, you never sleep this late. Second, you haven't answered your cell phone in two days. Where have you been?"

"We're divorced, Ali, remember? I don't have to report my whereabouts to you." Mark rolled over and stared at the ceiling.

"Excuse the hell out of me for worrying about you."

Mark groaned, fighting his growing irritation. "What can I do for you?"

"Are you okay?" she asked, sounding genuinely concerned.

"Yes, fine, but I'd like to get back to sleep."

"I wanted to make sure you were picking Jamie up at school on Friday. His bus gets in from science camp at about one o'clock."

"I don't need a reminder every time I have to do something for Jamie. I know my responsibilities."

"What's wrong with you?" she asked again. "Why are you in such a foul mood?"

Mark rolled his eyes. "Sorry, long weekend. I will get Jamie on Friday, one o'clock, at the school. I've got him covered. After I get him, I'm taking him to lunch and dropping him off at your house."

"I dropped him off with all his stuff this morning. He looked so grown-up with all his camping gear." Her voice hinted of a smile. "He's having a good time."

"Good, I wish I could've gone with him."

"I know, but he's a big kid now, doesn't want us hovering over him. God, can you believe it?"

Mark sneered, but with a smile on his face. "No, I hate it."

"Today they're going to explore the tide pools. It's gonna be a busy week for them." She grew quiet for a moment and sighed. "Anyway, thanks for picking him up. I'll see you Friday."

Now that Mark was more awake, he heard that telling tone in her voice that usually meant things weren't quite right with her. It wasn't the first time in recent months that he had heard it, either.

"Hey, Al..." Not sure what to say, he just pushed forward. "Are you okay?"

"Ah...yeah." Her voice grew softer. "I'm fine."

"You sound..." He sat up and shifted the phone. "Is everything okay with the baby?"

"I'm just tired. I spent most of the day yesterday trying to put the crib together."

"Carl didn't help you?"

She cleared her throat. "No, he went to Sacramento for a meeting."

"On Sunday?"

"Well, a meeting at the golf course."

"Why didn't you wait for him? You shouldn't do things like that on your own."

"It was fine. I like doing things on my own, you know. I never could with you—you wouldn't let me."

"Remember to ask for help when you need it. Take care of yourself and the baby."

It took her a moment to respond, but she finally exhaled heavily into the phone. "I gotta go, see you Friday."

She hung up the phone before he could say another word.

Freaking hormonal women. He shook his head and lay back down in bed, wide awake now. He might as well get up and get some things done.

ഌ൫

Mark waited until nine a.m. to go. He didn't think Sarah would sleep longer than that, considering she'd slept for nearly twenty-four hours the day before. He parked on the street and walked up the drive. The door to her Toyota truck was open, her leg sticking out. When he stepped forward, he had to dodge keys when they flew passed his head. A quiet curse and a sob followed the projectiles. She hopped out and ripped at the sling, tugging at the strap, still swearing under her breath. He wanted to laugh, but he'd been married long enough to know that temper tantrums had to be played out fully for everyone to get out safely.

He forced back the smile creeping at the corners of his mouth and approached her.

When she caught sight of him, she quickly wiped her face.

"Great. Just what I need," she mumbled under her breath.

He scratched his chin in an effort to hide his increasing grin. Her tear-streaked face shone red, her half-tucked shirt buttoned crooked, the collar sticking out of the top of the sling strap and poking her chin.

"Glad I amuse you," she said, slamming the door of the truck.

"May I help you?" he said, feeling a little guilty.

Finally giving up on the sling strap, she dropped her other arm to her side. "Why are you here?"

"Checking on you—and it's a good thing, you're a mess." He waved her forward. "Come here."

She stomped toward him, and he thought of Jamie at four when he needed a nap. Gingerly, he loosened the strap and lowered the sling to free her arm. She slipped out of it and tried to rotate her shoulder, wincing in pain as she did.

"Thank you," she said, rubbing at her shoulder.

"Where are you going?"

"I need to go to the DMV and take care of some other things."

Mark reached up, folded her collar down and started to fix her buttons.

She jerked away. "Excuse me!" His hands were still extended toward her, and she glared at them, then up at his face.

"What are you doing?" she asked, clutching the front of her shirt.

Mark smirked. "Relax. I'm trying to fix your buttons. They're crooked."

Sarah's head snapped down to look at her shirt, and her cheeks turned bright pink. "Shit," she said, turning her back on him.

A moment later, she smoothed the front of her shirt out and turned around.

"Sorry," Mark said, the humor gone from his voice. "I didn't mean to make you uncomfortable."

She waved off his apology. "It's been a terrible morning."

Her light brown hair was curlier than before and shiny in the morning sun with blond highlights that shimmered when she tilted her head. Mark wondered if they were natural highlights or the work of an expensive salon. The storm in her eyes settled as her anger faded. She looked better than the day before—stronger, almost fiery. "I would have stayed to help you."

She shouldered her purse with a tight grimace on her face.

She must have been sore after the beating she took from her attacker. Why did she think she could drive in her condition? Shoulder injuries took forever to heal and it'd only been a couple of days.

She blinked rapidly at him, as if surprised by what he said. "You couldn't have dressed me."

"No, but I can take you to the DMV. You can't drive with that shoulder." He reached down and picked up her keys, glancing at her sandaled feet and pink toenails. When he looked back up, he realized how slender and tall she was and how good she looked dressed in normal clothes. He hadn't noticed how beautiful she was before. Her heart-shaped face was angelic and delicate, which made her injuries all the more devastating.

"I can drive."

He raised his eyebrows in challenge. "Really?"

"With a few adjustments," she said, bracing her hand on her hip.

He walked over to the passenger door of her truck and opened it. "Just get in and let me help you."

She tried to cross her arms over her chest. It clearly hurt. The adorably angry expression on her face made him want to laugh, but he held it in and stood his ground.

She strolled over and stopped in front of him.

He leaned closer and whispered, "Please."

When she struggled to get in, he reached out to help her, but she pulled away. *Stubborn,* he thought, and reached over to click her seatbelt into place before she could refuse his help again.

He climbed in, clicked his own seatbelt, and looked over at her.

Sarah had leaned back against the headrest with closed eyes. Her face was drawn, and she wore the undeniable signs of defeat. After all the fighting she'd done to get away from that son of a bitch who had attacked her, now she had to deal with the recovery.

Anger rose up in him at the site. Given the chance, he'd kill the son of a bitch who hurt her.

Her bruises hadn't faded at all. They stood out menacingly on her delicate skin. The scratches were still there too, which surprised him. He would've expected her to cover them with makeup like most women.

He exhaled slowly, before reaching over and tucking a strand of hair behind her ear. "I know it sucks to be hurt."

She opened her eyes and repeated his gesture, running her fingers behind her ears to push the hair off her face. The look of defeat disappeared, her new expression one of stone, emotionless—a mask.

"Have you eaten anything yet this morning?"

She shook her head. "I don't have much of an appetite."

"You need to eat."

She studied him for a moment.

He braced himself for the telling off.

Instead she said, "I'm not usually so troublesome."

"The only thing troublesome is you not accepting my help." He started the truck, backed out of the driveway, and drove directly to the best breakfast house in town. She needed a good meal and a moment of peace to relax, and he would provide both.

Chapter Five

"I've never been here," Sarah said when Mark parked at Pegg's Western Bakery. She felt better, the aggravation of the morning melting away. The fresh air and sunshine helped. She wasn't trying to be difficult. It was just that Mark had a way of making her feel—inadequate. He seemed almost too helpful when she wanted to take care of things herself.

The small restaurant was warm, comfortable, and pretty crowded for a Monday. The beautiful, honey-oak woodwork was covered in a high-shine varnish, and the sun's reflection created a glow of morning light so nice Sarah could've stayed there all day.

They stood in the small lobby waiting for the hostess. The bakery was to the left of the dining room, and Sarah stared into the glass enclosure at the huge cinnamon rolls and morning buns, both bigger than the size of her entire hand. The sweet scent of fresh baked bread brought her appetite back with a vengeance.

"You should try the blueberry, cheese Danish," Mark said, smiling down at her when she leaned in to examine the baked goods.

"I've never seen muffins that big." She pointed to a chocolate muffin. "That's what I'm having." She smiled and said, "Chocolate cake for breakfast."

Unexpected fear gripped her when someone brushed up against her from behind. She straightened her back and shot upright, the smile slipping from her face. The person stood so close she felt his breath brush her cheek. She wanted to turn and face the person who'd approached, be brave and prove she wasn't afraid, but she froze, the heat draining from her body and her stomach lurching.

Without thinking, she reached for Mark and locked her trembling hand around his elbow.

Mark's eyes met hers, but she couldn't blink, couldn't talk, and couldn't breathe. Mark tucked her hand around his arm and stepped next to her, looking back at the people standing behind her. She felt the distance and the cooler air brush her back as the presence behind her moved away.

Mark rubbed her hand and whispered, "Take a breath, Sarah."

The sound of her name got her attention or the warm touch of his hand, she couldn't be sure. She inhaled and bowed her head, hoping nobody else noticed her discomfort.

Mark tugged her arm, and without looking up, she followed him. After pulling a chair out for her, he leaned in. "Do you want to leave?"

She shook her head and lowered herself into the chair. He sat across from her and ordered coffee for both of them. When the waitress left, Mark reached over and touched the top of her hand. "Sarah?"

She jerked away, knocking her silverware to the floor. "I'm okay, I just...thought this would be easier."

When she bent to pick it up, he stopped her. "Leave it. They'll bring you more."

She straightened and nodded but didn't meet his eyes.

"We can leave...order our food to go."

She fisted her hands. "I absolutely do not want to leave," she said, now looking him directly in the eye.

She had surprised him. The expression on his face was easy to read.

"I will not let that monster scare me out of living my life. *I am not going* to hide in my house like a coward." She pronounced each word fiercely, making her face hot with determination.

Mark smiled and looked at her with a new expression.

"What?"

"Anger is better than despair. I expected you to move on from terrified to pissed-off eventually. I just didn't expect it to happen so fast." He looked at her carefully. "But you shouldn't let your guard down."

"I *never* let my guard down."

Her hardness slipped into weariness under his gaze.

"I'm fine," she chanted more to herself than to him.

ഌ

After breakfast, Mark drove her to the DMV. This was an adventure all by itself. Mark took the liberty of explaining to the clerk why Sarah needed a replacement driver's license. Thankfully, he'd lied and said she had been mugged—the truth about her attack would've been too real for most people. As it was, people stared relentlessly at her—and if they weren't staring, they flat out refused to look at her at all.

Sarah wasn't sure which she preferred. When people stared, they got hard glances from Mark, but when they refused to look at her, she couldn't fight back the feeling of shame. This instinct was the one thing she'd had trouble shaking after leaving Kevin. He'd manipulated her into believing bad things happened because she deserved them—to feel guilty instead of victimized.

To this day she had trouble making eye contact with strangers, always afraid of what they thought of her. Kevin had filled her head with so much trash, she still had trouble deciphering sympathy from disdain.

Funny how clear the manipulation was to her now, eight years later. If only she could have figured it out before. That he still had even a little bit of control over her thoughts made her nauseous.

Mark pulled into her driveway, and she tried to force a smile when she looked over at him. "Thanks for taking me. I'm sure you had better things to do with your day."

"Actually I didn't." He climbed out and walked over to open the door for her.

She reached out for her keys, hesitating while she built up the nerve. "Do you...want to come inside for a while?"

Mark tilted his head and grinned. "Yeah, I need to show you how to use the system. I didn't get around to it last night."

His expression told Sarah that wasn't his only reason for showing up this morning...and she had no idea how to feel about it.

"Sorry, that's my fault for being so rude." She handed the keys back to him. "Will you get the door? I want to check the mail."

She walked to the end of the driveway and grabbed everything from the box. She flipped through the mail as she strolled back up the driveway. *Junk, junk, and more junk, what a waste of paper*. Except one envelope, blank, but sealed with a letter inside.

"What is this?" It was small, not a business-sized envelope. It must have been a note from one of her neighbors. She tucked her fingers under the lip and ripped at the seal as she climbed the steps to the front door where Mark waited.

The bold blue letters stood out fiercely on the white-lined paper. She tried to focus and read them, but blood rushed to her head, making her temples throb. She fought for air while she read the first line.

IT'S NOT OVER SWEET SWEET SARAH

Chapter Six

She heard her name from a distance, but she was fighting to keep upright. Arms came around her, pulling her to the sofa and her head was thrust between her legs.

"Breathe, Sarah," he said, holding her in place. "Take a steady breath."

When cool air burned her lungs, she threw her hands over her face to hide her tears. Her injuries seemed to have a memory, aching whenever she thought about the attack. The note had to be from him. He had her name, had been to her house. What if she'd been home alone? What if he had come across her in the driveway this morning instead of Mark? Her breath caught in her throat and she cursed. She didn't want Mark—or anyone—to see her like this.

He sat next to her and draped an arm over her shoulder. "Sarah, it's okay, take a deep breath."

She stood and paced to the window, crossing her arms over her chest. Willing herself to stop crying. God, she hated how incredibly vulnerable she must have looked to him. As much as she wanted comfort, she wouldn't let him see that. Once a man got a glimpse at your vulnerability, you've given him the upper hand, handed him the keys to your soul. She wouldn't go down that road again, no matter how comfortable she felt with Mark.

She took a shuddering breath and brushed the tears from her face.

"You okay?" he asked.

She nodded and looked around, pacing the room from window to window. "Sorry—I'm fine."

"I need to call the police. Can you handle that—if they come here?"

She nodded and walked over to pick up the note with a shaking hand.

IT'S NOT OVER SWEET SWEET SARAH.
WE LEFT THINGS UNFINISHED AND AFTER ALL MY HARD WORK. I OWE YOU ONE NOW. CAN'T WAIT TO SEE YOU AGAIN. UNTIL NEXT TIME...

"Sick bastard," Mark hissed.

She turned to find him standing behind her, the expression on his face hard and focused on the note.

When the paper fluttered in her grasp, he placed his hands on her upper arms and began to rub. "I have to call Brian. Please sit down."

Her body thawed slightly at his warm touch. If only she could bottle the feeling and have it around when she really needed it. It was scary how easily she felt herself getting closer to him. Wanting to be closer to him, even when she knew it was a mistake. She couldn't put herself in a vulnerable position again.

She walked back to the sofa, the note still clutched in her hand. Mark was talking into the phone, but she couldn't hear the conversation because a rushing noise filled her ears. She leaned back on the sofa cushion to get her bearings.

Pull yourself together. Stop acting like a frightened child. She'd faced worse than this before, hadn't she? She'd come out on top and managed to stay safe, hadn't she?

Mark snatched the note from her hand and stuffed it into a Ziplock bag with the envelope. "You don't have to face a bunch of cops, just Brian."

"Brian?"

Mark sat next to her again. "He's the investigating officer. He took your statement Friday night."

Sarah inched away, giving him room and fighting the urge to lean against him. "I don't remember much of anything from Friday."

"Probably a good thing," Mark muttered.

By the time Brian tapped on her screen door, her nerves had settled. Mark stood and opened it, greeting Brian with a nod.

She turned and focused on Brian's face. His hazel eyes stood out against his olive complexion and dark, curly hair. When their eyes met, his lips tipped into a smile, which contrasted against his agitated expression.

Brian reached a hand out to her. "It's good to see you again, Ms. Jennings."

She tried to maintain her focus, but flashes of memory rushed her thoughts—being pushed into the ambulance on a gurney, paramedics cutting the remains of her clothes off, lying in a hospital bed giving a description of her attacker, signing her statement with a shaky hand.

Mark at her side in every memory.

She blinked and reached out to shake Brian's hand.

"Yes, you too," she whispered as the memories continued to flood her mind. Sarah even remembered the argument Mark had with Brian when Brian wanted to take her statement. Mark insisted on staying with her, but only because Sarah didn't want him to leave. At her request, he adamantly refused to leave her side.

Sarah stood and excused herself. She needed to get out from under both sets of prying eyes and collect herself.

Once in the bathroom, she splashed water on her face and took several deep breaths. Why had she clung to Mark so tightly after her attack? What was it about him that broke through her defenses? It was as if he'd become her talisman, a source of strength, but she had no idea how or why.

When Mark knocked, she jumped and reached for a towel before opening the door.

"I'm fine," she said before he got the question out.

"What happened?"

"Seeing Brian triggered some memories...I got flashes from the hospital." She hung the towel over the front of the sink and faced him. "Thank you for being here for me. I wouldn't have gotten through...any of that without you."

She hung her head at the admission, but she owed him for being there for her. It couldn't have been easy for him.

Mark's expression sagged. "I couldn't leave you like that."

"And being here for me again this morning. I really don't deserve your kindness. I feel really bad for treating you the way I did yesterday. I shouldn't have acted..." She closed her eyes and shook her head. "I'm so sorry."

"It's my fault, I should have thought—I should have asked before I installed the system."

"Well, for what it's worth, thank you. It couldn't have been easy to sit through all that with a stranger."

"You needed someone. It wasn't hard to be there for you." He cleared his throat. "Are you up to talking to Brian?"

She hesitated and focused her eyes on the floor, not sure if she was.

"He's a good guy, Sarah. You can trust him. I've known him most of my life."

She nodded. "Okay, yeah, I can talk to him."

She followed Mark out of the bathroom and into the living room. Brian came back through the screen, scribbling in a small notepad at the same time.

"She's ready," Mark said.

Brian nodded. "I did a cursory of the yard, nothing looks disturbed. No signs that anyone approached the house." He gestured toward the sofa. "Let's have a seat."

She sat down and Brian took a seat across from her on the other side of her huge U-shaped sofa.

"I just have a few questions. I'll try to be fast."

"Thank you," Sarah said.

He clicked his pen a couple of times before looking up from the notepad. His eyes softened when they rested on her face. He smiled again and said, "Did you set the alarm when you left this morning?"

"No, she didn't know how to use it yet," Mark said from behind her.

"And what time did you leave?"

"A little after nine. I got here about nine," Mark said.

Brian shot Mark an exasperated look before asking Sarah, "How long were you gone?"

"All morning," Mark answered.

"Mark, shut the hell up before I throw you outta here. I'm not questioning you. I'm trying to talk to her."

"Don't shout like that. She's nervous and scared. I'm trying to help."

Sarah turned to him and said, "Thank you, Mark, but it's okay..."

"Mark, shut up!" Brian pointed his pen at him. "Don't act like you've never done this before."

Mark gave him a sullen look and leaned down to rest his hands on the sofa behind Sarah.

"Sarah, how long were you in the driveway before Mark showed up?"

"About ten minutes."

"What were you doing out there?"

"Trying to leave, but it's pretty damn hard to drive with one hand."

"You're not supposed to be driving. The ER doc put you under restrictions. No driving for at least three weeks."

Ignoring the pain, she crossed her arms over her chest. "I didn't know that."

"Your release papers are on your kitchen table. It has all the information," Mark said.

"As a cop, I have to warn you not to drive while under those restrictions. Do you have someone to call who can stay with you...or is Mark staying?"

She raised her eyebrows. "No—"

"I can stay. It's not a problem."

But it could too easily become a problem if she got any closer to him. She didn't need to complicate her life with a good-looking, yet overprotective man like Mark.

She turned to look at him. "I can't ask you to stay here. You've already done too much."

Brian leaned over and grabbed the Ziploc bag with the note inside. "What if he tries to carry out this threat? You're not exactly in the condition to fight him off again."

Her pulse kicked up at the thought, but she would not—could not—continue to rely on Mark. It was too much. "Why do I need someone here when I have the alarm?"

"The alarm will alert the police, not provide physical protection. There is a delay in response," Brian said. "Maybe you can stay somewhere else for a few days."

She stared at him, not sure what to say. *Dammit.* No way in hell was she calling her family. She'd rather chew off her own arm than call her parents, and her best friend, Ava, was out of town for work.

"No, I can't call—"

"I'll stay. It's no big deal," Mark said.

Her eyes swept the room before focusing on Mark again. He looked determined to stay. It was convincing too, but she just couldn't put herself in that position with him.

She glanced back at the note in the Ziplock. What if her attacker made good on his threat? She closed her eyes at the throbbing pain in her shoulder, knowing Brian was right. If her attacker came back, she couldn't fight him off now.

"Um...I can call my brother, Devon."

"Does he live nearby?" Mark asked.

"San Diego—he's the closest."

"He can't get here before tomorrow," Mark said.

Sarah's lips quirked into a smile. "You haven't met my brother."

"I would rather not leave you alone in this house," Brian said again, as if she wasn't grasping the severity of the situation.

"Okay, I know. I'll call him." She stood up, retrieved the phone handset, walked into her bedroom and closed the door behind her.

She sat on her bed, still debating. "It's Devon," she whispered, not her mother. She missed him anyway, and she could get Devon to swear not to tell Mama.

She blew her bangs off her forehead. God, she hated asking for help. He didn't want to take care of his little sister. He'd spent most of his young life taking care of her. She smacked her palm to her forehead and squeezed her eyes shut. *He's going to kill me when he finds out that I didn't call him right way.*

"Fine, might as well get it over with," she mumbled, dialing his number.

When her call went directly to voicemail, she hit the off button without leaving a message.

Sarah waited for another few minutes before dialing the number again. No answer. She was absolutely not calling Mama. She dialed Ava's number, praying Ava came home early from her trip, but it went directly to voicemail.

"Now what?" she whispered.

She thought about the nightmares she'd had the night before. No way was Mark staying when she couldn't sleep more than an hour without screaming awake. The new memories from the hospital coursed through her. God, she could not allow herself to get close to him, no matter how easy he made it for her...or how incredibly inviting it was.

She walked over to the nightstand and pulled open the drawer. Her gun sat directly on top of the case. She picked it up and checked the rounds. Between the alarm and the gun, she should be fine.

She turned and left the room. When she entered the living room, Mark and Brian were standing just outside the front door discussing the yard layout, pointing to the tall hedges, and judging the distance from the front door to the street.

"What's wrong?" she asked at the low murmurs.

Brian glanced back at her. "This place isn't very secure, too secluded. It wouldn't hurt for you to put a couple of cameras out here," he said. "Is your brother coming?"

"He'll be here sometime tonight." She looked at the clock. "He said he could be here by midnight."

"Good," Mark said, nodding his head. "I'll sleep better too if you have someone with you."

"Problem solved. I need to get this to the lab. It was nice to see you again, Sarah. I'll let you know what I get off this letter." He reached into his shirt pocket and pulled out a business card. "Please don't hesitate to call if you need me for anything."

"Thank you, Brian," Sarah said, fingering the card. "I appreciate you coming."

He waved one last time and stepped down off the porch.

Mark followed, but turned to Sarah first. "I'll be right back."

She nodded and returned to the sofa, plopping down, overcome with guilt. She'd lied to a police officer and possibly put herself in more danger, but at this point, she had to decipher who was more dangerous—the attacker or Mark. She'd leave catching her attacker up to the police, but she had to protect her heart all on her own, and that meant distance from Mark.

When Mark came back inside, her nerves kicked into overdrive. It was the whopping lie she had told them. She sucked at lying. Ava had always told her that. Her best friend was a master at making stuff up, but Sarah had too much of a guilty conscious to outright lie to someone.

"Are you all right?" he asked, sitting across from her.

"Please stop asking me that."

"All right, I'll lay off."

She rested her head back. "It's been a long day. I'm tired."

"Go lie down. I'll wait for your brother."

"No, you don't have to stay...although I need to learn how to use the alarm system."

"Oh right." He stood and walked over to the unit on the wall. "I'll show you."

She stood and joined him.

"I put a code in for you already, which you can change anytime you like." He pushed a button and made the system beep. "You have thirty seconds after you arm the system to exit and another thirty seconds to disarm when you enter. If you can't disarm it in thirty seconds, the alarm will sound. If the alarm sounds, you can still turn it off, but the monitoring company will call and ask for your password."

He punched in the passcode and pressed the off button. The beeping stopped.

His face lit as he explained the system, and Sarah couldn't help but feel a little lighter as she watched him—his excitement was contagious. He looked like a kid with a new toy. It was so cute. "What password do I use when the monitoring company calls?"

"Summors," he said, looking a little embarrassed.

She tilted her head. "Using the name of the company is pretty obvious."

"Well, the likelihood of someone guessing your password is slim, but like I said, you can change it."

"Okay, let me get this straight, if I accidentally set off the alarm, the password I give the person over the phone is Summors?"

"Exactly," he said, smiling. "Another great feature is the ambush code. If someone jumps out at you with a weapon and forces you to disarm the system under duress—this is important so pay attention."

When his grin disappeared, she held her hands up. "You have my full attention."

"If you're ambushed coming in the door, you must remember to type your code in backwards. This will disarm the alarm, but will send an emergency signal to the monitoring company. The monitoring company will immediately call the police. Your intruder won't know the police have been alerted. The monitoring company will not call the house to ask for the password, and the intruder will assume you entered the code correctly."

"Is that everything?"

"You need to understand, Sarah, the police often treat these calls as if they're false alarms or accidents. To get their attention, you need to use the ambush code. Otherwise, they assume it's breaking and entering, not home invasion."

"Okay." His stony expression made her a little uncomfortable, especially after his animated lesson. "You are really worried, aren't you?"

"Did you hear anything Brian said?"

"Yes, I heard and I understand."

"I should stay," he said, exhaling heavily. "I can sleep on the couch and make sure nothing happens."

She rested her hand on her chest, feeling a little overcome with his concern. "Thank you so much for thinking about me, but I have already taken too much of your time. Don't you need to get back to work? How can you run a business from here?"

"The security business practically runs itself."

She turned back to the sofa. "No business runs itself."

"True, but I have a couple of great managers. I only go into the office a couple of days a week. I do all the contracting for large accounts and agent contracts. I teach during the summer. That's my busy season."

"You teach? Really?" Surprised, she said, "What do you teach?"

"An academy for private security agents." He leaned back against the front door and crossed his arms over his chest. "It's a two-month intensive program covering everything from fighting to surveillance."

"What are security agents?"

"Basically, private bodyguards."

"Oh, well...," she said with a raised eyebrow, "that explains a lot. You seem to enjoy it. I've never seen anyone get so excited over an alarm system before." She curled her legs under her and sat back into the full sofa cushions.

"I do love my job. I used to be a cop, but my wife didn't like the constant worry." He shrugged. "I quit and started this company."

"You were a cop?"

"Yeah, actually Brian and I entered the police academy together with Shane, one of my best agents."

"And you quit for your wife?" This really surprised Sarah, never had she heard of a man putting his wife's concerns before his career. Mark was turning out to be quite an anomaly. "Brian isn't married?"

"He's married. Has two kids. His wife, Julie, is one of Ali's best friends. We all grew up together."

"Who is Ali?" she asked, confused.

"My ex-wife." He pushed off the door and walked over to sit on the sofa across from her. "Did you go to school here, in Santa Rosa?"

"I was born here, but we moved around a lot. I came back a few years ago. My oldest friend sucked me in and made me stay."

"I guess you like it here."

"Well." She looked around her house and wanted to cry. "It looks like my days in Santa Rosa are numbered...especially with everything that's going on."

"No, no, no, I recommend you don't make any life-altering decision right now. Besides, Brian will have that guy locked up in no time."

She ran her fingers through her hair. "I hope you're right."

"Who's this friend anyway and why isn't he here with you?" he asked, his eyebrows rising a little. "Maybe I know him."

"He is a she, and I don't think you know Ava."

He grinned wide. "Ava, as in Ava Mitchell?"

"You know her?" She couldn't believe it. What a small world.

"She was a few years behind me in school. She hung out with my sister, Angela."

"No kidding?"

"Why didn't you let me call Ava on Friday? She would've been here for you."

"She's out of town working. She's an international flight attendant. She's usually gone for weeks at a time."

"Right." He nodded. "I think I did hear that somewhere."

"Is it safe to say you don't make a habit out of rescuing damsels in distress?"

He laughed. "Only the ones who tackle me in parking lots, although, if I could, I would."

She arched an eyebrow at him, wishing like hell she didn't believe him. What was it her mama used to say, *if it seems too good to be true than it probably is too good to be true*. So was she missing something with Mark? Was he too good to be true too? "I think I believe that."

"Why wouldn't you believe that?"

She shrugged. "Most men wouldn't care, and you sort of...don't fit the stereotype. I mean, well." She paused, searching for the right words. "Most guys wouldn't devote this much time helping me without expecting something in return—unless you are expecting something in return?"

When his expression changed, she squirmed uncomfortably. So...maybe she wasn't missing something about him. God, what a bitch she was. Mark had done so much for her and she openly questioned his motives.

"Well, your stereotype sucks, Sarah. You might find it hard to trust people after what you've been through, but I'm only trying to help you feel safe in your home."

Mark's statement made her sick to her stomach. "You're right, I'm sorry."

"Forget it," he said, his tone laced with hurt. "I'll get out of your hair if you don't need anything else."

"Yeah...of course, go ahead." She tried to look at him, though she couldn't pull her attention from the floor. "Thanks again, Mark, for everything."

When the door closed behind him, she curled up and held her knees to her chest. Who had she become? A liar and a bitch who insulted good people who helped her.

Chapter Seven

On Wednesday morning Mark was surprised when Sarah's number came up on his caller ID. He leaned back in his office chair and answered on the second ring. "Hello."

"Mark, hi, it's Sarah Jennings." She sounded hesitant and used her full name as if he wouldn't remember her. Ha—yeah, like he could forget. He hadn't stopped thinking about her since he'd met her.

"Is everything okay?"

"I'm sorry to bother you, but ah...I wanted to apologize for my behavior before. The system is great...reassuring. I sleep better."

"Good, I'm glad. Your brother got there all right?"

"I'm sorry?"

"Your brother?" He bowed his head and shook it. "Didn't actually come up from San Diego."

"Oh, shit." She sighed heavily on the other end of the line. "No, um...he's not here."

"You've been alone the last two nights?" He stood, walked to the window and looked out at the traffic on Coggs Boulevard. "Why?"

"It doesn't matter. Nothing happened. I'm fine by myself."

"If only things were that easy," Mark muttered. "Well, you called, I guess you need something."

"Yeah." She laughed, but Mark didn't catch the joke. "I actually need a favor—I know, it's ridiculous. I treat you like a jerk, lie to you, and now I need a favor."

She laughed again, and this time Mark didn't miss the sarcasm.

"Feel free to hang up on me if you like. I'll understand."

"I'm not going to hang up. Come on, give me a break." He rubbed his forehead with his hand. "But you need to take this seriously. Your safety isn't a game."

"I promise to be more careful if you get me out of this freaking house."

Her voice elevated as she spoke, and Mark had to fight the same smile he wore when she threw a temper tantrum in her driveway.

"I can't drive, or exercise, or anything. I have a doctor's appointment today—but I can't drive."

He restrained his smile. "Do you need a ride?"

She exhaled heavily. "I'm sorry."

"Sarah, don't cry. I'll take you to your appointment."

"I'm not crying," she said through what sounded like gritted teeth. "I'm frustrated."

"What time?"

"Ten thirty. Dr. Davidson, he's on Sonoma Drive."

"I'm in my office across town. Give me fifteen minutes."

"Thank you. I appreciate it."

He hung up smirking and muttered, "And I thought Ali was stubborn. Why is it hard to simply ask for help without the drama?"

Sarah tried not to let it get to her. She hated relying on other people, and she tried to convince herself that calling Mark for help didn't mean anything. It certainly didn't mean she was afraid to get into a cab with a stranger. It didn't mean she was comfortable with Mark, and even if she *was* comfortable with Mark, that wasn't the point. And, most importantly, it didn't mean she couldn't have driven herself, she just didn't want to get caught. She'd already lied to the police once this week. She didn't want to push her luck further. Besides, she liked Brian. He'd treated her like a person, not like a victim. Giving things to her straight was what she wanted and Brian did that, which made lying to him even worse.

She watched from the window as Mark pulled into her driveway. When he climbed out of his truck, she couldn't help but admire his confidence. A lot of divorced men had a beaten and defeated way about them. Not Mark. He moved with purpose and strength, his broad shoulders back and his stride solid. And damn if he wasn't the best looking guy she'd laid eyes on in years.

Sarah wondered about his ex-wife. What was she like? Why divorce? Did he cheat on her? When his eyes locked on hers through the window, she almost blushed.

After a quick wave, she dropped the curtain and looked down at herself before opening the door.

"Hey," she said through the screen.

"You ready?"

"Yeah." She picked up her purse and stepped outside.

Mark stood still, staring at her like she'd forgotten something.

"I'm ready. Are you?"

He cocked an eyebrow. "The alarm?"

"Oh." She shook her head and squeezed her eyes shut. "Yes, sorry. I'm a little preoccupied."

She stepped inside, still mumbling excuses.

He followed her in and closed the door for her to set the alarm. "It's okay," Mark said. "But try to be more diligent."

"I know, I..." She shook her head and tugged the door back open when the beeping started. "How long do I have to get out of the house again?"

Mark stood too close to her, she couldn't think straight. He must have thought she was a complete nutcase. How odd that he had the ability to make her feel safe and comfortable, yet inadequate and weak at the same time.

"Thirty seconds." Mark followed her out and pulled the door shut behind him.

Sarah turned to lock the door, but her hands shook with nervous energy. At this rate, thirty seconds wouldn't be long enough. She fisted the keys, hoping Mark didn't notice. She'd hoped in vain.

He reached out and took them from her. "Here, let me do it."

She sighed and muttered a thank you, before stepping off the porch and walking to his truck.

He stepped ahead and opened the door for her. When he offered his hand to help her up, she accepted it. The warmth of his skin left a lingering pulse behind when he finally pulled away.

Her agitation grew on the ride to the doctor's office, forcing her to swallow back the nausea. It was ridiculous that at thirty years old, she was still frightened of doctors. She looked over at Mark and wondered how pissed he'd get if she puked in his truck. When he smiled back at her, his little dimple flashed, setting off another wave of nervous fluttering in her stomach.

When he caught her staring, she blurted out the first thing that came to mind. "How long were you married?"

Once the question was out, she could've slapped herself.

"Excuse me?" Mark asked.

"I'm curious," she said, hoping to smooth over her previous bluntness. "You said you're divorced. How long you were married?"

"Almost twelve years."

"And you didn't have any children?" She turned toward the window and let the bright, morning sunlight warm her face.

"Yes, I have a son...Jamie."

"Oh, I assumed since you hadn't mentioned—although we haven't exactly had time for normal conversation over the last few days." She turned back to him. "Do you get to spend a lot of time with him?"

"We split his time evenly. We didn't go through the big court battle for custody. It's been pretty civil considering the circumstances."

Sarah raised an eyebrow. "Circumstances?"

"It wasn't a pretty divorce." His smiled faltered a little. "He's away at science camp this week with his class."

"Oh yeah, our third graders went too. Does he go to my school?"

"No, he's at Highland."

"He must be, what, eight years old?"

"Yeah." His grin returned. "Eight is a fun age."

"Too bad they can't stay that age forever." She smiled wide, hoping he couldn't see through it. His enthusiasm made her feel a little vacant. While she loved and cared for her students, she couldn't pretend to understand what it was like to be a parent. She knew that kind of love was an entirely different thing.

"Ali and I met when we were eight." He chuckled at that and shook his head. "We got together in high school and were inseparable for a long time."

Sarah took the chance to satisfy her curiosity. She wanted to know how similar their stories were. Mark didn't seem like the type of guy who would hurt a woman, but abusers didn't exactly wear the label on their sleeve. "Why did you get divorced?" She waved her hand to stop him. "Um, none of my business—never mind—forget I asked."

He glanced at her with an amused expression. "It's okay. I don't mind talking about it." He turned back to face the road. "Ali had an affair."

The opposite of what she'd thought. Her heart thudded hard in her chest at the reminder of her own broken relationship. "I'm sorry you had to go through that, Mark. It must have been hard for you."

"Yeah." He nodded. "She joined a law firm in San Francisco. That's when we started to grow apart. She met Carl while working on a case for the State of California."

"Carl?"

"Her current husband," Mark said.

"And of course she had to kick you while you were down and marry the guy."

He gave her a sideways grin. "Of course."

They grew quiet. Sarah didn't know what to say and needed to give herself a moment to slow her angered pulse. She understood more than she wanted to, but she didn't understand why he was okay with it, so relaxed about his wife hurting him. Sarah wondered how many times Kevin had cheated on her before she had finally caught him. How different would her life have been if she hadn't caught him? Would her baby have lived and been raised, at least in part, by a monster?

Mark's story just proved to her that being alone was the way to go. Love wasn't worth the heartache it brought. Of course it was the good people who got hurt, not the cheaters. Even though he acted like he was over the divorce—over her—it was perfectly clear on his face that his ex-wife had truly hurt him.

At least being single meant you could do what you wanted without someone trying to control your life. Why fall in love, why marry, why live together if it was just going to turn out sour in the end? Between her relationship with Kevin and her mother's numerous failed relationships, she'd learned firsthand putting that much faith in someone just wasn't worth it.

"What's wrong with you?" he asked when she failed to look away from him. "You're staring at me like I'm a woman in men's clothes."

"Oh, sorry—you just surprised me. I don't meet many people who are so open about their past."

"I don't mind talking about it, why would I? I haven't done anything to be ashamed of."

She tried not to hear a double meaning in what he said. How would he know anything about her shame?

"How long have you and Ali been divorced?"

"About three years."

"So..." She grimaced. "How did you take it when you found out about the affair? You must have been devastated."

"I tried to work things out, but she didn't want to. Until then, we seemed pretty solid." He shrugged his shoulders. "I had to be strong for Jamie. He's the real victim. We agreed not to put him through a fight."

"So you get him, what, a couple days a week?"

"We rotate weeks. This is my week, but he's at camp."

"You won't get him next week, either?"

"I'll see him for a while on Friday before he goes back to Ali's."

"Sorry," she said, unable to articulate anything else. He seemed so civil when he talked about his ex-wife. Most couples were awful to each other after a divorce, but Mark had somehow managed to push all of that aside for his son.

"It's a daily struggle, but we manage."

Mark pulled into a parking lot next to a large warehouse.

"Where are we?" Sarah asked, sitting up in her seat to look around.

"This is Summors Security. Do you mind? I need to take care of a couple of quick things."

"Ah, okay," she said, staring out at the tall warehouse.

"This will only take a few minutes." He climbed out and opened her door.

"I'll stay here." She focused on her hands, not meeting his gaze.

"Why, is something wrong?"

"I jus...I'll wait." She glanced up at him. "I don't mind waiting."

He watched her for a second before realization softened his face. "Right...I guess you don't want to face a curious crowd."

"Do the people you work with know what happened?"

"Not everything, but since I installed your system and it's being monitored—actually, I can do this later."

When he started to close the door, she stopped him.

"No, go. I already feel bad enough for pulling you away to drive me around—"

"Don't."

The sharp tone of his voice made her look into his eyes.

"Don't do that. I want to help you."

She tried to give him a reassuring smile. The intensity he showed when it came to her comfort and her safety was extreme to the point of making her uncomfortable. She was not used to people caring about her like that.

"I won't if you go in there and do what you need to do and leave me here."

"I walked out with the gym keys when I came to get you and they'll need them while I'm out today." Mark surveyed the parking lot. "It'll only be a minute, if you need anything, call my cell. Oh, shit—forgot. Your phone is gone. Okay—honk the horn and I'll come right out."

"Yeah, I will. Honestly, don't worry about me. Hurry up or we'll be late for my appointment."

He took a few steps back, searching her face with his eyes. What he saw must have convinced him she'd be okay, because he finally turned and hurried into the building.

She smiled, wishing she could be annoyed with him, but the concern he showed made it difficult to be mad for long.

ꕥ

Mark came out ten minutes later, jogging toward his truck. "Sorry about that."

She waved away his apology. "Not a problem."

"I have a present for you."

His bright eyes made her smile. "What do you mean?"

He pulled a little, black cell phone out of his pocket.

"Here, it's one of our business phones. You can use it until you get a new one." He handed her the phone and a small piece of paper with a phone number on it.

"You're giving me a cell phone?"

"A loaner. It's not safe for you to be without a phone, and we have an inventory of phones for our field agents." He gave her a hesitant look. "Is that okay?"

Sarah felt a pang of guilt when she remembered the way she'd reacted to the alarm system. "It's okay." She looked at the phone. "I guess I should get a new one soon."

"Well, in the meantime, problem solved. I programmed my numbers and emergency numbers into the speed dial." He started the truck and drove out of the parking lot.

She opened the phone and reviewed the speed dial.

"What a thoughtful thing to do. Thank you." *Incredibly thoughtful actually, wow.*

"You're welcome. Now, let's get to your appointment."

Chapter Eight

As Sarah stood in the lobby of the doctor's office, she tried to ignore her anxiety and convince herself that everything would be fine, but she was losing the argument.

She hoped for some last minute reprieve, maybe a fire alarm or sudden earthquake—anything to get out of this appointment. The more she thought about it, the more uncomfortable she became.

Unable to sit still any longer, she walked toward the glass door leading to a small garden courtyard that separated her doctor's office from the neighboring one. She opened the door and forced herself to inhale as much fresh air as possible. The air burned her lungs and caught in her throat.

She kicked her way through the fallen leaves to sit on the park bench under a large, sycamore tree. Overgrown clematis climbed the exterior walls. She held her eyes closed and tried to focus on the scent, hoping it would calm her nerves.

When she opened her eyes, they focused on the crushed leaves under Mark's feet.

"What's going on in your head right now that's freaking you out?"

"I'm not freaking out."

"Hate to disappoint you, but you're a terrible actress."

She closed her eyes again and took a deep breath. "I don't want to go through an examination."

"I'm sure he's just going to check your injuries."

She lifted her eyes and saw his tightly knitted brow. She straightened and shook her head to push back the emotions. "I'll be fine. I just really hate doctors."

"I guess that explains your preoccupation earlier. Do you need a few more minutes or are you ready to go inside?"

She nodded jerkily. "I'm ready."

"Need an arm?" He held out his elbow for her to take.

She lowered her eyes and considered taking it, but before she could respond, the nurse stuck her head out and called for her.

The scent of ammonia and rubbing alcohol turned her stomach as she followed the nurse down the hall past the tiny sterile rooms. She swallowed hard and stepped into her own tiny room.

The nurse pulled out a sheet and gown for her. "Please remove your clothes. You can leave your bra and underwear on."

"Why...why do I need to remove my clothes?" Sarah asked.

The nurse flipped a page in the chart and said, "It says here you sustained injuries to your lower back. Dr. Davidson will need to take a look. It's easier if your jeans aren't in the way. Would you prefer to—"

"No, that's fine, I don't mind." Sarah said, feeling a little foolish now for asking. "Thank you."

When the door closed behind the nurse, she took a deep breath and murmured, "Okay, man-up, Sarah."

She removed her sling and the rest of her clothes, focusing on what she needed to do and not what came next. She slipped into the gown, leaving the back open, crawled up on the exam table, and covered the lower half of her body with the sheet.

Mark leaned against the wall in the waiting room. When his phone buzzed in his pocket, he pulled it out and flipped it open. "Hello."

"It's Brian."

"Hey, Bri, what's up?"

"I got a report back on the note Jennings found in her mailbox. No prints except yours and hers. We got his DNA off the envelope, it matches the DNA from the crime scene, but it's not in our system."

Mark's heart rate picked up. "Well, check this out. She didn't actually get a hold of her brother. She's been alone the last two nights."

"What? You're kiddin' me. How do you even know that?"

"I'm with her right now. She needed a ride to an appointment."

"Well, shit. I can't force her to get help. I guess she's on her own."

"No, she's not. I'll stay with her."

"Careful, bro. Don't get in too deep."

Mark ran his hand through his hair. "Too late. I can't let anything happen to her. I feel responsible."

Brian laughed. "Typical pansy-ass shit, Mark. You're a piece of work, you know that? Maybe your hovering is why she lied about her brother."

"Fuck you, Brian." He glanced around at the other people in the waiting room and lowered his voice. "I'm here because she asked me for help."

"Yeah, sure you are."

"Why haven't you caught this guy yet?"

Brian scoffed. "Oh, I will, don't worry about that."

"You think she's safe home alone?" Mark cleared his throat. "What are the chances he'll make good on his threat?"

"No, I don't think she's safe home alone. I already made that clear to her."

"Then how can I leave her alone? What if something happens?"

"I don't know, man. I'll up the patrols in her neighborhood."

Mark didn't respond. He couldn't help but worry about her. She still seemed so fragile.

"Talk to her, Mark. Make sure she's making these decisions fully informed."

"Right, talk to you later." Mark closed his phone and took a seat to wait for Sarah.

ꟈ

The nurse stepped back into the exam room, followed by Dr. Davidson. The doctor stepped forward and reached to shake her hand. "Hello, Sarah. It's good to see you again. Too bad it's under these circumstances."

"Hi," she said before pressing her lips together in a fake smile.

"It's been a rough couple of days for you, and I don't want to make things worse. This is Helen. She can stay if you prefer to have a nurse present?"

When Sarah didn't respond, he said, "Okay, if at any time you get uncomfortable, tell me to stop."

He talked slowly in that pitying, kindergarten tone people used when they felt sorry for you.

She straightened her back and looked him in the eye. The last thing she wanted from anyone was pity. "I'm fine, and I don't need Helen to stay. I'm perfectly comfortable talking to you alone."

"Okay." He turned and nodded to Helen as she let herself out. "I read the emergency room report and I don't want you to have to relive everything, but I have to say, you did an incredible job protecting yourself. Hopefully he'll think twice before he hurts anyone else."

Dr. Davidson gave her a half-smile and nodded at her shoulder. "Let's have a look at that shoulder."

He slowly pulled her gown down to get a good look at it. A yellow ring had developed around the edges of the huge bruise, and Sarah wondered if it would ever completely disappear.

"You need to start physical therapy. This type of injury usually takes a long time to heal. I expect your recovery to go a bit faster since you're in such good shape. Are you still going to the gym regularly?"

"Yes, about four times a week and I run four to five times a week. At least until this week."

"Well it's a good thing. I'd bet your workout regimen had a lot to do with your ability to kick the crap out of that jerk."

His smile was a mix of sympathy and awe as he eased the gown back up over her shoulder.

"Can you roll over? I need to examine the abrasions on your lower back."

With the doctors' help, she rolled onto her stomach.

"Do you know how you got these abrasions?"

Her pulse spiked. "He knocked me unconscious, pulled me into the bushes, dragging me by my left arm...on concrete and gravel, and dislocating my arm."

"But you were unconscious, so the police must have told you."

She nodded, praying he didn't ask for more details. She remembered just enough to know that she only wanted to forget. Not that she could forget—every time she rolled over in bed, her shoulder throbbed, and every time she stepped into a hot shower, the massive scratches and abrasions burned with a vengeance.

"Well, if you keep using this ointment, they'll heal with little scarring."

With a large cotton swab, he dabbed at the burning scratches down her back. His gentle touch to the area gave her a sense of vertigo, the injuries yet again reminding her of what she'd been through. She closed her eyes and willed herself to take a deep breath and push back the nausea.

"I'll give you a prescription so you can apply this at home. We can't do much about the bruising, but I have to insist you get some rest. No working out for a while—no hiking, no swimming, no running. You'll be off work for at least a month."

She scoffed. "A month. Why? It's only my arm. I can still work."

No way was she sitting around the house for a full month with nothing to do.

"*Rest*," he emphasized. "None of it until you're completely healed." He helped her sit back up. "Is there anything else I should know?"

"I'm having trouble figuring out what happened after the attack."

"Hmm." Dr. Davidson flipped through her chart.

"Some things have slowly returned, but very little."

"Do you have overwhelming feelings of guilt?"

"No."

"Do you feel reckless or impulsive?"

She shook her head. "No, not at all."

"Have you considered hurting yourself?" he asked.

"No," she said, taken aback by the question.

"Nightmares?"

Sarah's eyebrows shot up. "I've had nightmares."

"Are you excessively fearful of things?"

Sarah lowered her eyes feeling self-conscious now. "Not excessively."

But enough to keep her from getting a good night's sleep.

The doctor shook his head. "You don't have Post Traumatic Stress, although trauma can cause this sporadic memory loss.

Usually it's the event that's forgotten, but sometimes the after events are just as traumatic. Having your shoulder reset, giving your statement to the police..." He closed her chart. "I don't think it's permanent. You will probably remember in stages as your stress level returns to normal."

Just what she needed, slow and steady reminders flashing in her head *in stages*. "The sooner I get my life back to normal the better."

"I agree. I am concerned about your weight loss and high blood pressure. You've lost ten pounds since your last appointment"—he looked at her chart—"two months ago. You're usually healthy as a horse, but this incident has taken a toll on you." He stared at her intently. "You should join a support group or see a counselor."

"No." She shook her head, no way. She'd get through it on her own, just like she'd gotten through everything else in her life. "I don't need that. I just need to get on with my life."

He pulled a pamphlet from the chart in his hand and said, "Take this in case you change your mind. There are a lot of services for sexual assault victims. This hotline will connect you to victim support groups in the area. I'll leave it alone for now. But I want to see you back here in a couple of weeks with fuller cheeks and a healthy blood pressure, okay?"

"Okay."

"Stop at the desk on your way out to get your prescription and a follow-up appointment time. I'll see you in a couple of weeks, take things easy until then."

Chapter Nine

When Mark pulled into her driveway, she lifted her head off the back of the seat and wished to go anywhere but home. Restless to her core, she could hardly stand herself. She'd never spent this much time sitting around on her ass doing nothing, and to think, an entire month of nothing but the same.

"You okay?" Mark asked.

She rolled her eyes.

"Yes, I'm fine. But damn, I don't want to sit inside that house with nothing to do for the rest of the day." *Or the month, for that matter.*

"Where do you want to go?"

She pulled the door handle. "No, I've taken enough of your time. But thank you."

"Stop being so difficult." He slapped a hand down on the steering wheel. "If I wasn't willing to take you somewhere, I wouldn't have offered."

She dropped her head back again and exhaled heavily. "I'm sorry, I just feel like I'm taking advantage of you."

"I'll tell you when I feel taken advantage of. Where are we going?"

She thought for a minute, knowing exactly where she'd like to go. It was probably too much to ask, but a little sunshine would do them both some good. And a beautiful afternoon on the beach with him wouldn't hurt. She enjoyed his company. She could keep her distance and still spend the day with him...if he agreed.

"How about the beach?" she finally said, catching the surprise on Mark's face.

"It's the end of September, not exactly beach weather."

"Yeah, but it's still sunny."

He nodded. "You want to go to the beach?"

"If I could drive, it's where I would go."

"You'll feel better at the beach?" he asked.

"It's therapeutic. I go there all the time, although I usually go alone."

"I'm game."

A grin broke out across her face. When he grinned back at her, her stomach fluttered in excitement. "Thank you."

She jumped out of the truck, feeling better than she'd felt in days, and rushed into the house.

Mark closed the door to his truck, waiting to hear her enter the code to disarm the alarm. Almost at the same time, his cell phone rang.

He glanced at the caller ID. "What's up, Bri?"

"Is Jennings still with you?"

"Yeah...why?" Mark leaned against the side of his truck. "You got something new?"

"We have another victim."

"Wha...a rape victim?"

"A student over at the junior college, and I'm sure it's the same guy. I don't even need to wait for the DNA. He knocked her unconscious and beat the crap out of her before she could fight back. She also gave a description remarkably close to Jennings's attacker, *and* she looks just like your girl."

Mark had to slow his breathing to speak. "Is she okay?"

"She'll make it, but she's got a long road to recovery. You should push Jennings to call her brother again. This guy is not dormant."

"I'll talk to her." *Not today*, he thought. Not after he got a glimpse of her radiant smile. She needed a break, and if a sunny day at the beach would make her smile like that, he'd take her.

"All right, I'll call if I get anything else," Brian said before hanging up.

When Mark stepped into the house, he found Sarah in her bedroom packing a backpack full with accessories—iPod, books, towel, and a hat.

"What? You afraid I might make you talk to me?" he asked, picking up the second book.

"I'm packing some of this for you. I thought...," she said as she placed the book inside the bag and tilted her head, "since I've been so bitchy this week you might not want to talk to me."

He grinned. "Maybe I like the abuse."

She laughed faking a frown. "I'm sorry." She crossed her heart with two fingers. "I promise to cease all abuse for the rest of the day."

Mark couldn't respond. He was too fixated on her easy expression. Yeah, he definitely needed to keep her away from the news and let her enjoy the day before everything came crashing down on her again. The storm in her gray eyes settled, making it hard not to stare at her. "How about we pick up some sandwiches and eat on the beach?"

"Good idea. I already have everything we need in the car." She zipped up her bag and grabbed a sweater from the hook on the back of her bedroom door. "Do you have a jacket?"

"I have one in the truck. Here—" He gestured to her arm before unfastening the sling to help her with her jacket.

"I usually go the long way. It's a nice drive. Do you mind?"

"I don't mind," he said, helping her back into the sling.

Once the sling was fastened, she smiled again, nearly stopping his heart.

"Thanks," she said, tugging on the hem of her sweater and then tossing her backpack over her good shoulder as she left the room.

He followed her to the second bedroom, which was a makeshift office. She took a set of keys from her desk drawer and jingled them at him before leaving the room.

"What are you doing?"

"We're taking the car."

"What car?"

"My car. It's in the garage." She gestured toward the unattached, beat-up shack to the left of her house. "This is much more fun to drive to the beach. Come on."

Sarah unlocked the padlock on the double-hung, swinging garage doors. Both doors swayed forward, opening easily. Inside was a small car, concealed completely with a canvas car cover. She stepped inside and gripped the cover, tugging it until Mark reached down and pulled it back the rest of the way.

He stopped in his tracks. "What? Oh my God—is that a Shelby Mustang?"

"Yep. A 2008 Shelby GT500, and it's damn fun to drive to the beach."

"Holy shit, I'm gettin' a hard-on." The car was pearl white with vista blue racing strips, tinted windows, and it was in immaculate condition. He glanced over at Sarah who appeared almost excited as he was. Who would've known?

"Sarah, I didn't know you were a car guy."

"Ha, ha, ha, very funny."

"No wonder you take the long way to the beach—wait a minute, you can't drive." He pointed to her shoulder. "That means I get to drive this car."

"Whoa—wait a minute, cowboy. Pump your brakes."

"Nope, you can't drive...what? You don't trust me with your fifty thousand dollar car?"

"Honey, this car is worth more than that." She raised an eyebrow. "You need to try harder if you want to talk me into letting you drive it."

"Wait, you're a teacher?" Where the hell did she get the money for this?

"Yeah, so...I inherited some money from my grandma and I bought myself a present."

"And it never occurred to you to invest it instead?" he asked, leaning in to look through the windows.

"This car is an investment. It's only going to increase in value."

"Yeah, I guess you're right, and this is much more fun than stocks and bonds."

"Sure is, and yes, you can drive." She handed him the keys.

"Freaking awesome." He grabbed the keys and rushed to unlock the door before sliding into the soft leather seats.

Custom blue leather interior seats to match the racing strips and stark white leather piping. He was impressed. The Mustang had a built-in GPS system and an elaborate sound system. He couldn't wait to get out on the road and hear the motor purr.

"Don't get comfortable, we need one more chair and you need to move your truck."

"Hey, do you have some CDs we can take along for the ride?" he said. He wanted to check out the stereo *and* keep her away from any news reports.

"Yeah, what do you like?"

"Anything really, got any good driving music?"

He opened the trunk while Sarah grabbed another folding chair and placed it on top of the one already in the trunk.

"Wait, let me run inside and grab a couple more CDs. You might not like what I have in the glove box."

Mark moved his truck and pulled the Mustang out of the garage. He popped the glove box and looked at the CDs inside—Alanis Morissette, Avril Lavigne, Pink, and Kelly Clarkson. *I guess if that's what she likes.* He shrugged and returned the CDs when she opened the passenger door.

"101 South?" he asked, pulling out of the driveway.

"Yes. What do you want to listen to?" she asked, struggling to unzip her CD case with one hand.

"The glove box is full of angry girl music. Do you have anything else?"

"Angry girl music?" She opened the glove box and chuckled. "Very funny. I've never thought of it that way, but I guess you're right." She closed the glove box and flipped through the collection on her lap. "Do you like Matchbox Twenty?"

"Sure, put in some angry boy music instead."

"You got it," she said as he turned onto the freeway ramp.

He couldn't believe this car was hiding in that outdated dilapidated garage. He bumped his speed up to eighty and before he realized, they were already coming up on their exit.

"Can I ask you something?" Mark said, reaching to turn the music down.

"Sure, ask me anything."

"Why do you always go to the beach alone?"

"I like it. I can clear my head and it's peaceful," she said, staring through the passenger window.

"It seems like you do a lot of things alone."

"What's wrong with that?"

He shrugged. "Just trying to understand you."

"Give it up. I'm a deep pool of the darkest water you've ever seen. You don't want to go swimming, trust me."

"What if I do want to swim?" He was pushing, but she was in such a good mood, he wanted to get some answers out of her.

"You've already gotten your feet wetter than most people. Don't you feel the need to run away yet?"

"Do I look like I'm trying to run away from you?" He shrugged. "I just don't get you."

"What's to get?"

"What makes you tick—beside this awesome car?"

"Well, I love my job, and I'm pretty pissed the doctor is keeping me off work for a month."

"Yeah, that'd kill me too."

She smirked. "Why—you hardly work."

"Oh, I work, but being the boss has its advantages." He grinned. "What else? Your life can't be work alone."

"I'm a marathon runner."

"No kidding." He nodded his head in appreciation. "I like to run, but marathon running is a bit extreme for me." He glanced over at her. "That explains how you managed to take me down on Friday."

Her expression dropped.

"Fuck," Mark said under his breath. What the hell was he thinking bringing that up? "I'm sorry. I didn't mean to..."

"It's okay," she said on a gush of air.

"No. No, it's not. I should think before I speak."

She coughed out a laugh. "You did go down pretty easy."

"Adrenalin is a powerful thing." He needed to be more careful. He tilted his head in apology. "I'll keep my tongue in check for the rest of the day."

"Don't tiptoe around me." She brought her hand to her chest and rubbed up her neck to her jaw, as if easing the pressure. "It's okay. Let's talk about something else. What would you like to know about me?"

"Tell me about your parents."

"My dad lives in Nevada with his wife, Kim. He was once married to Ava's mom." Sarah looked away when she said it.

"That must make Ava your stepsister."

Sarah nodded. "When our parents divorced, we stayed close."

"And your mom?"

"Do you really want to know this stuff?" she asked with a nervous laugh, her cheeks turning a little pink.

"Don't feel obligated. Only curious." Okay, maybe this wasn't any easier than talking about her attack.

"My mom is a singer. She and her husband, Sean, own a nightclub in Portland and she sings there."

"Really? A singer. That's interesting."

"Interesting is an understatement when describing my mother."

He chuckled. "Yeah, why?"

"She has a tendency to make herself larger than life. I guess it's safe to say she likes being the center of attention. She was constantly moving us from one place to the next...always wanted to be the new best thing."

"I imagine that's a common thing for a performer."

"Is that it? Because I've yet to come up with a decent excuse for the things she does."

"Hell if I know." He chuckled, and Sarah laughed too. "But what an interesting way to grow up—with your mom being a singer and moving around like you did."

"Yeah, well, I've definitely seen a lot."

He pursed his lips and wondered exactly what that meant. What would it take to really get her to open up and talk? She was so closed off to people, it was no wonder she didn't have many friends. It seemed as if she liked it that way. "So where have you lived?"

"Portland, Boulder, Nashville. I went to high school in Flagstaff, Arizona. When I graduated, my mom moved back up to Portland with her new husband. I didn't want to move again, so I stayed and started college."

"You went to the University of Arizona?"

"Northern Arizona University is in Flagstaff, but I transferred to San Francisco and graduated from UCSF."

"Apparently you weren't too tired of moving since you moved to San Francisco and ended up here."

"Yeah, Flagstaff wasn't working for me."

Mark sensed there was more to Flagstaff than she wanted to tell him. Her voice grew quiet, and she turned away from him to face the window. She was clearly uncomfortable talking about her family, but she didn't have anything to be ashamed of. He wouldn't judge her based on her parents' mistakes.

"There's a bus stop up here on the right if you want to pull over to get out and run away. I'll understand, I warned you—dark water."

"What aren't you telling me, because I haven't heard anything too terribly dark. Lots of people move around a lot."

When she didn't respond, he said, "Would you feel better if I made up some outrageous stories about my mom?"

"No—geez! My stories are all true."

"It's going to take more than your mom to scare me, although now I understand why you're such a loner. Moving around so much would make getting to know people hard, much less have time to grow deeper relationships."

"Yeah, that's the reason," she said, sarcastic again.

He frowned. "What's made you so cynical?"

She was such a tough nut to crack. Never had he met a woman who kept herself so tightly guarded. Most people loved talking about themselves.

"Nothing, you're right," she said. "I told you this is a nice drive. Beautiful day."

"All right, I'll back off."

She didn't say anything else, which bugged him, but he accepted it. He'd agreed to come to the beach to brighten her spirits. Now, he didn't know if that was possible, not when she had such a dark outlook on life.

"What are you thinking?" he finally asked after a long stretch of silence.

"I'm thinking I'm an ass for ruining your good mood."

"That's funny. I was thinking the same thing about you." He gave her a thoughtful look. "We both need to cheer up. I've already decided you can't be miserable while riding in this car."

"And when did you decide this?"

"In the garage when I was trying to figure out what put you in such a good mood. I didn't understand it until I saw the car."

"I'm sorry I've been such a downer."

"Don't go there," he said. "I'm happy you feel better. Your eyes are brighter and you look...better." He looked at her, making eye contact.

"I didn't realize I looked bad before."

"No—I didn't mean—I meant...sorry. Ugh, this isn't coming out right." He gestured toward her. "You're beautiful all the time, but today you look a little less...miserable—not the word I'm searching for but..."

He looked at her again. She was breathtaking even with her dark moods.

She stared at him for a moment, clearly getting some enjoyment out of his discomfort.

"Was that a compliment?" she asked.

He laughed. "Okay, all right. I'll shut up. You talk—tell me more about your family."

She chuckled. "Hmm...let's see, I have two brothers. Devon is the oldest. As you know, he lives in San Diego. Robert is nineteen and at Stanford. My baby sister, Hayley, is fifteen and lives with my mom in Portland. She's a sweetheart but too much like my mom."

"You have two brothers and one sister? How long were your parents married?"

"My mom and dad were never married. It was just a fling. He married Ava's mom when I was little and then married Kim after divorcing Ava's mom. Robert is their child. He and I have the same father, different mothers. Devon, Hayley, and I all have the same mom, but different dads."

"Oh, so they're your half-siblings."

"I try not to label my family. It doesn't matter to me whether or not we have the same mother and father. I don't love them any less, so why use a disclaimer?"

He shrugged. "That's a good point. I never thought of it that way."

"I know, it's scary, huh? I warned you," she chanted halfheartedly.

"Not that scary and don't get cocky. We can't all grow up with interesting parents. You don't have to rub it in."

"Ha, ha, funny."

Mark's smile faded and he said, "So...if your parents were never married, have you ever lived with your father?"

"Nope. I spent a few summers with him when I was young. That's how Ave and I got so close, but other than a few months, I've never lived with him."

"It must have been hard not having a father around growing up."

"It was hard not seeing him every day. I imagine it's just as hard for Jamie when he's not with you. Being a teacher, I see a lot of kids going through that and it breaks my heart. They're so confused and always just a little homesick for one parent or the other. Especially the kids who only get to see their dads one or two days a month...it takes a toll on them."

He stared at her for a moment, realizing he had finally gotten through her wall, she was talking. No matter how self-conscious she was about her parents and her upbringing, something great had come out of it. The passion she had for her job and for kids came through loud and clear in spite of how she was raised. And now he finally knew how to get her talking.

"We try our hardest not to let Jamie feel like he's missing anything. It helps that Ali and I can still be friends."

"I think it's great that you consider his feelings. Most people are so hurt while going through a divorce, they don't consider their kids. Sometimes I think I'm lucky I didn't have to go through that as a kid. Since my parents were never married, I didn't have to live through their divorce."

Within the next few minutes, the road curved to the right and the coast came into view.

"Oh, there it is," Sarah said, lifting up to rest her eyes on the coastline.

Her face lit with excitement, and if he didn't know any better, he'd think this was the first time she'd seen the ocean.

"I'm glad you're driving so I can enjoy the view." She leaned toward him for a moment before resting back in her seat. "I would live here if I could. Right on the beach. People don't realize how lucky they are to live in California. I missed this when we moved away."

He grimaced. "Sorry, I'm one of those bad people who have taken this for granted. It is beautiful, though."

"I actually looked at a house out here to buy, but I talked myself out of it."

"How did you talk yourself out of it?"

"It didn't make sense." Her smile faded. "A single woman with no family owning two houses—a vacation house even. Seemed reckless and extravagant."

"If you're happy, who cares, and property is an investment."

"The road is up here on your left."

"I see why you drive the long way. The view from the highway is incredible," he said, turning after the Wright's Beach sign.

She was right about feeling better, and it wasn't just the car and it wasn't the beach—it had to be the company.

Chapter Ten

After Mark parked the car, Sarah jumped out and began grabbing things out of the trunk.

"Wait, stop, Sarah, hold on before you hurt yourself. I'll carry these." He handed her the blanket. "Here, take this and go pick a good spot."

She rolled her eyes and took the blanket.

He watched her disappear over the sand dunes and shook his head.

"Definitely a split-personality disorder," he mumbled to himself, grabbing everything else they needed and closing the trunk.

When he caught up to her, he laid out the chairs next to the blanket she put down.

"This is one of my favorite beaches. I like watching the high surf," she said.

Mark scanned the beach. "It's incredible. Perfect weather too. Crystal clear skies."

"Look—do you see the people up on that cliff?" she asked as she lowered herself into a chair.

There were two people high on a cliff that hung over the next beach. The spray from the surf splashed in the sun under them. "Yeah, how'd they..."

She pointed to the trailhead. "That's my favorite hiking trail. It's about six miles down to Goat Rock."

He shielded his eyes from the sun and examined the path. "You've hiked that?"

The trailhead started at beach level, climbed up and down through rugged terrain along the sea cliffs.

"Many times. It's awesome and the views are unbelievable."

"Who do you hike with?" He turned from the cliff back to Sarah.

She laid her head back and stared up at him. "What do you mean? I told you I like to come here alone."

"You hike that trail alone?" he asked as he pointed to the cliff, his voice growing hard, even though he fought not to show his irritation.

"Yeah, what's wrong with that?"

His pulse quickened. "Sarah, that's not safe. What if you got hurt?"

"I'd use my phone to call for help." Her lips quirked into a crooked smile. "Whadda ya think?"

"How do you dial if you're unconscious?"

"Give me some credit, Mark. I'm a good hiker. I kick that trail's ass."

He sat down and watched her, not sure what to think. "You shouldn't do things like that—hiking alone. It's not safe."

Why would she do such reckless things? He followed the trail with his eyes. This woman was totally backward in her view of things.

"That's more of a walking trail and I can handle it alone. As a matter of fact, I can handle a lot of things on my own." She raised her eyebrow at his stare. "What?"

"Nothing...just...nothing." He shook his head. "Forget it."

"Come out with it, geez."

Mark didn't laugh...nothing about this was funny. It was reckless for her to hike alone, especially out here. Why was her own safety something she took so lightly?

"You're fearless about some things." He hesitated, looking up at the trail again. "But other things—easy things seem to scare the shit out of you."

"Like what?"

"Like hiking that cliff. Like staying home alone when it's not safe." He stopped and scanned her thoroughly. "Yet when I've tried to help, it's like you're closed off to people...and not only me. You love this place, but you don't share it with anyone." He brushed a hand at her. "I've only known you for a week, but I don't need long to see how skittish you are around people."

She pulled the sunglasses off her face, and the sun glinted off her beautiful gray eyes.

He fought the instinct to grab her and hold on, protect her, and keep her this relaxed all the time. His heart skipped a beat in his chest. Oh man, Brian was right—this was dangerous territory. *She* was dangerous—his heart already hurt from it. He had never in his life met anyone like her before.

"And who the hell is Kevin?" he asked, unable to keep his mouth shut for another second.

"What?" she said with wide eyes, her voice dropping to little more than a breath.

"Kevin? You were screaming at him in your sleep the night I stayed with you, after the hospital." He held her gaze as the color drained from her face. "You told the police you didn't know the man who attacked you."

Seconds later her entire face lit on fire. "Do you think I've been acting? What? A game between me and an old boyfriend? Or do you just think I'm a complete whack job and a liar?"

"No—no, Sa-rah." He shifted in his chair to face her. "I was there—of course, I don't think you're lying. That's not what I meant."

Sarah leaned forward in her chair and rested her face in her hands.

He reached out and touched her arm. "I'm sorry. You've been through hell. I would never take that lightly."

"Do you think I like this? Do you think I'm looking for pity? I hate this. I hate being a victim. I hate having my choices taken away by someone bigger and stronger than me." She braced her hand on her knee and got to her feet. "I'm going for a walk."

And she was gone, walking toward the water, holding her sweater closed with her free hand.

Mark did a mental head smack. *Great job ruining the day, you jerk.* He wasn't even sure what he had just done, and he still didn't know who Kevin was. Maybe it didn't matter, but people don't scream like that in their sleep for nothing.

He dropped his head back, his eyes drifting up to the cloudless, bright blue sky. He understood why she loved this place. He wished he'd brought a tent so she could spend the night.

He lifted his head to watch Sarah. She walked along the waterline, and from his spot, it looked like the waves were taller than her. They crashed hard before spreading foam across the sand at her feet. To his right, waves beat against huge rocks, sending sea spray fifty feet up. The sounds of the waves and crying seagulls were seriously relaxing, and he hoped they did their magic on her, especially since he'd just ruined her mood.

Looking at her now, he was overcome with an intense urge to go to her, hold her, and feel her wrapped within his embrace. He wanted to know what her sweater felt like, and the faded jeans on her legs. Run his hands through her wavy hair and smell it.

God, he was losing it. How had this happened?

He stood up, unable to watch any longer. When he approached, she didn't turn. Her eyes were focused on the horizon, lost in what he hoped was a happy memory.

"Sarah..."

"I know." She bit her lip. "I overreacted again."

"And I had no right to question like that." He looked out to sea, not sure what else to say. When he looked back, her eyes were closed, the gentle breeze brushing her face. "If you want to talk about it, I'm a good listener," he said.

"But...I don't want to talk about it." She looked at him from the corner of her eye. "I want to forget about it."

He held up his hands. "Okay, I get it. I won't bring it up again."

ജ്ഞ

When the sun dipped into the ocean, they decided to pack up and head back.

"Can I buy you dinner?" he asked when Sarah laid her folding chair into the trunk. "The drive is at least an hour. We can stop on our way back."

"I would love that."

The gentle sound of her voice made his stomach flutter, and he had to remind himself to breathe.

His mind was full of her, and he tried to think about something else. It was no use. Her body language mirrored her feelings and attitude, and as the weight of the week lifted from her shoulders, she moved more fluidly and gracefully. He would pay every dollar in his bank account if he could keep her this happy.

When Sarah's tension faded, Mark felt lighter too. He usually took a long time to relax around women. He'd thought all those years wasted with Ali had ruined him. He'd dated since his divorce, but most of the single women out there were shallow and materialistic. Sarah seemed different, more real to him.

Mark started the car and followed her directions to River Road. It wound through the redwood trees along the Russian River, and even in the dark, it was a beautiful drive. They stopped at a little restaurant in Guerneville for dinner and sat in a small corner booth.

Sarah chatted animatedly through dinner, but he was preoccupied by the bad news he was keeping from her.

"Are you okay," she asked.

"Fine. Why?"

She chuckled. "You haven't heard one word I've said in the last five minutes."

"I'm sorry." He stared at her for a moment. "I had a good time today. I'm glad you brought me."

"Well, actually you brought me. I couldn't have come alone if I wanted to." She lifted her left arm when she said it. "But seriously, I feel a thousand times lighter now and I'm glad I shared it with you," she admitted, her cheeks going a little pink. "And thank you for dinner."

"You're welcome."

"Are you going to tell me what's bothering you?" she said.

"I talked to Brian this morning."

Her gray eyes turned stormy when he said Brian's name.

"He doesn't have any leads, but you're still in danger...it's not safe for you to be alone."

"It's been a couple of days since he left that note and I haven't had any trouble."

"That doesn't mean he's given up, Sarah. You need to take this seriously."

Her eyes narrowed. "What makes you think I don't take this seriously?"

"Your brother?" Mark said, raising his eyebrows.

She leaned forward, drawing closer. "I don't need a man around to protect me."

He let his eyes travel up and down her body, stopping on the sling. "Look at you, Sarah. Just because you got lucky once—"

"I didn't just get lucky. I defended myself and I'll do it again."

Mark leaned in too, nose-to-nose with her. "And what if you can't? What if he gets the better of you next time?"

The color drained from her face. She shook her head and rested back, fighting tears. "What am I supposed to—what do I have to do? Hide from him forever?"

"Give Brian time to do his job. And stay safe until then. Be smart and don't take any chances."

"I'm already going stir crazy." She opened her eyes and stared at Mark, as if pleading for answers.

Fear shadowed her stormy gray eyes. He'd never seen anything like that before. That old saying about people wearing their hearts on their sleeve was certainly true with her, only it showed in her eyes.

Goddamn, he'd completely destroyed her mood, and he hadn't even told her everything. He felt sick as the atmosphere between them changed. Everything she'd been feeling throughout the day was gone.

"Listen, I know this is hard, but you can't be complacent. You still need to be careful."

"Yeah, I know." She fisted her hand. "I fucking know it," she said, frustration squaring her shoulders and pulling her back within herself—closing the door to her soul.

Minutes before, he could feel her warmth, but she shut down and closed herself off. Cold again.

"Let's get out of here." He turned away from her to scoot out of the booth.

His instincts pushed him toward her. He wanted to comfort her, though she kept her distance. When he opened her car door, she stopped and stared up at the twinkling sky. The stars shone brighter away from the city lights.

Sarah took a deep breath, and in the glint of the parking lot light, Mark saw a tear rolled down her cheek. She turned and reached out, laying her head on his chest and wrapping her arm around his waist. It surprised him and relieved him at the same time.

He wrapped his arms around her and rested his head against hers. The sweet scent of honeysuckle mixed with sea air sent a jolt through his system, forcing him to close his eyes and focus on what she needed and not what he wanted. He'd gotten his wish, her sweater felt soft and her hair smelled great, and he knew as long as he was with her, nobody could touch her. She was safe.

He continued to hold her, hoping it was enough to help her get through. After a few minutes, she pulled away and wiped her face. Mark reached his hand up and tucked a strand of hair behind her ear. Even in the faint light, he could see how much lighter her eyes got when she cried.

The embrace felt good. Sarah's body seemed so delicate to him, and she fit perfectly in his arms. He couldn't remember the last time a woman had felt so good to him or smelled so good.

"I'm sorry."

"For what?" he whispered, wishing she hadn't pulled away.

"I'm such a basket case. I hate being like this."

"Being like what? This is real. Hell, I already know you're a bad-ass. You kicked the shit out of a rapist with one hand. You don't have anything to prove. Cry if you need to."

She shook her head adamantly. "I don't want to cry." She lifted her good hand to the back of her neck and rubbed at the tension, and Mark realized that she was worried about what he thought of her. As if he wouldn't respect her for needing help.

"You know what?" he said, resting a hand on top of the car and looking directly into her eyes. "Everyone has moments like that, moments of weakness. You're no different than me, no different from anyone else on the planet."

Mark wanted nothing more than to kiss her. He cupped her face. "Sarah, you're one of the bravest people I've ever met." He thumbed away one of her tears before moving his hand away. "It's amazing how well you're doing. It's only been a few days."

"Thank for saying that...and for the shoulder too." She looked down. "It's nice having someone around to talk to. It feels good. Thanks...thanks for being here for me."

"Yeah, well, I needed a hug, so...thank you for that." He smiled, trying to put her at ease. "Besides, I'm not thrilled with the idea of kicking around my big ol' stupid house alone. Spending the evening with you is much better than sitting at home."

He let go of her and helped her into the car.

Mark slid into the driver's seat, and when he reached over to snap her seatbelt into place, she waved him off.

He smirked. *Moment of weakness over – duly noted.*

Chapter Eleven

Mark looked over at the clock. After midnight. He'd dropped Sarah off hours ago and should've come home and gone to bed, but he couldn't shut his mind down. He dropped his head back on his shoulders and glanced around his home office.

They'd never planned to make this room an office. He'd envisioned a nursery when he and Ali bought the house. Of course, at the time he didn't know Ali was sleeping with someone else.

He had wanted something she didn't, a large family. *Ha.* Well, she'd wanted that too, but not with him. He threw his pen down on the desk. It didn't matter now. Why continue to stew over it?

His cell phone buzzed and rattled on the desk. He hit the talk button. "Seth, what's up?"

"The Jennings' alarm is sounding."

Mark jerked upright in his chair. "Did you call 911?"

"Yeah, but they're not too fired up. They asked if I called the resident yet."

"Did you?"

"I'm not getting an answer."

"Okay, I'll head over there. Get Shane and call Brian Hammel. Wake him up...he'll want to know about this."

ຈ໙

The loud, blaring sound vibrated through Sarah's body like a jolt of adrenalin. She jerked up and grimaced at the pain in her left shoulder. She scrambled off the side of the bed and landed hard.

"Shit, shit, shit," she said as she pulled the top drawer of her nightstand out and onto the floor, letting everything spill out. She grabbed her gun, braced herself against the bed, and peered over the top of the mattress, her eyes scanning the room. Even in the dimness of night, she had a perfect view of the bedroom door.

She couldn't see much else, but could hear someone banging around in her kitchen.

Sweat beaded up on her forehead, and her hands were slippery as the tip of the gun jittered in her trembling hands. She looked around for her phone. Oh God, she couldn't breathe, how stupid of her not to keep the phone nearby. She took several shuddering, deep breaths and tried to keep from hyperventilating.

Don't panic, Sarah. She didn't know what to do. Run, stay...hide?

Cursing and loud crashing came from the kitchen. The blaring alarm streamed through her brain and pounded along with her rapid pulse, making it impossible to focus. She heard the phone ringing but was too afraid to look around for it again. If she took her eyes off the door, she'd lose her line of sight in the dark room.

A large figure came into view. Sarah shrank behind the bed, extending her arms out with her gun gripped in both hands. Her body went ridged with fear. She couldn't tell if he had a weapon in his hand, but that didn't matter, his presence alone was threatening enough.

He panted like a dog in heat when he entered, his eyes searching the room, the narrow stream of light from his flashlight bouncing off the furniture and walls. The glow from the light skipped right over her head, and she hoped—prayed he hadn't seen her. Bile rose in her throat at the sight of him, and every instinct in her said to run like hell, but she couldn't move.

He peered into her bathroom before moving toward the closet. When he turned back, their eyes locked. The eye contact sent a rush of blood to her head. A wave of hatred mixed with fear coursed through her. She would kill him if she had to.

He took a step closer, and without the slightest hesitation, she pulled the trigger. The blast from the end of the gun lit the room. The power behind the shot jerked her hands up and sent a jolt of pain through her shoulder. She righted herself, not taking her eyes off him, ready to take another shot.

He pushed off the wall and grabbed his arm, leaning forward slightly. "Fuckin' bitch," he huffed. "You fucking shot me!"

He staggered out of her room, smashing something in the living room.

Sarah tried to hold still, her hands so sweaty the heavy gun nearly slipped from her grip.

When his feet shuffled on the wood floor, she froze again and braced for another fight, but heard him fumbling with the locks on the front door. The door banged open, slamming against the wall as his footsteps stormed out.

ജ്ഞ

When Mark pulled into her driveway, the alarm boomed through the open front door. His pulse accelerated at the sight of the dark house. Once he gripped the cold steel of his nine-millimeter, he calmed down and focused.

He inched toward the front door, listening for anything through the screeching alarm. The house was completely dark, but he caught the outline of the overturned table blocking the entrance in time to keep from tripping over it.

"Sarah?" he called as he inched through the house.

"Sarah!" he shouted more urgent this time with his gun extended into her bedroom. The bed was empty and the blankets trailed onto the floor. Mark took a breath to force back the panic.

"Mark?"

Oh, thank God. Hearing her voice settled him slightly. The whimper came from the other side of the bed, and when he looked closer, his eyes rested on the gun pointed at him.

"Yes...Sarah...it's Mark. Is he gone?"

"Oh, God," she breathed, but held the gun steady.

"Are you okay?"

Sarah began to sob, still clinging to the shaking gun.

The steadiness he'd felt moments ago was gone, the image of her scared and crouched on the floor hiding in her pajamas nearly broke him.

He stepped around the bed and carefully laid a hand on her wrist. "Put the gun down."

She dropped it and pulled her hand to her chest.

Mark knelt next to her, approaching her gently, hoping not to scare her further. "Are you hurt?"

Her shoulders jerked with her sobs, and she leaned into Mark's chest, gripping his t-shirt with her little fists. He scooped her up and leaned back against the wall, holding her in his lap.

She jittered uncontrollably in his arms, and her clothes were soaked through with sweat.

"It's okay, Sarah. I'm here. Take a breath." He pulled his phone out of his pocket and hit the speed dial for Summors' dispatch.

"Mark?"

"Yeah," he shouted. "I'm here, shut it down."

The alarm stopped, sirens replacing the noise.

Mark tried to take a deep breath before he said, "Seth, did you get Brian Hammel?"

"He's on his way. Everything okay?"

"She's fine." He closed his phone and stuffed it back into his pocket.

"Sarah." He looked down at her. She was curled in his lap, still clutching his shirt. "Let me look at you. Did he hurt you?"

"No," she sobbed, her body still trembling. "I'm okay."

"What happened?"

"I don't know."

"How about your shoulder? Let me check it." He pulled back and looked at her face first. She was stark white and shining with sweat and tears. He wiped her face and brushed her hair back. Relief swamped him, then guilt. Someone should have been here—he should've been here to protect her.

When she shuddered again, he pulled her tighter and whispered, "You're okay, Sarah."

He'd make sure of it.

ᘓᘐ

Sarah shivered while giving her statement to Detective Martinez. Mark had draped his jacket over her when he left the room, but she still felt chilled to the bone.

When Detective Martinez finished with her, she sat back on her bed and tried to relax, but she couldn't forget the fact that Mark's alarm system saved her life. He'd warned her about this and she didn't listen. All he'd wanted to do was help her, and she'd kept fighting him.

A few minutes later, he entered the room with Brian. She wiped the tears from her face, refusing to let all these cops see her cry.

"We found blood in the kitchen," Brian said as she sat up. "Have you been in the kitchen since he entered your home?"

"No," she said, trying to remember the chain of events. Everything happened so fast and waking up to the alarm didn't give her much time to think. "I heard glass breaking when he came in, I assumed he broke a window."

"He knocked over some dishes, must have cut himself. We'll compare this blood to the sample collected at Oakbrook on Friday. Then we'll know for sure if this is the same guy."

"I'm already sure he's the same guy—" She stopped talking when a huge, bald guy stopped in the doorway to her bedroom. She shrank back against the headboard at the sight of him, not sure what to do.

Mark and Brian both looked over when she stopped talking.

"Sarah, this is Shane Fields, he's one of my security agents," Mark said. "Shane was dispatched by me when I got the call from Summors."

Shane smiled at her. "Nice to meet you, ma'am."

She nodded at Shane, and she realized she owed Mark for more than just saving her life. "Thank you for coming."

"Anyway, Sarah, you said you're sure this is the same guy..."

"I recognized his voice." A shiver ran up her spine at the memory of his angry voice.

"What did he say to you?"

"He called me a 'fucking bitch.'" She put her hand over her mouth to hide her quivering chin and mumbled, "'You fucking shot me.'"

Brian's lips quirked into a quick smile. He pointed to the hole in her wall. "Is this his blood here?"

"Yes."

"Did you see where your shot hit him?"

"No, but he reached across himself like this." She demonstrated with her arm. "It looked like he grabbed his left bicep."

Brian examined the blood spot on the wall and pointed with his pen. "Look here," he said to Mark, "the slug."

Mark stood and peered over Brian's shoulder. "Flesh wound probably, went straight through," Mark said.

Sarah cleared her throat and they turned to her. "How did he get into the house if he didn't break a window?"

"He popped the kitchen window without breaking the glass," Brian said. "The weathered wood gave way, and the screws holding the sash lock stripped right out. You should consider upgrading to vinyl windows. They're a little more secure."

"Yeah, those old, double-hung, wood window frames don't stand a chance against someone who knows what they're doing," Mark said.

Brian snickered. "Yeah, well, let's not give him too much credit. He couldn't get his fat ass through the window without making a mess and alerting the victim."

Mark sat down next to her. "And now she's two for two."

"Do you think he's injured enough to get medical attention?" Sarah asked, wishing she'd taken better aim.

Brian shook his head. "No, there's not enough blood." He glanced from Sarah to Mark. "Don't fool yourself, man. He won't stop at this. If anything, it's going to get worse."

"Meaning...now he's really going to come after me." She closed her eyes, trying not to visibly shiver at the thought."

"You've escaped this guy twice, Sarah. I'm no psychologist, but it's pretty obvious you're in more danger." When she wrapped her arms around herself, Brian said, "We're doing everything we can."

Her eyes popped open, anger spiking her pulse. "Then why did it take so long for the police to get here?"

"Alarm systems go off all the time. Ninety percent of the time it's a mistake—someone's pet setting off a motion sensor or a door left ajar that gets thrown open from the wind." Brian leveled his gaze at her. "We're increasing patrols in the area. Dispatch knows the address, we'll be more diligent."

"You said that before," Mark said.

Brian shot Mark an angry look, and then glanced back at Sarah. "I'm sorry this happened to you, Sarah, but we made incredibly fast time considering the circumstances." His expression softened and he said, "I tried to warn you something like this might happen. There is a delay in response. This is why I told you to have someone here with you."

Sarah lowered her eyes, reminded of the lie she'd told him. He was right, she had been warned, and she should have listened to him and to Mark.

"It's a big city with lots of problems, we can't give everyone personal attention."

Mark stood and paced the room, stopping at the window with his back to them. They grew quiet, and it felt as if everyone in the room took a collective breath.

When Mark turned back around, she didn't miss the worry and regret outlined on his face. It hurt to see him so upset, especially knowing it was all due to her stupid choices.

"I guess it's a damn good thing she had that gun," Mark finally said.

"Yeah, but now I have to take it for evidence," Brian said.

Sarah whipped her head around to look at him. "No! I need my gun. You can't take it."

Brian's eye widened. "I have to. It was involved in a crime."

"That's not just *any* gun." Sarah couldn't hold back the pleading in her voice. She was helpless without her gun.

"I can see that. It's a collector's and worth a bundle. Custom Colt 45, right?" Brian asked, leaning against the wall crossing his arms over his chest.

"It was a gift. I want it back."

"A gift?" Mark said, sitting back down next to her. "Who gave it to you?"

"My mom's ex-husband, Charlie. He taught me and my brother, Devon, how to shoot and gave us our first guns."

Sarah looked up at Brian. "Charlie was a gun collector in Nashville, but I took care of the licensing when I moved back here. The gun is registered in California."

"Was? He doesn't collect guns anymore?" Mark asked.

"No." She shook her head, fighting the ache in her heart when she thought about Charlie. "He's dead. He was murdered a couple of years ago."

"Oh, wow." Mark whistled in surprise. "That's awful. I'm sorry, Sarah."

"How was he murdered?" Brian asked.

Her eyes dropped to the floor feeling sick with the memory. "He was stabbed by an intruder."

"They catch the guy?" Brian asked.

"No. I don't think they ever caught the murderer." She covered her mouth fighting the yawn creeping in.

"You know"—Brian looked at his watch—"we're about done and outta your hair."

He pushed off the wall and looked down at Sarah. "Do you plan to stay here? Can I make some calls for you?"

"Um...no, I..." She glanced at Mark.

"I'll take care of her, Brian. Don't worry about it."

A possessive statement like that usually would have bothered Sarah, but Mark saying the words *I'll take care of her* spiked another wave of appreciation...and something else resembling desire. From him, the phrase seemed more gallant than possessive.

"We'll keep a unit in the area. It's not likely he'll try to enter your home again, but you should be careful when you go out alone."

Sarah shrugged uncomfortably. "I'll be careful, thanks for everything, Brian."

When Brian and Shane left the room, Sarah turned toward the dark window. Was a maniac watching her? Even with a house full of cops, she felt so alone. She grabbed some clean clothes from the dresser and glanced over at Mark, who was now leaning in the doorway of her bedroom with his back to her, watching the police come in and out of the front door.

"Mark?"

He peered at her from over his shoulder. "You need something?"

"Are they done with me? I'd like to take a shower."

"They're finishing up. Go ahead. I'll make sure everything's locked up when they leave."

"Thank you. I'm sorry I kept you up all night again."

He turned to face her. "I should've believed you when you said you could protect yourself."

Sarah knitted her brow, staring into his eyes, hoping he understood how grateful she was for him. She had protected herself, but if it wasn't for him and his alarm, she might not have had the chance.

"No, you were right." She balled her clothes, rolling them in her hands, and lowered her eyes. "Things could have turned out much worse. Thanks for getting here so fast...and being here for me."

"You look exhausted," he said. "Are you sure you're okay?"

"I am exhausted," she murmured. "I'm going to take a shower and clean up. Will you be here when I get out?"

"Of course." He exhaled heavily and said, "We'll talk when you're done."

Brian poked his head in her room. "We're finished."

"Thank you," she said, and hobbled into the bathroom.

When she came out of the bathroom dressed in clean sweats and a tank top, she found Mark in the kitchen working on her window, with Shane handing him tools. The broken dishes were gone, and there was no evidence of the break-in left for Sarah to see.

"Hey," she said.

Mark turned over his shoulder to look at her.

"We secured the window. I reinstalled the lock and used bigger screws." He stepped down from the stepstool. "You should consider newer windows. I have a friend who owns a window company. I'll give him a call—whoa." He held up his hand. "What I mean is—do you mind if we call him and ask him to give us an estimate?"

When Shane snickered, she gave him a faint smile. "Thanks...that would be great."

Mark turned to Shane as he folded up the stepstool. "Can you give Greg a call in the morning, ask him to do the estimate and give him the address?"

Shane nodded as he closed the tool box. "Want me to hang out?"

"Ah...no, but do a cursory of the neighborhood and call me if anything stands out."

"Will do." Shane picked up the toolbox and headed out of the kitchen, stopping to say goodbye to Sarah. "It was nice meeting you, Ms. Jennings."

She halfheartedly smiled at him. "It's Sarah...thanks for coming."

Mark followed Shane to the door, and when she realized he intended to leave, she felt a jolt of panic.

"Mark?" She hugged herself, chilled with the knowledge that she'd shot someone in her house—in her bedroom. After all the bullshit she'd spouted about being able to take care of herself, now she couldn't stand the idea of being alone. "Will you stay?"

"I'm not leaving. I'm just walking Shane out..." He hesitated for a moment, his expression set. "I'll sleep on the couch tonight, tomorrow, we talk about serious protection."

She looked up at him and swallowed hard. Pride was a bitter pill, but she knew when to say when.

ഇര

Sarah helped Mark make up a bed on the sofa and took some pain meds. Her entire body ached from the adrenalin rush. She'd medicate herself into a coma if she had to. Sleep wouldn't come easy without it. She'd been too afraid to use the medication when she was alone, but having Mark there put her at ease.

She took one last peek at Mark on her sofa and wished she had something more comfortable to offer him. She briefly pictured him in her bed, keeping her warm and wrapping his strength around her. Embarrassed by the thought, her cheeks heated. She quickly closed the door on him and on her thoughts, leaving him to sleep and curling into her cold bed alone. The medication slowly lulled her to sleep.

Purple clouds stretched above her.

Her heart pounded and the gravel cut into her back.

A cold hand pawed at her skirt.

Hot, rancid breath scraped her face.

Sarah jerked awake and sat up as a strangled scream came out of her dry throat. When her eyes popped opened, so did her bedroom door with a loud crack.

When the dark figure came at her, she tried to scramble off the bed, but he grabbed her arm.

"It's okay." Mark clicked on the bedside lamp.

"Sarah, it's okay," he said gentler this time.

She wept, her relief overshadowing the embarrassment as her entire body convulsed into uncontrollable trembles. She lay back down, pulled the thick blanket over her head, and curled her knees to her chest.

"What can I do?" he asked.

Sarah couldn't stop crying long enough to give a coherent answer.

"Not all men are like him, Sarah."

The emotional weight pressed down on her chest as she sobbed, making it hard for her to breathe. Somehow this time she didn't care if Mark watched her fall apart.

She woke up a while later wrapped tightly in her blanket, sweating through her clothes. She poked her head out of the blanket and blinked at the lamp. Then she rolled over and saw Mark sleeping on the floor next to her bed. He was clutching the blanket from the sofa and fully dressed.

She gave his shoulder a little shake.

His eyes blinked open and met hers. He rubbed his face. "Do you need something?"

She nodded and her eyes filled with tears. "Will you lie down with me?"

"You don't want to be alone?"

She closed her eyes and shook her head. Mark stood and clicked the lamp off, before lying down next to her, leaving the thick blanket between them.

Sarah tried to catch her breath and stop crying, but couldn't.

"This is hard for you, isn't it?" Mark whispered.

Sarah nodded and wiped her face under the blanket.

"It's okay to ask for help, you don't have to handle everything on your own. You've been through hell. Nobody will think you're weak for needing a shoulder to cry on."

She nodded again and realized he might be right, no matter how hard it was to admit.

Chapter Twelve

The smell of coffee brought Mark out of his exhaustion-induced coma. He lifted his head and looked around the sunlit bedroom. This was not his bedroom. That was obvious by the sweet scent of vanilla and lavender. He stifled a moan and inhaled deeply while stuffing his nose into her pillow.

Lying next to her, inhaling her sweet scent all night had nearly sent him over the edge. He wanted to be here for her, but being here came with a price.

Anyone would have trouble dealing with what she'd been through. He knew firsthand how hard it was to point a gun at another human being and pull the trigger, no matter who the human was.

Now that he knew for sure she was being targeted, he wasn't leaving her alone at all.

The omission about the rape at the college weighed heavy on his mind, but at this point, he didn't think she could take much more.

Where were her loved ones? She had family...why wouldn't she share this with them? He glanced at the photo on her bedside table of Sarah with Ava, proof that she had someone in her life. There were other pictures around the room, too. Sarah's big, bright smile stood out amongst the others. It reminded him of how she looked on the beach, happy and lighthearted. She deserved to feel like that all the time, but it was obvious something had darkened her life, something besides the attack at Oakbrook on Friday.

He got up, rubbed the sleep from his eyes, and lumbered into the living room. "Good morning."

Sarah jumped, spilling coffee down her front. "Oh—hi," she said, wiping at the coffee spill.

He grimaced. "Sorry, didn't mean to sneak up on you."

"It's okay, I'm a little jumpy. Not used to having people here with me."

"How did you sleep?" he said over his shoulder, as he walked through the living room into the kitchen.

"Good, how about you? I didn't wake you, did I?"

"No, I didn't hear a thing." He pulled a mug from the cabinet and poured himself a cup of coffee.

"You didn't have to get up. I don't mind if you use the bed. It's the least I could offer after all the trouble I've caused you."

Mark sipped the rich brew and closed his eyes, silently thanking her for having fresh ground coffee instead of grocery store crap.

He waved her off as he walked back into the living room. "I got plenty of sleep."

He would much rather stay here and take care of her than sit home alone. He hated his house, hated being there. And with that vanilla and lavender scent burned into his brain, he'd never sleep as comfortably again without it. Sarah's house on the other hand was charming, inviting, and well...full of spirit.

He walked back into the living room and sat across from her. "We need to talk about some full-time protection, Sarah." He sipped his coffee. "Last night should be enough to convince you that you're not safe here alone."

Sarah stared at him, not speaking for a long time. Shifting her weight, she set her mug on the table.

"Mark...I don't want you feeling obligated to protect me. You have a busy life and a son to take care of."

He leaned forward. "You think I'm here because I feel obligated?"

Sarah looked down, chewing on her lip. "I don't know what to think."

Mark ran his hand over his head, wishing he could make her understand. "I don't do things because I have to. I do them because I want to."

"I'm sorry," she mumbled. "I just don't understand..."

"Look, Sarah, this is new territory for me. I've never dealt with this sort of thing before." He took a few sips of his coffee again, not sure how to explain his motivation to her, especially since he didn't completely understand it himself. "I'm not sure how to help...but I want to be here for you."

"You were a cop, surely you've seen this before, probably worse."

"You're right." He nodded. "Working as a police officer I had to deal with crime like this, but when you're on the job it's different. It's not personal, it's work. I was trained to distance myself from what I had to face." He closed his eyes for a split second and then trained his gaze on her again. "When I saw that terrified look in your eyes, it caught me off guard. It became personal to me." He stared at her unblinking for a moment. "And all of that was intensified ten-fold last night when I walked into this house and found you hiding in the corner with a gun. You *cannot* expect me to walk away after that."

Before Sarah could respond, there was a knock at the door. She bolted upright, the color draining from her face.

Mark walked to the window and looked out. A shiny red convertible with the top down sat haphazardly behind his truck. He turned and looked at Sarah's pale face. "I guess you're not expecting anyone."

She shook her head and got to her feet.

"Stay put, I'll get it." He peered through the peephole at a petite woman wearing huge sunglasses, carrying a white bag and a tray of coffee.

He opened the door and had to squint at the bright sun as it blasted through the door.

"Get up, you bum." The little woman nearly ran him over as she stepped into the house. "Whose big-ass truck is blocking the driveway?"

When she finally looked up, she yelped and ripped the sunglasses off her face. "Who the hell are you?"

Mark smiled. "Hello, Ava."

She was barely five feet tall with pin straight, blond hair and eyes that got stonier as they stared at him.

Her eyes went from his messy hair, to his bare feet, then to the mass of blankets on the sofa. An amusing smile jerked at the side of her mouth. "I know you," she said. "You're Angela Summors's brother, aren't you?"

"And that's my big-ass truck," Mark said as he closed the door behind her.

Ava turned and got a good look at Sarah. The grin dropped from her face. "Holy shit, Sarah! Look at you."

Sarah rubbed her face and brushed the hair from her forehead. "I'm fine, Ava. What are you doing here?"

"What am I—you fucking told me you were mugged. This doesn't look like a mugging."

"Mugged?" Mark crossed his arms over his chest, looking down at Sarah.

She rested her face in her hands. "I. Am. Fine. I didn't want you to rush home for nothing."

"You look like you've gone ten rounds with Mike Tyson." She walked over and set the drinks and bag of pastries down on the table next to the couch.

"If only," Mark said.

Sarah shot him a dirty look, and he felt bad for ganging up on her. "She's had a rough week."

"Why on earth wouldn't you tell me the truth?"

"Ava...don't, okay?"

"She was attacked Friday night leaving work. It was late, dark, and..."

Sarah glared at him again.

He waved a hand at Sarah. "You shouldn't lie to her. How would you feel if the roles were reversed—"

"Attacked. How?" Ava said, ignoring their sidebar. "Tell me everything."

"She got away from him, but he beat the hell out of her first."

When he saw the question in Ava's eyes, he answered before she could ask. "She wasn't raped."

Relief flashed in her dark eyes. "She told me her purse was stolen."

Mark walked over and sat back down on the couch across from them. "Technically, her purse was stolen. He got her house keys and all her identification."

"Why are you here?"

"I was at the school picking up my mom. When Sarah got away from him, she ran into us. I've been helping her out."

"Sleeping here?" Ava said, looking at the pile of blankets next to him.

"Someone broke in last night. I stayed so Sarah wouldn't have to be alone."

Ava's eyes grew wide. "Last night?"

Mark nodded. "Sarah shot him, tagged his arm. Lucky bastard, another few inches and he'd have a hole in his chest."

"I can't freaking believe all this happened last night and you didn't call me. You knew damn well I got home last night."

"I was here with her," Mark said. "There wasn't any need to call you in the middle of the night."

Sarah gave him a look of thanks when Ava backed down. "Is that Mocha for me?"

Ava chuckled. "Yeah, but I didn't know you had a hot guy spending the night or I would've brought him one too."

Mark fought to keep the color out of his face. It was definitely time to retreat. He reached for the bag, pulled out a blueberry scone, and stood. "If you two don't mind, I'm going to take a shower."

Sarah began to stand. "Do you need—"

"No, stay put, I'll find my way." He stopped short and turned toward Ava. "Maybe you can talk your friend into some full-time protection. She's not safe staying here alone, and she won't listen to me."

"Nice." Ava gave an appreciative nod as she watched Mark leave the room. "He certainly grew into his good looks."

"Shut up." Sarah shook her head, her eyes trailing Mark as he disappeared. She couldn't help but agree with Ava's perception.

Ava snickered. "He's like a real-life superhero."

Sarah leaned over to embrace Ava. "I'm glad you're here."

"Why didn't you call me sooner? You look like hell."

"I'm fine...but I shot someone last night, can you believe it?" It still didn't seem real to her. She'd owned that gun a long time, but she'd never imagined ever pointing it at another person and shooting them.

"Yeah," Ava scoffed. "I can." She pulled back and gave Sarah a good look. "I wouldn't want to meet you down a dark alley."

When Sarah didn't respond, Ava said, "So, you shot an intruder. You protected yourself, there's nothing wrong with that."

"Well I can no longer protect myself. The police took my gun."

"They took the Colt that Charlie gave you?"

"Yeah...needed it for evidence."

"I'm sorry, hon. I know that was important to you."

"God...I'll never forget the day Charlie gave me that gun."

"Wasn't that right before your mom divorced him?"

Sarah closed her eyes, wishing like hell she could forget that day. "Charlie took me and Devon to the shooting range...when we got home Mama was 'entertaining' some friends."

"What?" Ava raised her eyebrows in question.

"She had two men in our house and they were all drinking...two weeks later we moved to Flagstaff with one of them."

"Is that why she left Nashville?"

"Some guy, just like always. Charlie was heartbroken. I can still see the look on his face when we walked into that house." She dropped her head on her shoulders. "What is wrong with her?"

"You could waste your whole life trying to figure her out. Anyway, it doesn't matter, Sarah. She is who she is and nothing you do or say will change that."

"I guess you're right, but still..."

Ava rolled her eyes. "Oh, whatever. You try so hard to prove you're nothing like her, but who are you trying to prove it to?"

Sarah jerked her head up to look at Ava. "Ah! I do not." She shifted in her seat. "I don't have anything to prove, and I'm nothing like her."

Ava reached over for her coffee and then leaned back against the sofa cushions. "Yeah...so how many times have you starting packing since you were attacked?"

"That's not a fair question. You don't know what it feels like knowing some madman is stalking me."

Ava blew out a breath. "I'm sorry, you're right, I have no idea what you're going through right now." She leaned forward and placed her hand on Sarah's. "Why don't you stay with me? I'll take the week off. We'll hang out and come up with some cool revenge."

"You can't take a week off." Sarah considered the idea, but Ava was notorious for using every hour of sick leave and vacation as she earned it. "You don't have any vacation time."

"I'll work it out. I'm more concerned for you than that stupid airline."

It wouldn't hurt...maybe for a few days. At least that was better than calling Devon again. "Where do you go next week?"

"Guam."

"No," she shook her head, "that's good money for you. I can't ask you to give that up. Besides, what if it ends up being longer than a week?"

"Why don't you call Lily or Devon? I'm sure either would be here in a minute to help you."

"Are you mad at me? Geez. Forget that. I'm not calling Mama."

"What about Devon?"

"No, I feel bad asking him to rescue me again."

"That's what big brothers are for."

"No, it's not." Sarah dropped her head back in exasperation. "Do you know that it has taken every ounce of strength I have to keep from packing my bags and leaving the country? This is my home. I love it here. What kind of message am I sending if I leave? God! Why does everything in my life have to be so hard? I just want to live without the drama."

"If you don't want to leave, then ask Mark to stay."

"Ava! You know I can't ask him to do that." Sarah thought about what he'd said before Ava knocked and realized he might not take no for an answer.

"Not everything has to be hard. Maybe if you let people into your life once in a while, things might be easier. I think you should stop trying to prove something and be smart about this."

"I'm not trying to make a statement here. Do you really think I would put myself in danger to prove I'm not like Mama?"

Ava's eyes widened. "Ah...yes I do." She shrugged and said, "He seems to really care about you and you can use a man like that around."

"Having a man around isn't the solution to everything." And with her luck, having a man around was likely to cause her more trouble than solve anything, especially a man like Mark. He was just too perfect, too...soft. She thought about lying in bed with him last night. Yeah, he provided a little too much security.

"Sarah," Ava said in a low voice. "I've known his family for a long time. They're good people. *He* is a nice guy. Gawd, and the way he looks at you."

Sarah dropped her head to her hands. There was no use in asking her to stop—she didn't listen. "This isn't helping."

"What are you going to do? Stay here like a sitting duck? Wait for this fucker to come after you again?"

"That's a good question," Mark said.

They both jumped when they heard Mark's voice behind them.

"Excuse me?" Sarah said, trying to steady her racing heart. "Didn't your mother teach you not to eavesdrop?"

"I wasn't listening. I just walked in on the conversation. Although, I'm curious to see how you answer that question."

Sarah threw her hands in the air, wishing like hell she had an answer. "I don't freaking know what to do now."

She almost shouted it, but when the phone rang, she started at the sound. Then she sighed, feeling stupid for being so damned jumpy. She stood and walked over to answer, relieved to get away from the prying eyes and questions. "Hello."

"Hello, sweet Sarah. Did you think a bullet in the arm would stop me?"

Her blood went ice cold.

"Who is this?" she whispered as the room tilted. She braced herself against the table to regain her balance as the phone was ripped from her hand.

"Who is this?" Mark's face went red as he listened with a white-knuckled grip. "Ah! The coward hung up."

Sarah clutched her throat, rapidly breathing in and out.

Mark sat her down. "Take a deep breath, Sarah, before you hyperventilate."

She leaned back against the sofa and closed her eyes. What kind of sick person is this?

"Dammit!" she said after a few minutes of silence.

Now it was her turn to be the coward. She didn't want to let that monster chase her away, but he left her with little choice. She would not be his sitting duck.

She got up and went into her bedroom, pulling a large suitcase out of the closet. She started grabbing clothes from the hangers. He'd won, and that was okay with her. She'd happily admit defeat if it meant never having to look at that man ever again. If she'd learned anything in her life, it was how to retreat.

"Sarah?" Ava called softly.

She turned to look over and found Ava and Mark watching her with hesitant eyes. They wore the same expression. She almost wanted to laugh at it.

"What?"

"What are you doing?" Mark asked.

"I'm packing. I can't stay here with the son of a bitch taunting me."

"Good, you'll have fun at my house," Ava said.

"I'm not going to your house." She dropped some folded clothes into the suitcase. "I'm not letting you risk your job to babysit me."

"It'll be fine."

"No." Sarah shook her head. "I'm leaving town."

"I'll stay with you," Mark said.

"You can't put your life on hold for me either."

"I'll call Lily and see if she can take care of you," Ava said.

Sarah spun around, seething. "Don't you dare call my mother."

"Sarah, you shouldn't travel in this condition." His eyes rested on hers and he stepped closer. "I meant what I said. I want to be here for you."

Looking into his eyes, Sarah knew he meant it. He wanted to help her and protect her, but why? And what would it cost her?

Chapter Thirteen

Sarah felt the hours of sleep she'd lost clear to her bones. Mark was tired too, but he still took over the responsibility of making dinner. She tried to do it on her own. Of course she couldn't, which infuriated her. She had limited range of motion in her left arm, and the sling was driving her crazy. More than anything, she hated not being physically able to do everything herself. She wanted her life to get back to normal. Remembering the night before, she wondered if things would ever be normal again.

They ate dinner in the living room in front of the TV after agreeing on a movie. She took one side of the sofa and Mark took the other.

Halfway through the movie, Mark fell asleep. She watched him for a while, wishing she could sleep as peacefully. He was attractive. She nearly snorted out a laugh—attractive didn't begin to describe him. No, more like absolutely beautiful. Too bad he was a control freak, she shook her head. Maybe that was unfair. Mark wasn't controlling, she knew that. He was protective and that made him seem possessive. After the care he'd taken with her over the last several days, she was hesitant to group him in with other men. He deserved her respect if nothing else.

She couldn't remember the last time she'd let a man stay overnight. In the past, she didn't want anyone getting too comfortable in her house. She didn't like how men always managed to assume ownership over things—over her, her free time, her life. No, she didn't need a relationship like Ava seemed to think, but that didn't mean she couldn't be friends with him. She wasn't relationship material anyway. Kevin had ruined love for her and proved she was better off alone.

Sarah had spent the last eight years trying to keep history from repeating itself. She didn't feel comfortable in her own skin until she bought this house. It had been at least a year since she had thought much about Kevin. She rubbed a hand across the underside of her chin, near her left ear where the three-inch scar used to sit. Having that nasty reminder removed helped her forget, but these head-to-toe bruises brought it all up again.

She closed her eyes at the shame she felt having to sneak into Kevin's house to get her stuff after fleeing the hospital. His last words ringing in her head, *You killed our baby, Sarah. She's dead because of you.*

Her body had buzzed with adrenalin the entire time, knowing he'd catch her...yet knowing it was impossible because he was in jail. How did a person shake the fear of someone you knew couldn't reach you? Still she felt fearful when she thought about him.

That's what made the last year seem like such a huge accomplishment. Maybe she had actually recovered from the awful things she'd been through. Her eyes fluttered open, and she looked over at Mark again, trying to clear her head of the heavy memories. He looked peaceful, but chilled. She gently placed a blanket over him, hoping not to wake him up, and went to her bedroom to watch TV in bed.

Within minutes of turning the TV on, she found a good movie to watch and snuggled in with the remote control.

Before the first commercial break, Sarah felt herself dozing off.

Her throat was too restricted to breathe. She fought to inhale, but as his grip tightened, her fear became palpable.

"You want to leave, I'll kill you first. Don't ever think you can leave me."

He slammed her against the wall with his hand still clamped around her neck, holding her there while he screamed at her. His spit hit her face and his mouth contorted in a way she'd never seen before. He was insane. He had completely lost his mind and he was going to kill her. This was her only condolence, knowing that when it was over, she'd be dead.

"Let this be a reminder the next time you think about leaving me."

She stood on tiptoes, hoping to relieve the pressure of his grasp on her airway. When his massive fist came at her face, a quiet gasp left her lips and her wide eyes slammed shut...

Sarah woke up screaming, with a disheveled Mark standing over her. Her eyes darted from him, to the fuzzy TV, and around the room, trying to focus on something familiar.

"You scared the hell out of me," he said, sitting on the edge of the bed.

She blinked her eyes at the flickering lights from the TV.

"I need to..." She rolled out of bed and with trembling hands, pulled open the drawer of her nightstand. No gun. She stared into the open drawer until she could focus her thoughts and remember where the gun was.

"Sarah, you okay?"

"Yeah." She closed the drawer and stumbled into the bathroom.

With a cool washcloth, she dabbed her face and stared at her pale reflection, trying to steady her breathing. She dropped the washcloth and laid her hands on her flat stomach, the ache from her loss and the feeling of emptiness as fresh as if it had happened yesterday.

Stop this, Sarah—just stop it—get over it.

When she came out of the bathroom, Mark was waiting for her.

"Sorry if I woke you up." She walked over and turned off the TV, casting the room in shadows.

"You okay? Want to talk about your dream?"

She climbed back into bed. "I would much rather not relive it."

"You don't need the gun, Sarah. I'm not going to let anyone hurt you."

When she didn't respond, Mark whispered, "Good night."

He sounded exhausted. If she couldn't master herself, neither of them would get any sleep.

She covered herself completely with the comforter and tried to relax into her warm bed. Until this week, she hadn't dreamt about Kevin in a long time. Always the same dream—Kevin's hand around her neck, fighting for air, and praying for a quick death. She remembered his words clearly and the pain. She would never forget the pain.

How clever of her to think she'd gotten passed this. Instead of getting better, she had to live through that day again in her dreams. Kevin didn't even know where to find her and she had to let it go, but would she ever chase him from her nightmares permanently?

After several minutes of restlessness, she took her blanket from the bed and lumbered to the other end of the sectional sofa, letting Mark's steady breathing lull her to sleep.

Mark woke up early and glanced at the clock. Six a.m. He blinked in surprised at Sarah sleeping on the other side of the sectional sofa. He sat up and leaned over to see her face. Damn, she was beautiful.

When she slept, the fear disappeared and her beautiful face remained. He loved staring into those storm-cloud gray eyes, but she carried a lifetime of secrets and pain there. When she slept peacefully, the secrets and pain disappeared, and her beauty increased tenfold.

Her skin looked like porcelain and felt just as breakable. His eyes followed the line of her jaw and the curve of her cheekbone. He fought the urge to reach out to touch her. He could've watched her sleep for hours, but he got up, grabbed his laptop, and went to the kitchen.

When he finished reading his e-mail, he walked over to the bookcase in the corner of the living room to see what types of books she liked to read. Sarah's collection ranged from the complete Harry Potter series to classics like Jane Austen.

Tucked between two larger books was a high school yearbook from Central High. He flipped open the cover to read the Flagstaff address and then carried it to the kitchen table. Sarah's picture was amongst the seniors, but with a different name. Sarah Lange. *Hmm, why the name change?*

She shuffled into the kitchen with the comforter wrapped around her with only her small face exposed. She yawned and said, "Morning."

"Good morning," he said, looking back down at the book.

"What the hell are you doing?" She dropped her blanket and walked over to yank the yearbook out of his hand. She squinted at the page and then gave him a death stare as she walked across the room and dropped the yearbook into the garbage can.

"Why would you throw that away?"

"Why are you going through my things, reading my stuff?" she shouted.

"What's the big deal?"

Sarah grabbed her blanket off the floor and stormed to her room, slamming the door behind her.

He walked to the bedroom door and knocked. "Open up, please."

When she didn't answer after a few minutes, he went back to the kitchen and pulled the yearbook out of the trash can. She couldn't be angry over an outdated senior picture. He flipped through the book some more. Sarah was in the track team picture and the newspaper staff. It seemed like normal high school stuff, until he focused on one of the signatures.

Dear Sarah,

I didn't want to sign your yearbook, I was just checking to make sure no other guys did. I don't know why I bothered, it's not like you'd have your other boyfriends sign this anyway.

I'm glad school is out so we can be together without all the bullshit getting in our way. You belong to me forever now.

Love always,

Kevin Lewis

"Kevin," he whispered.

No, she couldn't have been screaming like that over a high school boyfriend. He flipped through the book, but couldn't find Kevin's picture, only another senior named Jeffery Lewis.

As he turned the pages, he realized how few signatures there were, and only one from a boy. He found a hand-drawn heart and scribble that said Kevin and Sarah forever. He turned this over in his head and thought of Ali, his high school sweetheart and ex-wife, who he still talked to almost every day.

"What did he do to you, Sarah?" he whispered before reading the entry again. *You belong to me forever now...*

Absolutely creepy. Goosebumps broke out on his arm. No wonder she tossed it in the trash.

He dropped the book back into the garbage and walked into her bedroom. When he inched the door open, he saw the lump under the covers.

He sat on the edge of her bed and pulled the blanket back to uncover her head. Sarah buried her face in the pillow.

"Sarah, look at me, please."

"No, I'm mad at you. Get out of my room—get out of my house!"

Mark took a deep breath to keep from chuckling. She was irresistible. How could anyone ever hurt her? The thought sobered him, and he wondered again where her fear came from. Did she really carry this around with her for all these years?

"I'm sorry. Look at me, please," he said, wanting to see her eyes. "I wasn't trying to invade your privacy, but I'm glad I did. You were pretty hot in high school."

"Shut up, I was fat in high school."

This time he did laugh. "No, not at all."

"It's not funny." She reached to smack him.

When she did, he grabbed her hand and turned her toward him.

"I am sorry. Will you forgive me?" he asked. "I won't touch anything else without your permission. How about you come to my house this afternoon and dig through my stuff?"

She jerked out of his grip, pulled the covers back over her head, and rolled back over on her side.

Mark lay down next to her and wrapped his arm over her, wanting to comfort her and needing to feel her next to him. If he could feel her, then he knew she was okay. Her nightmare had scared him last night too. Waking up to her screaming like that—it wasn't something he was prepared for.

"I really am sorry, and I'm sorry you couldn't sleep last night.

When she didn't respond, he said, "You should've woken me up if you couldn't sleep."

Sarah shook her head under the blanket.

He gave her a few minutes before trying again.

"Will you forgive me?" he asked in the sweetest voice.

When she nodded, he squeezed her until she said, "Ow."

"Oh, sorry." Mark started to get up, but she grabbed his arm and held him in place. He rested his head and lay still until her breathing steadied, and then he carefully removed the blanket off her face. *Damn, at least I'm capable of tranquilizing her to sleep.*

He didn't move. There was nothing worth doing that could compete with this. He snuggled in to enjoy her silent company.

ꙮ

Mark jumped when he realized Sarah was waking him up. "What's wrong?"

"What time do you pick up Jamie?"

"One o'clock?"

Sarah sat down on the edge of the bed next to him. "It's almost noon."

"Are you still mad at me?"

"No." She gave him a crooked smile. "But I am going to take you up on the offer."

"What offer?" he asked with a knitted brow.

"To go to your house. I'm sure you have a sofa I can sleep on."

"I'm sorry about the yearbook. I won't touch anything else." He held up his hands. "I promise."

"No." She rolled her eyes with a smile. "I don't want to go through your stuff. I just need a change of scenery."

"If you're sure, I'll drop you off on my way to get Jamie."

Mark lived in a track house in a newer development where the houses resembled each another—same shape and same color scheme.

Sarah had trouble hiding her chagrin when he pulled into the driveway.

"This is your house?"

"Yeah, what? You don't like it?"

"How many families live here with you? It's rather large for only you and one little boy."

"Yeah, it's ridiculous. Ali picked it out. I found out about her affair a couple months after I bought it...don't get me started." He frowned. "When the divorce was final, the housing market bombed and I got stuck with it."

Mark's house looked like a big box, almost completely square. She loved the colors though, soft gray with navy blue and charcoal trim—a perfect combination. The top floor had two large, symmetrical bay windows protruding out, and Sarah assumed those were two smaller bedrooms.

Before stepping inside, Mark stopped at the mailbox and pulled out a large handful of mail. He unlocked the front door and waved a hand for her to enter first. Sarah immediately heard a loud beeping coming from the alarm keypad located to the left of the front door.

She smiled when Mark entered the code. "So, Mark, what's your code?"

"Zero-nine-five-two," he said without hesitation.

She raised her eyebrows. "I was joking, you didn't have to tell me."

"I'm not worried." He smiled. "But I do have to hurry or Jamie will be stuck waiting outside his school alone."

He gave her instructions for his alarm system and his passwords before rushing back out the front door.

Chapter Fourteen

"Alone in a strange house—whose idea was this?" Sarah looked around at the entryway before walking into the large great room. The great room consisted of the family room, kitchen, and dining room, which were open to each other. A U-shaped island surrounded by barstools framed the kitchen, providing the only division from the other two rooms.

The open family room had a lived-in feel to it, very warm and inviting, and Sarah could see herself curled up with a book in the overstuffed chair. A big-screen TV sat opposite the sofa with a cabinet underneath for the DVD collection and a game console.

On her way to the stairs, she peeked in at the formal living room. Mark had it impeccably furnished with dark brown, plush leather sofas. Stained wood trimmed the latte-colored walls. Light poured in through the windows, creating a bright room, even with the shades of dark brown.

Sarah strolled up the stairs and was surprised to only find three bedrooms. Jamie's room looked like you would expect a little boy's bedroom. She loved the sea blue color and loved that Mark wasn't afraid of color. In the far corner sat a bookcase filled with books of all different shapes and sizes. Toys littered the floor, spilling out over the side of the toy bin to the left of his bedroom door. She smiled. This room was definitely lived-in.

An office sat across from Jamie's room, and Sarah could tell by the large cluttered, L-shaped desk that Mark did a lot of work from home. Opposite the desk sat a futon sofa.

Great candid pictures of Jamie hung around the office, mixed in with some of his school artwork. Sarah gazed at the picture of Mark's son, searching for a resemblance. Jamie had Mark's dimple and beautiful eyes, but lighter hair. What a lucky boy to have Mark as a father. If Mark was half as caring with his son as he'd been with her, then he was a wonderful dad. And for Mark to have such a beautiful little boy...she tried not to feel jealous, but that was impossible, especially with the way his face lit up every time he talked about Jamie.

After looking around, she moved on to the next bedroom. The master suite almost equaled the size of her entire house. To the right, a small seating area faced the fireplace, and Mark's king-size bed sat dead center between the two bay windows she'd seen from outside. The master bathroom had a two-person, spa bathtub and a huge walk-in shower.

"Wow, great bedroom," her voice seemed to echo in the large room. Regardless of how much Sarah hated track houses, this bedroom was incredible. She walked to one of the windows and looked out, expecting to see another house exactly like this, but instead she faced the neighborhood park. Beautiful eucalyptus and redwood trees lined the park and connected walking trail.

Sarah stared for a minute, not sure what to do with herself. Then she grabbed her bag and laid it on the futon in Mark's office. From the side pocket, she pulled out her most recent Stephanie Plum novel.

She took the book into Mark's room and stretched out on the sofa in front of his fireplace, wishing it was cold enough to justify a fire. Being here, in his room, seemed like an intrusion. She couldn't avoid thinking of his wife, and of this being the room they shared together. The thought made her lonely. She'd never shared warm memories with someone like Mark had. Even after a divorce, he still had a fondness for Ali. All Sarah felt for Kevin was fear.

Mark, Ali, and Jamie had been a family here, and knowing that...and being here, made her feel like she didn't belong.

These lingering thoughts made her wish she hadn't suggested he bring her here. She didn't need a reminder of what she couldn't have.

ꕥ

An hour later, the alarm system started beeping. She reached for the cell phone, but when Mark entered a code, the beeping stopped.

It took him about fifteen minutes to come up the stairs, and she wondered if maybe he was avoiding her. When he came in, her gaze was fixed on the lifeless fire grate. A few seconds later, the fire came to life.

"That's cool. I wish I would've figured that out an hour ago."

He grinned and pointed to the switch on the wall near the mantel. "You like that?"

"Yeah, that's the one regret I have about my house—no fireplace."

"I like not having to lug firewood up the stairs." He sat down on the end of the sofa and put her feet in his lap.

She jerked away and curled her knees to her chest.

"I don't bite, you know."

Her face grew hot. "Sorry, thought I'd give you some space."

"Is that a tattoo I see peeking out from under your jeans?" He reached out and grabbed her foot before she had time to refuse.

She didn't mind if he looked at the tattoo, but she wanted to tread more carefully with him, especially after sleeping in the same bed the other night...and again this morning. She'd slept better with him next to her than she'd slept in years. And that's what scared her.

When he turned her foot and tickled her, she squirmed and said, "It's a Celtic band."

"What does the phrase say?"

"*'Bíonn súil le muir ach ní bhíonn súil le tír'*. It's an Irish proverb, 'There is hope from the sea, but there is no hope from the land' or grave...depending." She shrugged her shoulders, praying he didn't ask why she tattooed that on her ankle.

"That's beautiful, but what does it mean?"

"I'm sure it means different things to different people. It helps me get through difficult times and"—her grin faded—"deal with grief."

"I guess it goes hand-in-hand with the Celtic Knot?"

"Yeah, helps me persevere."

"So does the knot have a special meaning?"

"It's protection, like a shield." She hesitated, trying to find the words. "It's hard to explain because it's so personal to me."

"Do you mind sharing?"

"No, it's just..." She looked at the tattoo before continuing. "This represents my family, my life. Having such a mixed family like I do." She pointed and ran her finger over the strands in the knot. "This helps me keep everything together. Each strand in the knot represents different aspects of my life interwoven into each other. Though each strand is individual, none can be separated from the whole, and all are never-ending. That's how it protects, like strength in numbers or strength in love. All aspects joined together to defeat the evils in my life." Her face grew warm again when she met his eyes. "I know, kinda corny, huh?"

"Corny—no. Thoughtful and powerful. It tells me where you draw your strength from, which is contradictory because you hate your family."

"I don't hate my family. Of course not."

"Okay." Mark lifted his hand. "Sorry."

"They're just...messy. I love them a great deal more from a distance."

"I can honestly say I've never heard anyone describe their family as messy," Mark said. "But after everything you've told me, I can understand why you feel that way."

Sarah let out a sarcastic laugh, glad he hadn't met her family. Messy was the perfect description for them. "I'll spare you the details."

He looked up from the tattoo. "Tell me about your house?"

"There's not much of a story there." She pulled her feet away again and tucked them under her.

"I love the way it's off the street and hidden away in a little nook. Hard to see if you're not looking for it." He shrugged and said, "It's beautiful, but not very secure."

"I love my little place," she said, her mood lightening. "Ava was dating a real estate agent, he told her about it. They showed me under the pretense that she wanted to buy it. I found out later she had no intentions, and instead, talked me into buying. She hoped if I bought a house I would stick around a little longer, and it worked. I'm still here."

"So, you must like Santa Rosa?" He turned and rested his arm on the back of the sofa.

She lifted her eyes to the ceiling, nodding. "Yeah. I only planned to stay long enough to get a couple of years teaching experience before moving on. But I bought my house and never got around to leaving."

"You've never been married."

She chuckled.

"Nope. I've managed to dodge that bullet." *Almost literally.*

"Then...," he said as he picked at a snag in the fabric on the back of the sofa, "why the name change?"

Sarah narrowed her eyes at him, the smile dropping from her face. How the hell did he know about that? "What are you talking about?"

"The yearbook...your picture said Sarah Lange? If you never married, why is your name different?"

She tried to relax again, but he was getting a little too personal for her taste. "Jennings is my father's last name. Since they never married, my mother gave me her name when I was born. When I moved to San Francisco, I changed it to Jennings."

"Is Lange her maiden name?"

"No, it's Devon's father's name. He was her first husband and the love of her life."

He lifted one eyebrow in question, making her laugh. Of course it sounded strange to someone who didn't know the story, Sarah understood that.

"Oscar Lange was her first love, but he died right after Devon was born. She's remarried a couple of times, but she's always kept his name."

Mark closed his eyes. "Wow. That is incredibly sad."

"The sad part is that Devon never had a father."

Sarah thought about Jamie and wondered how different her life might've been with attentive parents.

"Do you mind if I ask," he grimaced, "how old are you?"

She grinned. "Lacking the math skills to figure it out?"

He looked confused for a second. "Math? Oh right, the yearbook. Ah...twenty nine, thirty?"

"Thirty." She gave him a curious look. "And you're thirty-five?"

"Thirty-five." He dropped his head back against the couch. "Wow, do I look that old?"

She put her hand over her mouth and mumbled, "Sorry."

"Kidding." He snickered. "I just turned thirty-three."

She smacked him lightly and gasped. "Thirty-three. You literally got married right out of high school."

"We didn't wait. I never doubted that decision until the day she said she wasn't in love with me."

Mark frowned when he said this, which angered Sarah more than she wanted to admit. He had a broken heart and she could relate to his disillusionment.

"My parents have been married for thirty-five years. I wanted what they have. What can I say, I was young and stupid—and in too much of a hurry."

Sarah couldn't balk at that. She had been guilty of the same thing, young and stupid. God, the manipulation, and the emotional abuse Kevin put her through.

Her stomach quivered a little when she realized if her baby would have lived, she'd be eight now—the same age as Mark's son. How funny life could be, and how cruel. When she looked back up at Mark, he was watching her with those searching eyes again. She smiled in an attempt to hide her heavy thoughts.

"Wait a minute. You said just turned thirty-three, so you recently celebrated a birthday?"

The muscles in his jaw tightened. "A few days ago," he finally said without looking up.

She chuckled at his reluctance. "Well, happy birthday. So what day was your birthday?"

He looked up from lowered lashes. "A week ago today."

"Oh." She frowned, unable to hide how miserable she felt about that. "You spent your birthday taking care of me?"

"I promised my mom I would pick her up from work and have dinner with her and my dad. That's why I was at the school."

"I'm sorry I ruined your birthday."

"Don't be stupid...do you think I care about missing dinner?"

"Obviously, family is important to you."

"I can have dinner with my family anytime I want." He looked directly into her eyes now, holding her gaze. "Nothing that happened to you last week was your fault."

He was right. She didn't have control over what happened, and deep down she understood that. Sometimes it was hard to shut down the old programming.

"Please don't do that. You're going to make me feel bad," Mark said when she grew quiet.

She waved him off. "I won't feel bad, if you don't. How's Jamie?" she said to change the subject.

"He's fine. I took him to lunch and he didn't stop talking until I dropped him off at Ali's."

"I'm sorry he didn't get to come home with you."

"Me too, but you'll get to meet him next Tuesday."

"Why? What happens on Tuesday?"

"Ali agreed to let me spend the evening with him so I'm picking him up from school. I promised him the three of us would go out to dinner before I took him back to his mother's."

"Ah..." She was torn between curiosity and fear. Not once over the last few days had she considered meeting his son. "The three of us?"

"Yeah, I told him about you."

Told him what about me? "What exactly did you say?"

"I told him we were friends and that you'd had an accident."

"And did he believe you?"

"Of course, why wouldn't he believe me?"

Maybe because if her mother would have told her that story, Sarah never would have believed her. "You don't think this will be resolved by Tuesday. I can't live with a shadow over my shoulder forever."

Mark's expression dampened. "Brian is doing everything he can. Hopefully you can tolerate me for a few more days."

"No—you know that's not what I'm saying." This wasn't personal, she actually liked him and enjoyed his company. "I feel restless and..." She pressed her lips together, trying to find the right words to explain. "I hate—and I mean *hate* not being able to take care of myself."

Mark's mouth quirked into a grin. "Yeah, I caught that."

"It's not funny." She lifted an eyebrow. "I can't stand being cooped up all the time. I can't even go for a run in the park."

He nodded in sympathy, but there was no way she could explain the length of her discomfort without offending him.

"You have a target on your back, and this guy doesn't seem like the type to give up."

Her stomach did a little flip at that. No, she didn't want to be face-to-face with that guy again. She placed her feet on the floor and looked into the fire, not sure where to go from here. She didn't have her gun, she couldn't force Ava to take time off—her options were limited, to say the least. "I'm not sure what I should do."

"You're already doing it."

She slapped a hand on her thigh and stood. "That's the problem. I'm not doing anything. God, I don't want to go stay with my mother."

She closed her eyes and dropped her head, knowing she didn't have a choice.

He chuckled. "You don't have to call your mother, Sarah, just hang out with me for a few days...maybe a week. It's not a big deal. When you're recovered enough, I'll go running with you at Spring Lake." He grinned. "At least I'll try to keep up with you."

"That's nice, Mark. Thank you for what you're doing. I don't want you to think I don't appreciate all the help you're giving me."

He stood and approached her. "If you're so appreciative, then accept my help. It makes me feel better knowing you're safe...I do this for a living, remember?"

"What about Jamie?"

"Let's just take this one day at a time. If by Friday this attacker isn't in custody, we'll figure something out."

"Jamie didn't question your explanation? It's not like he's ever heard of me before."

"Oh, he asked tons of questions," Mark smiled. "Especially once he found out you're a teacher."

"I hope that's a good thing."

"I wouldn't worry. I'm sure he'll love you once he meets you."

Sarah didn't know how to take that. It sounded like she already had a strike against her.

Chapter Fifteen

Reluctantly, Sarah agreed to let Mark help her. They spent a couple of days at his house, and on Tuesday when Brian didn't have anything new on her attacker, she and Mark returned to her house. She found she didn't mind him sleeping on her sofa, but this arrangement couldn't go on forever.

She was having a difficult time being objective about him. It would've been easier if he wasn't so attentive and sweet to her. He never let her do anything for herself, and it was to the point of being annoying. She didn't want to get used to relying on him, and she didn't feel like she deserved his attention, especially after the way she'd treated him in the beginning.

He was also adamant about her having some protection, and she understood why. She wasn't ready to be on her own either, not after the break-in, the note, the phone call...the idea of facing her attacker again scared her senseless.

Sarah pressed the play button on her answering machine when she entered the house, while Mark carried in their overnight bags. After the long beep, Gabby's booming voice echoed out of the machine.

"Sar-rah, it's Gabby—where the hell have you been? I hope you're not sitting around getting fat on me, girl. Don't make me come over there and drag your hot, little ass out of bed."

Sarah grew warm with affection. Gabby, her personal trainer, was also a pretty good friend.

Gabby left two messages, and while listening to the second, she realized she'd completely flaked on their planned run around Spring Lake on Sunday.

She grabbed the handset and called him back.

"Hey, Gabs, phone tag, you're it. And no, I'm not getting fat." She laughed. "Sorry I flaked on our run Sunday. I hurt myself. Gotta take a break—doctor's orders. Call me back."

She clicked the phone off and looked up at Mark when he stepped back inside the house.

"You won't tell family about your attack—"

"I didn't tell Gabby either, and even if I did, he wouldn't freak out like my mother."

Mark smirked. "Gabby is a guy?"

"Yes, *Gabriel* is my personal trainer and a friend."

"Personal trainer? *Okay*." He handed her a stack of envelopes. "Here's your mail. No strange notes this time, but letters for Robert Jennings from Stanford."

"Ah, snooping through my mail, huh?"

"No, I just..." He stopped when he realized she was kidding. "Robert...brother, right?"

"Yeah, he's at Stanford. I need to go drop these off within the next couple of days."

"Drop them off?"

"I have to drop them off at my accountant's office."

His eyebrows lifted. "*Your* accountant—*you* pay your little brother's tuition at Stanford?"

"Yes, I do," she said, flipping through the mail, hoping like hell he didn't ask any questions. Some information she planned to keep quiet about, and her money was on a *need-to-know* basis only.

"I have to pick up Jamie from school at two-thirty. Do you want to come with me? He'll need to finish his homework before we go out."

"I think I'd like to stay here." She saw the argument dangling on the tip of his tongue and held her hand up. "Pick me up for dinner later. You can't be with me every waking moment." She smiled. "Go spend some time with your son."

"Fine, but I need you to take some precautions first."

She rolled her eyes. "Right, lock the doors, set the alarm to stay mode, and keep my phone on me at all times. I got it." She laughed. "Go on."

Chuckling, Mark headed for the door. "All right, I'll see you in a couple of hours."

He stepped outside with a wave, closing the door behind him. She punched the stay button and clicked the locks. When he finally backed out of the driveway, she inhaled deeply, glad to have a moment to herself.

She spent the afternoon on her computer, catching up with her family. She wrote messages full of lies about how well she was doing and how much she liked her group of first graders this year. She e-mailed Devon too, hoping to hear from him soon. When she had messages sent off to her mom and dad, she instant messaged with Ava until Ava refused to stop hinting about Mark, or the *superhero,* as she liked to call him.

Sarah liked Mark, but she knew she couldn't allow anything more than a friendship between them.

She pulled the borrowed cell phone out of her pocket and thumbed the buttons. He was thoughtful and caring—that was clear in the way he treated her. He also liked to make all the decisions.

His single dimple flashed in her head, making her smile. She hated to admit it, but she missed him. The stillness of the house bothered her when it'd never bothered her before. With a grimace, she hit the speed dial button to call him.

"Sarah, what's wrong? You okay?" he asked when he answered the phone.

"Ah—yeah, fine. What are you doing?" She curled into the sofa with the phone tucked under her ear.

"Everything's okay?"

"Yes, fine, stop freaking out."

"If nothing is wrong, why are you calling?"

"Oh, ah...when are you coming back with Jamie?"

The line went silent for a moment, and at first Sarah thought she lost the connection.

"So—you miss me, huh?"

She heard the smile in his voice. "Shut up—I'm going to hang up on you."

"No, don't hang up." He snickered. "We're done with homework. Do you want us to come over now?"

"Yeah, whenever you're ready." *Geez—mental head smack!* How stupid of her to try for breezy now.

He laughed. "Okay, we're on our way."

ꕥ

Sarah stood and clasped her hands behind her back to keep from fidgeting when Mark came in with Jamie. She felt a little silly for being nervous, but for some reason, meeting Mark's son was different than being with her students.

After spending so much time with Mark, she felt like she already knew Jamie, but Jamie didn't know her at all. What if he didn't like her? What if he hated teachers, or didn't want to share his dad with a woman? Would Mark reject her if Jamie didn't like her? Jamie had already been through so much with his parents, would her being in his life add to the stress already brought on by their divorce? Did it matter? It's not like she was dating Mark, even if it might appear that way to the outside world.

Was she overthinking this? Probably. She did a mental eye roll and smiled at Jamie, determined to focus on having a good time.

"Hello," Mark said with a smug smile, reminding Sarah of their conversation on the phone.

She returned his grin even when she didn't want to. She couldn't help herself. He was right, she had missed him while he was gone.

"Hi."

"Sarah, this is Jamie." He waved a hand at Sarah. "This is Ms. Jennings."

"No, call me Sarah. It's nice to meet you." Jamie's eyes darted to her face before dropping to her feet.

"Oh fine—clam up now, you wouldn't stop talking on the way over here."

Jamie's cheeks turned bright pink.

"Can you say hi to Sarah? You don't want to hurt her feelings, do you?"

She looked from Jamie to Mark. "That's okay. I don't want him to be uncomfortable."

"Where would you like to go for dinner?" Mark asked.

"Your choice, I'm not picky." She tried not to stare at Jamie—his smile was identical to his dad's, only smaller.

"Hey, buddy, why don't you go sit down and watch TV until it's time to go." Mark walked over and turned the TV on and handed Jamie the remote control.

Before he turned, Sarah got a good look at those beautiful, dark blue eyes. He had light brown hair that was cut short and parted on the side, neatly combed in place. She could see a sprinkling of freckles across his nose and cheeks. Big for an eight-year-old...eight years old. She closed her eyes when butterflies fluttered in her stomach.

Would my child have been like Jamie?

Would she be healthy, strong, and beautiful?

Would she take after me?

Sarah opened her eyes and looked into Mark's. "I...I'll be right back."

When the bathroom door closed behind her, she sat down on the edge of the bathtub, taking deep breaths. *What is your problem? Geez – get over it.*

She stood up when Mark tapped on the door.

"Is everything okay?" he asked.

"Yeah – fine."

"Are you sure. Can I come in?"

"I'm fine. I'll be out in a minute. You guys can figure out where we're going for dinner."

"Okay...," he said, and finally walked away several seconds later.

She splashed water on her face and stood for minute, staring in the mirror.

She didn't look like herself. The zombie complexion and hollow eyes made her want to cry. When did she stop caring about her appearance? Why did she let everything slide from her grasp? Her expression turned stony, and she wanted to slap the weak woman in the mirror staring back at her.

With a decided nod, she began applying her makeup and working on her hair. The process relaxed her, as if applying the war paint had given her a shield to hide behind.

Mark had never seen her with makeup. The realization surprised her. She'd easily opened up to him, which was completely out of character for her. She pictured him in the diner parking lot, after leaving the beach. She'd wanted his strength wrapped around her like she'd never wanted anything in her life before. That scared her more than she wanted to admit.

She glanced at her reflection again. The last time she'd made any effort to look halfway decent had been the morning before her attack.

No—no, no thinking about that tonight. Okay, only happy thoughts for the rest of the evening.

Less than twenty minutes later, she took one last look and plastered a smile on her face.

When she opened the door, Mark was perched on her bed waiting for her. From his position, he could watch Jamie and still see the bathroom door.

She smiled at him. "Sorry to make you wait."

He stood and walked toward her. "You okay?"

"Yes, of course."

"You're beautiful." His tense expression didn't soften when he said it and that made her nervous.

"Thanks, you too," she stammered, "no—I mean." She shook her head to clear it. "Not beautiful, you look good. Fatherhood works for you...he's sweet, like his dad."

They stood facing each other for a long moment before Mark said, "When you left the room you looked upset."

"I'm fine...I need to change my clothes. Jamie must have seen the bruises on my arms." She looked down at her wrists to avoid his eyes.

"I'm sure he didn't notice...but you should be wearing your sling." He took her hand and rubbed at the yellowing bruises on her wrist. He held her hand up to examine it. "They're finally fading."

"Yeah, and the scratches on my face are almost gone." She reached up and lifted the hair off her forehead to show him.

His expression changed, and he ran his finger across her eyebrow. "How did you get this scar? That's not recent, is it?"

"I got punched in the face." When the words left her mouth, she knew she shouldn't have said them.

His eyebrows snapped together. "Someone punched you?"

"Yeah, can you believe it?" She forced a chuckle, hoping he'd laugh it off too. "He split my face wide open, bled like crazy."

She turned toward her closet, holding the smile on her face...but damn, she'd said too much.

His voice went hard. "Are you telling me a guy hit you in the face?"

Without turning, she could picture his expression. She closed her eyes. *Stupid, stupid woman.* When she turned, his face was set and dangerous, exactly like she'd expected.

"It's not a big deal."

They both knew it was a lie.

"Son of a bitch. I thought you were going to tell me you fell and hit your head when you were a kid. Who the hell hit you, Sarah?" His teeth clenched when he said her name.

She waved him off. "It was a long time ago—it doesn't matter."

"It does matter—goddammit!" He marched over and took her face in his hands to get a better look.

Sarah felt the tension radiating through him as his quickened breath brushed her face. Mark rubbed his thumb over the scar until she reached up and touched his hand.

"It's okay, really." His concern touched her. She loved that he cared for her enough to be angry, but she felt bad for upsetting him.

"It. Is. Not. Okay." He took a shuddering breath and wrapped his arms around her. "I'm sorry someone hurt you."

"Stop, I'm okay." At first she stiffened at the embrace, but then melted into his warm chest. A lie would have been smarter. His question caught her off guard.

"I'm sorry, I'm stupid for telling you that," she mumbled into his chest.

"No, don't say that." He pulled away and stared into her eyes. "You're not stupid, don't do that. It is not okay when someone hurts you, *and* you can talk to me about anything—you can trust me."

"I'll talk to you, but not tonight. I want to have a nice evening with you and Jamie. Now get out, I need to change my clothes." She brushed him away, now thoroughly uncomfortable at the closeness.

Before closing the door, their eyes met for a brief moment, and Sarah felt the naked stare clear to her bones. She dropped down on the bed and rested her head in her hands, her stomach quivering with nervous energy. The things he did to her when he touched her. It'd been so long since anyone had stirred her like that.

Stop! Stop! Stop! Forget it, Sarah! He's bad news – this is a bad idea. She hugged herself for a moment trying to get her bearings, and then she stood and finished getting ready.

It took her ten minutes to decide on what to wear. She appraised herself in the full-length mirror. The black, twill, tight-fitting pencil skirt tapered down her legs to below the knee with a nice, little, center slit in the back. The tops of her high-heeled black leather boots got lost behind the bottom of her skirt. To add a little color, she chose a deep blue, button-up blouse that tapered in at her waist.

"Dressy enough?" she whispered with a frown. "Definitely not that dressy." But she didn't have the time or energy to look for something nicer.

When she came out of the bedroom, Mark and Jamie were on the sofa watching TV together. Mark looked at her, and his jaw dropped in slow motion.

"What?" she asked, looking down, thinking she'd forgotten something important.

"Wow."

"What?"

"You look incredible," he said, wide-eyed.

She raised one eyebrow. "Hmm, you sound so surprised."

"Ah—not surprised, struck dumb." He cleared his throat. "I've never seen you in anything but jeans and sweats. I guess we better pick a fancier restaurant, Jamie."

"Thank you, but anywhere is fine. I'm just happy to get out of the house, and you can hardly call this fancy." She walked toward her coat closet, feeling self-conscious now.

"We were thinking about cheeseburgers."

"I love cheeseburgers." She smiled over her shoulder at Jamie. He blushed again and turned away.

Before she realized he'd gotten up, Mark was at her side, helping her with the jacket.

When he rested it on her shoulders, he whispered, "If you want to get his attention, let's take the car."

"I'll get the keys if you move your truck."

Five minutes later, Jamie stared at her car with a big grin, unable to hide his face now.

"Cool Shelby Mustang! Is this your car?" he said in a sweet, little boy voice.

Sarah nodded and Mark laughed.

"Well, check it out—I get to drive!" he bragged.

"Awesome," Jamie said, looking up at his dad.

ꙮ

Mark was right, the car did it. Jamie started talking and didn't stop until they were driving him back to Ali's house.

Sarah realized when Mark asked Jamie if he was ready to go back to Mommy's house that she'd have to tag along with them. Her stomach gave a nervous jolt, but she didn't let Mark see her nerves. She'd had a good time with them and she felt good. It'd been a long time since she'd laughed so much.

She wasn't surprised when Ali's home turned out to be another big square track house in a new development. *Boring.*

Mark walked around the car to open Sarah's door and then reached in and took her hand to help her out. When she was out, he lifted the seat for Jamie. She turned to get out of Mark's way as a woman stepped out of the house.

The first thing Sarah noticed about Mark's ex-wife was that she was beautiful, even with a large protruding belly. She expected a monster, having prejudged her for cheating on Mark. Instead, she faced a very pregnant blond, dressed in sweats with her long hair pulled into a ponytail.

Sarah, despite her prejudice, tried to plaster a smile on her face, determined to behave herself.

Mark turned and was surprised to find Ali behind him. She held her arms crossed above her belly and looked thoroughly annoyed.

"Oh—hi," Mark said with the same big smile he'd worn most of the night.

"New car?" Ali looked at the car like it personally offended her.

"Ah...Sarah." He looked over at Sarah. "This is Jamie's mom, Ali. This is my friend, Sarah."

He placed his hand on Sarah's lower back when he introduced them.

"Hi." Ali nodded at Sarah without uncrossing her arms.

Sarah smiled at her and said, "Hello," in the sweetest voice possible.

"It's Sarah's car," he said, not giving in to Ali's accusatory tone. "Okay, big guy, give me a hug. I'll see you Friday night." Mark reached down and grabbed Jamie in a big hug.

"Goodbye, Jamie, it was nice meeting you," Sarah said, still using a sickly sweet voice.

When Mark came back to her side, they simultaneously reached out and grabbed each other's hand. Sarah suppressed an evil chuckle as she watched Ali's expression change from annoyed to pissed off.

"Bye, Sarah," Jamie piped in before bouncing into the house.

Ali turned without saying anything.

"Bye, Ali," Mark said.

Ali gave him a wave over her shoulder and entered the house.

When they were in the car, Sarah rested her hand over her mouth to hide the evil grin. "Sorry, I couldn't help having a little fun with her."

"Yeah, I enjoyed that a little too much, too."

"How can she have the nerve to be jealous after what she did to you?" Sarah said with a little edge in her voice.

Mark steered the car away from the curb. "She's usually much friendlier. I'm not sure what her problem is tonight."

"I guess she hasn't met any of the girls you've dated since the divorce?"

"Nope." he grinned. "Maybe I should have rubbed it in a little sooner."

"Does it bother you that she's pregnant?"

He glanced at her briefly and said, "Yes."

She felt a little pang with his admission but couldn't find the words to respond.

"Wasted time." He exhaled a long breath. "I always wanted a big family." He shrugged. "No big deal. If I only ever have Jamie, I can live with that too."

"So you're not still in love with her?"

He shook his head. "I'm not sure I was ever truly in love with her."

"What do you mean by that? You talk about her like you miss her."

"We were kids when we got married—best friends. Should have stayed that way. We kind of got our lines crossed and neither of us had the nerve to give up."

"Can men and women be just friends?" Oh God, had she said that out loud? What the hell was wrong with her mouth today?

She could've smacked herself. Wasn't she expecting that from him now? Friendship and nothing else.

He stared at her for a moment, and she knew she'd given him the wrong idea.

"You don't think so?" he asked.

She pretended to consider her answer. "Yeah, I actually have lots of men friends."

Of course they were all gay. Geez, this conversation was going downhill fast. Now she sounded like a hypocrite—or a slut at best.

Mark's mouth tightened into a frown. "Was it a *friend* who gave you the scar?"

"No." She snickered and rubbed her eyebrow. "Clearly he wasn't friendly."

"It's not funny. Domestic violence isn't funny."

This time she snorted out a laugh. "You're telling me."

"You're making light over the fact that someone you once loved and trusted punched you in the face. I don't get the joke."

"What else can I do? It happened. I can't change the past. But don't worry, you won't find me in that position ever again."

He chuckled now, though it lacked humor. "Oh...okay, now I understand." He shook his head and bit on his lower lip. "That's why you're such a loner. You cut yourself off from people because some asshole couldn't control his temper."

"You shouldn't assume I'm not happy with my life."

"Why don't you tell me what upset you—earlier when you met Jamie."

She turned toward him. "What are you talking about?"

"I saw the expression on your face."

"Let's go inside," she said, and reached for the door handle.

"What will it take to earn your trust? Why won't you talk to me?"

"There's nothing to talk about—nothing to break down and analyze. I'm only a victim of my own poor choices."

"Bullshit, Sarah." Mark shook his head and exhaled heavily. "That's a famous line spoken by battered women all over the country. No man should ever hit a woman—no matter the reason."

"It's more complicated than that." The heat from his anger radiated off him in waves. She wished she could open up to him. He had done a lot for her, but she didn't trust herself to talk about this. The wall she'd built wasn't strong enough to withstand letting him in and still maintain her own self-worth.

"Of course it is..." He pulled the door handle. "Let's go inside. It's been a long day." He got out of the car and came to her door to open it for her.

When she stood and faced him, their eyes met and Sarah took the chance to ask him something that had bothered her since they'd left Ali's house.

"Does Ali know why you and I are..." She lowered her eyes.

"Absolutely not, and I wouldn't tell anyone anything unless I had to."

She nodded. "It would make me sick to think about her feeling sorry for me."

"Don't worry. The only person she's feeling sorry for is herself."

Sarah's head shot up. "Why?"

"Ali likes being the prettiest girl in the room, and you...beautiful you," he said, poking her nose softly with his index finger, "have completely crushed her feeling of superiority."

Heat rushed her cheeks. "Thank you," she said, and laughed.

"Did I miss the joke?"

"The joke is," she leaned in close to his face and whispered, "I wasn't even trying."

He looked her up and down when she took a step back. "In that case, I can't wait until you try."

Chapter Sixteen

Sarah changed into sweats and joined Mark on the sofa. He picked up the remote and flipped through the channels until he found the news.

Spending time with Jamie improved his mood a great deal. Unfortunately, their conversation brought him back down a notch. She regretted that her past had ruined yet another day for her. She'd had a good time hanging out with Mark and Jamie, but she couldn't change who she was or where she came from.

When she heard the familiar sound of the Channel Two news anchor's voice, she looked up and caught the headline.

...third sexual assault in Sonoma County within a week, the police suspect a serial rapist...

Mark's phone vibrated on the side table and he snatched it up. "Brian..." He closed his eyes. "Yeah, it's on the news."

Sarah walked into the bathroom and paced, taking deep breaths to keep from being sick. When she felt more in control, she went back to face Mark.

She stood in the doorway to the living room and listened to Mark's side of the conversation. And as she listened, it became painfully clear that he hadn't been honest with her.

"Call me back when you have more news, I gotta go—" He began to stand, but froze halfway up. "Wait, what aren't you telling me?" His face paled a shade before he straightened. "Oh my God."

Slowly he closed his phone and turned to Sarah. His expression changed from trepidation to concern. "You okay?"

She gently crossed her arms over her chest. "You haven't been honest with me."

"What do you mean?"

"Really? Do you think I'm stupid?"

His shoulders slumped. "Sarah..."

"Tell me what information Brian just gave you." She inhaled deeply to regulate her breathing. "According to the news, there have been two other attacks in the last week, one today. Did Brian tell you about the second attack?"

She sat down before she lost her nerve and collapsed. She hated being lied to, and she wanted answers, honest answers. His lies scared her more than what she saw on the news.

"Let's sit down and I'll tell you whatever you want to know."

"I am sitting! Mark, did Brian tell you about the other rape?"

"Yes."

She shook her head in frustration. "Why didn't you tell me?"

"I didn't want to ruin your day. You were finally feeling better and..." His eyes lingered on the floor. He took a step back, stuffing his hands in his pockets. "I apologize for not telling you."

"What did Brian tell you on the phone?"

"They're sure it's the same guy that attacked you."

"What else?" she asked, clamping her hands together to hide her jumping nerves.

"He...uh...wanted to make sure I was keeping an eye on you. Brian believes you're still being targeted."

Sarah bowed her head and scrubbed her face with her hands. He was stalling—keeping things from her. Lying. She wasn't stupid. She could see right through his stammering bullshit.

Mark stepped forward and reached a hand out for her. "Are you all right?"

She pushed it away. "Why? Tell me why he believes that. What new information did he give you?"

He stared at her without speaking, obviously trying to get his lies in order before he said too much.

"I am not a child. Stop treating me like one. I don't like not knowing—this deceitful behavior isn't okay with me." She fought to control her temper, trying not to overreact. She wanted to trust him, but if he kept secrets, how could she?

She closed her eyes and shook her head. She thought he was different—but Mark was no different. He wanted to control her. Only he disguised it as protecting her. No, she wouldn't let this happen again—not again.

Sarah stood and walked from the room, pulling her borrowed cell phone out of her pocket. She went into her bedroom, closed the door behind her, and started dialing numbers.

"'Ello."

"Hey, Devon." Relief washed over her at the sound of his voice.

"Hey, Sis, what's going on?"

"Can I hang out with you for a few weeks? I need a change of scenery."

"What's wrong?"

"Why do you immediately assume something is wrong?"

"What should I assume when you ask if you can visit before you say a real hello?"

She rolled her eyes, bouncing her head back and forth. He had a point. "I miss you."

"You don't have to ask to visit me. You're always a sight for sore eyes."

His warm voice comforted her, but she couldn't hold in her unsettled, strangled giggle when she thought of giving up and leaving.

"What's up with you?" he asked.

"I need a break. I need a friendly face." Her voice broke when she said it.

"You can't lie to your big brother. Tell me what the hell is going on."

"Nothing I want to talk about over the phone. If you're sure it's okay, we'll talk when I get there."

"You can come here anytime. Don't be stupid."

"Thanks, I'll see you Friday."

Sarah hung up and pulled her suitcase out of her closet. She needed to call Ava and ask her to check on the house when she got back from her trip. Sarah lifted the suitcase on the bed, dialing Ava's number at the same time. Before she got the number dialed, Mark knocked on the bedroom door. She stuffed the phone back in her pocket and jerked the door open.

"Hey, listen—" He stopped midsentence, looking into her room at the suitcase on her bed. "What are you doing?"

"I'm leaving town until the police can get this figured out." She turned and unzipped the suitcase. "Thanks for everything you've done, but you don't have to worry about me. I have a safe place to go."

He stepped closer to her. "Where are you going?"

"I'd rather keep that to myself." She paced the room, pulling clothes from her closet and adding them to her suitcase.

Mark's voice tightened. "You said you didn't want to leave."

"I can't be stupid about this. I need to keep myself safe, regardless of what I want." The decision to leave relaxed her. Running was in her blood. She had her mom to thank for that. And not being able to trust Mark changed everything for her.

"No." He shook his head, his voice sounding panicked. "I can't let you leave."

She threw the sweater she'd finished folding into the suitcase. "Excuse me, but you don't have a say. I stopped listening to your opinion when you started lying to me."

When he came closer, she stepped around him, pulling clothes off hangers and carrying them to her bed.

"Sarah, don't leave. I promise I'll tell you everything."

"Too late. You should have already told me everything. Come on, Mark, aren't you sick of being here anyway? Aren't you sick of all of this? Don't you want to go home and back to your normal life?" She fought the painful regret surfacing. How could she have let herself get sucked into this? She wanted so badly to believe in him, to trust him.

"What are you talking about? I *want* to be here for you. Why don't you believe that?"

She threw her hands in the air. "Why? Tell me why it's so important to be here. Why do you have this masochistic need to protect me?"

"Because that son of a bitch could have attacked anyone." He ran his hands through his hair and made a fist, his eyes darting around the room, searching for the words he needed. "My mother was in that parking lot. My sister, Ali, any student could've been his victim. You—fighting him off—were incredible, and strong, and nobody else could have...but you did." He dropped his hands to his sides. "I need to do this. I need to make sure you're okay."

"You don't owe me anything. I don't want you to feel obligated to help me."

"Obligated...no..." He held his hands up. "That's not what I meant. I need to make sure you're okay because I care about you—not from obligation." He stepped closer. "Just stop packing and talk to me—give me a chance to tell you what happened."

"I trusted you, and you lied. How could you do that?"

He reached out, his arms engulfing her. "I'm sorry about lying, but you can trust me, Sarah.

Tensing, she stood stock still, not sure what to do. Once his warmth settled into her, she relaxed. Mark's embrace didn't relax, and she realized he was more upset than she'd ever seen him. She put her arms around him and some of her anger subsided.

"I'm sorry," he whispered. "Give me a chance to fix this." He moved his hand up to the back of her neck and his fingers threaded through her hair. Then he pulled back and looked at her. His intense stare traveled from her eyes to her lips as he leaned in and kissed her. She expected tender, but he was passionate, hot, and oh so goddamned sweet.

Mark's kiss melted her resolve. His warmth pulled her in and held her there, kept her warm and made her feel safe again. He would protect her even from her own fears. Her heart raced in her chest. God, how she wanted to enjoy his touch without hesitation, but she didn't trust her own judgment or her feelings. She pulled away, sucking in fresh air, hoping to clear her muddled brain.

"Shit!" He stepped back. "I'm sorry."

She stood with a racing pulse, searching for answers, searching for a reason to run away. Her heart said jump, but her head wasn't quite sure.

He stared at her and the sincerity in his eyes...in those deep blue eyes made her want to cry. His eyebrows creased and his cheeks were flushed. He placed his hands on his hips, leaning forward, inhaling fresh air. "Will you let me explain... please. I can't protect you if you leave."

"Or control me."

His head snapped up. "What?"

"I don't need you to protect me. I have the resources to take care of myself." She put her hand to her chest, trying to slow her pulse.

"Yeah, you can take care of yourself, but dammit, I am asking you to trust me."

The angry knot in her stomach tightened. "I can't trust you when you keep things from me. I have a lot more to worry about than this rapist." She stepped back, hoping he didn't hear the tremble in her voice.

Mark moved to her again and placed both hands on her face, kissing her, only slowly this time, allowing her to taste him fully. When her body curved against his, he pulled away enough to see her face.

"I will never hurt you." His lids grew heavy as he searched her face. His expression softened. "Stop packing and let me prove it to you."

He slid his hands down her arms and laced his fingers with hers to pull her back to the living room. She went with him willingly. The truth came through in his kiss, and she couldn't deny it. She still wanted to hear everything, but her doubt was fading.

Mark turned the TV off and sat on the sofa, facing her.

He told her everything, beginning with the rape from the week before. After Sarah heard the story about this first rape, her body went ice cold, and Mark didn't miss the change in her constitution.

"You okay?"

"Don't stop unless I throw up on you." She was serious, but she half-smiled at him as she leaned over and put her hand on top of his. "I'm fine, keep going."

"Brian suspects the rapist is obsessed with you because you escaped him. He's..." Mark's jaw flexed when he gritted his teeth and said, "had a taste and now won't stop until he gets what he wants."

"Brian said that before, but when he called tonight...what did he tell you?"

"The attacker's descriptions matched again, and both of the other victims looked like you. The attacks were similar, only while he raped her..." Mark cursed and looked down at their hands. His jaw clenched when he said, "While raping her, he said your name—he called her 'Sweet Sarah'."

"He—he said my name while raping this other girl?" Sarah barely got the words out. Bile rose in her throat, burning until she swallowed hard. She rested her head in her hands, concentrating on forcing the air in and out of her lungs.

"I'm sorry..." Mark cursed under his breath and reached for her hand. "Sarah?"

"Fine," she huffed, brushing him off. "I'm fine. I just...need a minute." When her breathing slowed, she leaned back with her eyes closed. After a few minutes, she stood and tried to shake it off as she walked into the kitchen.

She grabbed a bottle of wine and went to the drawer to get the corkscrew. After fighting with the cork, Mark pulled them both out of her hands and opened the bottle for her. He poured her a glass as she lifted herself onto a barstool. She couldn't talk yet.

They were silent until Mark said, "Are you staying?"

When she closed her eyes, he tried again. "I'm sorry about before. I hope you know now it wasn't done deceitfully."

"Having good intentions doesn't mean it wasn't deceitful."

He nodded. "I know...it got away from me."

"Mark, you have to give me the chance to decide for myself. I need you to respect my decisions and my right to have all the information. I will leave and not look back." She stared at him, hoping he understood.

"I won't keep anything else from you."

Sarah finished her glass of wine and refilled it before returning to her room to unpack. She thought about those other women. The things they'd gone through and the things they still had to face.

"I can't help but blame myself. What those poor women went through. It never goes away, that layer of filth and shame." This last part she whispered, though not low enough for him to miss.

Mark watched her unpack from a distance, as if he were afraid to approach. The space between them made her cold...lonely.

"You haven't done anything wrong or anything to deserve this."

"You can't understand what it's like to have the choice taken away, a man forcing himself on you. Not caring if you want or don't want...and that powerlessness. Not being strong enough to stop—not having any control. It's something that never goes away." Sarah hugged herself in a daze as if her words were thoughts being spoken aloud by accident.

"You're right," he whispered, "I can't understand."

She lowered herself to the bed and rubbed her hands over her face, trying to hide the tears building in her eyes. How stupid of her to cry after making such a big deal about being able to take care of herself. Mark must have thought she was a walking-talking contradiction.

"You are strong enough to get through this."

When he sat down next to her, Sarah jumped to her feet, putting distance between them. It was better to feel cold and lonely. It kept her out of trouble. She'd been alone for so long, she'd forgotten what it was like to have someone who cared, someone who wanted to listen to her. That's what Mark had touched on, something she didn't realize she was missing until it smacked her in the face.

She excused herself and went into the bathroom before her tears started to flow. Too much comfort, too much warmth. She needed a moment to have a breakdown without an audience—without his support. Because when he left, she'd need to keep moving forward alone.

After clicking the lock, she buried her face in a towel and sobbed, but not for herself—she cried for the rape victims who'd be scarred for life. What was she doing? How had she gotten herself into this mess—and how the hell did she get out of it?

When she had it out of her system, she washed her face, took a deep breath, and stepped out of the bathroom. Mark was leaning against the door frame between her bedroom and the living room, waiting for her.

"I'm okay," she said before he got the chance to ask.

"Ya know...I don't believe you."

She lifted her chin. "It's true."

He laughed and that pissed her off.

"What is so funny?"

"You are the most stubborn woman I've ever met." His grin faded. "There is nothing wrong with letting people in once in a while."

"In on what?" She dropped her shoulders and the strong front she'd fought to keep in place cracked. "What do you want from me?"

"What do I want?" He stepped closer to her. "Sarah, is it that foreign for you to have someone in your life who just wants to be there for you and help you? Someone who cares about you?"

"Yes," she said. "It is foreign to me."

"Well I'm sorry you haven't had that before...but you do now."

She raised a hand and rested it on his chest. "Thank you for caring, and I'm sorry if I seem ungrateful."

He took her hand and laced his fingers with hers. He was sweet—this simple gesture drew her notice more than all the muscle-bound protection he could possibly provide. She understood that he was staying with her to protect her, but did he realize he'd given her just as much—or more emotional support than she could've ever asked for. The image of their linked fingers made her eyes well up again.

She brought her other hand up to cover her eyes. God, she hated to let him see her cry. He pulled her close, held her against him, and let her cry. No words, no expectations, no advice, and no attempts to get her to stop crying—he simply held her.

Her tears slowed and when she looked up to thank him, their eyes met and then their lips.

When the kiss heated, Mark gently pulled back.

"Sarah, this isn't a good idea." Desire coated his voice.

She released her grip on him, lowering her eyes to the floor. She wanted to laugh at what a gentleman he'd always been, and now when she needed his touch, he wouldn't give it to her.

"I'm going back to the couch," he said, tucking a strand of hair behind her ear.

She looked up at him and tried to smile. "Sorry, I shouldn't have done that."

"I don't want to be another regret for you." He backed up a step, letting their linked hands slip apart. "Good night."

"Good night, Mark."

She closed the door and crawled into bed after draining her glass of wine.

ꕥ

Sarah woke up to Mark shaking her and calling her name. "Sarah, wake up—it's okay."

She opened her eyes and met his. One deep breath wasn't enough to relieve the pressure on her chest. Her body shook uncontrollably as she fought to relax and clear her mind of the nightmare. The blankets felt constricting and heavy. She pushed them off but trembled when the cool air hit her damp skin. Mark pulled the sheet away from the comforter and covered her with it, rubbing her arms to warm her.

"Take another breath."

She closed her eyes and shifted over so he could lie down next to her. She inhaled a shuddering breath and curled into his chest, trying to relax.

"It's all right," he whispered.

Mark's musky, sandalwood scent helped settle her. Even that didn't stop the flashing images of her attack when she closed her eyes. Mark's embrace didn't relax. She waited for him to drift off to sleep, but his breathing never leveled out.

After another few minutes, she whispered, "Are you awake?"

"Are you having trouble sleeping?"

Sarah nodded.

"Do you want to talk about your dream?"

"No." She lifted her head and tried to see his eyes. "Sorry I woke you up."

"Yeah, you're incredibly inconsiderate for sharing your bed with me like this."

Sarah chuckled and almost hiccupped with the effort. When the room went quiet again, she placed her palm flat against his chest. He held his breath, his body tensing for a fraction of a second before inhaling deeply, forcing her hand to rise with his chest.

Sarah slid her hand up to cup his shoulder and caressed her way up to his neck. He was tight and so damn strong. He tensed again, and she couldn't help herself from lifting up to meet his lips.

The kiss began tender, but when he pulled her closer, she grew hot and arched against him, moving her hands to his face.

Sarah pulled out of the kiss to touch him, to explore the texture of him. Her hand traveled to his forehead and then slid down his cheek and over his closed eyelids. The more she touched, the deeper his breathing became. Mark didn't move or react, as if he knew she needed to discover him in her own way. She wanted to memorize his curves and the softness of his skin. The act of touching him, feeling her way around his body and growing intimately familiar with him was relaxing and she felt as if she could explore a little more every day and never get enough to be satisfied.

She sat up, pulling him with her, and he kissed her again as they knelt on the bed together. She pulled out of the kiss to trace his perfect lips and jawline with her fingertips, making him shudder as she moved her hands to his shoulders, sliding them down his arms, lacing her fingers with his, unlacing, and moving back up to his shoulders. Her hands moved to his waist and tugged at his shirttail. When he realized what she was doing, he reached down and pulled off his t-shirt.

Mark felt so good under her hands. His firm body trembled as the tips of her fingers traced the inside of his elbows and drifted up to his broad chest, caressing his muscles before tracing his abs with her thumbs.

When she lifted her gaze back up to his face, his stunningly blue eyes focused on hers intensely. She could've looked into them forever, longing evident in their expression. To be wanted by a man like Mark, someone so soulful and caring, she felt undeserving yet so lucky at the same time.

They stared at each other until she cupped his face and pulled him closer, wanting to lick his lips and taste him. Mark slid his hands around her waist and tucked them under her shirt. The skin-on-skin contact sent a fever rush of blood through her body, her heart pounding with anticipation.

He moved to her jawline, tasting her, nipping her chin, and caressing her face with his lips. His hands were gentle yet purposeful as they moved over her lower back and traveled under the waistband of her sweats, cupping her and pulling her toward him.

When his hands traveled down the bare skin of her hips, panic surged through her. A cry caught in her throat, and she tried to focus on his whispering breaths, but she went cold. She clamped her eyes shut and whispered, "Stop."

"Did I hurt you?"

She gripped his shoulders for support, trying to steady herself. She wanted him—needed him. Why was she shutting down?

"No, I'm sorry..." Her head spun with dizziness.

"You look sick. What's wrong?"

She stood up and stumbled to the bathroom, closing the door behind her, leaving Mark alone in bed. She leaned over the sink, splashed water on her face, and tried to slow her heart rate. When the door opened, she jumped in surprise.

Mark rubbed a hand up and down her back. "I'm sorry, baby. I didn't mean to hurt you."

She shook her head and tried to laugh. Still, it came out dark and sarcastic. "You didn't hurt me," she said. His sincerity made her want to crawl into a dark hole and hide. "I'm not sure what happened."

"I shouldn't have pushed you."

"I'm the one that pushed." She dried her face on a towel and turned to him. His face was flush with heat, although the crease between his brows showed his worry. She looked away to hide her embarrassment. "Oh God, I'm so sorry. You must think I'm an evil tease."

"No, don't say that...too much...too soon. I'm sorry."

Sarah covered her face with her hands and leaned into his chest.

Mark led her by the waist back to the bed and sat her down, before kneeling in front of her. "I would never hurt you."

"Mark, it's not you, it's me." She reached out and touched his cheek. "You did everything right."

"We shouldn't have gone that far."

"I feel awful, I hope you don't think I'm—"

"The look on your face nearly stopped my heart. I know you're not playing." He squeezed her hand. "I'll go back to the couch."

"No—do you want to? Will it be too hard to lie down with me?"

He reached out and cupped her face. "No, I want to be with you."

She saw the sincerity again in his eyes and was thankful. His understanding meant everything to her. Nobody else would have been as forgiving. She crawled back into bed, and he lay next to her wrapping his arms around her.

Just before Sarah fell asleep, Mark said, "It seems like a lifetime ago, but thanks for going to dinner with me. I had a great time."

Chapter Seventeen

On Friday, they picked Jamie up at Ali's and spent the entire week at Mark's house. Every time she brought up staying home alone, he insisted she stay with him. When he admitted that he wouldn't be able to sleep through his worry, she knew she couldn't—and wouldn't—feel comfortable alone either. Not to mention, she loved being around Jamie. He had a kind spirit Sarah found irresistible. She thoroughly enjoyed being with him and his dad.

After an intense argument over sleeping arrangements, they'd settled in comfortably. Mark refused to give in and let her sleep on the futon. He insisted he worked late hours in his office, and if she slept in there, he wouldn't get any work done. If he intended to ease her guilt with this argument, he failed miserably. She just felt worse for taking him away from his work.

In the interest of letting Mark keep his male pride, Sarah gave in. She happily slept in his king-size bed the entire week, smelling him and wishing he was there with her. With Jamie in the house, that was out of the question.

She found that the first impressions she'd had of this being the room Mark shared with his wife had faded. It was all him when she looked at it now. It was a reflection of his personality—masculine and strong, yet caring. Sarah felt a sense of possessiveness she knew she shouldn't feel toward Mark, which excited her and scared her all at the same time.

Mark hadn't kissed her since the night they'd almost made love. They kept their distance from each other. She couldn't be sure if Mark regretted what had happened between them. She had mixed emotions about it. She feared getting involved with him, but was more afraid of how painful it would be if he walked away once the rapist was caught.

Mark drove her by her house a couple of times during the week to check on things. No new notes appeared in her mailbox. She had a couple of messages on her answering machine of heavy breathing, but nothing concrete to help Brian with his investigation. The phone calls reaffirmed Mark's fear of her being alone, and Sarah couldn't dispute it. The calls did their job and freaked her out enough to keep her from doing something stupid.

On Friday night, they dropped Jamie off at Ali's and shared a bottle of wine in front of his big screen TV.

"I'm sorry for being in the way all week. I'm sure you're irritated that I took up all your time with Jamie."

"Are you kidding?" He looked at her bemused. "It went better than I expected. I thought it would throw his schedule off, but everything went really well."

She leaned back in the overstuffed chair and brought her knees up to her chest. "I'm going to miss him. How do you do this every other week?"

"I'm thankful. Most dads only get weekends." He inclined his head as he studied her. "You're good with him. It surprised me, considering you don't have kids."

"I'm a teacher, you shouldn't be surprised."

"This was different, more...motherly. Have you ever wanted to have kids?"

She smiled. "I have kids, twenty-two six-year-olds. I get to spend my days with them and then I send them home to other people."

"I'm happy you have the joy of being with other people's children, but have you ever wanted to have kids of your own?"

"Have I ever wanted to have kids of my own?" She set her glass of wine down, stalling while she decided whether or not to answer the question. Finally, she nodded. "Yeah, once I wanted to...a long time ago."

"You're only thirty. What do you consider a long time ago?"

"In college, my early twenties."

"Why the change?"

Sarah stared blankly for a few moments, not sure how much she wanted to tell him. Mark had been completely honest about his relationship with Ali. Maybe this was her chance to tell him the truth. Was it worth hashing up old memories? Could a man like Mark ever be with someone as damaged as her?

She took a deep breath and let it out slowly. "I had a miscarriage at twenty-two. After that, I sort of gave up the idea of ever being a mother."

He bowed his head. "I'm sorry, Sarah, that's awful."

She shrugged her shoulders, trying to ignore the heaviness she felt in her heart. "Technically, she was stillborn. I was six months along, it shouldn't have happened."

"Did the doctor tell you that you couldn't have children?"

"They said it wasn't likely I'd be able to get pregnant again. They wanted to do more testing to confirm, but I wouldn't let them. I just wasn't meant to have a family."

"If you were pregnant at twenty-two...your child would be Jamie's age."

"Exactly Jamie's age." She looked away, trying to master herself. She didn't want to be emotional. She had given up any dreams of having a family long ago, nothing had changed, and she knew she had to live with it now.

He leaned forward. "Why did you have a miscarriage so late in your pregnancy?"

Her smile faded, and his question surprised her. She expected him to ask about the father of her baby, but it didn't matter. The answer would have been the same regardless.

She held up her index finger and pointedly ran it across the scar on her eyebrow. When his expression changed, she knew he understood.

"So"—he straightened his back and pointed a finger at her scar—"the same son of a bitch who gave you that scar caused you to have a miscarriage?"

She avoided his eyes at first, afraid of what she'd see. When he reached for her hand, she couldn't help but meet his eyes. The pity she saw felt like a blow to her midsection. That's not why she had told him the truth.

"Don't, Mark, it's not that bad." She pushed his hand away. "It's something I've recovered from. Just like I'll recover from what happened a few weeks ago." She shook her head. "It's certainly not something I'll ever have to go through again."

"Is that the reason you've decided you don't want children, because of what this asshole did to you?"

"No." She fought to keep her tone level despite the way she was feeling.

"Then why?"

"I never intended to get close enough to another man to want children with him."

Mark sat back on the sofa, creating a cold distance between them. "You have completely given up on your own happiness because some jerk beat on you?"

"No. You don't understand. This isn't *some jerk's* fault, it's mine. Don't be confused about that." Her voice hardened.

"You're right, I don't understand. I don't understand why after eight years you still believe what happened to you is your fault. You're a smart woman, Sarah. You should know better than this."

"No matter what I tell you I can't make you understand."

"Try," he said, leaning forward again.

Sarah rubbed her hands over her face, pressing her index fingers to her temples. "I don't think I'll be able to get the words out."

Feeling defeated, she lay back into the cushions. His disgusted expression told her that the words she'd spoken had done their job.

"You're letting the asshole who did this to you—you are letting him win! It's no different than letting that rapist chase you out of your home."

"You just don't understand..."

"Then help me. Make me understand, Sarah."

"I haven't made this decision because I'm afraid some guy will beat me up again. You are completely off target, listen." Her eyes pooled with tears as she tried to find the words. "I refuse to give anyone that kind of power again. He beat me because I let him have *me*." She poked her chest. "I wasn't strong enough to maintain my own identity. I wasn't strong enough to say *no* and walk away."

Agitated, she stood up. "I let him manipulate me. I let myself become his victim. I should have left early on, before I got pregnant, but I stayed and I let him mentally beat me into submission. I handed him my heart, soul, and spirit on a silver platter and he crushed them into a million pieces."

She paced the room trying to hold back her emotions before they took over.

"So you pick up the pieces. You can still have a life."

"I have a life!"

"A broken life," he said, standing to face her.

"There's no fixing this." Sarah couldn't look at him. When he reached out for her hand, she pulled away. She felt so disgusted with herself, she couldn't bear his sympathy.

"If I'd been stronger, if I could have maintained one ounce of self-respect, he wouldn't have been able to hurt me. Hell—even the beatings were nothing compared to the things I let him say to me. The words I believed when I should have cared enough about myself and been smart enough to walk away."

She raised her hands to her face, and then dropped them to her sides, exasperated. "If that's what love is, then I'm not interested in ever being loved by anyone again."

She turned, finally making eye contact with him.

Mark approached her and she held out her hand to stop him.

"I told you, fucking dark water. I warned you, but you wanted to know." Tears spilled down her face as she left the room. Mark called her name, but she didn't turn back.

Sarah wasn't sure how long it took for her to fall asleep, but her dream came fast and more vivid than any other she'd had before.

Jamie stood in front of her smiling. She smiled back at him, but when she leaned in to talk to him, his form changed. He morphed into a little girl just like Sarah, gray eyes and a heart-shaped face. She recognized her own smile immediately. The little, girl twin was different though, dark raven hair, long and straight – the exact color of her father's.

The atmosphere swirled and changed around them, and suddenly Kevin was with them. Sarah was scared for the little girl standing in front of her – scared for her child. Kevin approached the little girl with the same sick smile her attacker wore. He was looking at her little girl through Kevin's face with hunger in his eyes. Sarah screamed at him to leave the girl alone. He turned toward Sarah and lunged at her, wrapping his hands around her throat.

"You killed my child," he screamed as she struggled to hit him, to push him off and defend herself. She couldn't scream with his hands clamped around her throat. Kevin was finally killing her, just like he had always promised he would.

"Sarah—wake up!" Mark shouted at her, as she thrashed around and pulled at her throat, screaming.

He shook her and she swung her arms out to protect herself. When her screams turned into gasps, he screamed her name. "Sarah!"

She jerked up, breathing in and gasping again.

"Sarah, wake up, breathe—breathe."

Sweat saturated her clothes and glistened on her face. When her breathing calmed, she began to sob.

"Sarah, you have to breathe, baby." Mark fought for calm, his heart racing in his chest. It killed him to see her like this, but he had no idea how to help her. When he reached out for her, she pushed him away to scramble out of bed. Her body trembled violently, and Mark worried she'd collapse at any second. She paced with a hand clutched on her throat. Her wide eyes searched the room, though she appeared as if she was still in the dream.

"Where's my gun?" she sobbed, stumbling around in the dark until Mark grabbed her and drew her to him, not letting her pull away this time.

"Sarah, please stop. You don't need the gun. I won't let anyone hurt you."

Sarah surrendered this time, not fighting Mark's arms. He didn't loosen his grip, afraid she might sink to the floor if he did. As her sobs slowed, the crying turned into a whimper.

"I promise you're safe, baby."

She calmed, but she didn't speak. Mark helped her to the bathroom and sat her down on the toilet, draped his robe over her trembling shoulders, and ran a washcloth under cold water. Her eyes were glazed and unfocused as they stared at the floor.

He wiped away the tears and held the cold washcloth over the back of her neck and throat. He could see the red marks where she'd tried to free herself from an imaginary grasp. When her shivering slowed, he picked her up like a small child and carried her to the bed. He pulled the blankets off the floor and crawled in, wrapping his arms around her.

His heart broke for her as he lay there trying to make her feel secure enough to go back to sleep. She nuzzled into his chest, her body still taut with tension. It took over an hour for her to relax enough to drift back to sleep.

A few times during the night, her body went rigid, and she tried to push him away. He just pulled her closer and whispered reassurances in her ear until she relaxed.

This was his fault, dammit. He shouldn't have forced her to talk about it. She'd tried to avoid the subject, and he'd kept pushing, forcing her to bring up all those bad memories. He suspected something tragic had happened in her past. He'd guessed most of it, but never imagined a miscarriage—and the emotional abuse. Mark expected to hear how badly it hurt physically. Clearly, the emotional scars ran much deeper, and he wasn't prepared for that. Damn, how could she blame herself for being manipulated by a monster?

His soul hurt knowing this awful, abusive relationship had been what she'd based the decisions of her life on, a vicious cycle of abuse and loss. She didn't even know what love—real love—felt like.

Chapter Eighteen

When Sarah woke, she felt the strength of Mark's embrace. She stretched her arms out to push away from him. He eased his grip and looked down at her.

"Good morning," he whispered.

Her head pounded so hard it made her dizzy and unable to think straight. She looked down at their intertwined legs, and then back up into his eyes. He carefully reached up and brushed the hair off her cheek.

"How do you feel?"

She tried again to lift herself up, stopping when a sharp pain shot through her arm. "Oh—ow!"

"Careful, you may have hurt yourself last night."

Sarah stared at him, not sure how he ended up in bed with her.

Kevin.

She shot up and placed her hand on her neck. The vivid dream felt real, although everything after it clouded, as if the dream was reality and reality was the dream.

Mark rubbed a hand up her back. "Just a dream."

His unbridled concern and tenderness showed the true difference between a man and a monster. Mark was right, not all men were like Kevin. She should've been embarrassed for the way she behaved, but her gratefulness outweighed her embarrassment tenfold.

"Coffee?"

"Please."

His expression relaxed. "You shower, I'll fetch."

Fifteen minutes later, Sarah came out of the bathroom wrapped in Mark's robe with a towel on her head. At the same time, he walked back into the bedroom with two cups of coffee.

"I can't believe it's after two," she said, taking the cup he offered. "God, that smells good, thank you."

"You're welcome," he said, turning to sit on the sofa in front of the fireplace.

Sarah sat next to him sideways with her feet curled underneath her.

With one sip of the rich brew, her headache melted away. She sipped it again and then looked up at Mark. They stared at each other for a long moment before she broke the silence.

"Thank you."

He closed his eyes and shook his head. "Sarah, I'm sorry I pushed you last night. If I would have known..."

"If you would have known I'd have crazy nightmares about murderous ex-boyfriends?" She chuckled. "I didn't even know. I haven't had nightmares that bad in a long time." She let out a long breath. "God, I thought I was past this, moving on and living a normal life."

She moved her hand to her throat.

"I guess Kevin is the ex-boyfriend in question?"

She closed her eyes and nodded.

"Kevin Lewis from high school?"

Her eyes popped back open. "How do you know?"

"He left a creepy message in your high school yearbook. I couldn't find his picture, just Jeffrey Lewis."

"That's his brother. Kevin graduated with Devon the year before me. We started dating in my junior year, his senior. He was the cutest boy in school." She smirked at the memory of how thrilled she was when he asked her out, and how stupid she was for accepting.

How could she have known? Every girl in school wanted to date him.

"He was sweet then. Once he left school, things changed." She looked down at her coffee to avoid Mark's gaze.

"You don't have to talk about this. I don't want you to worry about him."

Sarah knew Mark was concerned about her, but she found she wanted to confide in him.

"At first his insecurity was endearing...*stupid, stupid girl.*" She shook her head. How naïve she'd been. "He controlled everything about me—and I let him."

Sarah's eyes were unfocused, staring into the fire.

"Sarah—"

"When I told him, he beat the hell out of me...accused me of cheating, because 'there was no way it could be his kid'. I'd never been with anyone else, and he still didn't trust me." She looked into Mark's eyes. "He beat me up, but I didn't lose the baby until months later."

Mark exhaled heavily. "Was that the first time he beat you?"

"He'd smacked me around a few times but never beat me until I got pregnant. Six months into my pregnancy, things were better. He proposed to me again. I hoped he was over the insecurities and I believed things were back to normal...at least until I caught him in bed with someone else. That's the day I lost my baby."

When her voice quavered, she kept talking. If she didn't get it all out, she'd lose her nerve. "I went home and started packing.

When he came home and saw what I was doing, he beat me—almost to death—and raped me, telling me the entire time he'd kill me if I ever left him."

Remaining silent, Mark leaned over to take her hand with both of his.

"It's true," she said, shaking her head. "I have no doubt he'll find me one day and finish what he started. He'll keep his promise." Her voice hardened, the quaver gone.

"Did you leave right after the miscarriage?"

"Kevin had been arrested. After a few days in the hospital, I left...went to Devon's. When I got there, I went to bed and slept for two days straight. I was bruised, sick, and completely spiritless."

"How did your brother keep from hunting the son of a bitch down and killing him?"

She shook her head. "He'd never leave me alone like that. He was so worried...and so pissed at me for not calling him. I was terrified that Kevin would come after me. With his parents help, I was sure he'd be out on bail or some stupid technicality soon enough." She waved dismissively. "It didn't happen, but I still didn't stay in San Diego for very long. Devon took me to stay with Richard. He lives in San Francisco."

She reached over and grabbed her coffee mug to busy her hands. *No turning back now.* She had to tell him the truth. The thought of that alone scared her senseless. Protecting her identity had become a major focus in her life.

"Who's Richard?"

"Richard Perry."

Mark's eyebrows lifted, but he didn't say anything.

"He's our attorney and sort of my grandfather."

"Sort of?"

"He married our grandmother and he's the controller of her estate." She paused to take a sip of coffee. "He set me up with good medical care...helped me transfer my school credits and hide everything from Kevin."

"Why the sudden need for medical care?"

She put her cup down. "When Kevin beat me...the baby died before I arrived at the hospital. Because I was over six months along, they induced labor."

She swiped a tear away, trying to master herself. "It was horrific, going through labor."

They sat quietly for a moment until Mark broke the silence.

"Sarah, I—I'm sorry. I can't imagine what that could have been like for you."

"Between the beating, the rape, and the emergency delivery—I developed an infection."

"Why didn't Devon take you to the hospital or to your parents? Why Richard?"

"I didn't realize how sick I was. I didn't want to go to the hospital. I just wanted to get far away from Kevin."

"I can understand that," Mark said.

"Devon didn't want Kevin to get his hands on the money." She shook her head with a faint smile. "Devon's more financially driven than I am. I didn't care about it, but he had the sense of mind to call Richard first. My parents don't really know what happened, not everything anyway."

"Sarah, did you have to go through that alone? The delivery, I mean?"

She nodded. "They took me directly to the delivery room. I didn't really have anyone to call anyway. Kevin had chased off all my friends."

Mark pursed lips. "Is Kevin the real reason for the name change?"

"Yes, but what I told you was true. I grew up using Lange. Richard helped me get it changed to Jennings after I left Flagstaff. Jennings is my father's last name."

She stopped talking and silence settled around the room. There was a certain freedom that came with confiding in Mark. She had no doubt about it being the right thing, telling him was a relief and lifted a burden she'd been carrying around for too long.

Mark laced his fingers with hers and the gesture made her smile. "I had a girl, a daughter. I named her Lillian Claire after my mother."

It'd been years since she'd said the name aloud.

Mark didn't say anything for a long time. Sarah finally looked up to see wetness on his cheeks. He pulled their entwined hands up and kissed hers.

"You are so brave."

The affection and understanding showed in his expression.

"If I were brave, and smarter, I would have left sooner." She closed her eyes and pulled her hands free of his. "Please don't praise me."

"I can't believe you actually feel guilty, like any of this could have been your fault."

"It's my fault for being in that position in the first place, and for letting him kill my baby."

He took her face in his hands, making her self-conscious about him being so close. "You're the strongest and bravest person I've ever met, and like I told you last night, none of the trauma this asshole put you through is your fault."

Sarah tried to shake him off, but he kept a firm grip on her face. When she closed her eyes, he moved his hands from her face to wrap his arms around her.

"You're wrong too," he whispered. "Kevin Lewis will never hurt you again. He's not going to keep his promise—that is my promise."

"Mark, you don't know what he is capable of. The level of manipulation he will go to in order to get what he wants, it's sickening."

"You don't know what I'm capable of when I want to protect someone I care about."

"You can't protect me from him. Kevin isn't some measly, two-bit, street rapist—he's powerful and dangerous." She hoped Mark never had to know just how dangerous.

"You once asked me not to underestimate you, and now I'm asking you not to underestimate me." He pulled out of the hug to meet her eyes.

They stared at each other for a long time, and she knew he would never let anything happen to her while he was around, but what if he wasn't always around.

"It must have been hard for you to share this with me. I hope one day to earn the trust you've given me."

"You've already earned it." She sat back and tried to relax into her coffee, glad it was over and she'd gotten it out of her system.

"I guess if Richard Perry is your grandfather, that means Catherine Connelly-Perry was your grandmother?"

She widened her eyes. "You've heard of them?"

"Richard Perry is the richest philanthropist in San Francisco. People like him often need security." He grinned a little and said, "We've met once or twice."

"I don't usually tell people I'm related to them and I'd rather the information not get out."

"Catherine died over ten years ago. Is that when you inherited the money?"

She nodded. "In high school. She left the money to me, Devon, and Hayley equally. She never trusted my mother and she wanted to make sure we were taken care of."

"Do you realize what the press would do if they found out that you were one of the victims of this rapist?"

"Oh yeah, but the press doesn't know who I am. Fortunately, when Richard retired, he got out of the spotlight. With him keeping a low profile, it makes it easy for us to keep a low profile. Not to mention, my grandmother disinherited my mother so long ago, we've sort of fallen off their radar."

"I take it the press didn't find out about the baby or Kevin?"

"The case was reported locally, but they never figured out who I was. They were much more interested in the local business owner's son on trial for domestic violence. His family is pretty well-known in that area." She scoffed. "They were so busy digging into the Lewis family and analyzing their lifestyle, they never paid much attention to me."

"Kevin was convicted?"

"His father's lawyer got him a plea bargain. He was convicted of domestic violence, a misdemeanor charge. He was sentenced to one year in jail." She rolled her eyes. "I was actually relieved."

"Why? You should have fought it, had the son of a bitch put away."

Mark shook his head, and she understood why.

"He should have gotten a manslaughter charge or even a second-degree murder charge for what he did, and attempted murder for the beating he gave you."

"I didn't have the guts to fight. I just wanted to stay away. The plea-bargain deal meant no trial. I didn't have to go back there. Call me a coward, but I couldn't live through all that again, and it would have put me in the spotlight. As it was, I should have moved out of the country. I'm too close, too easy to find here. I'll have to leave one day. I can't hide in plain sight forever."

"Sarah, I am so impressed with your resilience. I have never known anyone who has been through half of what you have endured and still manage to live a functional life."

"I am resilient, but I don't want your pity." She put both feet on the floor and leaned toward Mark. "Don't feel sorry for me. Nightmares or no nightmares, I've survived a lot, and this most recent incident will not keep me down for long, either."

"Speaking of nightmares." He gave her a searching look. "You scared the hell out of me, you were choking in your sleep—I couldn't wake you up."

She rested back against the arm of the sofa. "I'm glad you were there."

"Me too," he whispered.

"I want you to understand, Mark"—she looked intently into his eyes—"I don't regret not being able to have children—at least, I never did until I met Jamie, and that completely snuck up on me."

"What do you mean you don't regret—how could you not?"

"*'Bíonn súil le muir ach ní bhíonn súil le tír*—there is hope from the sea, but there is no hope from the grave'. Does this make sense now?" she asked as she moved her foot out to show him her tattoo. "I was devastated when I lost my baby, but imagine that man being a father." She shuddered at the thought. "I would rather never have children."

"Well, I hope you have the opportunity to experience the gift of a child's unconditional love." Mark rubbed her foot and ran his hand over the tattoo around her ankle. "I also hope that one day there will be a child lucky enough to experience your unconditional love."

Even though Sarah knew he meant it, it didn't change anything. He couldn't change what had happened any more than she could.

Sarah felt the weight lifting after she told Mark about her history with Kevin. She couldn't judge his reaction enough to say for sure that he wouldn't push her away now. Her feelings for him were growing stronger every day, and the butterflies in her stomach made her feel foolish, like a child. Of course, the last time she felt like this she was a child. Just seventeen when she met Kevin, but she felt more for Mark now than she ever had for Kevin, that she was sure of. When she remembered those first few months with Kevin, she was so sure about him, she cringed—and look how things turned out.

She couldn't distinguish what her real feelings for Kevin had been after the first year. Every emotion she ever had toward him seemed clouded with too much physical and emotional pain to be honestly evaluated or understood now. As if that time in her life were an emotional black hole, and when she tried to explore that hole, all she found were the awful words he always said to her.

Mark was the first man she'd ever met that was a stark difference from Kevin. Not that every man was evil, but most were single-minded at best. She thought back to the night she and Mark almost made love, proof again of just how different he really was.

Mark's ringing cell phone brought her out of these thoughts, and almost at the exact same time, her borrowed cell phone rang. They looked at each other confused and got up to get their phones.

"Hello," Sarah answered.

"Ms. Jennings, it's Randy from Summors Security. The back door contact on your home alarm system was tripped. We've also contacted Mark Summors."

"Okay, I'll get over there," she said, looking at Mark when he closed his phone. "My alarm is sounding."

"I know, stay here while I go—"

"Forget it. I'm not sitting here while you go over there without me," she said, unzipping her duffle bag to grab some clothes.

"Not a good idea—"

"It's my house. I'm going," she said, closing the bathroom door.

Ten minutes later, when Mark pulled down her street, the first thing Sarah noticed was the maroon Porsche Cheyenne SUV next to the police cruiser in her driveway.

"Oh crap—is there a Porsche in my driveway?" Sarah covered her face with her hands and sucked in a deep breath.

"Yeah, do you recognize—what's wrong?"

"It's Devon." She hopped out of the truck before Mark put it in park and went running into her brother's arms.

"Hey, Sis—hi," he said, and picked her up in a rib-cracking hug.

Chapter Nineteen

Mark approached the waiting officers. "Hey, guys." He pointed to Sarah and Devon. "They seem to know each other."

Officer Reed nodded to Devon. "He says this is his sister's house."

"Yeah, sorry for the false alarm."

"No problem, the city will send a bill." He smiled and walked back to his cruiser.

Mark turned in time to see Sarah cry out as her brother picked her up and swung her around. He looked Devon Lange up and down, unable to find the resemblance. Devon was taller than Sarah, though Devon wasn't as tall as he was. He had dark, almost black, shoulder length hair and deeply tanned, olive skin. He was athletic looking. Mark thought he looked like those Olympic swimmers, long and lean but strong.

Devon wore sandals with ragged, holey jeans and a tank top. Mark noticed the Celtic band tattoo wrapped around his upper arm, identical to Sarah's.

Mark wanted to be jealous of the clear affection she had for her brother, but after everything Sarah told him, he felt a kinship with Devon. As she pulled out of the hug, Mark noticed Devon's eyes. That's when he saw the resemblance. They were exactly like Sarah's, the same shape and the same stormy gray color. He had no doubt this was her brother.

"Stop crying. Aren't you happy to see me?" Devon asked, trailing his eyes from her head to her toes. "I thought you missed me," he teased.

"I do miss you," she said, looping her arm around his with a grin so big it lit up her entire face. "I'm glad you're here—why are you here?"

Devon leaned in toward her and said, "Dude, when did you start hangin' out with cops?"

"This is my friend, Mark. This is Devon."

Mark would let Devon have that dig since he'd made Sarah so happy after such a miserable night. He reached over and put his hand out to shake Devon's. "Ex-cop."

"Aha! Ex-cop, I can peg 'um a mile away." Devon laughed. "Nice to meet you—ex-cop-friend of my sister—Mark, right?" he said as he shook Mark's extended hand. "Sis, what is up with that alarm system? My key didn't work, so I tried to sneak in—then bam!"

"Yeah, the system is new..." Sarah grimaced and glanced over at Mark. "At least we know it works."

Mark raised an eyebrow. "We weren't in any doubt about the system working."

"Oh no, of course not, let's go inside," she said, changing the subject.

Mark walked up onto the porch and unlocked the door for her.

"Are you okay, you didn't hurt your shoulder, did you?" he asked as they entered the house, and he punched in a code on the alarm system.

"No, it's fine."

Mark's cell phone rang. He looked at the caller ID before excusing himself to the kitchen to give Sarah and her brother a moment to talk. "Ali, what's up?"

"What do you think you're doing having a woman over with Jamie in the house? He just told me that Sarah stayed with you all week."

"Excuse me? I'm sorry, divorced—remember?"

"I have a right to question anything you do regarding my son."

"Our son. And are you trying to say you don't trust me where Jamie is concerned?"

"What do you think you're teaching him, having a woman there?"

"For your information, I'm just helping out a friend. We didn't share a room, much less a bed."

"That doesn't matter."

"Yeah, well did it matter when you slept with Carl in our house, in our bed while we were still married? Don't you fucking dare talk shit to me about inappropriate behavior."

"I can't believe you're throwing that in my face now. If you're not careful, Mark, I'll go file for full custody."

"Don't threaten—Ali!" He pulled the phone away from his ear and looked at it as Sarah and Devon stepped into the room.

"What was that about?" Sarah asked.

"That bitch hung up on me," Mark growled.

"Mark—what?"

"It's Ali," he said before he opened his phone and dialed a number. "Oh fine, send me to voicemail."

"What's going on? What did she do?"

Instead of answering her questions, Mark looked at Devon. "Devon, how long are you staying?"

He shrugged. "At least tonight."

"Are you staying here?"

"Yeah, that's the plan."

"I have to go take care of this with Ali. Will you be okay with your brother for a while?" Mark looked between Sarah and Devon. "Devon, I need to leave, but I don't want Sarah left alone in this house. Will you stay with her until I come back?"

"Yeah, of course—what's going on?"

"I'll let Sarah tell you—it's up to her." He looked at Sarah, and a pang of regret and fear jolted his stomach. "Will you be all right if I leave?"

"Yes, I'll be fine. Is Jamie okay?"

"He's fine, he just has a big mouth, and Ali apparently doesn't like what he's saying."

Her eyes grew wide. "Oh..."

"It's fine, don't worry about it. She's hormonal." He looked over at Devon again. "Before I leave—Devon, tell me how you got in the house. Did you break any windows or anything?"

"No man, give me more credit than that. I picked the lock on the back door," he said, lifting his chin smugly.

"You picked the lock?" *Wonderful.* At least he had better skills than the last jerk who broke into her house.

"Yeah." He smiled wide. "It's an acquired skill, maybe I'll show you sometime."

"No need, but thanks." Mark pointed to the keypad. "Sarah, after you set this, make sure the back door is locked."

"Right, I know," she said as he opened the front door. "When will you be back?"

"I won't be gone long." He stopped and stared at her for a few seconds. "Maybe I'll try to call her again."

He pulled out his phone, knowing he was in deep. He hated the thought of leaving Sarah, even if only for a few minutes.

"Geez, I'm fine, just go."

Devon crossed his arms over his chest. "What the hell is going on?"

"Hold on, I'll tell you in a minute. Mark, go take care of Jamie and Ali."

He took one last look at her, before he reached down and pulled her into a tight embrace. "I'm sorry I have to leave. I know it's been a rough day—"

"Go. Don't worry about me."

"Stay out of trouble." Mark inhaled, taking in the scent of orange blossoms, and kissed her cheek near her ear before rushing out the door.

ꕥ

Sarah felt a little flustered after Mark's embrace, but she set the alarm once he left.

"What the fuck, Sis?" Devon asked.

"What?"

"Don't even—don't even pretend like—what the hell is going on?" He looked at her with a mixture of concern and anger. "You look like shit—that guy has a key to your house, your alarm code. You look like you haven't slept in a week."

"It's a long story," she said, turning away from the front door. "Let's get a drink first."

She went into the kitchen and grabbed a bottle of wine from the rack.

"All the phone calls," Devon said, following her into the kitchen. "First, you call and tell me you're coming to visit, and then you call and say never mind. I'm not stupid, something's up with you." He looked her up and down. "Spill it."

Sarah poured them each a glass of wine and told him about the attempted rape and about Mark. She didn't leave anything out, including the information about the notes and the other rapes. She wanted to make sure he understood everything Mark had done for her and why he was reluctant to leave.

"So, he's really been taking care of you? When I watched him unlock the front door, I about jumped out of my skin. I just thought." He rubbed his face. "I just thought *not again*. I couldn't believe it."

"Give me some credit. I'm smart enough not to get involved like that again." She sipped her wine and considered how much she should tell him. "I like him, and he seems to really care, which scares the hell out of me."

She looked down into her glass and laughed nervously.

"Do you care about him?"

"I do, but I'm not interested in anything serious and he has a really great kid. I don't think Mark and I are looking for the same things."

"Why don't you get over it already?"

"What?"

"Why won't you give up this *I'm never going to have a family* crap and just enjoy being with someone that treats you the way you deserve to be treated? Every time you hook up with someone, you chicken out when things get serious."

"Puh, you should talk. When is the last time you spent two nights in a row with the same girl?"

"Dude—shut up, you are so rude." He went straight-faced, and then laughed. "No, but really, why not? Why not this guy?"

"I don't know. I've been closed off to the idea for so long. I'm not sure I can trust myself. It would be different if I felt this way and he was, oh ugly, or stupid, or...I don't know—anything but incredibly hot." She kept her head bowed, the admission a little embarrassing. "Do you know what I mean? I don't know if it's my heart leading me or my libido."

"I don't think your libido would lead you anywhere so soon after someone threw you into the bushes and tried to rape you."

Devon always made Sarah feel like she was under a microscope. He knew everything about her and could always peg her feelings before she even knew how she felt.

"Try being honest about your feelings and leave Kevin out of the equation."

She nodded and the corners of her mouth turned down instinctively.

"Sis, think about your life. You insist you're happy, but you seem...incomplete, and it's obvious to everyone but you. You're letting Kevin win. You're leaving him with the best of you, and that fucking sucks."

"Mark told me the same thing. He said I shouldn't let Kevin win," she said, reaching for the hand Devon held out for her.

"Wha...you told him about Kevin?"

"Yeah, just today before you broke into my house."

"No kidding?"

"I felt bad for not being honest with him about everything, and it seemed to make sense at the time since he's been looking out for me."

"Clearly you trust him even if you don't trust yourself, otherwise you wouldn't have told him anything. Huge step for you, Sis." He hugged her, squeezing her and picking her up off the ground.

"Dev...you're hurting me...can't breathe..."

"Oh, sorry." He put her down and kissed her cheek.

ꙮ

Mark pounded on Ali's door, breathing in and out, forcing himself to calm down. This had to come from somewhere else...it wasn't like Ali to act like this.

He looked up when the door swung open.

"If you came over here to fight with me, you're wasting your time."

The wind gushed from his sails. God, she looked like hell, dark circles under her eyes, pale skin, and just plain tired. He felt anxiety churn in his stomach. "What the hell is up with you, Al? You sick?"

She rolled her eyes. "No, I'm pregnant, not sick."

"Bullshit, I know you better than that. Where's Carl?"

"He's not here."

Mark reached up and laid his palm on her forehead. Ali tried to dodge him but wasn't fast enough.

"What is wrong with you?" she asked, trying to get away from him.

"You're not fine. You look like hell, and you're acting like a crazed, hormonal bitch."

Her face turned pink, embarrassment adding some color to her cheeks. She tucked a strand of hair behind her ear.

"I'm sorry I did that. I missed Jamie and when he came home...he hasn't stopped talking about how great Sarah is." Her eyes welled up. "I can't do anything with him. I can't play with him like I usually do. I'm so freaking pregnant and tired and I..." Her chin quivered and tears leaked out of her eyes. "I'm sorry."

"You're having a baby, that's way cooler than being a playmate." He glanced behind her, into the house. "There's something else, Al. Talk to me."

"No." She wiped her face quickly and shook her head. "No, it's fine. I am fine. Carl's been working a lot. I've been stuck here alone, and my mother is driving me crazy. I'm sorry."

"It's all right, Ali. But it's not okay to use Jamie like that when you're pissed about something. If you need anything, you can call me, okay?" He stepped back. "Call me if you need to talk."

Mark waited for her to close the door before climbing back into his truck. He was glad she didn't ask more questions about Sarah. He had purposely avoided explaining his relationship with Sarah to Ali. He could have insisted they were just friends, but if they took the next step in their relationship, he didn't want to make a liar out of himself.

He drove home to do some digging on Kevin Lewis. If Sarah was right and this guy was looking for her, why hadn't he found her yet? She wasn't hidden well.

When Mark did the internet search, he realized how common the name Kevin Lewis was. His next try included the words Flagstaff, Arizona. *Lewis and Sons Wilderness Adventures and Training Center* came up first.

Mark tried it. He had no information on Kevin except what Sarah told him, and that wasn't much. He read the home page.

The Lewis and Son's Wilderness Adventures and Training Center is a comprehensive training program to prepare men for wilderness survival skills. Our year-round outdoor educational programs are conducted right here in Flagstaff, with courses that cover wilderness survival and desert survival. If you're not interested in taking our courses, but you want to experience a wilderness adventure of your own, then simply request a private tour with one of our experienced guides.

Mark clicked the link to see the tour guide bios. There were pictures. The first was of Kevin Lewis. Mark read the caption under the picture.

Kevin Lewis, age 31, 6 feet 6 inches tall, 240 pounds.

Next to the picture was a short bio. Mark read the bio holding his breath the entire time.

Kevin Lewis has been interested in outdoor survival since he was a child. His father lived on the land in the Alaskan bush for a decade before rejoining society at the age of twenty-nine. Kevin grew up learning about his father's passion for the outdoors. His experience and education include big game hunting, winter mountaineering, wilderness first-aid, and primitive survival skills. He is also an amateur boxer having won many fights in the heavyweight division before retiring to become a tour guide at Lewis and Son's.

Mark exhaled when he finished reading. "Holy shit." *I hope this isn't the bastard who beat on Sarah. What a Neanderthal.*

Mark followed the page and underneath Kevin's picture and bio was another.

Jeff Lewis, age 30, 6 feet 2 inches tall, 195 pounds.

Mark didn't need to read more. Sarah had said Kevin had a brother named Jeff who was Sarah's age. Mark's stomach rolled as he looked at the picture again. Kevin was built like one of those wrestlers on TV with huge shoulders and arms. His dark hair hung in curtains down the sides of his weathered face. Mark looked into Kevin's dark eyes and shuddered at the thought of him touching Sarah's delicate body.

"I can't believe this huge motherfucker beat on her."

Mark had an overwhelming need to be with her. He went to his room and packed a bag, and then gathered her stuff to return it.

As he locked up the house and walked to the truck, he pulled out his cell phone and dialed her number.

When Sarah answered, he heard the smile in her voice. "Miss me already?"

"You're funny." He laughed. "Actually, I do miss you, but that's beside the point. How you feeling? I'm worried about you. Last night was hard, not to mention our conversation earlier."

"I'm great, Devon and I just polished off a bottle of wine. When are you coming back?"

He grimaced at her drinking on an empty stomach. "I thought I'd grab a pizza, are you hungry?"

"Starving. Pizza sounds good. I haven't eaten anything today."

"Okay, I'll bring dinner. You want me to stay at my house tonight since you have another guest?" He prayed she'd say no. He didn't want to go home alone.

"Nah, Devon can sleep in the office on an air mattress. We already set it up."

"Okay, good."

"What happened with Ali?"

"She's having a rough time and needed a target for her frustrations. You don't need to worry, though, we worked everything out." He shifted the phone in his ear and hoped she didn't catch the worry in his voice.

"Maybe she's right about me staying there?"

"She's not right, and I honestly don't care if she has a problem with it. Once I reminded her that she slept with her current husband in my house, in my bed, she didn't have a leg to stand on."

The line went silent for a few seconds, and he wondered if he'd said too much. "All right, I'm going to Ace Hardware to get you another lock for the back door and then get the pizza. I'll be there in an hour."

"'Kay, see you then."

Her voice was so soft, he barely heard her.

Chapter Twenty

Mark arrived as promised within the hour carrying an extra-large pizza. He delivered the pizza to the kitchen before he stepped back outside to get the bags from his truck. He stopped to grab her mail. The only thing in the box was an unmarked sealed envelope. Fuck—he thought this was over. It'd been over a week since the last note. He carefully pulled it out and slipped it in the inside pocket of his jacket. His heart raced as he entered the house with the bags.

After one look at Sarah's smiling face, he felt sick, knowing he was about to completely ruin her evening.

"Thanks so much for dinner." She lifted the pizza box lid and closed her eyes as she inhaled the aroma. "I'm starving." She reached into the cabinet for three plates.

Taking advantage of the distraction, Mark slipped from the room to call Brian. He could at least let her eat something before he told her.

"Hey, Brian, I got something."

"What now?"

"I found a new note in Sarah's mailbox—unmarked and sealed. Can you come get it?"

"No kidding, it's been over a week. I thought maybe this guy was gonna give it a rest. You didn't open it, did you?"

"Nope, it went from the mail box to my pocket."

"Why your pocket? You hidin' it from her?"

"No, I'll tell her when I hang up the phone."

"I'll see you within the hour."

Mark stepped back into the kitchen just as Sarah finished her piece of pizza. It looked like Devon was reaching in the box for a second piece.

"Grab a plate before Devon eats it all," Sarah said, gesturing toward the box.

"Ha!" Devon pointed to his own chest. "Me? What about you, little piglet."

Sarah laughed and met Mark's eyes. The smile dripped from her face instantly. "What's wrong?"

He tugged the envelope from his pocket and held it up. Sarah's face paled, and she gently set her plate down on the counter.

"Brian is on his way over to pick it up...sorry." He dropped his head in defeat. "Sorry to ruin all your fun."

"What the hell is that?" Devon asked, reaching for the envelope.

"Wait." Mark pulled away and walked over to the drawer to pull out a Ziplock bag. After securing the bag, he handed it to Devon. "It's evidence. I don't want more fingerprints on it." He glanced at Sarah.

She shook her head. "I'm fine." She waved a hand at the note. "Thought...hoped he was done with this."

"Did you explain everything to Devon?"

"Yeah, he knows."

Mark took a step toward her. "Are you okay?"

She grimaced and slid down off her barstool. "Yes, God...I'm...it's fine."

She walked over to the corner cabinet and opened it.

The Patrón bottle she pulled out surprise him—he was expecting another bottle of wine. She twisted off the cork cap and lined up shot glasses.

Mark tilted his head. "What are you doing?"

"Drinking—want some?"

"Huh—yeah...but I should wait until after I hand this over to Brian."

She grabbed a lime from the fruit basket. "I'll try to save you some."

ஜ۩ஜ

As Sarah and Devon were taking their first shot, the doorbell rang.

Mark, Sarah, and Devon all stepped into the living room. Mark tugged the door and held it open for Brian.

He stepped inside and nodded at everyone. "Hello." His eyes froze on Devon.

"This is Sarah's brother, Devon." Mark said.

Brian stuck his hand out and said, "So the big brother does exist. Hi, Devon, nice to meet you."

"Devon, this is Brian Hammel. He's heading the investigation against the rapist."

Devon gave a curt nod to Brian and shook his hand. "Good to meet you. Thanks for watching out for my sister."

Brian chuckled but it lacked humor. "I'm trying."

He stuffed the note into his pocket and shook his head when Mark offered him pizza.

"No, I have to get this to the lab. I'll call you when I have the results."

He nodded to Sarah. "How are you doing, Sarah? You look better." He wagged a finger at her face. "The bruises have faded."

She forced a smile. "I'm better, thanks."

Brian ducked back out the front door, and Sarah went right back to the tequila bottle. She wanted to be numb for a while. Just forget about everything and enjoy her brother's company.

The tequila shot went straight to her head and now she was spinning. *Another note...was this ever going to be over?* She was tired—tired of being afraid, tired of seeing the worry in Mark's eyes, and now in Devon's.

Devon came up behind her and rested his hands on her shoulders. "I thought this was a party." He kneaded her shoulders and shook her a little. "Take a break and let it go for tonight."

"That's a good idea," Mark said. "Will you pour me one of those shots?"

She mumbled, "I will let it go tonight." She poured tequila into a shot glass for Mark and handed it to him. "What else can I do?"

She ate a couple more slices of pizza, and they continued taking shots of tequila while she and Devon shared stories about their life and about their mother's various husbands.

As if on cue, and after only a few shots, her southern drawl slipped right back into place. She didn't realize it until Mark's eyebrows lifted in amusement, and Devon pointed at her with a stupid grin.

"What are y'all lookin' at?" she said, pushing Devon's finger away from her.

Devon nodded at Mark in triumph and then glanced back at Sarah. "We're just lookin' at you, darlin'," he said with a drawn out, fake accent.

Sarah slapped a hand over her mouth and mumbled, "Shut up."

"Oh yeah, that's sweet," Mark said. "I didn't know that was hiding in there."

"Yep, she sounds just like our mama."

"Hah! I do nawt," Sarah said, punching at Devon's chest. "Besides, her accent is fake. The more men she has around, the thicker her accent gets."

"Yeah, she does know how to play the game."

"Knows how to play." Sarah snorted out a laugh. "Shit, she made up the rules herself."

"What do you mean by 'play the game'?" Mark said.

"Work what she has," Devon said, "bat her eyelashes, give a little hip shake and smile real big. Let's just say, our mama is the queen of free stuff."

"Yeah, all she has to do is purr a little and people jump at the chance to serve her. I don't think I've ever seen her pay for a drink."

"Or a meal," Devon added.

Sarah laughed at Mark's lopsided expression. He couldn't understand the life of a con artist like her mother. How could he—his parents were normal compared to hers.

"She sang in a lot of clubs so she was in tight with the owners, and they would always let us tag along." The smile slipped from her face. "Okay...not always. We spent many nights stuck in the car."

Mark held up a hand to stop her. "Are you telling me that your mother would leave you in the car while she drank in clubs?"

"Worked in clubs," Sarah said. "She didn't have a babysitter, so she brought us to work with her. She just happened to have a job where she was allowed to drink too."

"But we had some great times back then," Devon said. "Remember Patty Rose used to always let us hang out in her kitchen while she cooked."

"Yeah well, that was also usually the only time we had a decent meal."

"Mama was not exactly Holly Homemaker." Devon snickered. "Eventually we were old enough to stay home alone. But we survived, didn't we, Sis?"

Sarah nodded and downed another shot, realizing that if she were sober, she'd never tell anyone that stuff about her mother. "Somehow we survived."

After draining the remaining drops from the bottle, Devon stumbled into the office to crash, leaving Mark and Sarah on bar stools in the kitchen still talking. Mark stood up and left the room. She heard him checking the locks on the doors and windows.

When he reentered the kitchen, she was watching him, appreciating the way he moved. Damn she wanted him, and tonight she wouldn't chicken out.

"Do you need help?" he asked, reaching a hand out for her as she teetered on the bottom rung of the barstool.

She hopped down and into his arms before he was ready to catch her. He lifted her up and she wrapped her legs around his waist, making them sway against the wall with locked lips. She knew he'd catch her. He would never let her fall.

ନ୦ଓ

Mark's blood heated from the kiss—*fuckin-A, she was sweet.* He wrapped his hands around her hips, holding her to him, wanting to lay her down right here on the kitchen table.

"Wait...wait, Sarah." He tried to act serious, but he couldn't stop the wide smile that had taken over his face. Sarah's lips moved to his neck, making goose bumps break out on his arms.

She giggled. "Right, wait...wait for what?"

"We should move to the bedroom so your brother doesn't walk in on us." He forced a straight face and looked into her eyes. Her expression became solemn, and her eyes darkened with desire.

"Okay," she breathed. "Let's go into the bedroom."

"Are you going to be okay with this?"

She stared unblinking at him and lifted her finger to trace his lips. "This won't be a problem."

Mark gripped her firmly and stumbled into the bedroom, gently laying her down. He tried to go slow, but Sarah impatiently pawed at his clothes. He pulled his shirt off, and then tugged at her shirt buttons until they were unfastened. They rolled, and Mark shifted her on top of him. He unbuttoned her jeans, sliding his hands under the waistband while she kissed, nipped, and bit his lips.

"Sarah, oh God...you're killing me."

When his hands traveled over her hips to slide her jeans down, she stiffened and inhaled sharply. Mark glanced up to find her eyes closed. She was holding her breath and all the color had gone from her face.

His heat instantly cooled at the look on her face. He'd done something wrong again, but what? He pulled his hands away and shifted again to lay her down.

"No, keep going," she said, squeezing her eyes shut.

"I can't keep going, you're uncomfortable." He cupped her face and kissed each of her closed eyelids in turn.

"I don't want you to stop."

"I will absolutely not keep going. You're not ready for this." As if he would keep going after scaring the shit out of her. "I can wait."

She shook her head. "I *will* be okay."

"Stop it. I want to make love to you when we can both enjoy it. I shouldn't have pushed you."

Sarah covered her face with her hands. "God, I am so sorry I keep doing this to you."

Mark sighed and brushed his lips against her forehead. "Maybe I need a different approach."

She gave him a sad smile. "I like your approach just the way it is."

"Are you okay?" His buzz had melted and from the sound of Sarah's voice, so had hers. "Do you know what triggered it?"

She shook her head. "I don't know...I was really enjoying it..."

He stared at her for a moment and thought about everything she'd told him the day before. Any woman who'd been raped was bound to have some issues. He needed to know what he could do to help her overcome those issues.

"Maybe it wasn't a physical trigger."

"What do you mean?"

"Maybe it's psychological?" He twisted a few strands of her hair between his fingers. "What were you thinking about?"

Her cheeks turned bright pink. "What do you think I was thinking about?"

"Maybe it's a trust issue, subconsciously. Maybe in your heart of hearts you're not comfortable being intimate with me."

Mark had to figure out a way to help her come to grips with this or they would both go crazy. He moved up and sat cross-legged on the bed so he could give her some space.

"Let's just talk this out."

"Okay," she said, reaching for her discarded shirt.

"Are you comfortable talking about this?"

She nodded. "Yeah."

"Are you having trouble being intimate with me because you're unwilling to give up some of yourself to me?" He hesitated, trying to find a way to explain what he meant. "Maybe you're not comfortable enough with me to..."

"I want to do this. I don't feel pressured, if that's what your—"

"No." He reached for her hand, wanting to touch her. For the first time since he'd known her, he couldn't read her feelings by her expression. "Do you remember our conversation about those women who were raped? You told me that having a man force himself on you was a powerless feeling and that loss of control was something a woman never got over."

"And that's true, I'm surprised you remember all that."

"I couldn't forget it. Being that vulnerable has to be utterly frightening. I can't imagine it." He closed his eyes to push back the instant anger he felt at the thought of someone doing that to her, especially that Neanderthal, Kevin Lewis. The tequila in his stomach burned like fire.

"But, Mark, I don't feel like that with you at all."

He pulled her hand to his mouth and kissed it. "Good, I'm glad." He smiled and said, "I think between your past and this attack, the notes, the phone calls, this monster trying to get to you, breaking into your house—you've had me in your face, hovering and..." He took a deep, steadying breath. "Because of all that, you have lost some of the control you have on your life. Maybe this is your subconscious way of taking that control back."

He watched her face as she thought about everything he said. She didn't speak. She just looked into his eyes for a long time. Every emotion seemed to flash across her face in that lifetime of a moment.

"What are you thinking?" he whispered.

She shrugged and looked away.

"Did I get that completely wrong? Talk to me please..."

She shook her head and fisted her hand. "I don't know, but if you're right, I don't know how to fix it."

"I don't know either, but I'll help you. Maybe it just takes time." He waited for a moment. "Tell me what you're afraid of. What's got you worried?"

"Do you believe that I trust you?" she asked.

"I do, Sarah, but do you believe me?"

Her eyebrows drew together. "I'm sorry. I just feel like this is going to get old to you. How many times can we come so close just for me to chicken out? It's frustrating for me...I can't imagine what it's like for you."

"Do you think I'm only here for sex?"

"Of course not...," she said, droopy-eyed.

"Okay, then stop worrying about me leaving."

She nodded and whispered, "Okay."

Mark watched her for a few minutes, and then reached out and pulled her to him. "Let's go to sleep, we can talk about this again when we're both sober."

Chapter Twenty-One

When Mark woke up, his thoughts went directly to the note he found in Sarah's mailbox. With a full mug of coffee in his hand, he pulled out his cell phone and dialed Brian's number.

"Hey, Brian, anything yet?"

"No, man. It's been less than twelve hours. I told you I'd let you know."

"Okay, you're right."

"No wonder she's so tense, you're feeding it to her like candy. Take a break and let us do our job."

"Yep, okay. I get it." Mark shut his eyes and tried to relax. "You're right. Call me when you get something."

Mark closed his phone, and at the same time, Devon entered the kitchen, shirtless and looking for coffee.

"Morning. Right on—there's coffee already, thanks, dude."

"How's the air mattress?" Mark asked.

Devon looked at him with a raised eyebrow. "It's better than some other places I've slept." He sat down at the kitchen table across from Mark with his cup of coffee. "I'm actually glad I got up before her, I need to tell you something."

"What?"

"She told me she clued you in on Kevin Lewis. I didn't want to tell her, but he's been looking for her again."

"Again?" Mark sat up and gave Devon his complete attention. "You mean this isn't the first time?"

"Not even close to the first time. He calls me, leaves messages—fucking acting like nothing ever happened, like we're old buddies or something," Devon said, disgusted.

Mark considered him for a moment. "When was the last time you actually talked to him?"

"A couple of years ago, he showed up in San Diego. I told him Sarah and I had a falling out and hadn't been in touch in years, but that the last I'd heard she was somewhere in Tennessee. I tried to throw him off the California trail."

"Why Tennessee?"

"We lived in Nashville before moving to Flagstaff. He'd heard enough about Charlie to believe it."

"Charlie? Wait, the step-dad who gave her the Colt 45?"

"Oh yeah." Devon grinned. "You've seen the Colt?"

"Yeah, it's a nice piece. But I don't get it, if Kevin is really looking for Sarah, why hasn't he found her? All it would take is an internet search?"

"Hah, yeah." Devon nodded. "But this asshole is completely computer illiterate. He's a little bit of a conspiracy theorist. Thinks the government has too much control, he won't touch a computer." Devon chuckled. "Besides, she's lost in the sea of a common name. Try searching. You'll get like a hundred thousand results for Sarah Jennings, and she's super careful about how she uses her name on the internet. She doesn't use the social networking sites or anything like that." He brushed a dismissive hand at Mark. "Anyway, that dickhead is still looking for Sarah Lange, which is almost as common," Devon said.

"I did a little digging yesterday. Is he the same Kevin Lewis from Lewis and Son's Wilderness Adventure Center in Flagstaff?"

"One in the same, and they are no joke," Devon said, looking at Mark severely.

"I can't believe that guy was beating on her. He's a freaking monster—twice her size."

"I'm glad you know what you're dealing with just in case he comes knockin'. Speaking of...what's keeping you here? She doesn't need any more heartache in her life."

"You don't need to doubt my intentions, I won't hurt her," Mark said, looking Devon directly in the eyes when he said it.

"The woman can be a pain in the ass. You should know that going in."

Mark smiled in spite of himself. "Yeah, I've figured that out."

ꕥ

When Sarah came out of her bedroom showered and dressed, she glanced down at Devon's overnight bag already sitting near the front door. "You don't waste any time do you?" she muttered under her breath.

"I'll come back in a couple of months and stay longer." He looked down at his phone in irritation. "I have Lily blowing up my cell, wanting me there yesterday."

"Tell her to wait her turn," she said, and his cell phone rang again.

"You can tell her yourself." He laughed silently, teasing her as he held the open phone out to her.

She jumped back, wide-eyed, and shook her head violently. "No," she mouthed. "Don't you dare!"

Devon's eyes glinted and he put the phone to his ear. "Mama? Hey...I know. I'm leaving this very second—all right!" He dropped his head and said, "See you tonight."

After closing his phone, he glared up at Sarah. "You're such a brat! If you'd call her once in a while..."

He grabbed his bag and towed it outside, still wearing a teasing smile.

"I will call her, but not today," she said, stepping up to his car.

"So Lily...your mom?" Mark asked.

"Yeah, the one and only. Check it, dude. Call me if anything else happens. I can be here in a few hours." He rattled off his cell phone number, and Mark entered it into his phone.

"What's up with the SUV? What happened to the Carrera?" Sarah asked, examining the brand new SUV in her driveway.

"It's at home in the garage. I needed a car that could hold my surfboards and my skis."

"So you had to buy a brand new *Porsche* SUV? What's wrong with Chevy or Ford?"

"That's no fun, besides this is faster."

Sarah tried to maintain a smile when she said goodbye to Devon. She wasn't that good of an actress. She couldn't push herself out of the dark mood. One night with him wasn't enough. God, she missed him.

Devon hugged her. "Don't cry, Baby Sis. I'll be back in two months, okay?"

"Stay out of trouble."

"Ha! You stay out of trouble. Don't ever keep me in the dark about something like this again."

After she nodded a promise to him, he reached a hand out to Mark. "I mean it, call me for anything. I want to stay updated on what's happening here."

"I'll call," Mark promised.

Devon gave Sarah one more quick hug before he climbed into his SUV. When his car turned off her street, she put both hands over her face, fighting tears. It was stupid to be this emotional. She couldn't help herself. Watching him leave was like leaving home. He'd been her anchor and her rock for so long, and she mourned his absence now more than ever. She'd never admit aloud that she needed him there, but she couldn't deny it to herself.

When Mark came up behind her, she turned and rested her face against his chest.

"I'm sorry he had to leave."

"Me too," she said.

"Are you okay?"

She looked up into his eyes, and the fire sparking between them caught her off guard. When Mark tucked a stray hair behind her ear, she lifted up and kissed him. Her stomach fluttered as his hand cupped her neck, pulling her closer. When the kiss turned more passionate, she pulled back and looked into his eyes again.

He was so beautiful. Sarah wanted him and hated herself for ignoring her feelings and for fighting the attraction that pulled her toward him.

Devon had no idea how much his talk had helped her. Her big brother had saved her again, only this time instead of rescuing her from her bad choices, he kept her from making another one. And pushing Mark away would've been a huge mistake. She withdrew slowly and looked down into his chest, not sure what to say.

"Sorry," he whispered.

"Don't be, I like kissing you," she said. "But we need to talk about this before it goes any further." When she looked back up, she met his tender expression. "Now that we're sober."

"Let's go talk," he said, moving down her arm to her take her hand.

Sarah followed him into the house and sat sideways on her sofa, facing him. "I'm not sure...I don't know." She stopped for a moment, searching for the right words.

"It's okay, I understand." He pulled his hand away. "I'm here to keep you safe, not to—"

"Wait," she said, and her face heated. "Stop talking—let me finish." She pulled his hand back and held it with both of hers. "I haven't had a normal emotion in weeks. I've been on a roller coaster, and I'm not sure if what I'm feeling is a result of the ride or if it's real—but it seems real." She looked at him cautiously. "Do you understand?"

"I understand, it's been a hard couple of weeks for you and it's natural to be confused." He still didn't make eye contact with her.

"The last few weeks haven't been hard. The circumstances that threw us together suck, but I enjoy being with you, and I don't want to be away from you, that's something I'm sure of."

Mark's posture finally relaxed, and he reached over and pulled her into a gentle kiss. "I don't like being away from you, either," he said through their kiss. "I don't want you out of my sight, but not only because I want to keep you safe. Yesterday, when I was gone..."

"What?" she asked, holding her breath, waiting for him to finish his sentence.

"I'm afraid when I tell you...I don't want you to compare me to him."

"I swear to God," she grunted through gritted teeth. "Eight freaking years later and he is still interfering in my life." She put both hands over her face to rub away the anger she felt toward Kevin. "I'm sorry. Geez, I come with a lot of baggage. I don't blame you. I told you to run when you had the chance."

"Now you stop," he whispered. "My point is, my feelings for you are healthy, not controlling like his. I just want you to know that first, before anything else."

"I'm telling you now, I trust you, even if I overreact sometimes." She looked at him earnestly, wanting him to understand.

"Okay, I want you to know that I love being with you too. If I have to wait until this bad stuff goes away, I'm willing to wait. Last night I realized how much I was pushing and I don't want to pressure you."

"Ah...I'm not sure what happened last night. I'm sorry." Her face felt hot again. "I don't want to wait. I want to start over...I'm just not sure how."

He tilted his head. "Well, let's see," he said. "Yeah, we certainly aren't traditional considering we've pretty much been living together for the last couple of weeks."

"Exactly—now you understand," she said, relieved. "Maybe we shouldn't do that any longer."

"No. Not a good idea. Let's not forget you received a new note from this guy just yesterday."

"Yeah, you're right. What else then?"

"How about...we date?"

"Like, go out on a date together...like *a date*?"

He snickered at her reaction. "You have been on a date before, haven't you?"

"Duh, yeah, but how will that work when we go home together after the date."

"We're adults, we can handle this. It's not like we sleep in the same room."

"Well, not *every night*," she said, blushing at the memory of falling asleep in his arms last night. When her phone rang, she stuck up one finger. "Hold that thought."

She bounced off the sofa and reached over for the phone. "Hello?"

"*Sar-rrahh*...what? Are you mad at me or something?"

"No." She grinned at the sound of his voice. "What are you doing?"

"You don't call, you don't visit, and you stopped writing." Gabby laughed into the phone.

"I know, I'm sorry, what's going on, Gabs?"

"I'm throwing myself a twenty-nine-and-a-half year birthday party and you must come. It's Wednesday, at The Suite. Whadda ya say?"

"You are too much." She chuckled. "Any reason to throw a party, right?"

"I know—right?" he said, laughing with her. "I miss you...come out and play with me."

"Well, I have a lot going on."

She looked at Mark and smiled. "Gabs, do you mind if I bring a date?"

"Oh, I get it now, you've been held up with some hunk of a man. Bring him along—wait! Is he hot? Gurl...if he's hot, don't come without him," Gabby teased.

"What time?"

"Seven o'clock, The Suite, you'll break my heart if I don't see you."

"I'll see you then." She smiled and went back to the sofa, resting on her knees, next to Mark.

"What was that about?"

"That was Gabby and we are going to his half-year birthday party Wednesday night at The Suite."

"A party at a club, Sarah, that's not a good idea."

"Why not? It's not like I'm going alone."

"It's too volatile of a situation. I can't control what happens in a club with a bunch of drunk people around."

"So you believe this guy is going to follow us into a club and try to attack me again." She couldn't help the sarcastic tone in her voice. He was being ridiculous and way over protective.

"It's possible, Sarah. He's not going to give up, and the longer it takes him to get to you, the more desperate he'll get."

"I'm going. Sorry, I'm tired of being cooped up. I need some normal in my life right now."

"It's a bad idea. I'm telling you—it's not safe."

"I don't care. I would rather face him again than live my life trapped in this house." When she said it, she felt a flutter of nerves in her stomach.

Mark stared at her without expression.

Regardless of what he wanted, she wouldn't give in. "If you're some master protector, then you better come with me," she batted her lashes and leaned toward him, a little hip shake and a real big smile. "Come on, it can be our first date."

Mark reached up, wrapped his hand behind her neck, and pulled her into a hard kiss, sliding his other hand around her lower back as he moved up on his knees too.

Sarah couldn't think about anything other than him, his lips, and his body. Her head started spinning when he pressed against her. Mark moved his hand to her face and pushed her away very slowly.

"You have to stop doing that," he said, and they both took a deep breath.

"Apparently Mama was right about the eyelashes and the hip shake."

"You just can't be all sexy like that and not expect me to kiss you." He ran his hand through his hair as he sat back. "This is going to be interesting."

"So, we're going, right?"

"Ah, yeah, sure, if it's that important to you," he said, defeated.

She pulled him back toward her.

ꙮ

Mark leaned into her and into the kiss. Sarah's hands found his face and then traveled up through his hair.

"Sarah," he breathed.

She stopped kissing him and looked into his eyes.

"I don't think..." He gazed at her and knew it was the first time he'd really seen Sarah, the woman. Her penetrating stare filled him with pure desire, and he watched a rush of blood color her face. "You know...we haven't even had our first date yet."

She smiled at him. "I don't care."

"I have an idea if you're willing to try."

"I'm willing to try anything."

Mark kissed her again before leading her to the bedroom and closing the door behind him.

Sarah turned into him and covered his mouth hard with hers.

"Baby," he said, pulling out of the kiss. "Please slow down before we screw this up again."

"Okay,"

"Sarah."

She stopped and looked into his eyes.

"May I take off your shirt?"

By the glow of the sun behind the curtains, he saw a smile spread on her face and a slight nod.

Mark's eyes followed his fumbling fingers as they traveled down her shirt buttons one at a time. He had to fight for patience, giving her time to be comfortable with his touch.

After getting her buttons out of the way, he opened her shirt to lace and skin. He lifted his eyes to her lips before leaning in to kiss her gently, taking his time to taste her.

It was imperative he let her maintain control over her body and her actions. This was the only way he could think of to get past this paralyzing fear she had, and if that meant asking for permission before laying a hand on her, he could do that, and he would enjoy every touch she allowed him to have.

Mark lowered the sleeves of her shirt, letting it fall to the floor.

"Sarah, may I take off your bra?" The words came out in a quiet whisper, making her smile and nod again.

Mark breathed a sigh of relief. *Thank God*. He didn't think he could take another rejection like last night.

He unhooked her bra and slid the straps down her shoulders one side at time, exposing her perfect naked breasts. He took her face in his hands to kiss her again. He could feel her anticipation building as his lips trailed down to her chin and along her jawline to her ear. He carefully walked her backwards to the bed and laid her down.

"Sarah, may I touch your breast?" he asked, caressing her ear lobe with his lips.

Mark felt her mouth curve into a smile and she whispered, "Yes."

He cupped her breasts with careful hands. While his hands moved over her, his mouth moved back to hers, tracing her lips with his tongue, forcing a husky moan from her throat.

Mark's kisses traveled down her shoulders and followed the trail of freckles across her collarbone. Heat radiated off her skin like fire, and her breath quickened with each kiss. He worked his way down her shoulders, nibbling her sweet skin.

Sarah ran her hands through his hair and over his shoulders while she arched against him impatiently.

Slowly. He kept repeating this word to himself. He couldn't afford to lose his focus. At this point, she needed to get through this more than he did.

"Slowly, baby," he whispered, before he lowered his mouth to her breast. When his mouth surrounded her tight nipple, she gasped and dug her fingers into his back. Mark focused his attention on a steady pace. He had to take his time with her, let her build. Slowly.

"Mark—please." Sarah's urgent need was evident in her voice. He grazed her nipple with his teeth, teasing her as her breathing turned frantic and her body quivered under his. He went down her silky smooth stomach with gentle kisses and moved back up her body one kiss at a time until he reached her face. When he kissed her chin, she moved her mouth to his, lifting into the kiss with uncontrolled yearning.

"I can't—" Her hands fisted in his hair as she quivered under him.

"Sarah," he whispered to her lips. "I've got you, baby. I've got you, trust me."

"Please..."

"Sarah, may I take off your pants...*please*?"

She started nipping his lip with her teeth as he moved his hand from her breast to her lower back, pulling her closer.

He was losing it—slowly but surely he was losing his focus. Her lips felt like fire against his mouth, and if she kept doing what she was doing, he was going to explode.

"Yes—now—"

Thank you, he thought and with her permission, his hand traveled down and circled her waist, purposely moving slowly. He felt her inhale sharply, and he stopped to look at her.

"Sarah," he whispered again.

"Yes, Mark—you're making me crazy."

Crazy he could relate to.

Mark pulled at her jeans and felt the button and zipper give. She lifted her body so they could slide off easily, and he pulled one leg off at a time. He ran his hand up her leg as he went back to her lips to kiss her again.

She pulled at his clothes, sliding her hands under his shirt.

It took every ounce of strength he had to maintain an easy pace. If he had to stop now, it would destroy him completely. He pushed her harder by rubbing and grinding against her, testing the waters to see if she was ready for him.

Sarah wrapped her legs around his waist, arching up, nearly climbing him as she struggled to get closer.

He gripped her waist to lift her off the bed and into his lap as he sat back on his knees.

Sarah clung to him with her arms and legs as he sucked and kissed her breast, his hands holding her against him. She pressed her body against his, and he could feel her impatience as she leaned in and pulled away the neck of his shirt. She tasted him, nipping the skin along his neck and shoulder.

When he laid her back down, she jerked the hem of his shirt and pulled it over his head before he could stop her. She went for his collarbone, nibbling with heavy breaths, her face tucked into his chest. The skin-on-skin contact felt incredible.

Sarah's hands greedily gripped his waist...then went around him and under the waistband of his loose fitting jeans. His heart pounded madly as her hands traveled his bare skin.

"Sarah, may I take off your panties?"

She opened her eyes, giving him a look of pure passion. Her eyes were almost blue and so bright, the expression so trusting, he couldn't help but smile. He kissed her before he pulled back to memorize her face, sure he would remember this moment for the rest of his life.

Mark looked at her naked body with wonder, every inch of her more stunning than the last. His gaze traveled over everything, her flat, firm stomach, full breasts, and milky skin, pale as moonlight. His hand slid up her leg and followed the curve of her hip, the faint light glowing from the sun behind the curtains illuminating the room just enough for him to see her fully.

When she grabbed his hand to pull him back to her, Mark brought her hand to his lips and kissed it as he stared into her eyes. His heart raced. It was all he could do to keep from taking her that moment. *Slowly*, he chanted to himself again.

"Sarah?"

Before he could say another word, she moved to her knees and took his face in her hands, passionately kissing him. His blood boiled as her hands slid to his chest, slowly touching every inch. She pulled out of the kiss to explore with her eyes as well. Mark watched her, taking in her inquisitive features and flushed expression.

She let her fingers linger and tease, the tingle driving him mad while he watched her graceful, naked body come toward him completely unabashed. He reached down to unbutton his jeans as both pairs of hands simultaneously pushed them past his waist. Her hands traveled down his waist and hips, sending a surge of pleasure to his core. He fought to go slow. Her touch made it almost impossible to maintain control.

He gripped her hips and pulled her closer as he kissed her. When he felt a rush of air escape her lips, he opened his eyes, prepared to see that stark fear again, but he was greeted with desire. He lowered her back down on the bed and removed what was left of his own clothes.

"Easy, baby," he whispered, sliding his hand down toward her inner thigh as she arched closer him. "Sarah...may I touch you?"

She didn't speak, but the moan that escaped her lips was affirmation enough.

Mark lowered his hand and parted her, forcing her to cry out in pleasure. He smiled, watching her beautiful body wave and curve gracefully as he drove her to climax. Mark continued to move his fingers inside her until she finished, her nails digging into his flesh as she trembled beneath him.

"Mark," she cried, pulling him closer so her mouth could meet his. When her body tremors calmed, he slowly pulled his mouth away.

"Sarah, baby, may I—"

"Yes," she murmured, and groped for him too late, he was already lowering himself, pushing into her as he cried out in relief. When her wetness surrounded him, he felt a rush of panic, then relief, then pleasure with every surge forward. Her hands clamped on his hips as he moved, her body moving in sequence with his as he pushed her to peak again. He felt her tighten when she cried out, her eyelids fluttering, a satisfied smile spread across her face with each crest of pleasure.

Sarah clung to him, her nails cutting his skin, but the pain was pure pleasure because she was giving into him, letting go and trusting him more with every surge of pleasure.

"Baby," Mark cried out this time. "Sarah..." A feeling of completeness rushed through him at the same time as passion flooded her face and his name escaped her lips in a whisper.

Before he could take another breath, Mark flexed and released with one long, fluid motion. She joined him in his culmination, their bodies matching time perfectly. Sarah cried out with his last surge, and his body started to tremble. He collapsed on top of her. When he tried to move to her side, she held him in place.

"Wait," she breathed. "Just...wait." They were both breathing heavily, their hearts matching time, and he tried to look into her eyes but they were closed tight.

He carefully wrapped his arms around her and held her until her breathing slowed. "Are you okay?"

She nodded as a big smile spread across her face. She gave a deep, throaty chuckle before letting him go. Mark leaned in and kissed her forehead, before spooning her hips with his. With his arms around her, they lay quietly until their pounding hearts slowed.

Mark held her close. He was completely enchanted and could've held her until the end of the world if she would only let him. When he heard a quiet sniffle, he looked down into her eyes.

"Baby, did I hurt you?" Mark sat up on his elbow and cupped her face to look into her eyes.

She wasn't sad—her eyes were bright and wet, but she was smiling.

She reached up and traced his lips with the tip of her finger. "Of course, you didn't hurt me."

Mark took her hand and kissed it. "How *do* you feel?"

"Relaxed..."

"You..."—he carefully poked her nose with the tip of his finger—"are absolutely stunning, do you know that?"

"You are patient and caring and...*smart*," she said, not hiding her surprise. "What made you think of that?"

"I don't know. I was trying to give you control. I wanted you to feel comfortable with my touch."

"It worked, thank God," she said as she lifted her head to kiss him.

Chapter Twenty-Two

On Wednesday, Sarah talked Mark into giving her a couple of hours alone at home. She wanted to get ready for their date without him around, hoping to maintain some of the element of surprise that came with first dates. Mark was pretty easy to convince, which surprised her. He'd usually baulk at her being left unprotected, but then she realized he must have put one of his agents outside her house while he was gone. The thought irritated her but it wasn't worth fighting about. She was too excited about their date to care.

She checked Mark out thoroughly when he returned, from his brown boots to his stylishly messy hair. He wore a perfectly fitting khaki, knit, long-sleeve crew shirt, enhancing his well-formed, broad chest. With it, he had on a pair of even more perfectly fitting blue jeans. Sarah appreciated the well-fitting jeans and had to force herself to stop staring at him.

"What are you looking at," he said self-consciously as they climbed out of her Mustang.

"I'm looking at you, you look good."

"You are stunning. I should have chosen something other than jeans."

"Thank you, but"—she winked at him—"the jeans are perfect."

Sarah had decided on a slimming, V-neck, navy blue tank dress with gathered stitching to enhance her breasts. The tapered waist hugged her hips and then flared out at her knees.

They entered the club hand-in-hand, and when Mark expressed his surprised, she had to wonder what he was expecting.

The place was huge. With two stages and at least three bars, it looked like a small city. On one of the stages, a DJ played pop-ish, top-forty dance music, but nothing obnoxious. Around the dance floor, low-backed, round booths were lined up in a circular fashion to create smaller seating areas to accommodate groups of people instead of all being back-to-back.

They were inside for a couple of minutes when Gabby rushed her and sent her into a deep dip.

"Dahl-ling, where have you been all my life...," Gabby said as Sarah hung in his arms with her head inches from the floor. When he lifted her up, she gave him a big hug.

Sarah introduced Mark to Gabby and her friends. Gabby, Paul, Ryan, and Josh were all body builders from Sarah's gym. Gabby was the biggest of the quartette. He kept his long, blond hair in a ponytail at the base of his neck, and he looked immaculate in his black slacks and a pinstripe blue and black button-up shirt. While big, Gabby was harmless. He wore a big, goofy smile and constantly winked at people when he talked. It was obvious that Mark fought to suppress a smile when Sarah introduced them. She loved this group of guys, and she hoped Mark liked them too.

"So, gurl, where did you meet the hunk?" Gabby asked, smiling and looking Mark up and down.

The question surprised Sarah. "Ah, we met..."

"I installed the alarm system on her house," Mark answered for her.

"Gabby, where is everyone else, I thought this was a party?"

"Daniel and Scott are fighting again, so they're not coming, and I guess since it's Wednesday nobody else wanted to par-tay. Let's dance," he said, and held out a hand to Sarah.

"No, I need a drink first." She waved away his hand.

"Okay, girl, you owe me one." He grabbed Paul's hand and spun him gracefully onto the nearest dance floor.

Sarah was all smiles as she led Mark to the bar to buy him a drink.

"Hi, Robbie." She smiled at the bartender and handed him a gold card. "Can we have two draft beers?"

"Hey, sweetie, where have you been?"

"Oh, you know, school's back in session so I'm working and staying close to home." He placed the drinks down in front of her and then moved to help someone else.

"So...tell me again why you hang out with a bunch of gay men," Mark asked.

"I don't only hang out with gay men. We have other friends that are straight, but they didn't show up. We mostly know each other from the gym. Be happy Gabby didn't have his party at The Rainbow Mic."

"The Rainbow Mic, what the hell is that?"

"It's a gay karaoke bar." She laughed at his expression. "It's actually a lot of fun watching that group of guys get up on stage and sing Diana Ross songs."

"Gee, sorry I missed that," Mark said. He leaned close, inhaled, brushed his lips on her cheek, and whispered, "So let's go find a quiet corner to hang out in."

"I know the perfect place," she said, and picked up her drink.

She turned toward a glassed-in VIP lounge separate from the rest of the club. When the large, glass doors were closed behind them, she could easily see everything happening in the rest of the club, but the noise level dropped dramatically. They could also still here the music on the other side of the glass, though it was comfortably muted. The large, round room was quiet enough to have a conversation but still enjoy the music. It had a brick fireplace in the center of the room and a full bar along the far wall.

When they entered the lounge, Sarah pointed to a booth nearest the fireplace. They sat close and never released each other's hands. Sarah felt incredibly good with him. She remembered thinking of him as her talisman a couple weeks before. Touching him now felt much the same. It was Zen-like, very calming.

"So what do you think? Is this better than a crowded dance floor?"

"This is perfect." His breath brushed her ear, and he kissed her neck right below her lobe.

Sarah looked over his shoulder and out at the club where Gabby, Paul, and Josh were standing behind the glass, pointing and pretending to laugh. She felt her face grow hot as they entered the lounge and approached the booth.

"Okay, enough with the PDA. I thought this was my party," Gabby said when Sarah hid her face in Mark's shoulder.

They took the table directly across from her booth.

She laughed and felt like a little kid and had to tell them to shut up. She didn't want to make Mark uncomfortable with their teasing, but he ignored them, his attention focused solely on Sarah. When she looked into his eyes, the penetrating gaze he held made her nervous. Their eyes stayed locked on each other's until the cocktail waitress interrupted them.

"Can I get you two another drink?"

"I'll have another beer, my card's up with Robbie."

"Gotcha covered—and you?" she asked Mark.

"Nothing, thanks," he said without taking his eyes off Sarah.

When Gabby ordered a round of Patrón tequila shots from the other table, Sarah gave him an exasperated look.

He waved a hand at her. "Oh, stop it, you can handle one shot."

A few minutes later their drinks arrived. Sarah's beer and two shots sat in front of her and Mark. She took her shot with the other boys, but Mark still declined.

"Go ahead," he said, gesturing toward the second shot of tequila. Sarah gave him a sideways smile.

"Oh, sure get me drunk, you know what happens when I drink tequila."

Mark shrugged and flashed a sexy smile.

"Too bad for you—I'm not a first date kind of girl."

Mark's face broke out into a big grin as she shot the tequila. She set the glass down and sucked on a lime wedge, her eyes still locked with his.

"Would you like another?"

"Ha-ha, very funny." She stood. "Excuse me, I'll be right back."

He got to his feet. "Where are you going?"

"Ladies' room."

He reached out and grabbed her hand. "Wait, I'll go with you."

"To the ladies' room?" She pushed his hand away. "I think I can do it on my own. I haven't had that much to drink."

"Sarah, I don't think that's a good idea. I'll come with you and wait outside the door."

She pointed through the glass toward the other side of the club. "I'm just going over there, see the restroom sign, you can see it from here. It's okay."

"No, it's not okay."

Sarah frowned and leaned close to his ear. "Please don't do this in front of my friends." She met his eyes and said, "You can see me from here, you don't need to hover."

"If you're not back in five minutes, I'm coming to look for you," he warned, his expression dead serious.

"Okay, I'll see you in less than five minutes." She turned away from him and stepped out of the V.I.P. area, through the large, glass doors and toward the ladies' room.

She walked into the small waiting area that separated the club from the bathrooms. It was oddly deserted. She didn't see anyone until she pulled the ladies' room door open and was surprised by two women coming out. She moved aside for them to pass and then turned to enter. Before she could step inside, someone grabbed her from behind, twisting her left arm behind her back.

Sarah cried out, pulling away. Her stomach coiled from the smell of whiskey and cigarettes. She tried not to panic, but she couldn't breathe. The air caught in her throat and kept her from screaming. She reached up and grabbed for his face. She missed and ended up with a handful of hair at the base of his skull, where she dug into his neck with her fingernails.

He yanked her arm again, and she felt the sickening snap in her shoulder. She gasped and cried out, trying to turn out of the twist, but her arm went limp.

He released it and reached across her, restraining both her arms and body tightly against his chest with one arm. He was twice her size, and his arm reached all the way around to her right side, holding her easily. She squirmed to wiggle free as he pushed her toward the ladies' room. She lifted her leg, braced herself in the door jam, and pushed away. He started to lose his balance, but righted himself and squeezed her tighter.

"Didn't you get my note? You still owe me one, *Sweet Sarah,*" he said, panting his disgusting breath at her.

A thrill of terror raced up her spine at the sound of his voice.

"Please stop, don't touch me." She stomped hard with her heels on his feet. It didn't slow his progress. His cold hand up the back of her dress spiked her pulse in panic. At the same time, he started licking the side of her neck and shoulder. The hot wetness of his mouth forced a scream to come bubbling out of her throat. She squirmed away, shivering at the sensation. Sick with fear and anger.

"Get off me. Get off me. Don't touch me!" she shrieked as he clawed at her panties. Sarah pushed and twisted to free herself from his grip. Again, she managed to brace herself in the doorjamb, if he got her into the bathroom, she was dead. When they swung around, she let her knees weaken and tried to drop to the floor, but he pulled her tighter, lifting her off her feet this time.

Sarah threw her head back, hoping to make contact with his face. He slammed her face first into the wall.

"Bitch, if you fucking break my nose again, I'll kill you."

Sarah saw stars for a few seconds, and her face throbbed from the impact.

She felt him reach for his pants as he held her flush against the wall. His erection pressed into her thigh, and his hand came back up her dress. Sarah screamed again, desperately praying for someone to come. His grip was so tight around her torso she could hardly breathe.

When he ripped off her panties, blood pumped through her body, pounding in her head where her face hit the wall. She cried out again for help, but the sound seemed to echo in her head, and she wasn't sure if anyone could hear her. She tried to keep fighting, but she didn't have the strength. He was too strong.

Pins and needles broke out over her entire body when his hand reached between her legs, before she could react, she was pulled backward and knocked off her feet. Midway through her fall, someone scooped her up into a tight embrace.

Sarah looked up to see Gabby. He dragged her up by the waist and pulled her away from the fight happening behind her. Mark had the attacker by the throat against the wall, until the barrel of a gun was waved in front of his face.

"No—Mark—no!" She reached for Mark but gripped thin air. Gabby wouldn't loosen his hold around her waist. She was shaking and pushing at her restraints as she watched Mark back away with his eyes locked on the gun.

"No-no-no, Mark!" When she cried out, the attacker looked at her, and Gabby swung her around behind him and out of his sights.

The sound of a shot echoed around the room and her heart stopped. When she twisted out of Gabby's arms to find Mark, everything moved in slow motion. Within seconds, he had her in his arms and held her against his warm chest.

"Are you okay?" she cried as she ran her hand over his chest and then his face. "Did he shoot you—did he shoot Gabby?" she asked, looking around frantically.

"No, he shot at the ceiling. Are you okay?" he asked, obviously panicked as he examined her from head to toe.

Sarah nodded throwing her hand over her face to cover her sobs. "Oh my God—I thought he shot you."

She wrapped her arm around him, gripping him tightly, beyond thankful that he was okay. She inhaled his scent and started to cry again, unable to vocalize her relief.

"Baby, I'm fine." He held her close, keeping her from slipping to the floor when her knees gave out. "I'm sorry I wasn't here sooner."

ꟷ

Mark stayed at her side, holding her hand while the emergency room doctor set her shoulder. She tried not to cry out too much. She could see how difficult it was for Mark to watch. He looked just as beaten up as she felt, but he never left her, never released her hand.

They'd been there for hours. The sun was rising and all she wanted was her own bed. While they waited for her discharge papers, Mark kissed the bruise on the side of her face and then lightly kissed her shoulder. "I'm sorry I broke my promise," he whispered.

"What are you talking about?"

"I promised I would never let him hurt you again, this is my fault. I never should have let you out of my sight," he said with regret heavy in his voice.

"Stop—I should be able to walk myself to the bathroom. It's my fault. I'm one of those stupid women I usually laugh at."

"What?"

"I'm freaking stupid." Her eyes pooled with tears. She tried to push them away, but the medication was making her loopy. "I let myself get distracted. My stomach was full of butterflies and my head was full of you. I should have been more aware of my surroundings." She covered her eyes in embarrassment. "I can't believe I let myself—I never even saw or heard him coming. Stupid, stupid..."

"Stop calling yourself stupid." Mark pulled her hand away and leaned close to her face. "You don't really believe this is your fault, do you?"

"Of course, I do. I know better than that, and I should have been smarter and stronger than him. I can't freaking believe I let myself get victimized again."

She shook her head as her tears fell down her face.

"Sarah, you're being ridiculous, stop saying that. What if he would have put that gun in your face?" He put his hands carefully on her face and turned her, bringing them eye to eye. "He came prepared to win the fight this time."

"That's not the point. If I would have looked around at my surroundings, been more aware..."

She pushed his hands away, trying to hide her face again. Sarah knew she was right. She'd let herself get wrapped up in her feelings for Mark, and when she did, she let her guard down to the rest of the world.

Mark waited outside, watching through the window as Brian finished taking Sarah's statement. He couldn't stand to be away from her. This was his fault. He shouldn't have let her out of his sight—much less in a freaking dance club.

His feelings for her were clouding his judgment and he had to stop. But stop what? Stop protecting her or stop feeling for her? He grimaced at the term feeling, not yet ready to say love, but...it was there. It had been there for a while. He couldn't pinpoint the moment he realized it. Maybe when they were at the beach or when she'd told him about her past. Maybe when they'd made love. Sarah giving him her complete trust—God, and look what he'd done with it—he'd failed her.

If his feelings were clouding his judgment, there was only one solution. Another agent. He wouldn't leave her, but he could bring in someone else to take over the detail—if he could make her understand. Would she believe him now when he said she wasn't safe?

When Brian walked out, Mark nodded at him before turning to enter the room.

Brian put his hand on Mark's shoulder. "Wait, bro, I need a minute with you first."

"I don't want to leave her alone."

"She did okay, she's strong—she handled it well."

"Thanks, Brian." Mark reached for the door again.

"This won't take long. I have the information on the note you fished out of her mailbox." Brian reached into his pocket to pull out his little note pad and flipped it open to Mark.

"'An eye for an eye. A nose for a nose. A bullet for a bullet. We'll be together again soon, my Sweet Sarah.'"

Mark's stomach turned.

"Blue ink, all caps again, we got his DNA off the envelope."

"And...?" Mark asked, wanting to hear the rest.

"*And,* it's a match to the other rapes *and* to Jennings' attack on September twenty-second. When we get this guy, we get him on everything. Not to mention the DNA picked from under your girlfriend's fingernails tonight." Brian smiled in satisfaction.

"You have to catch him first," Mark pointed out, making his disappointment in the investigation clear.

"Yeah." He squinted at Mark. "And what the hell were you thinking? How did he even get to her tonight? You need to get your head out of your ass. You do this shit for a living. C'mon man, what happened?"

"Thanks, Brian—thanks for jumping right into my nightmare with both feet." Mark yanked on the door and turned his back on Brian.

"I'm just keepin' it real, man," Brian said before Mark closed the door behind him.

Chapter Twenty-Three

Sarah woke, wrapped in Mark's warmth. She wasn't sure if he was still sleeping. She gently turned her head to look at him. She wanted to reach up and touch his face, but her arm was tied up in a sling.

She wasn't confused this time, not like the last time she'd woke with a sling on her arm, although her arm hurt much worse this time. Everything hurt much worse this time.

Mark's relaxed face comforted her. He was like a blanket of safety she could wrap around herself. Even though it killed her to give him up, she had to do it. Yesterday she was ready to give it a try, but Mark represented a life she couldn't have.

He shifted and pulled her closer to him. She sucked air through her teeth and tried to hide her grimace too late. His eyes popped open and he released his grip.

"Sorry," he muttered as his eyes closed again. Then his eyes popped back open, and he looked down at her. "How are you feeling?"

"Like I've been beaten up," she said, her breath hitching again. "It pretty much hurts to do everything, even breathe. Other than that, I'm fine."

"I'll get you a painkiller." He kissed her forehead and slowly started to get up.

"No, don't move yet, please." She gripped him and held him in place.

"What's wrong?"

"I'm not ready to face reality, wait please." She breathed in deep and sighed in pain again. He slid his arm out from around her to get up. "I'm okay really. You don't have to get up."

This would be the last time she'd let him hold her, and she wasn't ready to let go of him.

"No, it's not okay if you're in pain. I'll be right back."

He returned a minute later with a glass of water and a pill. "What time is it?" she asked after she swallowed the pill.

"It's about three o'clock in the afternoon. Are you still tired?"

"No, since you're forcing me to face reality, I really want a shower. I feel kind of gross." She slowly lifted herself off the bed.

"We can certainly accommodate a shower."

"I don't understand why everything hurts much worse today. I feel like my ribs are broken and my arm's been ripped off." She grimaced as she looked down at her bruised arms. "Back to long sleeves."

"I'm sorry...you were just starting to feel normal again." He came up behind her and wrapped his arms around her. She shook him off and went into the bathroom, closing the door behind her.

When her clothes were off, she stared at herself in the mirror, starting at her feet and up to her face. As bad as the body bruises were, it was the bruises on her face that really broke down the sturdy façade she'd been wearing.

The bruising traveled up the side of her face, around her cheekbone, to her forehead, and both eyes were black. Sarah looked at herself as memories of her past flooded her mind.

She remembered the weeks she'd spent with black eyes, heaviness in her heart, and pain so bad she wished for death. For weeks, every morning she'd awaken and cursed God for making her spend another day in a world without her child.

Sarah started to sob and had to suck in painful breaths as her chest heaved. The pain in her ribs forced her to cry out. She turned the water on so Mark wouldn't hear her cry. He'd feel worse if he saw how wretched she was. If she could just have some time alone to get it out of her system, she'd be stronger when she had to face telling him.

Now she had to find the strength to take back everything she'd said the day before. The thought of losing Mark made everything in her body ache worse. She sobbed mercilessly, knowing she would hurt him and hurt herself in the process.

The tears continued to stream down her face, mixing with the flow of fresh water as she stepped into the shower. She hoped the water would rinse away the horrible feeling of loneliness she felt at having to walk away from Mark.

She scrubbed and scrubbed, trying to rid herself of the nasty layer of filth and heavy thoughts that consumed her. When the water went cold, she turned the shower off and stepped out, all the while trying to push away her emotions and face her decision with certainty.

Her scrubbing left raw and red marks all over her body, enhancing the black and blue from the bruises. Sarah gently toweled off and dried her hair hoping the extra few minutes would give her time to rebuild what little was left of her façade.

She tried to dress herself without calling for help, but when she couldn't pull her injured arm through her shirt, she gave up. She had her sweats on and one arm in the shirt when Mark entered the bathroom. He helped her get both arms through the shirt and hooked the sling.

"What happened here?" he asked, gesturing to the red and irritated skin above her collar. She turned and looked in the mirror, rubbing at the marks on her neck.

"I scrubbed a little too hard with the washcloth," she said, lowering her eyes.

"I guess so." He put his cool hand to the irritated skin. "Why did you do that?"

"He..." She cleared her throat and shrugged away from him. "He touched me there." She waved her hand at her neck where the attacker licked her. The look on Mark's face told her that he understood.

He pursed his lips and tried again to put his hand on her neck. She pulled away to get some space between them. She wasn't ready. Her emotional grip was slipping away and she needed a couple more minutes.

"I made breakfast. You should feel better after you have some coffee."

"Coffee sounds good. I'll be out in a minute."

Mark turned and walked out of the bathroom, and Sarah could tell she'd hurt his feelings.

She waited a few minutes before stepping out of the bathroom. When she went into the kitchen, she poured herself a cup of coffee without saying a word to him.

"Did I do something wrong?" he asked as he put a plate of food down on the bar for her.

"No," she said, still unable to look at him.

"Clearly there's a reason you're giving me the cold shoulder."

This made her glance up at him.

"Have you been crying?" Concern clear on his face, he reached for her hand. She pulled it away before he could touch her.

She lifted herself onto a barstool, wincing at the pain. Then she pushed the plate away. Smelling the food made her stomach roll. She rubbed her forehead, trying to gather her courage.

"This isn't going to work out."

"I'm sorry?" He tilted his head forward. "*What* isn't going to work out?"

"This." She gestured between the two of them. "You and me—and the dating thing."

"I don't understand?"

"I was careless and I should have been more alert and careful—"

"Wait—you don't want to be with me because..." He stopped to catch his breath. "You seriously believe this happened because you weren't paying attention? Sarah, look at me...*babe*." He said it so tenderly, she couldn't help but do what he asked.

"You didn't have a chance this time, paying attention or not."

A lump formed in her throat when she remembered that gun pointed at Mark's face. She shook her head and looked away from him.

"That's not the point. It could've been anyone who came up behind me. I need to get my act together—back together." She swallowed hard, willing herself to keep talking. "I've been living in a bubble for all these weeks and I need to just...stop...get back to normal and stop living in the clouds. I'm sorry, Mark. I'm not trying to hurt you..." her voice broke.

"Then don't," he said earnestly. "If you don't want to hurt me, then don't—it's a choice."

"You're right. It is a choice and I'm not making this decision lightly," she said with wavering resolve. His sincerity was slowly breaking her heart.

"Don't be a coward, if you walk away now, you'll never know what could've been."

Sarah didn't have the strength to continue arguing with him. She covered her face, losing what little control she had over her tears.

"Can you honestly tell me you don't have strong feelings for me? Dammit—just don't give up so easily."

"You d—don't understand," Sarah stammered.

"Oh, yes I do. You're afraid to let someone into your safe, little sheltered world. I've gotten too close and you've allowed yourself to develop real feelings for me and now you're running scared."

His sincerity had turned to anger, and he was trying to provoke her into fighting with him. How could she argue with him? They both knew he was right.

Massive tears spilled over her lids just as Mark stepped in front of her and pulled her hand away from her face.

"Sarah, good things in life are hard to find. When you find them, you should hold on."

The hurt in his voice left her speechless. He reached up and wiped a tear from her chin.

"Yesterday was perfect until..."

The look in his eyes, his emotions were clear too, and it wasn't just anger that he felt. She pulled away from him and stood up, bypassing him to get some distance. She couldn't stand the feel of his skin or bear to look at his face any longer. Regardless of how hard she fought to stay calm, hysterics were building deep in her chest. She couldn't take this, couldn't stand what was happening to them. Why did she let it go this far? He was right, good things in life were hard to find, but they were impossible to keep.

Mark grabbed her hand and pulled her back. "Don't run away from me. Talk to me—tell me what's going on inside your head."

"I don't know!" she screamed, and yanked her hand away flailing to stop him from touching her. "I—I don't know what to do. Things are all fucked up. I don't know what the right answers are." She squeezed her ribs to hold in her painful sobs. "He's free while I'm trapped—unable to live my life. I don't know if I'm coming or going anymore. I haven't felt this lost in—*dammit*!" she yelled as she leaned against the wall to brace herself. "He's contaminated everything in my life. I can't...work. I can't drive. I can't sleep. I can't run—and now...I can't even dress myself. Everything normal in my life has been taken away from me. I'm grasping at straws to just...breathe. I'm *trapped* and I can't...*breathe*..." She began to hyperventilate, her chest heaving in an effort to regulate her breathing.

"Take a deep breath, Sarah—a deep breath please." He grasped her hand, but she pulled away again.

When her breathing mellowed, he leaned in and took her face in both hands. There was so much passion in his eyes. It hurt to look into them. He was so sincere and she was so broken, too broken to handle him and her life at the same time. She didn't know how to be with him.

"I'm sorry you're going through this, but pushing me away isn't going to fix things."

"I can't do this anymore." She sucked in air, and then flinched in pain.

"Sarah, you're not feeling trapped because of our relationship, it's a result of what happened to you." He lowered his hands to cup her neck. "Baby—you and me together—what we've found is the only good thing that's come out of this, don't ruin it." He pressed his lips to the top of her head and held her until her breathing slowed. "I love you, Sarah, and I will take care of you."

She flinched at his words.

He leaned back and looked into her eyes. "You can try to push me away, but I'll push back. I'm not giving up on you." With her face in his hands, he gave her a deep, passionate kiss.

She relaxed and gave into him, clinging to his body, enjoying the warmth, wishing she could have him.

He wiped her tear-streaked face. "I'll back off *for a while*...but I'm not going away."

She took a deep breath again and pulled her arm around her torso.

"It really does hurt to breathe, doesn't it?" His eyebrows furrowed with concern.

She nodded and squeezed her eyes closed.

Mark led her to the sofa and helped her lay down. "Stay there."

He came back a minute later with a fresh cup of coffee, a glass of water, and another pill. "Do you want to try an ice pack around your ribs?"

"No, I'm fine. Stop worrying about me."

"Can't help it when I'm the reason you're so upset." After she swallowed the pill, he said, "I'm going to go take a shower...give you a few minutes. Will you be all right?"

She nodded and tried to smile.

"Come get me if you need anything," Mark said as he left the room.

When Sarah heard the running water, she jumped up and ran to her bedroom. As quickly as she could, she packed a duffle bag, scribbled a note to Mark, and raced from the house as she flipped open her borrowed cell phone.

Mark took a long shower to give Sarah time alone. After everything that had happened to her over the past couple of weeks, she had every right to freak out. He didn't want to minimize what she was going through, and yet pushing him away wouldn't make things easier for her.

He dressed and went into the living room. She was gone and the room was empty. He walked through the house and into the backyard, and then raced to the front door, which he found unlocked.

"What the fuck?" His pulse elevated as his worst fears coursed through him. He went back to the bedroom and grabbed his cell phone.

"Bri, Sarah's gone!"

"What?" Brian said. "Where are you?"

"I'm at Sarah's. When I got out of the shower she was—" He stopped when he saw the scribbled note on the bed. "Hold on." He snatched up the note and scanned it quickly.

Mark,

I had to leave, I'm sorry. I'll be in a safe place. Thanks for taking care of me. This—everything was a mistake. I am sorry.

Sarah

He read it until the words sunk in. "Oh my God..." He lowered himself to the bed before his knees gave out. "She's gone."

"What are you talking about?"

"She left a note. She...left," he said as the realization tightened into a knot in his chest.

"What does the note say?"

"I'll call you back." Mark closed the phone and ran to the window to look out. The Mustang and her truck were still in the driveway. Was she wandering around the neighborhood? Did someone pick her up?

He dialed her number. "Voicemail—shit—Sarah, what the hell? Come back so we can talk. It's not safe for you to be out alone. God dammit! What are you doing?" He closed his phone and grabbed his keys.

Chapter Twenty-Four

When Devon picked her up from the Portland Airport, she didn't say a word, and as if he knew she wasn't ready to talk about it, he didn't ask until they were in the car.

"Are you okay?" he finally croaked, after several tense and silent minutes.

"Yeah, I'm fine. Thanks for picking me up. I'm sorry for the short notice."

"Are you going to tell me what happened?" he finally asked.

Sarah shook her head and closed her eyes, consumed with self-loathing. He'd never understand. How could any man understand her life, much less the reasoning behind her decisions?

"Can you at least tell me why you're so beat up? Who do I need to kill?"

Reluctantly she told Devon about the attack at the club, leaving out all the extra stuff about Mark. She couldn't let her mind venture into thoughts of him or what she'd done. Her voicemail was full, and all the messages were from him.

"I have an idea, if you're up for it," Devon said when she grew quiet.

Sarah looked at him wearily.

"I was thinking about renting a beach house in Newport for a couple of months. What do you think?"

"Newport, Oregon?"

"Yeah. Lily, Hayley, and I spent last summer there. The place is incredible. You can walk out the back door right onto the beach. I met this cool chic, Chloe, and I thought you and I could hang out there for a while."

"You met a girl and you want to see her again, *really*?"

"Yeah, well, the surfing is awesome and the house is available. Some peace and quiet might do you some good."

"Some peace and quiet might do me some good," she repeated, her tone defeated. "Tell me about this girl."

"She lives in the house next door with a couple of roommates—they're all super cool."

"I would love to meet your *girlfriend*," she teased.

"Don't get ahead of yourself. I don't have a girlfriend. She's just a cool chic, okay."

"Fine, whatever. I would rather stay at the beach than stay with Mama. It's only a matter of time before we're at each other's throats."

"Yeah, I made a bet with Hayley already. If you can make it until Sunday, I win."

The next morning, Sarah sat up and blinked her eyes at the light shining through the curtains and the rain as it splattered on the windowpane. She couldn't believe she'd slept until noon. Her first night without Mark had been miserable, and she wondered how he was.

Her mother's guest room looked like a floral nightmare. No wonder she couldn't sleep. The pink walls with floral curtains and the matching pink floral comforter on the bed explained why Devon took the couch instead of fighting for the bed.

When she entered the kitchen, Lily and Sean were sitting at the table chatting quietly. They both stopped talking when she entered.

"Don't let me interrupt. I only came for coffee."

"Well, darlin', we can't talk about you behind your back while you're in the room." Her mother smiled as she said this.

"Great, once I have my coffee, I'll get out of your way so you can continue to talk about me," she said, thoroughly irritated.

"Actually, we would like to talk to you, if you don't mind?" Sean said. Her stepfather had all the manners that her mother lacked, and Sarah wondered what he saw in Lily.

"Sarah, you don't need to be so sensitive, I'm only kiddin' with you."

"I know, Mama, but I didn't sleep well, and I feel like I've been through the spin cycle in your washing machine."

Sarah slowly lowered herself to a chair and looked at her mother. Lily hadn't changed at all since the last time she'd seen her. She had deeply tanned, olive skin and pin-straight, long, dark hair, the complete opposite of Sarah.

"What's up?" she asked, sipping her coffee.

"Well, sweetheart, we would like for you to stay for a while. There's no reason for you to go back to Santa Rosa, and you don't really need to work." Lily placed her hand over Sarah's. "We would love to have you here. We miss you."

"Mama, thank you, but I like Santa Rosa and I love my job." She sighed and bowed her head. "It hasn't stopped raining since my plane landed last night."

"Sarah, we have some great schools in Portland. You can easily get another job, and you can stay here until you find your own place," Sean said.

"Aren't you already looking for a new place, especially since you walked out on that new man in your life?" Lily smiled. "Sarah, maybe you need to settle down. Devon told me about Mark and what he's done for you. Why did you leave?"

Sarah threw her hands in the air. "God, Mama—you know. Why can't you believe I'm happy on my own? I've built a life for myself—for myself and by myself."

"Lily, you're not helping. Sarah's not you, she wants to be on her own and there's nothing wrong with that."

"Thank you, Sean," Sarah said, relieved to have some backup.

"For a while I thought you might be a lesbian. I'm thrilled that you have a boyfriend." Lily shrugged. "I wish you would get married, have some babies—"

"Mama! Jeez-us!" She stood and snatched up her coffee mug and nearly ran Devon over as she left the room.

Chapter Twenty-Five

Mark looked at the clock and rolled out of bed. Why waste time lying in bed when he couldn't sleep. He went downstairs and put on a pot of coffee, and then he looked around his kitchen.

"Man, what a mess." He needed to get a grip.

He felt sick at the thought of her. Would she ever understand the hell she'd put him through by running out on him? The last week had been the worst of his life, even worse than what he'd been through with Ali.

When the doorbell rang, he plodded to the door. Shane's hulking form nearly took up Mark's entire front porch.

"Took you long enough. You got it?" Mark asked, holding the door open for Shane to enter.

"Yeah, bro, you look like shit." Shane looked Mark up and down. "Maybe you should shower and shave first."

"Not now," Mark growled. "Give me the address. Are you sure it's the right one?"

"The mother's club checked out. This is Lily Lange's home address, and this is the nightclub. She co-owns it with her husband, Sean Metzger. She's a singer and he manages the business."

"That doesn't mean that's where Devon and Sarah are."

"Trust me, she's there. My contact did some snooping and Lily's been bragging all over town about her kids visiting. It's no secret, every regular from that club knows about Sarah and Devon being there. Devon's even been to the club a few nights."

"Great security." Mark shook his head in disgust. "It's amazing this rapist hasn't found her yet."

Shane lips tipped into a smile. "He doesn't have me looking."

"Thanks, brother...I seriously owe you one."

"Nah, you could've done it yourself if you pulled your head out of your ass. You going to Portland?"

"No, you are."

Shane scoffed. "Too chicken shit to face her yourself?"

"I'm not going after her. She knows where I am if she needs me. If I keep chasing her, she'll keep running and I can't take that."

Shane's brows lifted. "She's done this before?"

"No, but only because I've talked her out of it." Mark bowed his head, feeling stupid for letting her get the best of him. As much as he loved her, he wouldn't chase her. She loved him, too. He was sure of it. Maybe she just needed a little time to figure that out.

"You want work or not? I could leave you on disabled status if you prefer." Mark shrugged. "I'm sure Randy would like the easy work."

"I'm not dragging your girlfriend home from Portland for you."

"No, asshole, I want you to keep an eye on her. If she wants to come home, she'll have to do it on her own."

"Ha, yeah, easy work." Shane rolled his eyes. "I got this."

Mark smirked. "Yeah, okay, big guy, but you let anything happen to her, don't bother coming home."

"Here." He handed an equipment order to Shane. "Give this to Seth when you get back to the office."

Shane looked over the schematic and the order. "You're going to install cameras on her house without her permission?"

"She can sue me when she gets back if she wants. I want this fucker caught."

Shane held his hands up. "All right, I got my orders. I'll keep in touch."

Sarah rolled her eyes at her mother's exuberant exclamation at how beautiful the beach house was that Devon rented. She acted as if she'd never been there before. But that was Lily. She went overboard on everything, even her praise.

Devon met Sarah's eyes and they both snickered.

"Mama, you've been here before," Devon said when she gasped at the view.

"I know, baby, but it's so beautiful. I can't help myself."

"You didn't have to come. I'm fine with Devon, Mama."

"Sarah, you're a mess. I'm not about to leave you injured and brokenhearted in the hands of your flaky brother."

"Ha." Devon laughed a sarcastic and loud laugh. "On that note, I'm going next door to say hi to Chloe. I'll be back by morning." He kissed Sarah on the cheek and muttered, "Have a nice evening."

"Well, Dev wants the downstairs room, why don't you go ahead and take the master suite? You'll love the room, and I know how you like your privacy, so I'll settle into the third bedroom."

"I can sleep anywhere. Mama, you can have the master if you want."

"No, no, I wouldn't hear of it. You go on up and get yourself settled in and I'll get started on dinner."

Grateful for the escape, Sarah climbed the stairs to her room. Her mother had been right in her praise though—the house was over-the-top gorgeous. It was tall and narrow with three floors, fully furnished, and stocked with all the linens they would need.

Sarah found the top floor and entered the master suite in awe of the beautiful room. The first thing her eyes landed on was the double-sided fireplace, one side enjoyable from the bedroom, the other from the sitting room. While staring into the lifeless grate, she thought of Mark and clicked the switch on the wall, a gas fireplace just like his.

Thinking of Mark siphoned every ounce of energy out of her. It'd been a week since she left him...a very long week without him. She walked over and sank onto the bed. With her face in her hands, she inhaled, trying to fight the tightness in her chest. She hugged herself, wishing she could push him out of her mind, but she couldn't turn it off. His smile, his frown, his touch...his deep, beautiful blue eyes and the way he looked at her. God, what had she done?

She dropped back and turned over. That's when she saw the spectacular view through the large picture window. A huge stretch of beach and the never-ending Pacific Ocean was shadowed by dark, angry storm clouds. She lay there and watched the surf until she fell asleep.

Sarah woke up hours later to pounding thunder that shook her senseless. She watched the light show for a few minutes, and then got up, washed her face, and went back downstairs.

She found her mother sound asleep on the sofa with a movie on the TV. She tiptoed to the kitchen, following the scent of food. On the stove was a fully prepared meal of fried chicken, mashed potatoes with gravy, and green beans. In the warm oven sat a dozen homemade, buttermilk biscuits to die for.

"Ah, yeah, sometimes it is nice to come home for a visit," Sarah muttered.

"What's that?" Devon said, coming up behind her.

Sarah jumped, slamming the oven shut. "Dammit, Devon!" She smacked him as he laughed hysterically, bending over, grabbing his sides.

"Sorry." He cleared his throat and tried to remove the smile from his face. "I'm really sorry. I wasn't trying to scare you."

"No, right, that's why you tiptoed in here and told me to be quiet," Chloe said.

Sarah straightened and looked around for the person who went with the voice. Behind Devon was a pretty, young woman with an amused smile. Sarah watched her for a moment and wished like hell she had a reason to smile like that.

The girl's light blond hair had a few pink, blue, and purple streaks through it. The super-short bob cut came down to frame her face in the front. Her beautiful smile and bright green eyes softened her perfectly square face. She seemed to be exactly Devon's type.

"Hi," Sarah said as she peered around Devon.

"This is Chloe."

"Hi, Chloe, I'm Sarah, it's nice to meet you." Sarah had some trouble pulling off a smile.

"How are you, Sarah?" Chloe asked.

Sarah dropped her pretense of a smile and looked at Devon.

"I'm fine. I guess my big mouth brother told you."

Chloe nodded. "Sorry." She grimaced. "Honestly...the black eyes would've clued me in."

Sarah threw her hand up to her face. "Yeah, they're hard to hide. I look worse than I feel," Sarah said, and hoped they believed the lie. "I'm fine, really. Thank you for asking."

"I know you don't like the sympathy, but if it gets me some action, I'm using it," Devon said smugly.

Sarah laughed at that. "I'm glad my misfortune has given you an advantage with the ladies."

"My roommates and I are having a little get together tonight—would you like to come over with Devon? We live right next door."

"Thanks, but I don't think I'm up for a party yet."

"Chloe, I'm gonna hang with my sister tonight. I don't think she should be alone," Devon said as he gave Sarah a long look.

"No, Devon, go have a good time, I'll be fine. Besides, Mama's here." She didn't mention that their mother was passed out on the sofa. She looked forward to being alone. "You guys should eat, Mama cooked up a feast."

Devon looked under the pot lid. "Oh damn..."

"I know, I can already feel my arteries clogging," Sarah said. "It was nice meeting you, Chloe.

"You, too. I hope you feel better soon."

Chapter Twenty-Six

Sarah looked out the window at the bright blue sky. She'd been at the beach house for over a week, and this was the first sunny day she'd seen.

After changing, she snuck downstairs, hoping to get out before her mother saw her. No luck. Lily sat at the kitchen table with a mug of coffee.

"Morning, darlin', want coffee?"

"Morning, Mama. Thanks, but I'm anxious to get some vitamin D while the sun's out."

"Excuse me—I hope you're not planning to run on that beach in your condition. You got three more weeks before you're healed enough to do anything like that, Sarah Jean."

Sarah rolled her eyes. "No, Mama. I'm just going for a walk."

"Please be careful."

"Will do," Sarah said, and rushed out the sliding glass door toward the beach.

Instant freedom, beach for as far as her eyes could see. So why didn't she feel better? She jogged over the dunes and went to the water's edge, ignoring the pain in her arm.

The wave of homesickness and loneliness hit her hard as the sea air brushed her face. She could no longer deny how much she missed Mark. Their day on the beach together was so like this one. He had been incredible to her. God, she was stupid. What had she done by walking away? And, damn, how it hurt that he stopped trying to call her. Her phone hadn't rung in days.

She pulled out her borrowed cell and fingered the keypad. Willing it to ring, wishing like hell she could take back what she'd done. She plopped down on the sand and lay back as her eyes darted over the cloudless sky. Then she lifted the phone and dialed his number.

When his voicemail came up, she listened intently on the sound of his voice. She missed hearing it, missed his whispered breaths on her cheek.

"Hi, it's me. God, Mark, please call me. I miss you and I'm worried about you and..." She painfully inhaled a sob. "I really miss you." She quickly closed her phone before breaking down completely.

She lay there for a long time—too long. It sickened her how pathetic she was.

"Get over it," she muttered. "Get up and move on, Sarah." She lifted up, watched the surf for a while, and then stood and got moving. She needed to work her muscles to clear her head. That was the only healthy way to move on. When she felt better, she'd be better.

❧

"So what's this update you were so fired up to give me?" Mark asked when he stepped into Brian's office.

Brian gestured. "Close the door." He waited for Mark to sit. "You find your lady yet?"

"Yeah, I got Shane on her." He sat in the chair across from Brian.

Brian's lips curled into a crooked smile. "You sound like a fucking stalker. I should arrest you."

"Don't start with me." Mark frowned. "You of all people should understand why I'm doing this."

"We've all been stupid in love before. I get it." He flipped open the file on his desk and tossed Mark the picture on top.

"Oh—hell!" He fought the coiling in his stomach. It was a crime scene photo of a dead woman, her throat slit from ear to ear and her eyes wide open. The resemblance to Sarah was uncanny. Her face was slightly narrower than Sarah's but the curls, the shape of her eyes, everything else was eerily similar. "Who the hell is that?"

"Our guy's latest victim." Brian snatched the photo out of Mark's hand and tossed it back in the file. "You didn't see that."

Mark's blood ran cold. He knew what it meant...and he knew how much trouble Brian would be in for showing him.

"You need to call Shane and get him on guard."

"He's graduated to murder...oh my God." Mark closed his eyes, trying to get the image of the dead girl out of his head. "I can't believe how much she looks like Sarah."

"Considering the notes that have been left in her box since she's been gone...she's in a lot of danger if he finds her."

"I'll let Shane know. Thank God she's not here." He lowered his head, hoping Brian didn't see the look in his eyes. He missed her so much, he could hardy drag himself out of bed every day, and hearing updates from Shane didn't help.

"You should head up there too. Stop licking your wounds, get away from this, and work some shit out with her."

Mark would love to. After seeing that picture, he wanted nothing more than to hold her close, inhale her scent, and keep her in the circle of his arms forever. But he couldn't, she needed to come back on her own. She had to make the choice to be with him.

He shook his head. "She's the one who ran away. I'm not chasing her, and I'm not forcing her into a relationship she doesn't want. She'll come home when she's ready, and until then, I'm backing off."

Brian stared at the file on his desk for a long time, his expression hard, disdainful. "If you love her, you'll fight for her. Sitting around feeling sorry for yourself is just wasting time. Trust me, I know." He leaned forward and looked Mark dead in the eye. "Don't you think she might be worth a try?"

Mark stood. "I gotta go."

"Mark!" Brian shouted before Mark could leave the office. "Don't get any ideas with this guy. If you get him on camera, call us. Don't be a fucking hero."

Mark climbed into his truck and heard the chime on his cell phone. He reached over and took it from the cup holder where he'd left it. One missed call.

"Son of a bitch...she called." He dialed up the voice message and listened with a sinking heart, surprised that he could feel any worse than he already had.

He needed to warn Shane, maybe get Randy up there to help with the detail. He put his Bluetooth to his ear and hit the speed dial to call Shane before starting his truck.

"'Ello," he panted into the phone.

"Hey, how's it going? Why the hell are you out of breath?"

"Sarah decided to go running on the beach today. I'm trying to keep up with her."

"She's injured—not supposed to be running."

"How the fuck do you suggest I stop her? Come on, man, this is only the second time she's stepped out of the house all week."

"How does she look? Is she in any pain?"

"She's broken, Mark. Sat on the beach and cried for fifteen minutes, then jumped up and took off running—oh thank God, she's slowing to a walk."

"Don't let her make you."

"No, she's not paying any attention to me...ah...she's crying again."

"Dammit." The one time he leaves the phone in the truck, she calls. "She—" He gritted his teeth and fought to keep calm. "She called me and I didn't have my phone on me."

"Ouch." Shane sucked air though his teeth. "Well...that's progress. At least she made the first move."

"I have an update from Brian," Mark said, changing the subject on purpose. "Our rapist is now a murderer."

"That changes things."

"He's also still leaving notes in her box—notes that get more graphic every day. You need to be on guard. I'm thinking about sending Randy up there to relieve you." Mark angled his truck into his driveway and turned the engine off.

"Don't yet, give it another day or two. If she doesn't leave the house, then you'll just be wasting your money."

"I don't give a shit about money. She's what's important here."

"Then quit dicking around and call her back. I gotta go, she's on the move again."

Mark slammed his phone shut and wanted to fucking punch something.

"Dicking around, fuck me!" He threw the truck door open, slammed it behind him, tugged the mailbox open, and froze, unable to break his gaze from the small, unmarked envelope staring back at him.

After several seconds, he snatched up the envelope and ran into the house for a Ziploc bag. He stood in his kitchen, looking at the envelope in the bag, knowing without a doubt that things had changed. This message proved she was in more danger than he had ever imagined.

Pictures of a dead girl flashed in his mind. He took a deep breath and stepped back outside to his truck. He needed to get this to Brian, but first, he had to hear her voice. He had to know that at this very second she was okay.

He pulled out his phone and dialed her number. It rang several times, and he was about to hang up to avoid her voicemail, when she finally answered.

"Hello?"

"Hi..." Fuck, now what. "Ah, I saw that you called."

"I did."

Her heavy breathing scared him. She was supposed to be recovering still. "Are you okay? You sound breathless."

"I'm trying to run." The whine in her voice made him want to reach out and touch her. Do something to make things easier for her. "I'm not getting very far though."

"Doesn't your doctor still have you on rest?"

"He does, but I'm going stir crazy with the rain. I'm in Oregon."

He nearly said *I know* but stopped himself. "It's a little late to let me know where you are, don't you think?"

"I guess so."

"I'm not sure what I'm supposed to say to you...I tell you I love you and you run out on me."

"You have every right to be furious with me."

"Yeah." He wanted like hell to rant at her but that would get him nowhere, and regardless of how pissed off he was, he still loved her and missed her.

"How have you been?" Her attempt at sounding breezy pissed him off even more.

He slammed his hand down on the steering wheel. "Just peachy. How the fuck do you think I've been?"

"I miss you...you're all I can think about."

He sat quietly for a few seconds, waiting for his stomach to stop tilting. All the anger in the world couldn't hold up against those few words. What was he doing picking a fight with her when he was just happy to hear her voice again?

He squeezed his eyes shut and tried to get the same words out, but all he said was, "Me too."

"I'm sorry for leaving without saying goodbye."

"Right—right! You're sorry for not saying goodbye—that's exactly what I needed to know. Thanks for calling. I gotta go."

"No! That's not what I meant—I'm sorry for hurting you—I'm sorry for running away when I should have talked to you."

Mark opened his eyes and stared up at the roof of his truck. "You're a coward—is that what you want to talk about? Let's put it out there—let's just throw all our cards on the table. You're scared because you have feelings for me and that fucks up your tight, little controlled world."

"I don't blame you for being angry with me...don't know what else to say but that I'm sorry."

"You don't know what to say but that *you're sorry.*" He couldn't help shouting. Even now she closed herself off to him. "How about talking to me for real? Just talk! Tell me something other than I'm sorry. Instead of walking away, tell me you're scared or tell me you need space. Anything!"

"When I tried to talk to you, you didn't want to hear what I had to say."

"Bullshit, Sarah, I told you I would back off. I agreed you weren't ready for this. Do you have any idea what the last two weeks have been like for me, not knowing what happened to you? You never considered how I would feel when I realized you were gone."

"I have a pretty good idea what you were going through. I was alone and worried, too."

"I didn't have a choice, though! You cut me off cold...left a fucking note that didn't say anything!"

"I'm sorry for all the words I didn't say."

He'd been hard on her, but he couldn't push back his anger. Not over the phone. God, he wanted to touch her—pull her close and bury his face in her curls.

"I'm sorry for all the words you didn't say too."

The line went dead before he got the sentence out. He stared at the phone, not sure what to do next. Call her back? Go to Oregon? Drag her ass home and show her that she loved him too, even when she was too chicken shit to admit it?

No. He shook his head, knowing his main concern should be getting this envelope to Brian and installing cameras on his house like he'd done Sarah's. The only way to guarantee her safety was to catch this fucker, and since the police weren't having any luck, he'd do it himself.

Chapter Twenty-Seven

Sarah didn't know how long she sat there, watching the surf. She and Mark were over, and she had to face the fact that she'd screwed things up beyond repair. He was too angry to see how she felt, and besides, it's not like he could ever understand her. He could never understand where she'd come from or what she'd endured in her life. How stupid of her to believe she had a chance for anything normal—any semblance of a normal life for her.

She held too much baggage—too many hurts and too many hurdles to jump. She slowly walked back to the beach house and climbed the stairs on the back deck. As she turned to go inside, she noticed a man off in the distance. The beach wasn't deserted. The great weather had brought everyone out, but this wasn't the first time she'd noticed him since she'd left the house. The hair on her scalp prickled. Even from this distance, she could feel his eyes on her.

All the years she'd spent looking over her shoulder for Kevin had given her a sixth sense about these things. That's why the attack at the club scared her. She'd never seen it coming. Another reason for her to get her act together, get back in shape, and maybe talk Gabby into teaching her some self-defense moves.

ꕥ

Sarah's new outlook on life started here. When she stepped off these stairs and into the kitchen, she'd have a new mindset, new workout routine, new everything. She would get Mark out of her head, even if she had to use a freaking crowbar. In a few weeks, she'd go home and meet him as a friend only.

Mark would meet a woman without the baggage, and Sarah could go back to her simple life—she couldn't wait to get back to work. She'd had very little time with her new class before the attack, and she craved their attention and their open, little minds. That's one of the things she loved about teaching first grade. She got them before the prejudices in life got into their heads. They were like clean canvases, and she could paint a pretty picture and teach them value, not just numbers and words.

Sarah turned to the stove and faced a pan of the most beautiful enchiladas she'd ever seen. "Oh my God, Chloe, did you cook these? They look incredible."

"Yes," Chloe said from behind her. "It's my father's recipe. He was such a fan of Mexican food."

"Patrón shots!" Devon said from behind her, filling four shot glasses.

"You're going to do a shot too, Lily?" Chloe said.

"Oh, darlin', yes. I'll show you how it's done. These kids were raised around clubs. Where do you think they learned it?"

Devon and Sarah's eyes met, and she felt the heat rise in her cheeks, feeling an embarrassment that she hadn't felt in a long time. Her mother bragging about what an awful parent she'd been was too much. Devon shook his head and she understood. He didn't want a fight tonight. Sarah didn't want a fight either. She had a new lease on life and fighting with her mother wasn't part of her plan.

Before they began eating, Devon filled their glasses with margaritas and passed around another full round of shots. Sarah thought maybe he wanted to keep everyone good and tossed to avoid the sour words that she and Lily were so famously good at throwing at each other. But Sarah kept her mouth shut. She wouldn't fight with her mother tonight.

When their plates were empty and their bellies full, they all stood to clear the table. Sarah couldn't remember the last time she'd eaten so much. She had a new respect for Chloe. Everything tasted excellent.

Devon stood with his plate and said, "Shots!"

"No, I think I'm done for the night." She tilted her head. "But y'all go ahead."

"Oh come on, baby," Lily said. "We don't get much of a chance to be together, let's enjoy it."

Sarah looked at Devon and he held up one finger and mouthed, "One more."

She nodded. "Just one more."

As they laid the empty shot glasses down, Lily's cell phone rang in her pocket. She snatched it up and smiled as she answered. "Hi, sweet girl."

Sarah stepped over to the sliding glass door and stared out at the rain that had started to fall. She sighed. So much for the nice weather.

"Hayley, tell Sean I said it was okay...no...no, he won't. Tell him what I said."

Sarah turned, startled by her mother's raised voice.

"I'm hanging up, either tell Sean what I said or go home. It's up to you. I love you. Call me in the morning." She closed her phone and then dropped it on the table.

"Isn't it kinda late to be arguing with Hayley?" Sarah asked.

"Oh that girl, she's spending the night with her boyfriend, and she's afraid Sean's going to be pissed at her."

"What? Mama, she's only fifteen. Why would that be okay with you?"

"Well, she loves the boy. You know how teenagers are." She walked toward the sink and said, "Chloe, you cooked, so you don't get to do the dishes too."

"Mama, you let Hayley spend the night with her boyfriend?"

"What's the big deal? You had a boyfriend at her age."

"How old is this boy? Where are his parents?" Sarah asked.

"He's in college. He lives in a big house with a bunch of roommates."

Sarah placed her hands on her hips. "You are letting your fifteen-year-old daughter spend the night with a man? What the hell are you thinking?"

"You were the same at her age. Remember Kevin? Why would I have different rules for her than for you?"

"I was two years older than Hayley, and Kevin was the biggest mistake of my life. Hayley isn't old enough to make mature decisions yet. What do you know about this boy? He could be abusive or—God, Mama, what if she gets pregnant?"

"Hey—I thought we weren't going to fight tonight," Devon said, stepping between them.

"Maybe Hayley is a little smarter than you, Sarah. I'm not going to punish her for your bad choices," Lily said.

"It's not punishing her. It's to protect her." Sarah felt her heart pound like a base drum inside her chest. "Why aren't *you* trying to protect her, Mother?" Sarah's indignation felt like fire licking the inside of her stomach.

"Do not talk to me like that, Sarah Jean, grown or not, I am still your mother."

Sarah scoffed. "Mother, huh, yeah."

Lily took a step back with wide eyes. "Excuse me?"

"Please," Devon said. "Stop."

"Now you're blaming me for your poor choices?" Lily dropped a hand to her hip. "Now it's my fault things didn't work out with Kevin?"

"Work out? What the hell are you talking about? Kevin beat me and emotionally abused me." She felt the tears come as the fire in her stomach rose to her throat.

"He nearly beat me to death. He killed my baby." Her mother wasn't there...she was never there when Sarah needed her.

"If you were any kind of mother you would have protected me. You of all people should have recognized the patterns of abuse!" She fought back the scream in her throat. "He hurt me...and you never noticed because you were too wrapped up in your own life." Sarah wanted to punch her mother's blasé face.

"If it was that bad, why didn't you leave him, Sarah?"

A rush of memories overwhelmed her, things she hadn't thought about in years. Staring at her mother now, it was so clear to her. Her feelings of never belonging anywhere, always being homesick, but never knowing where her home was.

Kevin had given her a home. It was broken and abusive, but it had been a home and she clung to it.

Ava's words echoed in her head, *You try so hard to prove you're nothing like her, but who are you trying to prove it too?* Ava was right. Sarah remembered wanting to prove that she could hold on to a relationship when her mother couldn't. She had clung to him even when he beat her—because she wanted a place to belong—*a home.*

"I stayed because of you, Mama," she whispered, her eyes still focused on Devon's and the tightness around his eyes softened. "I was needy and stupid. I wanted to be important to someone and be loved...oh my God." Sarah broke the eye contact with Devon and felt the walls closing in on her. "I need to get out of here—fresh air."

The atmosphere around her mother, even around Devon was suffocating, she needed space and air. Room to think.

"No!" Devon grabbed her arm. "Don't leave."

"It's okay, I just need some air." She pried his fingers from her arm and vaulted out of the sliding glass door into the rain.

Sarah inhaled and forced her lungs to take in the air even as they fought against it. She hit the beach on a run, happy for the darkness and the sound of the waves crashing around her.

She thought of every cruel word Kevin had said to her. The nasty things he'd accused her of. All this time she blamed herself for staying and not running away.

If Kevin thought she was stupid and useless, why did he want her? Why the manipulation? She would've stayed forever if he had treated her right.

Sarah remembered the disgusted look on Mark's face when she told him about Kevin and about the baby. His questions, how hard he'd tried to understand her self-blame. One question stood out in her memory, and at the time, it didn't make sense. Now she couldn't get it out of her head.

Kevin didn't want me. He wanted money—he wanted to control her money. That's why he was so furious with her for postponing the wedding date. Why he felt the need to break her down and destroy her spirit. He'd wanted her submissive, to strip away her confidence so she believed she'd never survive without him or have the strength to leave him.

Sarah stopped running and leaned over to throw up. Her lungs burned, she tried to catch her breath as she braced her hands on her knees.

Kevin had come so close to getting what he wanted. She'd eaten everything he'd fed her, believing she was the problem. The memories of him sickened her. She had been a naive child and blamed herself for years and for what, for nothing.

Losing her child had been the catalyst for saving her life. And much as it hurt, she'd survived, but what had she done with her second chance? Squandered away the best thing that had ever happened to her. Look how she'd treated Mark when all he'd done wrong was love her.

When she could breathe normally, she pushed the wet curls off her face and ran to the dock, crouching to get out of the rain. From the corner of her eye, she saw someone coming toward her. Her heart began pounding faster. She spun to head back toward the house but tripped over a piece of driftwood. Sand stuck to her wet body and face. The jolt sent a stab of pain through her arms when she tried to catch herself.

Ignoring the pain in her shoulder, she jumped up and dug her heels in to run, but he grabbed her from behind. She cried out and fought against him but stopped abruptly when she heard his voice.

"Sarah! It's okay. I'm not going to hurt you."

She pushed off him with her elbows and spun to face him. She squinted in the dark, trying to focus on his face.

"It's Shane. Are you all right?"

"Shane?" She couldn't remember how or where she knew him from.

"Shane Fields. I work for Mark Summors. Did you hurt yourself?"

She leaned forward, relief flooding her senses. "You scared the crap out of me. What are you doing here?"

"Did you hurt yourself?"

"No..." She winced and tried to get the sand off her face. "I'm fine, what are you doing here?"

"Let me help you back. Do you need to go to the hospital?"

"What are you doing here?" she shrieked, taking a step back. "Did Mark send you here?"

"Let me take you back and we can talk."

"I'm not going anywhere with you until you tell me why you're here."

Shane bowed his head and shook it, and then leveled his dark eyes on her. "Mark sent me to make sure you're okay."

Anger and elation surged through Sarah at the same time. If Mark sent someone to check on her, that meant he still cared. "Why didn't he come? How did you get here so fast?"

"What?"

"I just talked to him a couple of hours ago." She stopped and thought about it. "How long have you been in town?"

"I've been following you since Portland. You shouldn't be out here at night."

"Whoa, wait a minute. You've been watching me?" That must be why Mark stopped calling—he'd had eyes on her since she got to the beach. She started laughing—laughing like a crazy person.

"Oh my God!" She paced in circles, laughing a little crazier with each pass. Mark followed her. This whole time she was under surveillance. How did he know where to look? She pulled the phone out of her pocket and stared at it. Of course...stupid woman, she should've known Mark would find her.

"He cares about you. Do you realize what kind of hell you've put him through?" Words like that sounded a little funny coming from such a big man. How sweet of him to be concerned for his boss's feelings. She never would have expected something like that from someone who got paid to be a bodyguard.

She stopped pacing and looked at him. "Oh, I know—he let me have it on the phone today. Let me know exactly what I'd done." She chuckled again and felt lighter than she had in months. She felt like she could actually run that marathon now. "I gotta go."

"What? No." He reached for her as she turned away. "Let me take you back."

She stopped suddenly and spun to look at him. "That's a great idea. Take me back."

Chapter Twenty-Eight

Within twenty-four hours, Sarah was staring at Mark's front door, shaking with nervous energy. The house was pitch black and for a fleeting moment, she almost chickened out.

When they arrived, she asked Shane to stand in the shadows. He'd kindly escorted her back to Santa Rosa without any argument. She was worried that her stunt might jeopardize his job, but he insisted he wasn't worried and said he'd kept her safe and that's all Mark cared about.

She pushed back the nerves. She didn't know how Mark would feel about her being there, especially in the middle of the night without any warning. He'd made it pretty clear that he was done with her when they spoke on the phone. But that was before she realized she loved him. Now, she was the one unwilling to give up—she was the one asking for a chance with him.

Ringing the doorbell, she felt a flutter of butterflies in her stomach. He was at the door at a surprising rate considering he should have been in bed. When he thrust the door open, tears instantly watered her eyes.

Sarah cleared her throat and fought for a smile. "Hi."

He swayed a bit in surprise. "What are you doing?"

Ouch, she deserved that, but it still hurt. "It's nice to see you too."

Mark glanced around her, his eyes stopping on her suitcase, and then on Shane. "What the fuck, Shane?"

"Talk to your lady. She's here, she's safe—now it's on you."

Oh God, she needed to throw up. Mark didn't want her here. She shouldn't have come. Mark stepped outside and she could smell alcohol. "I don't understand what's going on."

She blinked heavily and fought the heat of embarrassment that flushed her face. "I ugh...came to apologize to you."

He stared at her and she didn't know what to do next.

"Shane was kind enough to bring me back...sorry. I guess I shouldn't have come. You're clearly not interested." She turned to leave, but he caught her arm.

"Sarah, why did you come here?"

"I told you..." She bowed her head and closed her eyes. "It's okay, I'll leave you alone."

"That's it? You came to apologize and now you're leaving?" His words were slurred, and she felt bad for being the reason he was drowning his sorrows.

"No, I came here to tell you that I am sorry, and that I want to be with you. Since you don't want to invite me in, I'll assume I'm too late."

"Stop fucking around with my feelings. You come here hat in hand and say you want to be with me, but what happens the next time you have to face something difficult?"

She reached over and grabbed her suitcase, throwing it down at his feet. "There's another one in the trunk. Does that prove anything to you? This *is* difficult for me, Mark, I am—*right now*—facing one of the most difficult moments in my life, and I'm handling it—not running. I'm fucking trying here. Will you give me a chance?"

She took in a deep, sobbing breath. Her heart ached like nothing she'd ever felt before. Now, standing in front of him, she knew just how much she loved him and how much losing him would hurt her. "I told you, I don't know how to do this." Her eyes darted around searching for the words she needed to make him understand. When the words wouldn't come, her heart sank.

"Forget it...I guess this was a mistake."

She took the handle of the suitcase and turned to leave. Mark reached out and grabbed her arm again. She raised her free hand to cover her face as her chest heaved in an effort to hold in her tears.

"I don't want you to leave." He tugged on her arm. When she turned, he nodded toward the house. "Come inside, I'll get your bags." Mark gently pulled her hand from her face. "It's okay, come in and we'll talk."

Sarah nodded and stepped inside but abruptly stopped. What a complete pigsty. Her mouth dropped open at the sight of his beautiful house in complete disarray. She stepped forward carefully and looked toward the glow coming from the stove in the kitchen It was the only light on in the house, but it was enough to see the mess. She felt sick and placed a hand over her stomach. At the end of the bar was a half-empty bottle of scotch and a small glass.

"I'm so sorry."

Mark stepped in and looked at her shocked face. "I wasn't exactly expecting company."

Sarah's stomach rolled again and she rushed to the bathroom.

When she rested back on her heels, Mark came through the door, his face stark white. "It's not that bad in here."

She waved him off. "I'm not sick because of the house."

He helped her up and gave her a clean wet wash cloth. It reminded her of the night she had that awful nightmare about Kevin. Mark was so gentle with her, caring, and thoughtful. She wanted that back. She wanted him back...she wanted things to be like they were.

"I'm sorry—I am a coward—I panicked. I feel like every time things get really good, then something else happens."

Mark's expression was surprised. He looked as if he was taken aback by the outburst. He turned and left the bathroom and went to the bar to get a drink.

"Do you want me to leave?"

"No," he mumbled. "I didn't want you to leave the first time."

"I know. I'm stupid, childish. I freaked out and ran, but I never stopped thinking about you." She waited for him to finish pouring his drink. "I've never had these feelings before...I'm trying to accept us without the old prejudices sneaking in, but then I start doubting everything." She rubbed her face and pushed her bangs back, her heart aching at the distance and the pain she felt from him. "I don't know how to be part of a couple."

He slammed the glass down on the bar. "What feelings? You haven't shared any feelings with me. I shared mine and you took off."

"I love you." Her eyes widened at the relief she felt just saying those words to him aloud. "I love you."

He shook his head slightly as if he didn't understand. "What did you just say?"

"I love you...and I'm sorry it took losing you to figure that out."

His anger deflated. "Did you say you love me?"

She nodded and tears dripped from her eyes.

He put a hand to his chest. "Are you sure, because my fucking heart can't take this."

"It's the only thing I'm sure of. I love you, and I'm so sorry I hurt you."

He stepped to her and she launched herself into his arms. He held her tight, tighter than she could take. She had to pull away to breathe, and when she placed her hands on his face, she felt the wetness on his cheeks too. "I'm sorry."

Mark's lips found hers, and he lifted her off her feet and took her upstairs.

Mark wanted to throw the phone across the room when it woke him up. If he didn't have a kid to worry about, he would. He looked at the caller ID and realized it wasn't his kid, or his ex.

"Why are you waking me up so early?"

"We need to talk."

"I hope so, Brian, otherwise I'm kicking your ass for waking me up."

"Do you feel secure with Shane? Can he handle things with his injury?"

"What exactly do you mean by *things*?"

"If our rapist finds Jennings, can Shane handle it?"

"It's a moot point. She's here with me." Mark got up and carried the phone into his office to avoid waking Sarah up. "What's going on?"

"Our guy is getting a little desperate and we both know what happens when sociopaths get desperate."

Every muscle in Mark's body tensed. "What the fuck?"

"That last letter...the one he left in your mailbox..."

"Yeah..."

"'There will be more blood spilt if I don't taste Sweet, Sweet Sarah soon.'" Brian recited the words, then said, "Yeah, a real poet this one...she needs to be in protective custody."

"Shane and I have her covered."

"You can't cover her. Get another guy."

"It's fine, Bri."

"Yeah, fine huh? What happened the night you two were out at that club? You've got your head in the clouds and you know it."

Mark knew Brian was right. He still fought the guilt that occasionally crept up on him for letting that bastard get to her in that damn club. "Fine, I'll take care of it."

"Smart move. I'll push for more patrols in the area too. Make sure you call us if you get something on this guy."

"I know, 'don't be a hero,'" Mark mocked. "We'll call you if he shows his face." Mark closed his phone and called Shane.

Pulling on Mark's robe, Sarah hobbled her way downstairs and turned into the great room. She stopped at the strange man standing in her path. "Ah, hi..."

He turned and held up his coffee mug in greeting. "Mornin'."

Sarah continued to stare at him, trying to figure out what she'd missed. Her brain frantically shifted through the last twenty-four hours, searching for a memory of this person, and how he ended up in Mark's house. She squinted as she thought about it and realized she should be afraid of him. He was a hulking man, at least six feet five and almost six feet wide.

"Hey, babe."

She turned toward Mark's voice.

He was standing in the kitchen holding out a mug of coffee. "Good morning."

Sarah looked from him, back to the man in front of her, then back to Mark.

"That's Randy. He's here to keep an eye on things."

"Things...like?"

"Come have coffee and I'll explain."

She padded around Randy and reached for the mug Mark extended out to her. She sniffed, and her stomach instantly turned upside down. With her hand over her mouth, she rushed to the bathroom.

When she finished retching, she dropped the toilet lid and sat down, waiting for the nausea to pass. Mark knocked and came into the bathroom.

"Do you have the flu?" He touched her forehead. "You don't have a fever."

"It's stress."

"Since when does a cup of coffee stress you out?"

She reached up and laid a hand over his on her forehead, enjoying the feel of the skin-on-skin contact.

"It's everything...traveling, dealing with my mother for an extended period of time."

"I'm taking you to the doctor."

"No...no, I'm fine. Tell me about Randy." She hoped changing the subject would make him forget about the doctor.

"Randy is going to hang out with us, just to keep an eye on things."

Her eyes grew wide, and she twisted to lift herself up off the floor. "You didn't fire Shane, did you?"

He chuckled. "No, Shane will be back tonight. Randy will be here during the day."

"You can't do days?" she said, leaving the bathroom to return to the kitchen.

"Nope. I'm on boyfriend duty. I can't do both."

Randy caught her eye, and she couldn't stop staring at him. He was unnaturally huge, like one of the body builders at the gym, only scarier and considerably taller.

"Don't worry, he doesn't bite."

When she didn't turn away, he said, "Do you want to try eating something?"

"Um...yeah," she said, finally looking over at Mark as she climbed onto a barstool. Their eyes met, and she had to push back the self-consciousness she felt at being there. He'd forgiven her, but that didn't erase the hurt he still must have felt.

"Are you going to be okay with having a tag-a-long?"

"I'll deal with it." She cleared her throat and lowered her eyes. "I'm sorry, I'm so sorry about what I did. I know you're going to be a little gun-shy around me now, but I will do whatever I have to in order for you to trust me again."

She heard the front door close and turned. Randy was gone.

"He stepped out to look around. Are you sure you can handle having people around?"

"I can handle it," she whispered.

Mark picked up her hand and held it to his cheek. "Stop feeling bad. It's okay. I'm just glad you're here and safe."

"Me too." She took a sip of her coffee and said, "Where's Jamie?"

Mark lowered his eyes and mumbled, "He's with Ali." When he looked back up, she caught the unsettled expression on his face. "Some things have changed since you left."

"Some things?"

"I received a note from the attacker in my mailbox."

Sarah placed a hand to her chest and held her breath for a split second. "And now you can't have Jamie over here."

"Don't!" He held a finger up to her. "It's not your fault."

"Oh my God, Mark. I'm so sorry I've put you and your family in the middle of my mess."

"What? Come on, Sarah." He slammed his mug down. "You're a part of my family now. We're in this together, dammit. Don't tell me you love me then treat this like casual sex."

Her pulse spiked at his outburst, but she deserved his anger for what she'd done. She'd spend a lifetime making it up to him if that's what she needed to do. "I'm sorry. You're right, thank you for saying that." She reached out for his hand. "I do love you."

ജ്

After three weeks of having Shane and Randy tailing her, Sarah couldn't help but feel annoyed as she waited for Randy to come out of her bathroom. Mark watched her pace, but she refused to complain. She had no idea how much Mark was paying these guys to protect her so she *would not* complain, not after everything he'd done for her.

"Maybe we should go back to my house. It's bigger and has two bathrooms."

"Maybe," she said, tightening the tie on her robe. "I have my doctor's appointment today. Are you going with me?"

"That's today?" His eyes shadowed. "I made plans for us to go over to Ali's to see Jamie."

"Oh, Mark, I don't want to miss that. I'll reschedule the appointment."

"No. You need to go. Baby, you should have seen the doctor weeks ago. I'll call Ali and see if I can do it tomorrow."

Sarah shook her head. "No, you haven't spent any quality time with him in weeks. You go see him. I can go to my appointment alone."

"Are you sure?"

"Yeah...well, I'll have Randy with me. He'll keep me company." She smiled at the look on his face. She liked to see that little hint of jealousy he got when she was friendly with his guys.

"Ha, ha! Very funny." He pulled her close and nibbled on her ear. "I'll miss you today. Hey, have Randy bring you by Ali's after the appointment, and then you can see Jamie for a little bit."

"Okay. I'll see you after."

When the bathroom door opened, Mark looked up to glare at Randy.

"Sorry," Randy said, sneaking back into the living room.

Chapter Twenty-Nine

"Good afternoon, Sarah," Dr. Davidson said, peering over his reading glasses to look at her. "I'm sorry to hear you've been sick. I was hoping things would start getting easier for you."

"I think it's from stress, but Mark insisted I come in."

"He's right. You should have come in a couple of weeks ago. You've been vomiting and what else?" He pulled his stool closer and sat down.

"I'm really tired all the time, and I've had some headaches."

"And the vomiting, how often?" he asked.

"Almost every day. I tend to be sick when I'm nervous or stressed."

"Sarah, that can't be from stress alone." He looked her over. "How often do you have headaches?"

"A couple times a week."

He jotted some notes down on his notepad. "When was the first day of your last menstrual cycle?"

She blew her bangs off her forehead and looked up at the ceiling. "Um, I don't know. Do you have a calendar?"

"How about an educated guess."

"Late September?" She smiled nervously at his expression.

"You haven't had a period in over two months?"

"My periods have always been irregular. I don't usually go that long, but I'm sure that's due to stress too. There's been a lot going on."

"Yeah, stress can do funny things to your body. Your period would regulate if you took my advice and started a birth control regimen. Have you been sexually active?"

"Yes."

"Could you be pregnant?"

"No." Her stomach did a little flutter. "I can't be pregnant."

"I know you've been told you couldn't, but I can run some tests." He put his notepad down and slipped off his reading glasses. "Do an ultrasound, take a good look at your uterus if you wanted to be sure."

"No, I don't—no." She shook her head. "I'm sure it's a virus or something like that. I'm not pregnant."

"You may be anemic, that could cause you to be tired, but not the vomiting. Although, considering you haven't had a period, you shouldn't be anemic. We'll check your thyroid and hormone levels too."

"Have you noticed any particular types of food that make you sick?"

"No, sometimes I wake up sick."

"Really? And you don't think it's possible for you to be pregnant."

"No, I'm not pregnant. I am absolutely not pregnant," she repeated, pounding her knee lightly with her fist in hopes to pound out her nervous energy.

"Okay. I want you to start a food journal so we can trace it and pinpoint what might be causing it. Also, keep saltine crackers next to your bed and nibble on a couple before you get up. That tends to help with the nausea."

"Okay, that sounds easy enough. Do you think I can go back to work now?"

He chuckled. "No, we already agreed. I'm not going to release you until after the first of the year."

"I'm fine though. I'm working out with Mark. He's teaching me self-defense and I'm back to running. I don't understand why I can't work."

"Sarah, the kids are going to be out on holiday vacation in a week anyway. Why don't you just enjoy your time off?"

"I'm restless. I've been cooped up for months."

"It's just a few more weeks. In the meantime, I'm sending you home with anti-nausea pills, and I want you to take care of yourself. Don't stop eating to avoid being sick. Start taking some vitamins to help boost your energy."

"I can do that," she said.

He gave her a long look. "I'm doing a pregnancy test just in case."

"Okay, but you're wasting your time."

Dr. Davidson smiled at her. "We shall see." He stood and reached for the door handle. "Don't forget to visit the lab before leaving."

༄༅

When Sarah got in the truck with Randy, she rested her head back and closed her eyes. *Pregnant,* she thought, *gimme a break—please.*

"You okay?" Randy asked.

"Yeah, fine." She thought of Ali's huge belly and for the first time in years, she felt envious. *Get over it, Sarah. Shake it off and get over it.* "Mark wants us to meet him at Ali's house. Will you drive me there please?"

"You got it."

When Sarah knocked, she didn't get an answer. She reached to knock again but jumped when the door was thrown open.

"Hello? Oh well, hello there." His eyes widened and he looked her up and down with a grin that made Sarah's skin crawl. At least the pervert had managed to suppress the whistle that went along with his expression.

"Hi, I'm Sarah. I'm here to see Jamie."

"Oh, right. You must be Mark's new girlfriend. I've heard about you." He leaned against the doorframe and stuck his hand in his pocket, staring at her like the cat that ate the mouse.

He was older than her, though not much taller, and a little thick around the middle. Sarah had to wonder if this was Carl. God help Ali if he was. This man couldn't compete with Mark in his wildest dreams.

Her pulse spiked when he looked her up and down again.

"I'm sorry, but who are you?"

He held out his hand for her to shake. "I'm Carl Hayes, Jamie's step-dad."

Not Ali's husband but Jamie's step-dad. Hmm. She ignored his hand. "Is Jamie here, I believe he and Mark are expecting me."

He tilted his head over his shoulder. "They took off a little while ago."

"Is Ali home?"

"No, she stepped out. Would you like to come in?" He held the door wide.

Sarah glanced around the large foyer, and then she shook her head. "No, I can wait here."

"I can get you a glass of wine, maybe a beer. You don't want to have a drink with me..."

"No, thanks," Randy said, stepping up on the porch behind her. "The lady is just looking for Mark. Where is it that you said they went?"

Sarah smiled her biggest most sarcastic smile. "This is Randy. Randy, this is Carl."

Carl's mouth froze half-open, and Sarah thought for a moment that he might have peed himself. "He, ah...they went to the park around the corner."

"Great," Sarah said. "Thanks. We'll go catch up with him there." She turned on her heel and walked away, wondering what in the hell Ali was thinking when she hooked up with that pig.

When she climbed into the truck with Randy, she tried to push away the uneasiness she felt after meeting Carl.

"You okay?" Randy asked.

She nodded and looked over at him. "Thank you."

"Next time, I pound his face in."

She smiled. "Next time *I'll* pound his face in." Her smile dropped. "Please don't tell Mark. I don't want him to have to worry about this on top of everything else."

Randy gave her a long look. "I won't mention it unless he does it again."

"That's good enough for me. Thank you."

ജ്ഞ

The next morning Sarah woke to her front door closing hard. She jerked awake and then got up to see what was going on. Before she got her robe on, Mark came around the corner with a big grin on his face.

"Who's here?"

"No one." Mark reached out to cup her neck, pulling her close. He kissed her with more force than she was expecting.

She pushed him away. "We're not doing that with Randy in the next room."

"I sent him home. It's just you and me," Mark said, taking her mouth with his again.

She smiled into the kiss. "We're alone?"

"Yeah, I thought we could all use a break."

"What about—"

"I think I can handle your security for one day, don't you?" Mark lifted his eyebrows and said, "Besides, I don't plan on leaving the bed, much less the house."

He kissed her hard and then withdrew quickly, taking her by surprise.

"There is something I've wanted to do with you since the first—second time I saw you, maybe now you can oblige me."

"You want to take a shower with me?"

His eyes grew wide. "How did you know that?"

"I've got you all figured out, cowboy."

"I'll be right back."

He rushed to the bathroom and came back a minute later, lifting her nightgown up and over her head.

Before she was ready, he swept her off her feet. She shrieked and grabbed hold as he carried her into the bathroom and stepped into the shower. When he released her, she slid down his body. The hot water was another shock to her system, running in sheets down her back and saturating her hair.

Mark's lips sought hers, and then traveled across her jaw in a trail of soft kisses. His blue eyes filled with passion as he cupped her breasts. He explored, pinching her nipples and letting his palms glide across her wet skin. His hand slipped between her legs, parting her, entering her, and massaging her. Before she realized what he was doing, she was pressing against him, moving with his touch as heat radiated from her core and traveled outward through her body until it reached her fingers and toes.

She held onto Mark's arms, afraid her legs would give out. He drove her closer, stopping just before and pulling away. When she moaned in protest, he hoisted her up by the hips in one fluid motion. She couldn't react, taken aback when he was suddenly hard inside her, stroking slowly, letting the water flow between them. It'd been weeks since they'd made love, and now they were making up for lost time.

Sarah made fists in his hair and locked eyes with him. His gaze held hers, the desire in his stare mesmerizing. She felt a stir in her soul like nothing she'd ever felt before and a connection so strong it consumed her. She couldn't look away, and with every stroke he drove her higher.

Unable to hold back, she arched and dropped her head, leaning against the shower wall, wanting to feel him fully. Mark drove faster, harder. She couldn't hold on, couldn't wait for him. Her climax rushed through her with an ache so sweet she didn't want it to end. Within seconds, Mark was crying out too.

He leaned forward, resting on the wall as Sarah collapsed on his shoulder, trembling, and breathing in spurts, wanting to cry from the pleasure. She clung to him, not sure she could hold herself up if he let her down.

He held on and whispered in her ear. "I love you, Sarah."

Chapter Thirty

Mark pounded the keyboard and switched camera views again. When he heard a noise, he peered around the corner and listened for Sarah's footsteps.

They were both exhausted after a day of lovemaking. She was still sleeping, but his mind wouldn't slow down long enough for him to enjoy the afterglow. He turned back and glanced at the pictures sitting on Sarah's desk. When he glimpsed one with her and Devon, he picked it up. Her smile so bright she almost looked like a different person. He wanted that smile on her lips every day, dammit.

"Fuck! C'mon, bastard." He cursed to the empty room. *She can't live like this forever—we can't live with Randy and Shane shadowing our every move forever.* He switched camera angles again and then looked up at the clock and out at the darkening sky. Shane would be there any minute to cover the evening shift. At least he and Sarah had been able to spend the day together without an audience.

He stood to go watch for Shane, but before he turned, something on the screen caught his eye.

With a racing pulse, he stared at the dark figure as it skirted the driveway, with Shane lurking fifteen feet behind him.

Mark rushed out the backdoor and inched around the house toward the front drive. He peered around the corner and saw a man, ski mask covering his face. One hand held an envelope, and the other a small gun. As he reached out for the handle of the mailbox, Shane inched silently closer.

Got him, yes! Mark could hardly contain the adrenalin racing through his veins.

After the letter had been placed in the box, Shane shouted, "Don't move, scumbag!"

Mark's eyes jetted back and forth between guns as fire blasts erupted from each pistol in the darkness. He couldn't tell if either hit their intended targets. He reached for his own gun and then cursed. He'd left it next to the bed.

When he didn't hear more threats from Shane, he felt a gripping fear in his chest. *God dammit, Shane, where are you?*

The masked man turned and ran back down the driveway. Mark took off after him and jumped him from behind. They both fell to the ground as the gun went flying. The man rolled over with Mark clinging to his back. He rammed his elbow into Mark's ribs numerous times while Mark held him in a headlock.

After struggling for several minutes, Mark felt a cold blade slice through his shirt sleeve and the warm gush of blood as it spread down his forearm. He jerked away to avoid the second swipe. When the attacker scrambled to his feet, he reached out and slashed at Mark's chest, missing him.

Both men turned when Sarah yelled, "Stop!"

She stood in the middle of the driveway, pointing Mark's gun at the masked man with a steady hand. He scrambled to his feet and took off running down the street.

Mark ran to Sarah and snatched the gun out of her hand. "Call 911 and Brian!"

"I already did, they're on their way."

"Get back in the house and lock the door—now!"

Mark sprinted down the driveway and he could hear the sirens approaching. As he turned onto the street, an engine came to life.

He pointed and shot, emptying the gun into the windshield of the car as it barreled toward him.

ꙮ

She sat there, scared out of her mind all night, but when Mark started to finally stir, her heart raced with relief. He reached for her but didn't seem to have the strength to lift his hand up enough. She laced her fingers with his. "Mark... honey, look at me."

"Sarah...Where am I?"

"You're in the hospital." She fought to put a smile on her face. He slowly lifted his lids and met her eyes. His were both black and bloodshot.

"Mr. Summors, how do you feel?" the nurse asked.

Mark lifted his head. "What happened?"

"You're very lucky. Only a concussion, no broken bones. You're going to be sore for several days."

He reached up to touch the bandage over his left temple. "I don't feel very lucky."

"Ten stitches and you'll have a scar, but it should be fine."

Mark jerked up quickly. "Shane?" His face paled even further, and he slowly drifted back down on his pillow. "Shit—what happened to Shane?"

"Relax. He was shot in the shoulder. He'll be fine though."

"Oh God. I have to call his—"

Sarah squeezed his hand. "Seth made all the calls. Shane's girlfriend is with him. He's alert and feeling fine, although he's a little worried about you."

"Where's my phone?" Mark looked around. "Give me a phone. I need to call Brian."

"Brian's out in the hall. He's been here all night."

When Mark started to get out of bed, the nurse stopped him. "Stay put, Mr. Summors, you're not ready to stand yet."

"I need to talk to Brian."

"Fine," Sarah said. "I'll get him if you stay still. She stepped out and saw Brian with his back to the door, jabbering on his phone a mile a minute. She touched his shoulder and he quickly turned. "He's awake."

He nodded. "He's awake, Jules, I gotta go." Then he closed his phone and followed Sarah into the room, wearing a huge smile.

"You got him, bro!"

Mark put his hand over his face, and his head dropped back down to his pillow.

"The uniforms showed up just in time to see you roll over the guy's windshield. What the hell were you thinking?"

Mark shook his head and looked over at Sarah. "I was thinking about killing the bastard." He slowly sat up. "Did I?"

"Yeah."

Mark stiffened. "He's dead?"

Brian nodded. "Yes, he's dead. We need you two to come down and make a statement. I don't want this murderer to become a victim. We need to start on the self-defense case ASAP."

When Brian's cell phone rang, he held up one finger and left the room.

Mark looked at Sarah and waved imperiously for her. "Come here, baby."

She laid her head on his chest. "I'm so glad you're okay. I was so scared when I saw that car plow into you."

"It's over, it's finally over." He kissed the top of her head and engulfed her in his arms.

When the door was thrown open, they both turned.

"We have a problem," Brian said, carrying a newspaper in one hand and his phone in another. He held up the paper, showing the bold front page headline.

Sarah's Grandmother's name stood out in huge, bold print. Under it was a picture of herself and the headline.

CONNELLY-PERRY HEIRESS RAPED?

Her breath came out in spurts as she snatched the paper from Brian's hand. A second later he was shouting into the phone about a leak, investigations, and wrong information. Sarah couldn't follow his words because her pulse was pounding in her head, filling her ears with a loud buzz. She scanned the first few lines.

> *Sarah Jean Jennings, granddaughter of deceased San Francisco socialite Catherine Connelly-Perry and philanthropist Richard Q. Perry II, was one of the victims of the serial rapist Rupert Maylyn…*

"Oh my God." She whipped her head around to meet Mark's wide eyes.

He held up a finger. "I know what you're thinking. Don't!"

She clutched her now turning stomach. "I have to..."

"No, you don't. We'll work it out."

"Work what out? You can't protect me from this. This won't blow over for a long time. Reporters are like cockroaches, they multiply uncontrollably and they can't be killed."

"Stop and think about this."

She covered her face in her hands, an overwhelming sense of loss forming a pit in her stomach. There was no way around this. "I have to leave, Mark."

"No, you don't! You promised me, Sarah. You promised you wouldn't do this again."

Her cell phone rang and she pulled it out.

"Give it to me," Mark said, reaching for the phone. He accepted the call on speaker and waved for Sarah to answer.

"Hello," she said.

"Ms. Jennings?"

"Yes. Who's calling?"

"This is Jasper Lovelund from KTVU news. We'd like your permission to report your information in our Santa Rosa Serial Rapist story. May we schedule an interview with you—"

Mark closed the phone and pulled the battery. "Dammit. How did they find out?"

"I haven't figured out how they got your name." Brian sighed and stuffed his phone in his pocket. "They don't usually use names, but they're not likely to hold off when the Perry name is involved. It only takes one sleazy paparazzo to start." He looked over at Sarah. "I wish you would've told me."

"I thought the less people who knew, the safer."

He bowed his head and said, "Is there any possible way someone in your family leaked this information? I would hate to think someone in my department would give out a victim's name."

"It's doesn't matter now, it's out there, everyone knows." Sarah couldn't fight the trembling in her hands. Her quiet life, her privacy, her anonymity were all gone. She badly wanted to retreat, to run like hell and get out of town.

She looked Mark up and down and her heart sank. He needed her, he had never left her side when she was injured, and here she was planning her way out. He'd nailed her on it too. He told her she'd want to leave again at the first signs of trouble, and he was right. She bit her lip and thought about the consequences of staying...her mind couldn't grasp anything beyond losing Mark. She couldn't—wouldn't lose him again.

"Only locally, Sarah. This is a Santa Rosa paper," Brian said.

With her hand on her stomach, she nodded and said, "I know, but it's just a matter of time before it gets out further."

"Let me try to put a lid on it. Most journalists won't report a victim's name unless they have a release form."

"I know...but most victims don't come from a Connelly or a Perry." She met Mark's eyes. "We'll work it out. I'm not leaving."

Mark's expression relaxed and he closed his eyes. He looked utterly exhausted. "Brian, do you think you could give us a ride to

Mark's house. I rode with him in the ambulance and...well, I want to get him home to rest."

Brian lips moved into quirky smile. "Yeah, I'll pull the car around."

"Thanks."

When he was out of the room, Mark reached for her and pulled her close. "We'll deal with this together, okay?"

"I love you and I am *not* leaving you." She meant it too, even if staying meant losing a part of herself to the rest of the world. "I'm going home with you and taking care of you."

Chapter Thirty-One

"It's part of the game. You've been through this before—fucking red tape," Brian said, facing down Mark at his angriest.

"We're victims here, we shouldn't...especially Sarah. She shouldn't have to continually face this questioning. We've spent more afternoons in the DA's office over the last two weeks than I care to count."

"I agree, but Maylyn's family is putting the pressure on the District Attorney, he's up for reelection."

"Rupert Maylyn was a serial rapist! Fuck him and his family."

Sarah laid a hand on Mark's shoulder, hoping the contact would help him calm down a little bit.

He sat back and rolled his neck, fighting against the tension. "I'm sorry. I just don't think she should have to face this again."

"It's not that big a deal," she said.

"It is a big deal." Mark stood and paced the room. "We're getting a lawyer. Maybe even file our own suit against the DA."

That made Brian smile. "Good. I hope you nail the bastard's ass. I'm sick of him shredding my cases and not fighting harder to get the right convictions."

"We'll never get the press off our lawn if they don't conclude their investigation."

"At least they stopped printing Sarah's name," Brian said.

When Sarah's cell phone rang, she looked at the caller ID and then excused herself.

"Hello," she answered, leaving the family room and turning into the kitchen.

"Sarah?"

"Yes, Dr. Davidson, is something wrong?"

"You missed your follow-up appointment on Friday."

"Yeah, sorry, I've had several meetings with the District Attorney and the police department. I rescheduled for next week."

"I didn't want to wait that long to give you the test results."

"Is something wrong?" she asked again, looking around to make sure she wasn't being overheard.

"That depends on how you feel about it."

"Excuse me?" she asked, ducking her chin to her chest trying to mask the conversation from Mark and Brian.

"You're pregnant, Sarah."

"What?" She jerked upright and spoke much louder than she intended. "What did you say?" she whispered this time.

"You are pregnant." When she didn't respond, he said, "I'm sorry to give you this news over the phone. I thought you would be happy." He sighed heavily. "I wasn't expecting to have the *alternative* conversation with you."

"Ah, I'm not sure...no, of course...if I am pregnant...I want the baby. If that's what you're asking." She tiptoed into the dining room to get more distance from the family room.

"You are pregnant, I have no doubt. I want to schedule an ultrasound ASAP so we can determine your due date and check the overall health of the baby."

Sarah heard him talking, although she couldn't take in all his words. When her stomach fluttered, she moved her hand down in an attempt to rub away the sickness. If only it was possible, but she knew it wasn't.

Her eyes fluttered down to her hand and hoped sparked, and the words *what if* echoed in her head. She took several deep breaths and swallowed hard to hold back her tears.

"Are you sure?"

"You have one good ovary, and when we do the ultrasound, we'll be able to see what condition your uterus is in." He sighed. "I think we can already label it high risk, but if you're careful and take good care of yourself, everything should be fine."

"Will you do another test please?"

"My medical assistant, Jenny, will call with the ultrasound appointment. If this is a mistake, we'll know after that."

"I would rather get it over with sooner than later. I have an appointment with my boss tomorrow for lunch. Can we set it up for the afternoon?"

"What time?"

"Around one?"

"I'm sure that's fine. If that time isn't available, I'll have her give you a call. You should consider bringing the father with you. He might enjoy seeing the ultrasound too."

She smiled, wiping at the stray tear that fell from her eyes. "Thank you for taking the time to call me."

"Take care of yourself, Sarah. Please don't do anything risky in an attempt to deny this."

"Okay," she said as Mark's hand slip around her waist from behind. "Thank you."

"Goodbye, Sarah."

She closed her phone and turned to Mark.

"What's wrong, baby?" Mark asked.

The word baby repeated in her head, and she bit her lip at the lie she was about to tell him. "That was the doctor. He wanted to know why I missed my follow-up."

"Is something wrong? Did your tests come back?"

"I'm anemic. I'll pick up some iron supplements when I meet with Nancy tomorrow."

"Anemic? That wouldn't make you sick." He looked at her closer. "Why are you crying?"

"I'm not." She smiled, trying to put him at ease. "Anemia causes fatigue."

Mark's eyebrows drew together. "Fatigue, but not vomiting. Did he reschedule the follow-up?"

"Yes, next week."

"I'm going with you this time. I want to talk to him."

"Okay," she said, smiling again.

When Mark went back to the family room, Sarah snuck upstairs to have a few minutes alone. She stood in front of the mirror and looked at herself.

"This is a cruel joke," she whispered. "*Dammit...*" Why couldn't this be happening? Why couldn't life be this simple? Why couldn't she tell Mark the good news?

Because life doesn't work out like that for you, Sarah.

She put one hand over her mouth, struck suddenly with a wave of nausea, and then ran into the bathroom.

"Sarah." Mark startled her when he said her name. She didn't realize he'd come upstairs. "What else did the doctor tell you?"

"I told you," she said, looking at him through the bathroom mirror as she finished brushing her teeth. "There isn't anything else."

When she finished washing her face, she turned to leave the room.

Mark grabbed her arm and turned her around. "I'm scared, you're worrying me."

"Don't you think if there were something to worry about, I would tell you?" She shrugged out of his grip and walked away from him and then stopped, turned and walked back.

"I'm sorry." She rubbed her forehead, staring at the floor. Lying to Mark about this was cruel, but what if the doctor was wrong? Getting his hopes up for nothing would be worse. "I'm just tired and grumpy."

"Lie down, take a nap." He brushed his fingers across her cheekbone. "I'll come wake you up in a little while."

She walked to the bed and lay down, letting Mark toss a throw blanket over her.

He kissed her cheek and muttered, "Get some rest."

Then he left her alone in the room.

God, what if she were pregnant? Admitting she wanted a baby meant living with the disappointment of losing a baby. *What if I am pregnant?* She thought again, and her hands moved to her stomach. She actually felt bigger. Her defined abs felt softer, but she could attribute that to her lack of exercise. She'd spent the last several weeks stuck in the house avoiding the press.

What about Mark? And another *what if* echoed in her head...what if he wasn't ready to be a father again?

He'd talked about more kids...he'd also said he was happy just having Jamie. All these questions swam in her head as she caressed her stomach, the memories of her last pregnancy still fresh. Last time, as her stomach had grown, so did her excitement. Until she'd had to give birth to a lifeless baby.

What if that happened again?

She suddenly felt so vulnerable—almost breakable. She shook the thoughts from her head and closed her eyes.

ೞ

When Mark shook her awake, she jerked up. "Sarah, wake up."

"What's wrong," she slurred, still half asleep.

"Carl called, Ali's having her baby." His eyes were bright with excitement. "I have to go pick up Jamie at the hospital."

"That's great," Sarah said. "Are you bringing Jamie back here?"

"Yeah, well, we are," he said, his smile fading. "You'll go with me, right?"

"No, Mark..." Sarah didn't know how to verbalize her excuse for not going. She stared at him, hoping he would understand without an explanation.

"Jamie's going to be a big brother." His eyes looked right through her, as if he had no idea what she was feeling, all he could think about was being with Jamie and the excitement of a new baby.

"Okay...of course I'll go," she said, trying to get her bearings.

When they arrived at the hospital, they found Carl in the waiting room with Jamie.

"Daddy," Jamie said, running at Mark.

"Hey, buddy. What's going on?"

Jamie jumped up and down. "Mommy is having a baby."

"I know. That's why I'm here to pick you up."

He stopped jumping and his shoulders slumped. "I have to leave?"

"It could take a long time for her to have the baby and you can't sit out here by yourself. Carl has to go help Mommy."

Mark squatted to be eye-to-eye with his son. "I'll bring you back after Mommy has the baby, okay?"

"Well, okay..." He looked around at Sarah, and then at Carl, trying to hold in his tears.

"Your dad can take you in to say goodbye to Mommy. I'll wait out here," Carl said.

Jamie nodded his head and took the hand Mark offered.

Mark and Jamie left Sarah in the waiting room with Carl. She ignored him as she sat in the nearest chair.

"So, Sarah, how are you?" he asked.

She looked up at his smug smile. "I'm fine."

He sat next to her and leaned toward her.

"You ready to have that drink yet?" He leaned further over the arm of the chair to make eye contact.

"Nope, not interested," she said, squeezing past him to get out of her chair. What did it take for this jerk to get the hint? She walked over and leaned against the wall next to the entrance of the waiting room, keeping Carl within view, but pretending to be interested in the news show blasting from the TV mounted in the corner of the room.

He stepped in front of her, still wearing his *Carl, The Pig* smile. "You know, Mark may be awhile. We could just," he paused, as he brushed the tips of his fingers across her jawbone, "sneak away."

Sarah smacked his hand away and glared at him. "I am truly not interested."

He leaned closer and Sarah held her hand up.

"Back off, Carl." The breath caught in her throat when he lifted his hand to touch her again. She inhaled, fighting for air.

When the tips of his fingers touched her collarbone, she laid both hands on his chest and pushed him hard, and then she pulled back her fist and punched him before he could step toward her again.

Carl grabbed his face. "Bitch!"

Sarah's heart pounded in her chest as she rushed out of the waiting room and directly into Mark's chest, just as she had the first time she'd been attack by Maylyn.

She yelped and stumbled before meeting his eyes. "I'll meet you in the truck."

She huffed out between heavy breaths as she skirted around him and down the hall.

Mark called out to her, but she rushed into the open elevator. As she punched the button for the ground floor, she inhaled deeply trying not to hyperventilate and telling herself to breathe.

By the time she reached Mark's truck, her face was covered in sweat. Not having the keys, she paced as she waited for him, shaking away the pain in her right hand.

When Mark and Jamie walked up, the look on Mark's face had her recoiling. He unlocked the door, helped Jamie in, and then he closed the door.

He pulled her into a fierce embrace. "Are you okay?" he asked.

She nodded into his shoulder. "I'm sorry, I didn't mean to..."

"Why are you apologizing?" Mark pulled back to look at her.

She shook her head and lowered her eyes, unable to look at him.

"Do you think I'm blaming you? Dammit, Sarah. I'm not Kevin Lewis."

She closed her eyes and rested her forehead on his chest.

"I'm sorry I left you alone with him. I had no idea he would do that."

Sarah lifted her head to meet his eyes. "Let's go home."

Chapter Thirty-Two

After her appointment, Sarah drove back to Mark's house on autopilot. She sat in the driveway, wanting time to reconcile her feelings. She touched her stomach and looked down at the ultrasound picture in her hand. *My and Mark's baby. Will he be happy?*

The memory of Kevin's reaction came back painfully.

She pushed away the thought and focused on her baby, and Mark...then Jamie, her new family...a real family. Something she never thought she could have.

"My baby," she whispered. "Nothing is going to happen. We'll protect you and keep you safe."

When the front door opened, she slid the picture back into the envelope and stuffed it in her purse. Her pulse jumping as she met Mark's eyes through the windshield.

He walked around and tugged the car door open for her. "Hey, babe, what's going on...what happened?"

"What do you mean?" she asked, fighting her nervousness.

"Did something happen with Nancy? You look upset."

With the ultrasound, she had completely forgotten about her talk with Nancy. Normally, that would've been forefront on her mind. She nodded. "I was fired...Nancy fired me."

"They can't fire you. You're on leave." He helped her out of the car and closed the door for her.

"She called it *extended leave*, but they don't want me to come back until next fall." Sarah slid out of the truck and walked with Mark into the house.

"Maybe we should take legal action against them."

"No, I don't want to drag down their reputation. God, could you see that on the six o'clock news airing right after..." She sighed and shook her head. "I'm not sure if I want to go back now."

She moved her hand to her stomach again. Maybe it was a blessing. She looked down at the hand covering her baby and realized she wasn't as upset as she should have been. At the time, she was so angry at Nancy, she didn't consider what it would mean to be out of work during her pregnancy.

"Are you feeling sick?" he asked, noticing the gesture.

Before she could answer his question, his cell phone rang.

Mark cleared his throat as he flipped the phone open.

"Hello." His jaw flexed. "Yeah, what?" After a long pause he said, "No, don't come to my house. I'll bring him there." He shifted and adjusted the phone. "Too fucking bad. I'll bring him to you. I want to talk to her anyway." He laughed and said, "You should have thought about that before."

Mark closed his phone and then tossed it on the table before turning back toward Sarah.

"Who was that?"

"Carl. Ali had the baby early this morning. It's a boy, she named him Micah."

"Oh, she had another boy. I guess Jamie will be disappointed. Should we go tell him?"

"I have to drop him off in an hour at the hospital."

"Are you going to tell Ali what happened?"

"Yeah, I just don't know when. I don't think now is the best time."

"She's going to hate me."

"No, she is not going to hate you. She's no fool to what type of man her husband is." He closed his eyes for a second. "Are you going to be okay on your own for a while?"

"Yeah, I'll be fine. I have some Christmas presents to wrap and I might drive by my house and pick up some things."

He gave her an apprehensive look, and her stomach did a weird flip. "Unless you're starting to feel crowded with me here all the time."

When he smiled, his little dimple winked at her. "I would love nothing more than to make this a permanent living situation." He tugged her hand to pull her closer. "I was planning to ask if you wanted to look for a house together, but I wasn't sure how to bring it up without making you feel pressured."

She chuckled. "Sorry, I make you walk on egg shells all the time with my stupid insecurities."

"So what do you think?"

"About getting a house together?" She watched light dance across his hopeful eyes. "Yeah...I would like to live with you and Jamie."

"Seriously?" Mark's smile took over his entire face, and she knew it was the right decision—pregnant or not.

"We should probably wait until after the holidays. Now doesn't seem to be the best time to move, but I do want to be with you."

He pulled her closer and kissed her lips. "Oh my God, I'm so happy right now."

"Me, too," she said smiling, feeling every bit as excited as he was. Keeping this secret was going to be harder than she thought.

The last meeting with the DA was particularly stressful for Sarah and for Mark. With Sarah being one of Rupert Maylyn's victims, it made his death look like a crime of passion. This was an angle the press loved. They could report on Mark but still include her in their story. They didn't outright use her name, but her and Mark's relationship had become a key point in the DA's investigation, which Sarah and Mark both knew was the reason behind the investigation to begin with. The DA was campaigning for reelection and headlines were the cheapest form of advertising.

The whole idea of Mark being accused of murder was too much for Sarah. He'd done nothing but protect her from day one, and now he was being scrutinized in the media as an out-of-control boyfriend. She could show them an out-of-control boyfriend—and it wasn't Mark.

Even now, Mark was protecting her, only this time it was from the *official questioning* that always seemed to be swayed against the two of them. And that in itself was a point against them, because whenever they asked Sarah a particularly difficult question, Mark would get angry and lash out at the attorney's questioning them.

They finally hired a reputable attorney of their own, one recommended by Richard. She found it interesting that once she'd hired Christopher Rhodes, the DA suddenly stopped harassing them and became sickeningly polite. Thanks to Christopher, the DA agreed to conclude his investigation by the end of the following week and agreed to let them know right away when his report was ready.

One of Mark's clients had given him tickets to the Christmas ball at the Sir Francis Drake Hotel in San Francisco. Sarah couldn't think of a better way to spend a Friday night, and she couldn't wait to spend a stress-free evening out with him. She felt like she could breathe without worry, and she decided it was time to finally tell Mark about the baby. The Christmas ball would be the perfect place to do it.

Sarah finished her make-up and hair and then stepped into Mark's walk-in closet and unzipped the garment bag holding her dress.

It was a pewter gray, silk halter dress that pulled in at the waist and gathered at her lower back, leaving a flow of fabric to trail behind her.

The front came down into a V between her breasts and tied behind her neck leaving the long, thick, silk straps to fall down her bare back. She slipped into the silver strap stilettos and looked herself over in the mirror, turning to see how the dress trailed behind her. The long, flowing skirt gathered at her lower back and fit snugly in the front.

Sarah rested her hand over the small baby bump where the dress formed around it. It wasn't much of a bump yet and Mark hadn't even noticed the slight difference in her size. She had always been proud of her flat stomach and defined abs, but today she felt proud and beautiful knowing her body was capable of such a miracle. Her smile widened when she heard Mark call out to her from the bedroom. The sound of his voice sent an electric sensation through her system. Yes. Tonight was definitely the night to tell him about the baby. She felt strong enough to share her news with him and confident of his happiness.

She stepped out of the closet. "What's wrong with you?"

He froze, his eyes traveled from her toes to her face, and his expression made her stop in her tracks.

"Do you like it?"

Mark pulled the tie off as he moved to her, pulling her up into a kiss so deep she could hardly hold herself up. "We are not leaving this house."

One hand moved up her back and into her wild curls, and the other cupped her hip. His lips went straight to her bare shoulder and trailed kisses down her arm.

"Stop—we are going to this party." She inhaled sharply when his right hand found her breast, and she actually considered staying home with him.

He smiled a crooked smile. "You're not wearing a bra."

"With this dress?"

He cupped her breast and rubbed his thumb over her hard nipple. "I love your hard body and I can't believe the way this dress brings out your stormy eyes."

Sarah laughed and tried to pull out of his clutches, pretending to be annoyed, but loving his attention.

"I hope you love me for more than my body." Because in a few months she was going to be really fat and loving every second of it.

When she turned, he grabbed her from behind and wrapped his hands around her, resting them on their baby. "I love everything about you. Don't forget that."

He cupped her small bump, and she held her breath, waiting for him to comment on the little bit of weight she'd gained, but he didn't seem to notice.

"Hurry up or we're going to be late." She moved away from him and went back to the closet to get her wrap and add her jewelry.

A few minutes later, she came out of the closet and was greeted by Mark, fully dressed in the Armani tuxedo he didn't want to wear.

"You look...wow!" She grinned at him. "Do you feel better about wearing it now that it's on?"

"If I get the pleasure of peeling you out of that dress later, I can tolerate this suit."

When they arrived at the Sir Francis Drake Hotel, Mark handed in their tickets and checked his coat.

"You're freezing," he said, rubbing her arms trying to warm her.

"I'll warm up in a minute. Let's get a drink." She pulled him to the bar.

"One cranberry juice and seven-up, one shot of Patrón with lime, and a Tequila Sunrise."

"I don't get a shot?" he asked.

"The shot is for you. I'm not drinking so I can drive us home."

"We could always get a room here."

"Maybe...but I'm still not drinking." He reached around, picked up her drink, handed it to her, and then he drank his shot of tequila. "Since when do you not want to drink?"

"I want to remember every moment of this night," she said, pulling him to a table. "I love this. I love being here with you and enjoying your company without the distractions."

"You don't think all these people and loud music is a distraction?"

"Here, nobody knows us, we're anonymous. No questions, no onlookers, no cops, and no security agents following us around."

"That's true, but if we hide the car in the garage and pretend we're not home, then I can get you out of this dress."

"Hmm, there is that." She winked. He was right, but being out in public with him and not having all their troubles hanging over her head felt like a different experience to her.

She took in the sights. The crowded room had big, bright silver and blue balloons and streamers everywhere she looked. They made the place look like a winter wonderland, although instead of cold, it felt warm and comforting.

All the women were dressed for the red carpet, and all the men could have given James Bond a run for his money. The confetti that littered the stark white tablecloths sparkled when the light touched it. People in their formal wear moved around the dance floor, and before she could lean in to ask him, Mark was pulling her to her feet.

Sarah laughed as he dipped her low and kissed her bare shoulder. When she looked up, she noticed the balloons littering the ceiling in every shade of dark blue to simulate the night sky. Here and there were a few white balloons standing in place of the stars. The effect was breathtaking.

After dancing through several songs, Mark led her off the dance floor and into an embrace that made her heart stop. The drinks were starting to get to him. He couldn't wipe the big grin off his face and his cheeks were flushed.

"I love you," he breathed in her ear. "I could eat you alive I love you so much. Will you marry me?" he asked before kissing her and nipping on her lower lip.

Sarah drew back and stared into his eyes, not sure if he was serious or not.

Mark released her and pulled a little leather pouch out of his pocket and handed it to her.

She pulled the strings and let the ring drop out and onto her palm.

"Sarah, I love you and I know this seems sudden...I want to be with you and take care of you. I want you to love me and take care of me. I want you to marry me."

Sarah gripped the ring tight in her hand, placed it over her stomach, and then lifted her other hand over her mouth.

His eyes never left hers and sweat beaded on her forehead. Marriage, something she swore she'd never want. From everything she'd ever seen, marriage only ruined good relationships. Look at her parents...they were a complete disaster as had been nearly every relationship her mother had ever had. After everything that had happened to her in her life—abusive boyfriend, a lost child, name changes, moving around and always feeling lost—and now a pregnancy when she never thought it was possible. But what did she want for her child? A family...a mother and father in love, a brother like Jamie, and God how she'd love to be a mother to that sweet little boy.

"You're breaking my heart here," Mark said, interrupting her thoughts. "Say something please."

"Mark, I..." She rubbed her face. "I...I've never believed in marriage. Look at you and Ali—look at Ali and Carl."

"I get that, but I have to believe that you have faith in me...this is you and me, baby. You can't compare this to anyone else. It's just us. We're already moving in together...let's just do it right and make it legal. We'll be a family—me, you and Jamie."

He reached down and took the fisted hand she held over her stomach and pried the ring from her tightly wound fingers. He held it up and said, "If you need time to think about it, I can wait for an answer."

As he said this, his smile creased into a slight frown, and that slight frown was all the convincing she needed. She wanted to make him happy and she wanted happiness for herself. A family—this family—was exactly what she wanted.

"I don't need to think about it, I will marry you."

Mark froze. "What did you say?"

She laughed and said, "I will marry you."

Mark picked her up and spun her around, forcing people to clear a space for them.

"Oh my God, I thought you were going to say no." He pulled back to look into her eyes. "Do you mean it?"

"I mean it. I want to be your wife."

"Let's get a glass of champagne and toast," he said, pulling her to the bar. He handed her a glass, took one for himself, and then led her to a quiet corner where they could have some privacy.

When he found a quiet spot, he turned around and pulled her close, lifting his hand up the bare skin of her back.

"To your beautiful eyes." He held up his glass. "The windows to your beautiful soul." He tipped his glass toward hers and leaned in, kissing her.

She pulled back. "My turn."

She looked down at his chest and thought for a second. She wanted to tell him about the baby, right then, while he still wore that stunning smile, but she knew it should wait until they were alone and he was sober.

Her eyes lifted to meet his. "You've taught me what love feels like and you've given me a home in your arms. This is to you, to our future, and to a long life together."

They stared into each other eyes, clinking their glasses again before Mark pulled her into a tight one-arm embrace. She moved her hands around his neck, letting the champagne glass dangle as she leaned in, feeling the length of him.

"Sarah Lange!"

Sarah felt the atmospheric shift she'd been waiting for. Her champagne glass slipped from between her fingers and her own words rang in her head, but they were morphed as if spoken in slow motion. *Kevin Lewis will find me and he will finish what he started. He will kill me.*

She didn't hear her champagne hit the floor, but it shattered into millions of tiny, diamond-size pieces of glass as it smashed at Mark's feet.

Chapter Thirty-Three

Mark withdrew, still smiling and met her panicked eyes. It felt like a lifetime before she could turn her head toward the person whose voice she had heard so many times in her nightmares.

"It is Sarah Lange."

Sarah slid her arms from around Mark's neck, and a tremble traveled through her body.

"Kevin Lewis." Her voice shook like a frightened child's.

Mark stiffened next to her and shifted his body between her and Kevin with a protective arm across her front, clapped on her hip.

"Sarah...it's been a long time." When he said it, a murderous look crossed his face, and his dark eyes focused on Mark's hand.

"Yeah." She forced a steady voice while her insides writhed in nervous energy and discomfort. "What are you doing in San Francisco, Kevin?"

"I'm staying here at the Sir Francis Drake on invitation from a high-dollar client." He gave her a seething look. "What are *you* doing in San Francisco? I thought you were in Tennessee?"

"Ah—I was, but now I'm ah...staying in Colorado. I moved there about eight months ago. I'm visiting friends...for Christmas."

"Is this your husband?" he asked, staring Mark up and down.

"Not yet," Mark said in a tone that prickled down her spine.

"This is Mark...Son-ders," she stuttered. Mark looked at her sideways, not bothering to hold out his hand to shake Kevin's. "He's a police officer in Denver."

"Her fiancé," he said, finishing her introduction.

"Mark, this is Kevin Lewis, he...we were..." Her voice cracked from the dryness in her throat. The more she tried to talk, the more her chest felt as if her lungs were full of ice.

Sarah had both her hands wrapped around Mark's arm with a death grip to hide the shaking in her body. Her instincts told her to run, but her feet felt like concrete blocks holding her in place.

"Sarah and I were engaged once...a long time ago," Kevin finished for her. "You look good. I'm glad to see you're taking care of yourself." He looked her up and down, and every muscle in Mark's body flexed in protest.

"I went to Nashville and tried to look you up but I couldn't find you. I met Charlie. It was a nice surprise since I'd heard so much about him."

"Charlie died," she managed to get out.

"Yeah, I met him *just* before he died," he said pointedly. "Charlie didn't seem to know where you were, even though I told him I was sure you were in Nashville." His eyes darkened. "I don't know why he would lie."

"I wasn't in Nashville. I lived in Memphis," Sarah said, trying to pull off confusion.

"Memphis...hmm, you don't have much of an accent." He chuckled and looked at Mark. "When I first met Sarah, she had a heavy Southern twang. Sometimes I couldn't understand her. It took about a year for her to lose it." He let his eyes drop to the floor and his expression saddened.

Sarah relaxed a little. Maybe he was a different person than the one she had left all those years ago. This thought was washed away when he looked back up at her. Their eyes met again, and she saw the hunter she remembered, the monster that had beaten her and killed her child.

Sarah straightened her back and looked at him with all the contempt and hatred she had buried for eight years. She loosened her grip on Mark's arm and said, "Excuse us, Kevin, but we were on our way out."

Mark smiled and turned into her, putting his arm around her waist and pulling her away from Kevin. She gave Kevin one last look, but cringed when his eyes focused on Mark's grip around her waist.

"Well, I'm sure we'll run into each other again soon." Her body stiffened at the threat, but she kept moving with Mark.

"We need to leave," she said, fighting to control her trembling. Her steps were hurried, but Mark held her back from running.

"I know, baby. I've got you."

"We need to leave."

He squeezed her hand. "We're going. Please stop running. I'm not going to let him hurt you."

When they were in the parking lot, Mark handed the ticket to the valet, and then Sarah handed him a one hundred dollar bill. "Hurry."

"Sarah, it's going to be okay."

"It's not okay," she shouted and balled her hands into fists. "It is not okay."

When the car came around the corner and stopped in front of them, Sarah took the keys from the valet and slid into the driver's seat.

Mark gripped the dashboard when she ripped out of the parking garage. "You need to slow down."

"I will when I get out of the city," she said, angling the car onto the Golden Gate Bridge. She pushed the gas pedal of the Shelby Mustang and held the steering wheel with a white knuckled grip. "I need to get as far away from that city—as fast as I can. If you want me to pull over and let you out then I will."

"Wow—seriously! I can just get out. Get out on the side of the fucking freeway."

"What do you want me to do?" she shouted before taking a deep breath, trying to calm herself. "Let me get home, okay?"

"Sarah, I know you're afraid." He reached over and stroked her hair. "I won't let him hurt you."

"And who's going to protect you, Mark? You don't know what he's capable of." She was on the verge of hysteria as she went over their conversation in her head.

He visited Charlie...

He knew Charlie lied...

He knew Charlie was dead...

"I think he killed Charlie." The realization brought tears to her eyes.

"What—why?"

"Didn't you see him? The look in his eyes—Kevin said he visited Charlie right before he died." Her heart was doing sprints in her chest. She could feel it pounding and pumping the adrenaline through her system.

"You need to calm down and think about what you're saying."

"He nearly beat me to death without so much as flinching. He killed one baby already. I have to..." She ran out of breath, forgetting to inhale.

"Sarah, pull over." He wasn't asking. She recognized the tone in his voice. It was the same tone he used when he directed his security agents.

"Fucking stop before you kill us both by crashing the car."

She shook her head, making tears drop from her eyes. "I'm sorry, I can't stop."

When she exited the freeway in Santa Rosa, she drove through town toward her house instead of his.

"I have to pick something up at my house." She felt calmer now. The few moments of silence gave her a chance to plan. "This won't take long. You can wait here if you want." She jumped out of the car and ran into the house.

Sarah rushed to her closet, but then turned and paced, her agitation growing with every turn of the room. She had to leave. Kevin would kill her when he found her; it was there in his eyes. She wasn't in any doubt about this fact. She stopped pacing and stared down at her engagement ring, and at the same time, tears dropped from her eyes.

One way or another, she was going to lose everything.

"What are you doing?"

Sarah jumped at the tone in Mark's voice. Without turning to look at him, she went back to her closet to grab a shoulder bag. "He's going to kill us both if I don't leave."

"Sarah, what the fuck are you doing? You promised you wouldn't do this to me again." He grabbed her left hand and spun her as he held it up. "You agreed to marry me."

She stared at the floor, unable to respond. What else could she do? It wasn't just her life to lose this time. Mark, Jamie, her baby, they were all in danger. He'd kill them just like he killed Charlie. If she left, Kevin would come after her and Mark would be safe. She could hide again. She'd managed to hide from him until now, and she could do it again.

"You're not fucking leaving me." He grabbed her chin and lifted her face, trying to make her look at him.

She flinched and jerked out of his grip, all her composure slipping away when she saw the angry expression. "I'm pregnant!" she screamed.

"You're pregnant?" His eyes grew sad as he looked down at the bag she was packing. "You were just going to leave and not tell me?"

"I planned to tell you tonight," she said, holding in her sob.

"We're having a baby and you want to leave." Mark stepped back and the hurt look on his face broke her.

"If I don't leave, he'll kill all of us!"

"Why don't you believe that I can protect you from him?" Mark jerked forward, forcing her to take a step back. "I told you, I knew you were going to do this—I can't go through it again." He got right in her face. She quailed again as his shouts brushed across her face. "You're not using him as an excuse to leave me."

When she flinched, he paced away from her.

"Mark, come with me."

After a few minutes of silent pacing, he turned toward her, his voice now calm, almost too controlled and in complete contrast to his angry stance. "Do you expect me to choose between you and our baby—or Jamie. I can't take Jamie away from his mother."

Sarah didn't know what scared her more, the controlled quiet or the shouting.

He stared at her, searching her face. "I won't uproot my life for your ex-boyfriend." When she didn't speak, he shouted, "Fine! Fucking fine! You've made your choice, now live with it. Goodbye, Sarah."

She hardly heard his goodbye over the sound of his footsteps as he stormed out the door.

Sarah watched as if in slow motion, and her mind raced with the reality of what she had done. When the front door closed, she let out an aching, body wrenching sob that pulled at every part of her soul. She fought not to hyperventilate on her own cries. When the car door slammed, it was like a knife slicing right through her.

She stopped breathing and looked around, placing both hands on her stomach. He was right. She would have to live with the choice. *Live*? There was no choice to make, she couldn't live without Mark—she would rather die.

Sarah ran for the door as she heard the car start. She yanked it open and started screaming for him as the car began rolling.

"Stop! Mark...Stop!" She saw the brake lights and pounded down the steps of the porch. "I'm sorry. I love you—just stop." She sobbed as he jumped out of the car.

He came at her and pulled her off her feet. Her legs wrapped around his hips and her mouth crushed his as the tears streamed down her face. Her hands clasped around his neck, pulling him to her and feeling like she couldn't get close enough. She'd never let him go again, never again.

Mark moved his hands up her dress and clutched her hips, holding her against him with such force it took her breath away. He flung her on the car and pushed against her.

"If you want me—it's forever. I'm not playing games." He was out of breath from kissing her. "You know the deal." He gripped her lace thong and tugged it down so hard, it ripped in two. "If you want me, tell me now, Sarah...tell me you want me or tell me to stop."

Sarah held on, wanting him more than she'd ever wanted anything in her life. He unlatched his tuxedo pants and yanked on the zipper. "What do you want? Tell me now!"

She sucked in air as he yanked the front of her dress up. "I want you," she cried. "I only want you. I only want to love you."

When he opened her with his fingers, she arched against him, taking them without hesitation.

"Tell me to stop if you want me to stop." He grunted and massaged her with his fingers while he nipped at the skin between her breasts. He reached up with his other hand and untied the straps of her dress.

Sarah wanted nothing more than for him to take her. She was open to him and needed the safety of his arms and the strength of his hands.

When his mouth found her hard nipple, she cried out again. "Mark, don't stop. I don't want you to stop. I just want you." Her head dropped back, and she propped herself up on the hood of the car as he tasted her breasts one at a time. "I love you," she gasped arching to him.

When she shuddered, he pulled her closer. "Tell me to stop, Sarah." He said her name from his throat, the harsh tone sending a jolt through her system. "Either give me all of you or tell me to stop—now!"

She shook her head trying to form the words as he pushed her toward her peak.

"No...I want...Mark!" She shrieked out his name, her body moving with his touch. "I want you. You can have all of me...everything." Her fingers fisted in his hair as the climax slammed into her. When her body arched against him, he pushed himself into her so hard and fast it made her gasp.

He gripped her hair, tugging her head back so he could suck and bite her neck. His fingers were wrapped in her curls and his body pushed, taking her wantonly without hesitation or apology. He throbbed and pulsed, thrusting one more time and moaning her name as he released inside her.

When she collapsed on his shoulder, he wrapped his arms around her. As Sarah's tears came, so did his. They cried together, holding each other with an unrestrained grip.

"I just love you," he whispered as his chest heaved and his body trembled against hers.

She pulled him closer, wanting to crawl into his warmth. "I love you. You have me, all of me...forever."

Chapter Thirty-Four

Sarah found Mark lying on the bathroom floor in boxer shorts as white as the tile underneath him and hugging a bath towel as if it were his lifeline. At first, she felt a twinge of panic, but then she remembered the tequila. She knelt next to him and laid a hand on his forehead.

"Go away." His voice was harsh, and she fought to suppress a smile when he pulled the bath towel over his head. "I don't want you to see me like this."

"I am not leaving you on the floor in this condition." She tugged on his arm to get him upright. When he didn't move, she grabbed his robe off the back of the bathroom door, laid it over him, and then sat down.

"What are you doing? Get off the floor."

"If you're going to stay down here, so will I."

"No, go away. Leave me to die in peace."

She laughed and stood back up, pulling on his arm.

"Okay, fine, just—just let me do it before you hurt yourself." He slowly sat up and pulled his arms through the robe before standing. When he swayed, she reached out to help steady him. Mark pulled the robe tighter as he shivered and hobbled to the bed.

"I'm never drinking again—remind me to never drink again," he said still with a hoarse voice.

Sarah went to the dresser and pulled out a thin, white box with a pink ribbon and then slipped back in bed with him. "Mark, I have something for you."

He turned to wrap his arms around her and found her sitting up. "A hangover cure?" he asked, blinking up at her.

She handed him the box. "It's sort of a Christmas present. I wanted to give it to you last night."

"What's wrong with you?" he asked at her shaking hands.

"Open it."

"Okay." He scrubbed his face with his hands and slowly sat up to examine the box. "It's not Christmas yet," he murmured, and pulled on the end of the pink ribbon. It drifted slowly to the bed as he lifted the lid. He ran his finger over the black and white ultrasound picture of their baby, fascination lighting his eyes.

He swallowed hard and looked up at her. "Is this our baby?" They stared at each other for a long time.

"It's our baby."

Mark's eyes filled with tears. "I can't believe we made a baby." He cupped her neck and drew her to him. "I thought you couldn't...are you okay?"

"I really didn't think I could get pregnant. I would have been more careful. I'm sorry," she said, gripping him to her tightly.

"You're apologizing? Sarah, is it safe for you to carry a baby?"

She shrugged her shoulders.

"You don't know?" he asked, fear creeping into his voice. "When did you find out about this? When did..." He looked at the picture. "This is dated over a week ago. Why didn't you tell me sooner?"

"I wasn't sure how," she said. "I didn't want to lie to you, but I didn't know how you would feel and I wanted to be sure first. Mark, are you happy?" she finally asked.

"Am I happy? Baby, of course I'm happy. Are you happy?"

She nodded quickly, ashamed that she'd had any doubts about Mark being happy.

"How far along did they say you are?"

"Nine weeks today."

"Nine weeks?" He appeared to calculate in his head. "So the first time?" he asked with a smile.

"I think so."

"I guess this explains why you've been sick. It's morning sickness."

She threw her hands in the air with a slight grin. "Who knew?" Her smile faded. "I have to go back next week for some tests. Do you want to come with me?"

His mouth quirked into a smile. "Yeah, I want to go to every appointment. Tell me everything the doctor said." He took both her hands. "He didn't say anything about you not being able to safely carry a baby?"

"It is high risk...I have to avoid stress."

Mark gave her a significant look, and she knew he was thinking about the night before.

She shook her head. "I'm scared. I've been drinking, and working out, running, the self-defense lessons." She covered her face with her hands. "I'm glad you know now. I was going crazy wanting to talk about it."

Mark drew her closer.

"I don't want to lose another baby. What if something goes wrong?"

"Shh, babe, don't get worked up. We'll take it one day at a time. You're not alone this time. I'll be here to take care of you and the baby." He kissed the top of her head. "I love you...and we're having a baby."

ᘓᘐ

Sarah's words cut right to his soul. She'd never openly admitted to being scared of anything—or anyone.

Mark prayed God would not put her through losing another baby. The cruelty of that was unconscionable. He would do whatever necessary to keep her healthy and safe.

He thought about the night before and Kevin Lewis. His chest tightened at the memory of her packing and then of the cameras trained on her driveway. He released her and got out of bed.

"Where are you going—don't leave," Sarah called after him.

"I'll be right back. I have to do something in the office." He rushed in and signed onto the server. Within a few minutes, he'd deleted the last twenty-four hours from the DVR that housed all the video from Sarah's house.

He went back and crawled into bed with her.

"Where did you go?"

"I erased the porno we made in your driveway last night before the guys at work found it."

"What?"

"The cameras are still up from when you were in Oregon. They would've gotten a good show if they decided to look at the surveillance video."

She put her hand over her mouth to hide her grin.

"They have no reason to go looking, but I erased the last twenty-four hours just in case."

"And did you watch it before you erased it?"

He smiled. "Only the good parts." His smile faded and he lifted up the blankets, but she yanked them back. "Stop, I want to see if I hurt you."

She gripped the blanket firmly. "You can ask me."

He tilted his head. "Did I hurt you?"

"No, you did not hurt me."

"I don't believe you."

"You didn't hurt me, but you scared me when you walked out on me."

Mark felt the squeeze in his chest again and looked away from her.

"He is going to come after us." When he didn't respond, she said, "You've never been on the receiving end of his fists. You don't know what he can do."

He looked up and the expression on her face melted his anger. "You can't let him continue to dictate your life." He pulled her closer. "What happened to that woman I met that insisted she wasn't scared of anything."

"She was a liar." Sarah bowed her head further into his chest. "Afraid of everything, but she didn't want you to know that."

"We have everything now, each other, the baby, Jamie. We can't let him interfere with what we have. You have to shake free of him, Sarah." He pushed her back to see her face. "It's just you and me. Don't let him in."

"What if you're wrong this time?" she said earnestly. "I'm pregnant—this could be my last chance to have a baby, your baby, Mark."

"You're torturing yourself over this and that will do more harm to the baby than anything else right now." He sighed as he looked into her frightened eyes. "Will it make you feel better if I call Brian and have Kevin checked out? Tell him about Charlie?"

She held her breath for a moment then nodded her head. "Will Brian do it?"

"Baby, Brian would walk on glass if you asked him to. He cares about you almost as much as I do." He glanced over at the clock. "I'll call him...I thought I would be enough to make you feel safe, but I can see now that I'm not enough." He shook his head and closed his eyes. "I can't stand to see that fearful expression in your eyes."

Sarah's shaking hands moved to her chest and she sat up on her knees. "Did you see the look in Kevin's eyes when you touched me? He would rather see me dead than see me with someone else." She placed her hands on her belly. "If he comes after me while I'm alone, he'll kill me. He's strong—he hits too hard—I can't fight him like I did Maylyn."

"It's okay, baby, I'll do whatever I have to—we'll talk to Brian and see what we can do." When she didn't relax, he said, "Sarah, you're my life now...you're everything to me. Please stop trying to leave me. Stop and let me take care of this."

Sarah looked down at her stomach. "I could lose everything. Now that I have you, what I would do if I lost you? It would destroy me."

He drew her to him again. "I understand more than you know."

Mark forced her to eat breakfast by threatening to call the doctor. Dr. Davidson would put her on bed rest if she didn't take care of herself. After eating, she felt more in control, but she constantly fought the nausea at the thought of having to tell Brian everything about her past.

When they were seated in the family room with a cup of coffee, Brian said, "I'm glad you called, I have good news."

"We could use some good news right now," Mark said.

"Internal affairs and the DA concluded their investigation."

Mark straightened in his seat. "What's the verdict?"

"The DA will not press charges, reasoning Maylyn's death was an act of self-defense."

"Oh thank God," Sarah said, glad not to have that hanging over their heads any longer.

"What about IA?" Mark asked.

"We have a meeting set for Monday. But it's fine. Martinez and I ran a clean investigation. I'm not worried," Brian said. "Rupert Maylyn was not murdered."

Mark bowed his head and sighed in relief meeting Sarah's eyes. If it wasn't one thing it was another, and Sarah was as tired of drama as he.

When they grew quiet, Brian's gaze went from Mark's to Sarah's with concern. "Mark told me you guys had a problem that I can help with. What's going on, Sarah?"

Sarah stared at him, not sure what to say, and then her eyes dropped back to her coffee mug unable to force the words out.

When she didn't speak, Brian tried a different tactic. "Mark told me the good news. Congratulations."

"There's more," Mark said smiling.

Sarah wasn't sure which news Brian was talking about, and for the life of her, she didn't understand where Mark found the strength to smile.

"Sarah is pregnant."

Sarah looked back up to see Brian's face break out in a big grin. "You guys are having a baby—that's awesome."

He shook Mark's hand before leaning in to kiss Sarah's cheek. "Congratulations, Sarah. If anyone deserves this it's you guys after what you've been through."

"Thanks," Sarah said, enjoying his enthusiasm.

"You don't seem very happy about it." He turned toward Mark. "I guess now I get the bad news."

"We're ecstatic about the baby and about getting married...there's something else though. We hope it's not a big deal." Mark glanced at Sarah. "We have to explain before Brian can help us. I don't know how much you want me to tell him."

Sarah closed her eyes and thought about how she had spent her entire life constructing a wall to keep people out to protect herself. Now she was breaking down the wall for the same reason. Everything somehow felt backwards, like the sun shining on a rainy day. For some reason Mark was the rare exception to whom she let see through her wall, as if he were her rainbow that shown on those sunny-rainy days.

She opened her eyes and looked into Brian's, searching for the reassurance she needed from him.

"Sarah, I'll do whatever I can to help, but you have to tell me what's going on." After another moment, he said, "You can trust me—Mark and I have been friends since we were kids. We don't always see eye-to-eye, but we've always had each other's backs."

"It must be nice to have friends like that," she said quietly.

"You do have friends like that. I'm not here because Mark needs my help. I'm here because he said you needed me."

Sarah nodded. "Thank you, I'm sorry for being overdramatic about this."

"You don't have anything to apologize for, stop doing that." Mark looked back at Brian. "Sarah's been pregnant before, eight years ago. The father of the baby nearly beat her to death when she was six months along and she lost the baby."

Brian's face burned red and he closed his eyes for a second.

"She had been with the guy for several years. He was really controlling, verbally abusive, and physically abusive to her throughout most of their relationship..." He paused and said to Sarah, "I'm telling him everything. I want to make sure he understands what this means to you."

"I know...tell him whatever is necessary for him to understand."

Mark told Brian the story of how she lost her baby, the beating, the rape, everything, including the way she left the hospital to get away from Kevin.

Brian rubbed his face with his hands, and Sarah could see the same hard expression she'd seen on Mark's face when she'd first told him the story.

"She developed an infection and by the time she'd gotten proper medical care she was really sick. To make a long story short—the doctors told her she would never be able to get pregnant."

Brian relaxed a little. "Now she's pregnant. That's great."

"The problem is the ex-boyfriend. She's been hiding from him for eight years. He threatened to kill her if she ever left him—he's a mean son of a bitch." Mark reached out for Sarah's hand. "We ran into him last night at the Christmas ball."

"Aw fuck!" Brian said through clenched teeth. "And now he knows where you are."

She nodded and tried to smile at him. It was a pathetic attempt.

"No wonder you're terrified."

Sarah sat in a daze with a pounding headache while Mark explained the rest of the story. She forced herself to put on a brave face. She could see the wear of her emotions on Mark, and she didn't want to pull him down into her dark pit.

"Sarah, I need you to write down everything you know about Kevin, date of birth, last known address, nearest relatives. I'll check him out. I can have a friend at the airport check see when he flies home from San Francisco. We can make sure he's on that flight. Do you have a picture of him?"

"No, I left everything like that behind."

"His family's business has a website and his picture is on it with a short bio. Let's go to the office and I'll bring it up for you."

Sarah's head shot up.

Mark stood to take Brian upstairs, but before walking away, he turned to her. "Are you going to be okay by yourself for a few minutes?"

"Yeah, can I talk to you for a quick second?"

"I'll meet you up there, Brian."

Brian nodded and bounced up the stairs.

"What's up?"

"How did you know about his family business and the website?"

"Did you think I wouldn't check him out myself?"

Sarah leaned over and gave him a tight hug. "Thank you. I'm sorry for all this. I don't mean to be so much trouble."

He held her, inhaling deeply and holding her for a moment. "Please, don't apologize to me again. I love you. I'm sorry you've had to go through this. You should be able to have everything you want...you should be a mommy and a wife and you shouldn't have to live with your life being threatened at every turn." He pulled back and framed her face in his hands. "I've seen how strong and resilient you are. Give yourself time, baby, and stop feeling guilty."

He stood up and gave her a faint smile before leaving the room.

Sarah took a deep breath and tried to focus on what he said. "I have to be resilient—stronger," she told herself.

She considered what kind of an example she'd be setting if she were a mommy. That pissed her off and made her hate Kevin even more. Mark was right—she needed to stop letting Kevin into her life, *their life*, and into her nightmares. It was one thing to let him affect her, but it was wholly unfair to let him affect Mark's life, Jamie's life and her baby's life. She leaned over and reached for the notepad and pen to write down all the facts she had on Kevin Lewis.

Chapter Thirty-Five

"Son of a bitch, Mark. That guy beat on her? She's lucky to be alive." Brian and Mark stared at the picture on the screen. "No fucking wonder she's freaked out."

Mark moved to the other side of the desk and sat down on the folded futon, giving his desk chair to Brian. "I told you he's a mean son of a bitch. The things he did to her..." Mark closed his eyes and tried to contain his anger. "She wakes up from vicious nightmares of him strangling her."

"Mark, man, she needs to take care of herself. If she's not sleeping and the stress—"

"What can I do? She's so exhausted she can't even think straight." He ran his hand through his hair. "Things were supposed to get back to normal now."

"Okay, let's summarize here. He doesn't know her last name and he doesn't know she lives in Santa Rosa. He thinks your name is Sonders—or something like that. She told him you're a cop from Denver."

"Did the cop thing deter him at all?"

"No, he didn't seem to care at all." Mark thought about the entire conversation. "Oh, and they talked about her step-dad—which is another issue entirely." He thrust his hand out gesturing to the computer monitor. "She believes he murdered her stepfather. He was murdered a couple of years ago and they never caught the killer."

"Right." Brian snapped his fingers as if trying to recall the conversation. "The gun dealer. I remember her mentioning him."

Mark went on to explain Sarah's suspicions. When he finished, Brian focused on him with a calculating stare.

"What do you think? When he mentioned the step-dad in conversation, did he act guilty?"

"Brian, I was on my fourth or fifth shot of tequila. Honestly, I don't know. He's definitely jealous. He stared me down when I put my hands on her and his parting words were, 'I'm sure we'll see each other again soon' or something to that effect. It scared her; she saw that as a threat."

"Maybe it was a threat, it is kinda creepy." Brian looked at the monitor again and scratched his chin. "Okay, let me make a couple of calls." He pulled out his cell phone and his little note pad.

While Brian talked on the phone, he also copied the information from the website with Kevin's bio. When he closed his phone, he went back to asking Mark questions.

"What's the step-dad's name?"

"I'm not sure, Charlie...something, I'll ask Sarah—"

"Charlie Wyman," Sarah said coming up behind him.

Mark turned to her. "You look like you feel better."

"I do." She smiled as she handed Brian the piece of paper with all Kevin's information. When the computer screen caught her eye, her smile faded.

"Sit down. I'll tell you what I have," Brian said. "I called my friend at the airport. After some smooth talking, I got her to check on his flight. He leaves tomorrow, Southwest Airlines at 9:15 a.m. If I call her after 10:00 a.m. she'll confirm whether or not he got on the flight. My theory is, if he's coming after you here in Santa Rosa, he'll do it between now and then, or he won't be on that flight tomorrow. If he's going to look for you in Colorado, he'll change his flight. We'll know for sure tomorrow."

"There is one more thing we haven't considered." Sarah looked at Brian, then Mark, and then back to Brian. "What if he saw the two of us in the paper...or on the news? The news stories have died down, but there is still a good chance he's seen it."

"Either way, Sarah, if he's coming after you, he won't be on that plane tomorrow. We can't do much until we know for sure."

She got the sense now that he was placating her and she felt a little silly. "Am I overreacting?"

"Considering what you've been through in the last few months, considering this guy"—Brian pointed his pen at the computer screen—"and considering everything Mark's told me, no, you're not overreacting. Mark should put another one of his guys in this house until tomorrow afternoon. We can wait it out and see what happens. Until then, I'll check out what's going on in the investigation for Charlie Wyman. Can you give me more detail on that, maybe the date of his death, full name, things like that?"

"Yeah, I'll write down what I remember." She reached over for the same piece of paper she'd handed him and jotted down the facts she had on Charlie.

Sarah could hear the doubt in their voices. As if they couldn't believe Kevin was capable of murder. Sarah felt the anger rise with the bile in her throat. What made them think they knew him better than she?

"Kevin is into knives. He collects them, hunts with them, and uses them to scare people—he likes guns, too—but knives were always his favorite when he really wanted to terrorize someone." Sarah didn't look up at them, didn't want to invite questions. "Someone broke into Charlie's house and stabbed him to death. When Kevin talked about him last night, he pointedly said he met Charlie *just* before he died, which was an odd thing to say. Kevin always bragged about the game he'd hunted, and he had the same attitude last night when he talked about Charlie."

She was calm when she said it, but the memory made her want to throw up.

When she looked up, Brian was watching her. "Did he ever threaten you with a knife, Sarah?"

Brian came right out and asked without hesitation, and it surprised her. Mark seemed to have a way of getting information out of people without them realizing they were giving it. But not Brian, he threw it right out there. She looked at him for a long time not sure how to answer.

"Yes," she finally said. "Sometimes he used a gun. It was a game to him. He would wait until I cried and then he'd pull away, call me a baby and laugh at me." She didn't look away when she said it. She wanted to be what she needed to be—stronger, more resilient. She could hear Mark's breathing increase as he lifted his hand to rub his face.

"I don't know," she said to Brian's unasked question.

Brian's eyebrows drew together. "You don't know what?"

"You wanted to ask me why I didn't leave...I don't know why."

"Sarah, I don't need to ask, he's a manipulator. Most abusive men are narcissistic. They do it for control. They want to lift themselves up by bringing you down. It's a power game. Rapists don't rape for the sex, they rape for power. He's no different. I'm sure he told you how worthless you were on a daily basis, made you feel like you needed him, and couldn't survive without him. That kind of abuse is no different than being chained to a bed and starved—same effect on people."

Mark and Sarah both stared at him. Sarah felt like she'd been punched in the stomach, but she didn't get up. She would not allow herself to run away from Brian's gaze.

"It's nice to know I'm a textbook pathetic, stupid woman."

"You're not stupid, pathetic, or textbook. Actually, you're the opposite of textbook. Most abused women end up dead or in prison for murder. You were strong enough to get away and get your life together. That's not luck, Sarah. It's pure, unadulterated strength of character and drive. You can continue to put yourself down, but your time and energy would be better spent concentrating on your new family."

Wow—he didn't pull any punches. Sarah wasn't sure how she liked that. Mark and Brian's relationship made better sense now that she understood their complete opposite personalities. She finally looked over at Mark's pale face and saw the nausea he felt.

"Are you okay?"

"I'll be right back." He stood up and rushed out of the room.

"He drank a lot last night."

Brian chuckled. "Yeah, I heard."

"I'm going to go check on him."

She went into the bathroom and found him splashing water on his face. "Are you okay?"

He looked at her and nodded as he dried his face on a towel. "You didn't tell me about the knives." Mark wiped the clamminess from his neck and rubbed his face again.

"Maybe I shouldn't have now, but I wanted you to understand why I think he may be the person who killed Charlie."

"You should tell me everything. I want to know so I can understand you better and help you deal with this."

"You already treat me like a glass doll. I don't want you to tiptoe around me, always afraid you're going to hurt me."

He stepped back, sat on the closed toilet, and covered his face with the towel. "I hurt you last night."

"No." She knelt in front of him. "You did not hurt me last night. Last night was real, you finally didn't hold back. If I would have said no or asked you to stop, you would have, right?"

"Of course, I would have stopped. I just drank too much and I was upset. I'm sorry."

She grinned. "I'm not sorry. I enjoyed last night."

"Did he really put a gun to your head?"

"It doesn't matter now, Mark."

"It does matter. It explains everything. God damn, no wonder you want to run away...and the nightmares. I never imagined he did things like that to you. It might have been a game to him, but to you, it had to be terrifying." He closed his eyes tightly. "It makes me sick to think about it."

"It makes me sick, too. We have to stop thinking about it." She nodded toward the office. "Come on, Brian is waiting for us."

They walked back into the office and Brian was typing on the computer.

"I'll do some checking in Nashville. Make some calls and see where their investigation stands with Wyman." He stopped typing and stood to leave. "When I hear from my contact at the airport tomorrow, I'll call and let you know."

ꟷ

"I feel guilty that Shane sat up all night while we slept," Sarah said, fixing the collar on her shirt in the bathroom mirror. She tried to hide her agitation from Mark.

"Don't feel guilty, he's well paid, and he got a free breakfast out of it."

She turned from the mirror to face him. "Telling me he's being paid to sooth my insecurities doesn't ease my guilt."

"Your insecurities are well founded. Stop feeling guilty. I'm just hoping Kevin"—he looked at his watch—"got on that plane twenty minutes ago so we can have a nice quiet weekend."

She sighed. "I would love a quiet weekend."

"Let's go downstairs so he can go home."

She nodded and followed him out.

"Thanks for waiting, Shane. You can take off now," Mark said, refilling his mug. "Brian should be calling soon. We'll let you know what's going on for tonight, get some sleep just in case."

"Okay, but don't call me until this afternoon. I'm going straight to bed when I get home." He yawned as he walked toward to door. "See you guys later."

"Thanks again, Shane," Sarah called to his back as he left. She rubbed at her neck, trying to ease some of her tension.

When the phone rang, she stiffened up again.

"Hello," Mark answered.

He sighed in relief. "What now? Do we still need to worry about this?"

Mark's eyes met Sarah's. "Okay, thanks, man." Mark hung up the phone. "He boarded the plane. Brian is on his way over with the information he's dug up on him."

"Okay, so...this might be over soon?"

"Yes, if this goes well, you'll never have to worry about him again." Mark reached for her and she rested her head on his chest, unable to hide her relief. "He sounded like he had good news."

When the doorbell rang, she tensed again.

Mark gave her a sad smile and walked over to get the door for Brian.

"Hi, guys. Good morning."

"That was fast," Mark said, gesturing to a chair.

"You look better today," Brian said to Sarah as he took his seat.

"Thank you. I finally got a good night sleep."

"I had a talk with an old friend of yours, a cop in Nashville."

"I don't know any cops in Nashville."

"He wasn't a cop in the eighth grade, but he's a cop now, a regular good ol' boy too." Brian chuckled.

Sarah stared at him for a moment. "I'm afraid to ask..."

"John Bennett."

Sarah thought about it for a few seconds. "I don't know...wait, do you mean *Johnny Rhay* Bennett?"

Brian gave her a funny look and nodded his head. "Yeah, he did call himself Johnny Rhay, but I thought it was a joke. Sounds like a Nascar driver if you ask me."

"Johnny Rhay...oh my God! He's a cop?" She smiled. "I'm a little surprised."

"He had some pretty good stories about you, this good ol' boy liked to talk."

"We don't need to go *there*," she said, feeling the blush rise in her cheeks.

"Oh come on, don't get embarrassed now. *Was* he the first boy you kissed? 'Cause he *reckoned* you were the first girl he kissed." Brian laughed at the look on her face.

"Anyway, Charlie being a gun dealer, all the cops liked him. He was a friend of the department. They're all interested in finding his killer."

"Yeah, Johnny Rhay knew Charlie well."

"I told him the story and he's very interested in Kevin Lewis, although that has more to do with you than Charlie."

Sarah stood up quickly. "You told Johnny Rhay?"

"Don't panic, Sarah," Brian said.

"Brian, give her a minute. This isn't something she likes to talk about," Mark said.

She paced the room for a minute, trying to reconcile her thoughts.

Brian rolled his eyes at Mark. "She's fine, give her some credit. Sarah, if you sit down, I'll tell you exactly what I told him, which wasn't very much."

Sarah willed herself to relax. It wasn't that big of a deal, right? One more person knowing about her past wasn't the end of the world. When she felt ready, she sat back down.

"Are you okay?" Mark asked, surveying her expression.

"Anyway," Brian said, ignoring Mark's question. "I gave him zero details about the abuse, or the baby, or the length of time you were with the guy. I only told him what he needed to know about Kevin and our suspicions about the Charlie Wyman case." Brian smiled at her. "He was pretty curious about you though, asked if you were single. You must have been a hot item in the eighth grade."

"Johnny Rhay was my first boyfriend. He and Devon were best friends." She smiled now too.

"He is all over this. He's getting warrants for Lewis's travel records, and he's pulling out all the evidence from the case to compare everything. They hit such a dead end with this case, they're anxious to find out about Lewis. They didn't know anything about him until I called."

"No, they wouldn't. Charlie and Kevin never met. The only reason Kevin knew anything about Charlie was because of my gun."

"You mean the Colt 45?"

"Yeah, Kevin wanted that gun. I bet he was pissed to find out I took it with me when I left. He was lucky he never saw the barrel end of that gun—as often as I was tempted."

Brian grimaced. "Don't say that in front of me, please. I'd hate to have to arrest you if this asshole ends up dead."

"You don't need to worry. Mark hides the guns from me here. He's scared I'm going to shoot him." She smiled.

Brian laughed. "Funny..."

"Yeah, you think it's funny, but she has nightmares about this guy and she goes looking for that gun in her sleep. Believe me, it's best she doesn't have access to firearms right now."

He held his hand up in defense. "Okay, you may be right."

"What does all this mean to us right now? How long will it take for them to find out about Kevin and arrest him?" Sarah asked.

"We should know in a couple of days. They were hot for this, it could be sooner. Until I get more news, I wouldn't worry about Kevin anymore."

"Is there anything else?" Mark asked.

"Nope, Kevin Lewis is on an airplane with Jeff Lewis. I bet they've landed by now, and in a few hours he'll find out Nashville Metro is investigating him." He looked at both of them and smiled. "I'll keep you guys informed. Sarah, try to relax and have a nice weekend."

He stood to leave.

"I'll walk you out," Mark said, following him to the front door.

ꕥ

When Mark came back inside, he caught her smiling, lost in thought.

"What are you grinning about?"

"Johnny Rhay, oh my God, that brings back memories. I can't wait to tell Devon." She laughed.

"So *was* he your first kiss?" He gave her an innocent smile.

"Yes, my first kiss, and my first make out, and my first...up the shirt grope." She gasped as Mark's hands traveled up her shirt. "But they were much smaller back then," she said, looking down at her breasts.

"He was always the gentleman, never trying to go further than under my shirt but over my bra." She smiled again as he kissed her.

"Well, I'm glad some of the guys you've known are decent, and it's nice to hear you laugh. I miss the sound. I haven't heard it in a couple of days." He pulled her off her feet again and kissed her until she gave into him with a deep moan.

Chapter Thirty-Six

"So?" Mark asked, fighting the agitation while they waited for Brian to give him the news.

"I didn't want to tell you this over the phone." Brian placed his coffee on the table next to the couch. "Lewis was in Nashville the day of Wyman's murder. He'd been scheduled to fly home the same day but missed his flight and flew home the day after the funeral."

"Oh my God..." Sarah inhaled sharply and closed her eyes. After a couple of deep breaths, she opened them.

Mark took her hand and asked Brian, "What happens next?"

"Bennett is flying to Arizona tomorrow to question him about the murder. I'll keep you informed. We should have something solid by tomorrow night."

"Thanks for letting us know. I appreciate everything you've done," Mark said.

Brian stood. "It feels good to solve a cold case and get another asshole off the street." He smiled and turned to leave. "I'll call when I hear more."

For the rest of the evening, Sarah couldn't get her mind off Charlie. The thought of Kevin hurting him was more than she wanted to believe. Charlie had been an innocent victim in her drama-filled life. She realized it could have been anyone, Devon, her mother, Sean, or Hayley.

"Stop," Mark said, walking into their bedroom later that evening.

"What?"

"I'm sorry you feel badly, babe, but you should be grateful you didn't attend the funeral. I have a feeling he was waiting for you to show up."

"I'm grateful I followed my instincts all these years. Kevin murdering Charlie is proof that I had every right to be afraid. Now you know I'm not crazy."

"I never thought you were crazy, but I am sorry I didn't take you more seriously. I should've listened."

She leaned down and placed her head in his lap. "It's a moot point now... right?" She closed her eyes and said, "Is Jamie in bed?"

"Yeah, out like a light. Can you do without me tomorrow?"

"Why, do you need to go into work?"

"Shane and I are meeting with a new client in the morning. I need to be there at eight. Do you mind taking Jamie to my parents' house? They want to spend some time with him while he's on Christmas break."

"Of course, I don't mind. Will you be gone all day?"

"We're meeting with the developers of that new shopping center downtown. I expect it to take most of the day." He brushed the hair off her face. "It's a big job with big money."

ഇൻ

Sarah woke up to the sound of the shower on Wednesday morning. She heard Jamie bouncing around his room and went to check on him.

"Are you ready for Grandma and Grandpa's house?"

"Yeah," Jamie said from under the blankets.

"Really? Did you brush your teeth?"

"No," he said, lifting the blanket to reveal the mass of army men in the bed with him. They were all lined up for battle, green on one side, brown on the other.

"Don't forget."

"Okay." He gently shifted and slid off the bed, trying not to knock the men over.

She walked back into the bedroom in time to see Mark come out of the bathroom in a towel.

"Maybe we should stay in bed all day." She gave him a sexy smile and wrapped herself around his naked body.

"That is so unfair, you big tease." He crushed his mouth on hers and pulled her closer. She moved her hand down and yanked his towel off. "So unfair."

He kissed her again and dropped down on the bed with her on his chest. He moved his hands up her shirt and teased her nipples. When she groaned and straddled his body with her legs, he laughed. "Stop...oh my God, you're killing me."

"We will finish this later."

"Yes ma'am, that's a date. I'll meet you right here at bedtime, if I can wait that long." With a grimace, he shifted her off his lap and on her back, then leaned in, kissing her again, slowly this time.

"Take care of yourself today, and take care of my baby." He moved down and kissed her small belly.

"I promise I'll take care of both of us. You better hurry or you're going to be late."

He groaned and lifted himself off the bed to dress.

She went back to check on Jamie, and then returned to the bedroom to throw her hair into a ponytail and change into sweats.

"I'm going to the gym after I drop Jamie off. I have an appointment with Gabby."

"Keep it easy."

She frowned. "I already promised I would take care of us today."

"I'll see you later. I won't be answering my phone, but you can text me."

"Okay, I love you. I'll check in after my workout."

Saying goodbye to Mark left her with a strange feeling in her gut. She hadn't spent a day without him in a long time, and she already missed him. A few months ago, she spent all her time alone and now she couldn't imagine it. She took off her t-shirt and changed into one of his. If she couldn't see him, she could at least smell him. She smiled, inhaling his musky, sandalwood scent.

"I'm ready," Jamie said, knocking on the bedroom door.

"Me, too. Let's go."

She got Jamie loaded in her truck and drove to Mark's parents' house.

"Bye, Sarah," Jamie said, jumping out of the truck and into his grandparent's house. Sarah waited for him to close the door behind him before driving back to Mark's house to get her gym bag.

She clicked the garage door opener and pulled into the driveway. She could have kicked herself for forgetting her gym bag. Now she was late. She entered the garage but stopped when a large figure moved toward her. She looked up quickly.

"Hi, Sarah."

Her throat shriveled up, too dry to speak. She lifted her hand to her neck to relieve some of the pressure. "Kevin...what are you doing here?"

Dread swamped her when she looked into his eyes and down at his military fatigues. Her heart pounded so hard it made her ears ring. She had no doubt he was going to kill her.

"You're so stupid, giving me that Colorado story after your boyfriend's face was plastered all over the local newspapers. I caught your picture in the paper the first day I got here. I knew that was you, you haven't changed at all. Did you really think telling me he was a cop would scare me away?" He stepped closer. "If anything, it just pissed me off even more."

She swallowed, trying to create some saliva so she could talk. A tremble of fear or adrenalin started to overwhelm her system. Kevin reached across her to hit the button on the automatic garage door. Sarah fought to suppress the flinch at his closeness.

"Kevin, why are you here? Why are you dressed in fatigues?" A trapped feeling set in as the large door closed, locking her inside with him—a murderer.

"I hid in the yard, waiting for you to be alone. When your boyfriend left, I started to come in but saw the kid."

"How ah—how long have you been waiting in the yard?"

"Got back to town early this morning."

"Why are you here?" she asked again.

"I went to jail because of you. Did you think I'd let you get away with what you did?"

"What I did?" Her stomach coiled into knots. "Are you kidding me? You spent only a year in jail for *killing* my baby.

"That bitch lawyer had my father wrapped around her little finger. He insisted on hiring a woman attorney, said it would look better if a girl represented me. Dad forced me to accept that shit deal, but I didn't need it. I didn't kill that baby." He sneered at her. "If you wouldn't have tried to leave, everything would've been fine."

"You're delusional. You beat me and raped me." Her pounding pulse pushed heat to her cheeks. The gall to act like it was her fault.

"That wasn't rape. We always did it like that. You liked it."

"No, Kevin. When a woman screams to stop, she's not enjoying herself. Don't play stupid with me. You can't play games with me. I'm not a kid anymore. I know what you did and you know what you did."

"Sarah, I'm ready to forgive you. I want you to come home."

"I am home." She stepped back as far as she could, trying to break through the vortex that had surrounded them. She needed air to think. "*This* is my home."

Kevin mirrored her image, stepping forward. He carefully reached out for her arm, the grip soft at first, but it tightened like a vice when she tried to pull away. "You're coming with me."

"Let go of me. You don't have any right to touch me."

Before she could react, Kevin smacked her, sending her sprawling to the ground. The concrete floor bit into her hip and she could taste the blood pooling in her mouth.

Oh God, she had to keep her cool. If she could just maintain and keep him calm, maybe she could talk herself out of this.

She swiped at the blood on the corner of her mouth, and the bright red color fueled her anger. Years of running and hiding, months of pushing away the greatest thing that had ever happened to her, all that time wasted because of this bastard. No, she could not talk her way out of this. There were no rational discussions with maniacs. She'd learned that years ago.

She tried to clear her head as she slowly got up off the garage floor.

"You're coming with me today, Sarah. We're going home and getting married." He grabbed her arm and pulled her up. "Or I could just kill you. I spent a year in jail for you, you fucking bitch. Now I get what I want."

Sarah got to her feet and looked at him defiantly. "Why would I go anywhere with you when you hit me like that? I'm not marrying you, and I'm not leaving with you." When the words left her mouth, the air left her lungs.

The blow across her cheek sent her flying over the hood of the Mustang and back onto the concrete floor. She gasped to catch her breath as her mouth filled with more blood.

"You're going with me. You—are—going—with—me." He got louder as he repeated himself. "Don't fucking fight me, bitch."

Sarah's mind flooded with memories, her senses clouding. He hadn't changed, but she had. No longer would she cower and flinch away from him and follow his orders.

She moved slowly, her body ached from the impact of the car and the ground. She lifted the back of her hand to her face and felt the heat from the swelling.

"Kevin, let's sit down and talk, okay?"

"Bitch, you need to do what you're told." He grabbed her arm, pulling her off the floor. "We're leaving now!"

She pulled back and punched him with all the strength she had. As if she hadn't touched him, he grabbed her around the neck and tightened his fingers, pushing her against the car.

The punch she'd landed to his face didn't even leave a mark. She went through the motions, following the careful instructions Mark had given her to protect herself but nothing worked. Kevin lifted her to the hood of the car in the seated position. With his free hand, he grabbed her shirt and started ripping the material. She felt the panic set in as she struggled to breathe and fight.

"You look good, girl—you've been working out. Yeah, nice, tight ass. I was checking you out in that dress at the party. You're going to get fucked right here on this car. I bet your new, little boyfriend would love to know I fucked you on his car." He leaned closer. She used every ounce of strength she had to push him off and pulled at the fingers around her throat. His grip was just tight enough to slightly restrict her air and hold her in place.

She tried to kick him, but he pinned her legs to the car with his bigger legs. "Kevin, Kevin...stop!" She gasped, trying to get him to look at her eyes. "Kevin, please...let's talk first."

He chuckled at her. "Talk? What would you like to talk about?" He carefully released her throat, but kept his tight grip on her breast under her shirt.

"We can talk while I...ah...pack. I can't leave without my things. I need to pack."

"Cool, we can talk, but don't fucking try to punch me again." He let her go and leaned over, grabbing her keys off the ground where she had dropped them.

"Here," he said, throwing her against the closed door and thrusting her keys at her. Her head smacked the door and stars erupted in her vision. She tried to focus on the keys, but her hands shook and she dropped them. Tears burned her eyes, and she thought hard about Mark, hoping he would have some sixth sense that something was wrong.

When would he realize something was wrong? Would it be after Kevin killed her and her baby?

She slowly turned the handle and opened the door. The loud beeping of the alarm system almost stopped her heart. She still had a chance.

Kevin slammed her from behind, grabbed her by the hair, and hauled her into the house by her ponytail. "Nice trick, bitch, now turn it off." He slammed her face into the keypad, still gripping her hair. "Turn it off now—or I slit your throat right here."

Sarah felt the cold blade against her neck.

"Okay, I need my hand," she cried as he held her against the wall. *Think Sarah—ambush code—think! Mark's alarm code backwards, right?*

"Turn it off," He grunted and pushed her harder into the wall, pressing her lower back with his knee.

"Okay, stop! Okay." She reached up with her right hand and entered 2590. *Is that right?* She questioned herself as she pressed the off button. When the beeping stopped, she let out a strangled sob as Kevin pulled her away from the wall by her hair.

He pushed her toward the kitchen, slamming her into the bar. Sarah's hands slapped onto the counter, leaving a smear of blood on the gleaming white countertops. Her ribs smacked the high counter of the bar, knocking the breath out of her.

"What time is boyfriend getting home? Maybe I should wait for him? Take care of him before we leave? Wouldn't want him trying to track you down like I did."

"No, no, he'll be gone all day," she huffed, trying to catch her breath.

He grabbed her arm and shoved her into the kitchen around the bar. "Maybe I should fuck you here in the kitchen. I'm sure the blood will be a nice greeting for him when he comes home and you're gone. He turned into her and backed her into the corner against the counter, smothering her mouth with his.

Kevin pinned her with his hips and tangled one hand in her hair. With the other hand, he slid the knife up, cutting what was left of Mark's shirt off her and slicing her skin at the same time.

Sarah gasped as she felt the rush of blood. "Kevin, you're hurting me...please...stop!"

The cold steel of the blade forced her to suck in another sharp breath when he wedged the knife under her bra and cut it away. Kevin then shoved the blade down the waistband of her sweats. The tip of the knife penetrated her skin as he tugged to cut through the sweats and slide it down her leg.

She frantically looked around for something to grab but couldn't see with Kevin holding her head in place by the hair. She reached out for anything she could find on the counter, her breathing hitched as her hand wrapped around something. She realized it was the table knife Jamie had used for his toast. She reached up and thrust the knife into Kevin's back. At the same time, his knife stabbed further into her thigh as he dropped it to reach for his back.

"You fucking bitch!"

Sarah pushed him away and ran for the nearest door.

Chapter Thirty-Seven

Mark looked over at Shane when his phone buzzed again in his pocket. "I guess I better answer this. It's the fifth time Seth has tried to call me."

"He's calling me now too, it must be important," Shane said.

Mark stood and looked across the table at his new client. "Excuse me, James, I really need to take this call." He stepped out of the large, glass door, into the hall, and flipped his phone open.

"Seth, what the hell, we're— "

"It's Brian, Mark."

Mark pulled the phone from his ear to look at the caller ID.

"Mark! Are you listening to me? Lewis is gone."

"What are you talking about?"

"I called Flagstaff PD this morning to have him checked out. They can't locate him."

"Mark's phone beeped and he pulled it away from his ear again to look at the ID. "Brian, hold on." He hit the button to answer Seth's call. "Seth, what's up?"

"Ambush code from your house!"

"What!" Mark turned and caught Shane's eyes through the glass door.

"I have an ambush code from your house, four minutes ago." Seth took a deep breath. "What do you want me to do?"

Mark turned back into the conference room and waved Shane out of his chair. "James, I'm sorry but I have an emergency."

James looked at Mark's face and nodded quickly. "No problem, we're almost done anyway. Call me and we'll set the date for the install," James said as Shane followed Mark out of the room.

Mark turned, and without thinking about what he was doing, rushed toward the parking lot with Shane close on his heels.

"Maybe it was a mistake—did you try to call?" he said into the phone.

"No, it's against policy."

"Try now, but if someone answers, act like a friend instead of the alarm company."

"Okay, hold the line."

Mark clicked back over to Brian's call. "Seth has an ambush code on my house."

"Fuck!" Brian said, "You're not home?"

"No, Sarah's alone. Meet me there."

"I'm on my way," Brian said as Mark clicked back over to Seth's call.

Shane reached over and snatched the keys from Mark's hand. "I'll drive."

"No answer, should I call the uniforms?" Seth said, coming back on the line.

"Yes! 911. We're on our way." Mark climbed into his truck. "Pull up the cameras on my house, maybe we can see who—"

"I'm pulling up the surveillance, Randy's on with 911." Thirty seconds later Mark heard Seth gasp.

"What?" Mark felt his heart leap out of his chest.

"I have a very large man dressed in fatigues sneaking into the garage behind Sarah."

"How long ago?" Mark's airway constricted in his panic. "Shane, hurry!"

"Ten...minutes ago."

"What the fuck are you looking at? Tell me everything you see."

"He...ah...he's hit her a couple of times and knocked her to the ground. She got up and they're talking. Oh fuck...she's bleeding. Mark, hurry up. He's got her trapped against the car with his hand around her throat and he's pulling at her clothes." Seth sounded breathless as he explained. "He's trying to, no-no-no, son of a—"

"Stop and tell me what the fuck is going on!" Mark screamed into the phone.

"She's trying to fight him off, but he's too strong. Shit! It's just making him mad. Wait, he's letting her go. Okay, okay, good girl. Whatever she said to him, made him stop. He's letting her up. Okay, she's getting up and unlocking the door to the house. Oh man, Mark, he dragged her into the house by her hair. I can't...they're out of sight. Randy took off to meet you there and the uniforms are on the way."

"Seth, keep watching, call me if you get them back into view." He closed his phone, feeling completely out of breath. "Fuck!"

"We're two minutes away."

"He'll have beaten her to death before we get there at this rate. I'll kill that fucker. Drive on the sidewalk if you have to. Just get there!"

Mark's heart pounded so hard he felt like it would jump out of his chest. Helplessness had never hurt so badly. He swallowed and scrambled to dig his gun out of the glove box.

"Fuck!" Mark growled. "Shane, did you bring your gun?"

"Yeah, I stuffed it under the seat." Mark pulled the gun out from under the seat and handed it to Shane before checking the rounds in his own gun and sticking it in the back of his jeans.

Mark's phone buzzed and he nearly jumped out of his skin. "Seth," he shouted into the phone.

"I have them back in view. He chased her into the backyard. She was running from him, but he caught her and threw her to the ground. He's straddling her—"

"Where the fuck are the uniforms?" Mark cursed when Shane pulled in front of the house. "We're here, Seth!" Mark closed his phone and dropped it into his pocket as he grabbed his gun. When they got out of the truck, they heard Sarah screaming from the backyard. Mark felt a thrill of terror race down his spine when he heard her.

"They're in the backyard." Mark quickly pointed Shane to the right side of the house and rushed toward the left. As he turned to the yard, Brian's car pulled to a stop in the middle of the street. Sarah's screaming stopped, and Mark now heard the police sirens.

He thrust himself onto the fence and looked over. Sarah wasn't in sight, so he scrambled over and ran to the end of the house. He peered around the corner and had a perfect view of Kevin straddling Sarah.

Before he could react, a crash came from the house, and then Brian shouted, "Let her go, Lewis. Put the knife down." Kevin looked up at Brian who was standing, gun extended at the back door of the house.

"Fuck you! I'll slit her fucking throat right now. Back off!" He lifted Sarah's head by the hair. She was face down on the ground, naked and unconscious—or dead. Fear coursed through Mark when he looked at her face. She was bloody and swollen. Purple marks ran across her eyes, forehead, and chin. With his only thought being to get to her and protect her, he pulled the trigger. At the same time, he heard shouts and two other shots.

Chapter Thirty-Eight

"Mark, sit down," Shane said.

Mark dropped back down. He couldn't talk. Bile rose in his throat and his stomach burned. He had to squeeze his eyes closed to fight back the tears as the worry consumed him.

When Ava came around the corner, she looked as bad as he felt.

"Mark...where is she, how is she?" she said in a worried sob.

Mark's resolve broke when he looked at her. He shook his head unable to talk.

"Where is she?" she shouted.

"She's being treated now by her doctor. Relax. She's stable, but really beat up," Shane told her.

Ava let out a shaky sigh of relief as she walked over and hugged Mark.

Mark laid his head on Ava's shoulder. "It's all my fault, I'm sorry."

"It's not your fault, brother. Don't do this to yourself. She's going to be okay," Shane said. "Do you want me to go check?" he asked, trying to get Mark to look at him.

Mark nodded against Ava's shoulder.

"She tried to tell me this would happen, but I left her alone anyway. It's my fault. She's going to hate me."

"Mark, she's alive. That's what's important." Ava tried to sooth him through her sobs. "How did he find her? What the hell happened?"

She pulled out of the hug and grabbed a box of tissues for them both.

"We ran into him at the Christmas ball."

Ava's face paled.

"She told him she lived in Colorado."

"Colorado. Mark, if he was in the Bay Area, he would have seen the two of you all over the news reports. He had to have known she was lying."

Mark stared at her, the realization of how badly he'd let Sarah down killing him. "I know—we knew that, but we tracked him back to Phoenix. Dammit!" He looked down at his bandaged hand to hide his shame. "I'm so stupid. I didn't think he would turn right around and come after her."

When he looked back up, Shane came in the room, followed by Dr. Davidson. Mark jumped up to greet him.

"She's stable. We're running tests to check for brain injuries. She has a broken hand and several lacerations."

"Is she awake?" Mark asked.

"She woke up screaming and fighting. We needed to sedate her."

Mark felt the blow to his stomach when he heard this. Sarah was stuck alone in her nightmares.

"Doctor, the baby?" Ava sniffled.

"The baby is fine, no distress."

"The baby is okay?" Mark asked.

Dr. Davidson nodded.

"Did he...was she?" The pain in his chest took his breath away, keeping him from finishing his sentences.

"It doesn't look like she was raped. You must have gotten there just in time." He reached over to put his hand on Mark's arm. "I'll come get you when she's back from—"

"No, I want to see her before you take her...let me talk to her. It'll calm her down."

"She's calm, trust me, the medication is working."

"Please, please just for a minute."

The doctor nodded. "We have to hurry. If she has a head injury, we need to know ASAP."

Mark rushed after him toward Sarah's room. When he entered, the sight of all the monitors and machines stopped him in his tracks until the sound of the static heartbeat coming from the baby monitor drew him forward.

Sarah lay naked under a sheet, her skin pale where there were no bruises. She had a blood pressure cuff on one arm and a tube in her nose for oxygen. The baby monitor stood out, a small square strapped to her belly and hidden under the sheet.

Mark inhaled sharply as he examined her bruised face and matted hair. Her lip was cut in two places, both of her eyes were black, and both cheekbones bruised up to her temples. He leaned in and kissed her forehead, and then both her cheeks.

"Baby, I love you," he whispered in her ear. "Sarah, can you hear me? The baby is safe. It's okay, he can't hurt you anymore." He leaned in close to her face, and her eyelids flickering slightly when he talked to her.

Mark placed his hand on her small belly. Tears stung his eyes again as he forced them back. When the doctor appeared in the doorway, he kissed her gently again. "Sarah, my love, Sarah...just know that I love you." He heard the monitor beep and looked up quickly. The doctor stepped inside and looked at the readout.

"You're right. It did calm her down. Her blood pressure is lower and her pulse normal." He smiled at Mark. "She's doing better. Now let me take her for the tests."

Mark nodded weakly as he turned to leave the room. He wandered back to the waiting room in a daze. He could hear phones ringing and people talking. None of it meant anything to him. His head and heart were with Sarah.

"How did she look?" Ava asked when he entered the room. He looked at her, confused. "Mark, did she look okay? Tell me something."

"She looked...hurt. Her face is bruised and cut. She looked hurt." He slumped into the nearest chair and lowered his head to his hands. He tried to remember the last time he'd seen her smile...laugh. This morning—just this morning when she was safe and whole. They'd made a date for tonight. She'd promised to take care of herself and the baby. She'd tried. Seth said she'd tried to fight back.

Sarah had warned him this would happen. She had said she couldn't fight him off. *He's too strong...too big.* Mark hadn't listened to her. He shouldn't have left her alone. *Why did I leave her?*

He sat there for what felt like hours. He could hear Ava and Shane both on the phone. It was hard to pay attention to them. His mind was too overcome with regret and fear.

He heard Brian's voice but didn't look up. "Mark, how is she?"

"She's stable. They took her for some tests," Shane said.

"Bennett is on his way here. I called him when you left. He had just landed in Arizona. Never even made it out of the airport."

Mark nodded, not really paying attention.

"He should be here anytime now, it's a short flight."

The room grew silent, but Brian's sharp tone forced Mark to look up. "Lewis is dead."

"Good."

"Two shots to the torso, one to the head."

Shane snickered. "That was Mark's."

"You know it, brother." Brian smiled. "He's always gone for the head shots, never the chest. He got him right between the eyes as if his lady wasn't under the bastard. You'd think it would have thrown his shot off a little."

"It'll never happen." Shane's chin jutted out. "At least he's in Hell now."

"I'll have an officer take both your statements later," Brian said.

The doctor entered and all heads turned in his direction.

"Mark, you can come in now."

He nearly jumped out of his chair and headed for the door with Ava right behind him.

"I'm sorry ma'am—"

"I need to see her, we're family." She grabbed Mark's arm. "I won't get in the way."

The doctor looked at her concerned face and nodded.

"We'll wait here, Mark," Shane said.

Mark looked up at the sound of his name. "Jamie needs to be—"

"I already called your parents and Ali, don't worry about it."

"Thanks."

When Mark entered the room, he carefully lifted Sarah's small hand and kissed it. "I'm here, baby. I won't leave your side again, I promise."

He looked up when Ava sobbed. He couldn't comfort her. It was all he could do to keep from sobbing himself. He laid his head down on Sarah's hand and prayed.

Mark didn't move again until he heard his name. He looked up, squinting at Brian.

"Mark...bro, how is she?"

Mark shook his head. The only response he had ready.

"This is Detective John Bennett from Nashville Metro."

Mark put his hand out to shake Johnny's. "Thanks for coming."

"Call me Johnny, please."

Mark wasn't surprised to see that Johnny was tall and good-looking. As an ex-boyfriend of Sarah's, he expected it. But he didn't expect the scruffiness with a five o'clock shadow and longer hair. He certainly didn't look like a cop and nothing like Mark.

"It's good to meet you, Mr. Summors," Johnny said in a drawling accent. Mark fought to suppress a smile and remembered Devon teasing Sarah about her sometimes reoccurring accent.

"You, too."

They approached the bed and looked down at Sarah. "Mark, man...I'm sorry if I gave you guys a false sense of security." Brian shook his head. "I should have parked a patrol outside your house. Damn, I'm sorry. She looks awful."

"I shouldn't have left her," Mark said in a cracked voice. "I should have listened to her. She was scared and I..." Mark looked from Brian to Johnny's pale face as Johnny stared at her.

"That motherfucker!" he raged.

It didn't sound as scary with the accent, but Mark could relate to Johnny's feelings anyway.

"How could he do this? Look at her, she's so tiny."

"Mark, how's the baby?" Brian asked.

Mark looked over at the fetal monitor. "Hanging in there, she did a good job protecting her stomach."

"She's pregnant?" Johnny asked with a hint of a smile.

Mark nodded.

"I went over to Summors' and had a look at the video. She didn't go down without a fight. Did you teach her all those self-defense moves?" Brian asked.

"Yeah. A lot of damn good they did her."

"Dude, she stabbed him with a butter knife. If only she would've gone for the throat. You need to teach her that." Brian gestured a stab to the neck.

"I'll try to remember that."

"What's her prognosis?" Johnny asked.

"She has a concussion and several lacerations. He beat the hell out of her...bruises all over her body and a couple of broken fingers."

Johnny raised an eyebrow. "Broken fingers?"

"She punched him a couple of times," Brian said smugly. "She has a hell of a punch. She broke Maylyn's nose with that punch."

"Yeah, she hurt Carl pretty bad too." Mark lifted her hand and kissed it. "Kevin's the person who taught her how to throw a punch. He was an amateur boxer."

"Motherfucker," Johnny muttered.

"He cut her clothes off with that damned hunting knife. That's where the cuts came from," Brian explained. "Too bad she didn't break his nose, the bastard."

When Brian said this, Sarah started to move around and tried to open her eyes. Mark leaned in. He wanted to make sure he was the first thing she saw when she woke up.

"Listen, we'll get out of here and check on you guys later," Brian said, backing out of the room.

Mark could hear her murmuring as she tried to open her eyes. "Baby, can you look at me. Sarah, open your eyes." When he said her name, she stopped struggling and batted her eyes open. When they met Mark's, they filled with tears.

"You're safe, baby, he can't hurt you again," he whispered.

She let out a heartbreaking sob as she squeezed his hand.

"Sarah, relax or they're going to medicate you again and make you sleep." Her eyes calmed and her mouth started moving. He felt her hand flutter toward her stomach.

"The baby is fine. She's fine...I promise. You kept her safe."

She took a deep, ragged breath of relief and nodded.

"I love you. I'm so sorry I left you alone."

She shook her head, looked at him with concerned eyes, and murmured a faint, "I love you."

Chapter Thirty-Nine

It was nearly nine o'clock at night when Mark wandered into the waiting room to find Ava, Ali, and, his parents still waiting. He took the seat between Ava and Ali.

"How's Jamie? Did you tell him what happened?" he asked Ali after a few minutes.

"I told him she was hurt and in the hospital, but no details. He's worried, but Mom is keeping him busy."

They all turned at the same time when Johnny Rhay walked into the waiting room. Mark stood up to greet him. "Hi, Johnny."

"Hey, Mark. How is she?" he asked. Johnny was moving slower than earlier, clearly exhausted.

"She's awake but the doctor is in with her now. You can see her if you don't mind waiting." Mark looked around the room and then introduced everyone. "Johnny, this is Sarah's best friend, Ava. These are my parents, Beth and Phillip, and Ali." When he finished, Johnny gave them all a very charming, southern greeting stopping at Ali.

"It's lovely to meet you, Miss Ali."

"Johnny is a detective from Nashville and an old friend of Sarah's."

"Yes, she was my very first girlfriend," he said with a charming smile that irritated Mark.

"Oh, are you Johnny something?" Ava asked, wagging a finger at him.

"Yes, ma'am, Johnny Rhay Bennett," he said, shaking her hand.

"I've heard about you. I bet I still have the letters Sarah wrote me when she was in Nashville."

"Oh, Sarah Jean wrote you letters, huh? That's a hell of a lot more than anyone else got."

Mark turned when he heard rushing footsteps coming up behind him.

"Mark, what's going on? How is she?" Devon said.

"I can't believe you got here so fast."

"I left as soon as Ava called. Is Sarah okay?"

"She's better. When the doctor is finished, you can go in."

"Devon?" Johnny drawled from behind Mark. Devon's eyes squinted, and he turned to peer around Mark.

"Son of a...Johnny Rhay, holy shit." Devon smiled big and jumped into Johnny, doing a body slam that almost shook the room. "What the hell are you doing here?"

"I was investigatin' Kevin Lewis, but he snuck away from me."

"Investigatin'," Devon said, mocking his accent. "What are you talking about?"

Mark smiled. "I guess you better get your radar fixed, Dev. Don't you recognize a cop when you see one?"

Devon's eyes widened. "I don't believe it."

Mark left the room so they could catch up. He didn't like being away from her, but he wanted to stay out of the doctor's way. He stood in the hall and waited alone until Ali came out of the waiting room.

"How are you holding up?"

"Barely," he said as she hugged him. "This is all my fault. I shouldn't have left her alone."

"Don't beat yourself up. She's going to be okay."

Mark leaned against the wall trying to avoid her eyes. She was right but that didn't lessen his guilt.

"You really love her, don't you?"

He tilted his head and glared at her. "Why do you sound surprised?"

"I'm not surprised. She's beautiful, smart, sexy, and rich."

"Ali—"

She held her hand up. "She loves Jamie...and she loves you, too." She smiled at him. "She's timorous—I imagine that has a lot to do with Maylyn—but even as timid as she is, it's obvious she loves you."

"Ali, why are you here?"

"I came to show my support. It's the least I can do after what Carl did to her."

Mark looked up at her sharply. "He told you?"

"Two black eyes and a bloody nose left him with little choice." She let out a humorless chuckle. "I wanted to believe the *I walked into a wall* story, but I'm not stupid."

"Sorry," Mark said.

"No, you're not, and neither am I. Did you give him the black eyes?"

"Nope, I didn't have the pleasure. Sarah did it when he cornered her."

This time her laugh was full of humor. "Good for her. I guess I shouldn't be surprised."

"What are you going to do about it?"

"I threw him out. I don't want a man like that around my sons. Carl and I assumed Maylyn raped her. We didn't know the details...at least not until today. How he could so easily victimize her again...it's disgusting. I can't imagine what she's going through."

"I'll take care of her."

"I hope she lets you. If anyone can help her heal, it's you." Ali hesitated for a long time, staring at the floor. "I owe you an apology, Mark."

"Don't, Ali." He waved her off. "We're beyond—"

"I'm sorry for what I put you through. I'm sorry I let him into my life."

"You can't regret him when he gave you Micah."

She smiled again and it lit her face up. "Micah is a gift."

"It doesn't matter anyway. I know now that my feelings for you were only a shadow of what they should have been. It would've ended eventually."

"Your feelings for her are that strong?" she asked.

"Stronger—" He thought about the way Sarah looked in her hospital bed and it turned his stomach. "I've never felt like this. If something happens to her..." He made a fist and slightly pounded his forehead to push the dark images away. "She's pregnant, I left her alone, and let a maniac have her."

"Walking around with all this guilt will not help her recovery. Don't do this, it's a vicious cycle, you feel guilt and that'll make her feel guilty, just stop."

Mark nodded, she was right. "What are you going to do now? Will you be okay with the baby on your own?"

"I've been on my own for the last nine months. Carl never wanted a baby. He hardly spoke ten words to me since I told him about the pregnancy. He would have eventually left anyway."

Mark shook his head. "Why didn't you talk to me?"

"I couldn't. Hell, Mark, with everything that happened between you, Carl, and me, I couldn't come crying to you."

"You can always come to me. I'll always be here."

"But I couldn't ask you this time. I couldn't..."

"If you need anything, especially now, call me."

"I will. Thank you." She gestured to the waiting room. "Who's the cowboy?" she asked.

He smiled and thought about Sarah again.

"He's a cop from Nashville. He's investigating the murder of Sarah's stepfather, Charlie. We suspect Kevin Lewis murdered him trying to get to her—"

Mark stopped when Sarah's doctor came out of her room.

"Hey, Ali, will you go tell Devon he can come back now. I'll meet him in there." She nodded and went back into the waiting room.

He walked into Sarah's room and found her propped up on pillows trying to sit up.

"Hi, babe." he smiled at her. "Are you ready to see Devon?"

Her eyes grew wide. "He's here?"

"He raced down here as soon as he got the call."

"Hey, Baby Sis," Devon said from behind Mark.

Devon propped himself on the edge of her bed before carefully leaning over to hug her.

"He's dead, Devon, Kevin is dead. Mark killed him."

ꕥ

Devon stayed until Mark reminded them about the other people outside waiting to see her. When Devon left, Mark walked out with him.

"Johnny, do you want to come back now?" Mark asked, breaking up his and Ali's conversation.

"Yes, thank you." He stood up and followed Mark out of the waiting room.

"Does it bother you if I make conversation with your ex-wife?" Johnny asked as they walked toward Sarah's room.

"Not at all, converse with her all you want. I'm not her keeper."

When they entered Sarah's room, she gasped and tried to hide her face. "I didn't know you were coming," she shrieked. "Johnny Rhay, how the hell are you?" she asked, reaching her arms out to him.

"Well, I'm better 'n you darlin'," he said, drawling out his accent a little too deeply in Mark's opinion.

He hugged her and then pulled back, pouring his long body into the chair next to her bed. "You seem to be feeling a bit better now."

"Yeah, I might survive."

"Sarah Jean, why didn't you call me when all this trouble started?" He leaned forward in his chair to look into her swollen eyes. "I could have helped instead of you spending eight years hiding from the bastard. You should have called me."

She shook her head. "I couldn't call you. I took off to freaking Flagstaff and got into this trouble on my own."

"Don't be foolish, you moved cause your mama moved. I know the story. And don't forget, I know you, girl...and where you come from."

"Yeah, but I was never going back, Johnny. That's why I couldn't stay in touch. It was too hard." She frowned, unable to finish her sentence.

"You don't have to tell me," he muttered. "There's no reason for you to miss a place like that, it wasn't meant to be your home. Things were hard for you there, I remember."

He smiled his charming smile back at her. "Sarah Jean, you were always a lady even at thirteen. Too classy for The Park, that's for sure...and you still are. Some things never change."

"I wasn't the only one, you didn't belong there either. A detective now, huh?"

"Yeah, well, back then we were both just a couple of lost orphans trying to find a home and a place to be." He smiled halfheartedly at the memory.

She'd found what she was looking for. She belonged with Mark.

"I've finally found my place," she whispered.

"You sure did, darlin'. Your home is wherever that man is." He gestured toward Mark when he said it. "I see it in your eyes and I see it in his when he looks at you."

She smiled and followed it up with a little yawn.

"That's my hint to leave." He stood up slowly and leaned in to kiss her cheek.

"Is it alright if I come back tomorrow?" he asked, looking from Sarah to Mark.

"Of course, she'll still be here. Hey, do you have a place to stay tonight?"

"Yeah, I'm in a motel up the street." He walked toward Mark and handed him a business card. "Will you call me if there are any changes? I'll be working with Detective Hammel tomorrow."

"Yeah, I'll keep you updated. Thanks for coming out and checking into Kevin Lewis for us." Mark reached out, shook Johnny's hand, and then followed it up by handing him his business card. "Our home number and Sarah's cell number is on the back."

When Johnny Rhay was gone, Mark yawned too, resting his forehead on hers.

"Sorry I ruined our date," she said.

"It's not ruined, just postponed." He lifted his head and gave her a seductive smile.

"Are you going home?"

"Not without you."

"That's not necessary...you need some rest."

"No, I'm not leaving you alone."

She nodded, and he could see her eyes water.

"Baby, you never have to be alone ever again. I promise."

"Will you lie down with me?"

"Of course, scoot over—*carefully*." He helped her as she slowly inched over to make room for him. He slipped out of his shoes and crawled into the bed next to her, spooning her hips with his.

"I love you." Mark rested his hand on her belly when he said it. "More than my own life, I love you, baby." He squeezed her softly and inhaled, taking in the scent of blood and dirt. The smell reminded him of how close he came to losing her.

"I'm so sorry. I should have listened to you. I broke my promise and I let that monster get to you. I'll never forgive myself." His chest heaved when he said it.

"Don't. We both thought he was gone. I'm fine and the baby is fine. That's what's important."

"When I saw you unconscious, I thought you were dead." Mark was overcome again, burying his face in her hair against her neck.

Sarah turned her body to face him.

"Stop, it's over. Kevin is gone and he can't hurt us again. I love you, Mark." Sarah's eyes swam with tears as she cupped his wet cheeks and smiled at him. "You gave me my life back."

"It's going to take me forever to make this up to you," he whispered.

"I guess it's a good thing we have forever." Sarah kissed him before curling into his chest, hugging the warmth.

They lay in the quiet for a long time and held each other. Mark could hear the flutter of their baby's heartbeat coming from the monitor, and the sound combined with Sarah's steady breathing comforted him.

He thought she had fallen asleep, but she said, "What are you thinking about?"

"How important you are to me, and how much I love you and our baby. How about you?"

"Johnny Rhay. He seemed sad. I hope he's this happy one day."

"What did Johnny mean by 'The Park'?"

She laughed and then groaned in pain. "The trailer park."

"Oh." The conversation made much more sense to him now. "Why did he say you were both orphans?"

"Well, my mama was never around for me and Devon. We were alone most of the time. Johnny lost his family in a house fire when he was a kid. After they were killed, he lived with his aunt, uncle, and cousin."

"Wow, that's awful."

"It's amazing he's managed to do something with his life. He's always been a good guy though, even when he was a delinquent."

"He really seems to get you."

"It's a different world where he comes from. He helped me get through a lot of stuff."

"Sorry to keep you talking, go to sleep." He kissed her hair.

"I'll go to sleep if you promise to be here when I wake up."

"Is that why you're not sleeping?" he asked, trying to look at her face.

She nodded into his chest.

He pushed the hair off her cheek and looked into her eyes. "I promise to always be here when you wake up."

When Mark brought Sarah home from the hospital several days later, the house was full of people. She groaned when she entered and saw everyone. She tried to be gracious, and she was thrilled to see Ali's new baby, but she wanted to be alone with Mark.

Catching her subtle hints, people slowly trickled out. Johnny Rhay and Ali lagged behind. Sarah suspected Ali wasn't in a hurry to go home alone, but she wasn't sure why Johnny Rhay was still in town.

"I'm surprised you're still here. Haven't you had enough of California to last you a lifetime?"

"I kinda like it here...and I need to talk to you and Mark before I leave." He handed the baby back to Ali. "Kevin Lewis killed Charlie. We compared the DNA and it's a match. The case has been closed."

Sarah held her breath for several seconds, and then let it gush out in a long exhale. "I...I knew when I looked into his eyes at the party." She bowed her head. "Poor Charlie."

"Now, Sarah, Charlie wouldn't want you to feel like that. Y'all were his only kin. He would have done anything to protect you. Don't ruin his legacy by feeling sorry for him."

She nodded and looked back up. "You're right. I loved him too. He was a good man."

"Johnny, thanks for staying to see this through," Mark said.

"It's been my pleasure. Y'all have a great group of friends and family out here. It's a nice little town...not at all like the Metro, maybe I'll visit again. Devon promised to teach me how to surf, although I don't think I want to be eaten by sharks." He reached in to hug Sarah. "Can you keep in touch this time?"

"I will e-mail, how about that?"

"Sounds real nice," he drawled.

"Mark, it's been good to meet you. Take care of this girl."

"I will. Come back to visit anytime."

"I just might do that." He turned to Ali. "Miss Ali, may I buy you a cup of coffee before you go home?"

Ali looked surprised but nodded in agreement.

Mark walked them out and then snuck up behind Sarah to nuzzle her neck. "I have something for you." He held her engagement ring out to her. "They gave it to me to take care of when you were in the hospital. I've been so distracted I forgot to give it back to you."

Sarah let him slide the ring on her left hand and whispered, "I love it."

He swayed with her for a moment, enjoying the quiet of the house and said, "It's just you and me."

"Just me and you," she said, hugging the arms he held around her. "Just me and you, Jamie...and pretty soon...baby."

CPSIA information can be obtained at www.ICGtesting.com
Printed in the USA
BVOW081438231012

303734BV00001B/106/P